Henry Hall

American Navigation

with some account of the causes of its recent decay, and of the means by

which its prosperity may be restored

Henry Hall

American Navigation
with some account of the causes of its recent decay, and of the means by which its prosperity may be restored

ISBN/EAN: 9783337423544

Printed in Europe, USA, Canada, Australia, Japan

Cover: Foto ©Andreas Hilbeck / pixelio.de

More available books at **www.hansebooks.com**

AMERICAN

NAVIGATION,

WITH SOME ACCOUNT OF

*THE CAUSES OF ITS RECENT DECAY, AND
OF THE MEANS BY WHICH ITS PROS-
PERITY MAY BE RESTORED.*

BY

HENRY HALL.

"I am for ruling America for the benefit, first, of Americans, and the rest of mankind afterward."—Mr. Morrill, of Vermont.

REVISED AND ENLARGED.

NEW YORK:
D. APPLETON AND COMPANY,
1880.

PREFACE.

THE object of this pamphlet is to set forth the causes of the decline of American shipping, and the arguments pro and con on the subject of free ships, subsidies, and the propriety of maintaining the Navigation Laws of the United States. A first edition of this dissertation, printed last winter, was received with some encouragement. The author ventures to put the pamphlet forth again, in a revised and enlarged form, in the hope that it may assist those who wish for information on this interesting current topic, to form an opinion on the merits of the questions at issue.

The original purpose was to show why American ships are not employed to a large extent in the immense foreign trade of this country, and to indicate what might be done to effect a change for the better. Two or three years ago, the topic which most engaged attention was the causes which had led almost to the extinction of the great fleet of beautiful clipper ships and swift ocean-steamers, which, in 1857, had become the pride of our country and the admiration of the whole maritime world. The public were then first beginning to be painfully aware of the growing ascendency of foreign shipping in the trade of all our harbors, and of the fact that the export trade in American manufactures was shackled by the lack of American steamers plying direct to certain coasts with which the United States ought to have a large commerce. The first question which arose in all minds was, naturally, how did this decay of American shipping in the ocean commerce come about. There were almost as many opinions on the point as there were men to utter them. Views differed according to the interests of the several authorities and the amount of pains each one took to investigate the subject. The first edition of this pamphlet was printed as a contribution to that discussion ; and, as it was intended not so much for ship-owners and ship-builders as for practical business men, merchants, manufacturers, farmers, and others, whose welfare is linked with the welfare of the merchant marine, but who seldom pay any attention to the causes affecting maritime activity, some of the more elemental facts involved in the subject were set forth for their information.

The scope of the discussion has latterly been extended somewhat. It is now seriously proposed in Congress to repeal the Navigation Laws of the United States, and to bring down upon vessel-owners in the Mississippi river valley, on the northern lakes, and in the coasting trade, the fury of competition with a multitude of hungry foreign vessels, now out of employment, and eager to get admittance to our rivers, lakes, and coasts, as well as to subject our builders from Maine to Alaska to the competition of foreign builders. " Free ships" is the cry. Concurrently, the policy of establishing American steamship lines to foreign countries by mail contracts is more vigorously opposed than ever, while, on the other hand, the friends of American shipping are now advocating a general government policy in favor of mail contracts to all the lines which it may be expedient to establish. In view of the enlarged scope of the discussion, a chapter has been added to this edition, presenting the arguments on the question of Free Ships and Subsidies.

The whole subject of the state of our shipping interest is discussed here in the light of foreign policy. No correct explanation of our former prosperity or recent decay can be given except by so doing. No intelligent action can be taken for the future benefit of our navigation except by understanding what other nations have done and are willing to do in competition with us. There has been too much indifference for the last thirty years in regard to foreign policy. We have suffered from it, but paid no attention to it. The time has come for a change. We need now to study foreign policy attentively, and must do so before even undertaking to decide what policy we shall adopt for ourselves.

This pamphlet advocates a protective policy in regard to our shipping. It claims that the United States has reached a point in its history when the opportunity is placed before it to embark in the navigation of the Atlantic and Pacific on a large scale, and that the Government should actively aid the people by mail contracts to steamship lines and otherwise, to take advantage of the situation. Prompt action is needed, lest a great opportunity may be lost. It also proposes that there shall be a general investigation of the whole subject of American navigation, trade, and manufacture, in order to place before Congress the facts upon which an intelligent and aggressive policy can alone be founded.

In the words of General Key, in a recent speech in the West, " The time has come when our farmers and businesss men must take interest in these questions, if the fountains of our prosperity are not to be dried up."

HENRY HALL.

TRIBUNE OFFICE, NEW YORK, *October*, 1879.

AMERICAN NAVIGATION.

I.

THE SITUATION.

THE United States now makes to the ocean-carrying trade of the world its most valuable contribution. No other nation gives to commerce so many tons of bulky commodities which have to be carried such long distances across the sea. The extent of our commerce, in tons of articles carried (2,240 pounds to the ton), is as follows : [1]

EXPORTS.

YEARS ENDING JUNE 30th.	Ag. Produce.	Oils.	Provisions.	Manufactures.	Metals, etc.	Total.
1869	1,404,642	455,857	104,764	198,605	318,283	2,482,171
1870	2,190,957	538,491	110,525	170,200	362,531	2,372,704
1871	2,524,005	651,938	180,981	204,419	477,960	4,039,302
1872	2,683,213	505,492	347,715	277,582	627,398	4,501,400
1873	3,837,967	852,687	424,030	201,649	725,882	5,542,165
1874	4,567,184	1,114,521	411,600	258,779	926,346	7,278,430
1875	3,681,202	989,900	353,511	253,405	707,505	5,985,523
1876	4,400,907	1,088,158	371,639	306,241	751,889	6,918,834
1877	4,658,839	1,896,623	553,969	262,500	904,769	7,721,700
1878	6,463,150	1,549,390	633,150	217,200	758,620	9,616,540
1879	7,947,230	1,564,600	699,430	190,600	747,800	11,149,160

IMPORTS.

YEARS ENDING JUNE 80th.	Ag. Produce.	Manufactures.	Metals and Minerals.	Chemicals.	Miscellaneous.	Total.
1869	1,222,726	617,588	1,385,625	170,786	55,427	3,452,152
1870	1,258,570	738,981	1,429,461	161,910	64,588	3,653,460
1871	1,292,217	696,772	1,658,465	175,853	149,645	4,002,452
1872	1,527,050	698,296	1,901,681	185,308	180,000	4,437,385
1873	1,818,905	909,429	1,522,546	240,297	112,791	4,603,968
1874	1,759,410	759,917	1,222,540	217,751	54,896	4,018,014
1875	1,786,467	685,099	951,689	216,283	65,759	3,705,297
1876	1,777,170	605,429	870,427	163,708	181,467	3,548,201
1877	1,725,066	602,161	927,078	202,458	127,046	3,593,804
1878	1,755,900	567,900	906,020	220,880	251,900	3,702,500
1879	1,944,800	574,770	869,980	282,030	111,500	3,782,530

[1] These figures, if not exact, are at least a very close approximation, obtained by a condensation from the tables of the Bureau of Statistics.

These goods are exchanged with continents and lands lying from 3,000 to 5,000 miles distant and farther. Our commerce is, therefore, carried on by means of the long voyages which in every age have been eagerly coveted by a maritime people, and which are productive of employment to the greatest tonnage of shipping. The value of the goods entering into our commerce by sea amounted in 1877 to $1,173,-000,000, of which $694,000,000 were exports and $479,000,000 were imports. Twenty-five years ago this commerce amounted to less than $500,000,000.

Twenty-five years ago American shipping was almost supreme in our commerce. In 1851 $316,000,000 of the exports and imports were carried by vessels belonging to this country and built upon its shores, against $117,000,000 carried under foreign flags. The most valuable freights were secured by American ships; and they got better pay for their services in competition with foreign vessels. To-day American ships actually carry less than they did in 1851, or in any year thereafter until the war broke out, 1852 alone excepted. Yet commerce by sea has more than doubled. In 1877 American ships carried $315,000,-000 of the imports and exports by sea. Foreign ships carried $858,-000,000, over seven times as much as in 1851.

If the larger proportion of this commerce consisted in the importation of articles of foreign growth and manufacture, it would not be strange to find foreign ships enjoying the larger share of the business. The ships of other lands would naturally have the preference in their own ports for the exportation of goods to the United States. The remarkable fact is, that the larger proportion of the goods go from our own shores. This is shown both by the above table and by the record of the custom-houses along the coast. Of the 17,000 ships which enter and clear at our ocean-ports every year, 4,600 enter port empty, seeking a cargo, and only 2,000 sail from port without a cargo.

In New York Harbor 800 vessels and more constantly lie at the piers or at anchor in the bay, taking on or discharging cargo. There are one hundred departures a week for foreign lands. Yet it often happens that a fortnight passes without a single ship with an American flag at the peak clearing from the port for the British Isles, with which the largest commerce of New York is transacted. At the same time an average of twenty-five foreign vessels clear from the same port every week in that trade.

For the last fifteen years a sum of money has been paid by the United States to foreign ship-owners for the transportation of mails, passengers, and goods, which cannot in any one year have been less than $20,000,000. It now amounts to $50,000,000 a year. Practical shipping-men have estimated it as high as $75,000,000 a year. It is $50,000,000 at least. As far as freight is concerned, this refers to the import trade alone. In the export trade, only seventeen per cent. of which is now transacted in American vessels, we again have to pay heavy tribute to foreign ship-owners. Owing to the low prices prevailing abroad, we sometimes have to pay a part of the ocean freight to get our goods to market ; that is to say, we have to take lower prices for our goods in American ports, which is the same thing as paying a part of the freight. The United States accordingly pays a tribute of from $50,000,000 to $100,000,000 yearly to foreign ship-owners. These immense sums of money do not return to us in any useful manner. They are not invested in American goods. There is plenty of evidence of that ; and, considering what our exports are, it is not probable that we would sell less of them in the future, if the whole of them, and the imports, too, were carried in American ships, and all the freight-money earned by Americans. Those sums are not invested in American labor. Their disbursement to foreigners certainly does not tend, either, to the accumulation of capital in this young country, which needs capital so much. There are only three possible ways in which we can derive any benefit whatever from this drain upon the national wealth. One is, that a portion of the money may be loaned to us again to build our great railroads from the interior to the sea-shore, which Englishmen seem as anxious now to control as they have been in the past to get possession of the steamship lines, which run from the termini of those roads to other lands. Another is, that the money may be invested in our Government bonds. A third is, that the heavy drain of specie, which has amounted to $780,000,000 in the last fourteen years, $360,000,000 of it being for freight-money, has tended, as far as it has had any influence whatever, to bring down the prices of labor and goods, and to enable us to export on a larger scale. In the first two cases the benefit to this country is small, and is more than counterbalanced by the fresh drain of specie which has been created for the payment of interest. In the latter case there may have been a small benefit to the country in the way of increased exports ; but this, again, is more than offset by the suffering which a fall in the value of labor has brought about, and by the check to national development and civilization. It is confidently asserted that the money paid by this country to foreign shipping is a useless and disastrous drain upon our resources. The $50,000,000 to $100,000,000 of money paid out every year is thrown to the winds, while, if paid to our own citizens, it would be an inexhaustible source of blessing to every class of our countrymen.

One advantage of living in a republic is, that the taxes there are lighter. The government is run at less expense. There are great economical advantages to a people in having a republican government on that account. This is well understood in the United States, where, to secure the full advantages of our free political institutions, there is a constant striving after a sparing expenditure in public affairs. Yet our people are incurring a loss every year in reference to their shipping interests, which no saving in government expenses can possibly make up, simply because they are paying no attention to the subject. They might, by spending $5,000,000 every year in compensation to American steamship lines, save $50,000,000.

In the last two hundred years the tonnage of the world has increased enormously. According to Seabright's statistical annals, the tonnage of Europe in 1676 was 2,000,000, owned as follows: In the Netherlands, 900,000 ; in England, 500,000; in Hamburg, Denmark, Sweden, and Dantzic, 250,000; in Spain, Portugal, and Italy, 250,000 ; and the rest here and there. Now Europe owns 13,700,000 tons of shipping, and the world owns over 19,000,000, of which 15,600,000 tons is in sailing-craft, and the rest in steam-vessels. This includes only sea-going vessels, and does not take in river-craft. The distribution is as follows: Great Britain, 7,300,000 ; the Netherlands, 500,000 ; Norway and Sweden, 1,800,000; Italy, 1,300,000 ; France, 925,000; Germany, 540,-000 ; the United States, 3,500,000 ; and the rest here and there. The greatest increase has been within the last forty years. The tonnage of the world has tripled in that period. Its efficiency has increased in a greater ratio. It is now six times as great as forty years ago, owing to the fact that steam has been utilized in ocean-commerce within that period, and that a given tonnage of steam-shipping performs a service equal to three times the amount of sailing-tonnage. Shipping has increased faster than commerce and travel, and a great deal of it has been rendered idle and useless by steam, the employment of the telegraph throughout the world, and the opening of the Suez Canal.

A growing proportion of the ocean-commerce of the world is being transacted by steam-vessels. This is an important fact in the situation. The cost of operating steamships has been cheapened one-half within twenty years. Steam can now compete with sails, and it is gradually and surely superseding sails in all important trades. Trade loves rapid dispatch, and as steam has made itself able to transact business three times as fast as the craft propelled by the winds, and at little or no greater cost, it is rapidly gathering up not only all the mails, passengers, and finer classes of freight, but the bulky staple goods, which, twenty-five years ago, statesmen said would never in the world be carried in anything except sailing-vessels. There are some figures to show how rapidly sailing-vessels are being displaced in ocean-commerce. At the port of New York, to which are brought three-fourths of all the imports to the United States, steam-vessels import nine-tenths of all the goods coming from countries from which steamships run. They bring all the passengers and mails. Of the exports from New York Harbor, three-fifths of the whole go by steamer. Mr. R. K. Sanford, the intelligent chief of export statistics at the New York Custom-House, kept for a few months in 1876 an account of the exports by steam and sail to the special countries to which steamers run. For six months his record was as follows:

SPECIAL COUNTRIES.	Steam.	Sail.
England	$55,741,203	$18,487,682
Scotland	8,921,132	969,785
France	5,449,055	3,804,644
Germany	10,595,748	6,272,795
Cuba	3,026,473	1,485,058
Netherlands	5,061,920	2,241,389

Had a record been kept at Boston, Philadelphia, and Baltimore, the same increase of steam in commerce and the same displacement of sailing-tonnage would have been shown.

This result was clearly foreseen in Europe, and foreigners shifted their capital from sailing to steam tonnage. They have put two hundred steamers into the trade to the United States. On the other hand, the United States has neglected the new mode of transportation in its foreign trade, and has less than fifteen steamers running across the Atlantic and Pacific Oceans. It loses ground in the carrying-trade, therefore, year by year. It neither employs the modern style of ship, nor is able to compete for business with its sailing-craft. It suffers the double loss of not having a share of a profitable business, and of seeing tens of thousands of tons of sailing-vessels lying idle in its harbors. A revival of our shipping interest must take place principally in the direction of our steam marine. It is only with the most modern description of vessel that we can win back our old-time supremacy in the carrying-trade.

With the decay of our foreign navigation there has been a corresponding decay of our ship-building. In 1857, when our marine was the most prosperous, $25,000,000 was being expended annually in the construction of new vessels, and a far greater sum in the repair of old ones. Only an infinitely small part of this expenditure was for raw material. It was nearly all for labor. The amount spent annually in building new vessels is now about $11,000,000, and the disbursements for repairs are proportionately reduced. The falling off is more than half. Except for the wise regulation that none except American ships shall take part in the coasting-trade of the United States, this profitable branch of manufacturing industry would have died out in this country. As it is, with twice the tonnage employed in our foreign trade, ship-building has fallen off one-half in twenty years. There are thousands of men starving in this country to-day because they cannot get work. There are large numbers of our young men growing up who cannot find any field of employment that is not overcrowded. What a boon it would be to our country were the Government to pursue a policy with reference to shipping which would lead to the old activity at the ship-yards, and make a fresh demand for the services of our laboring population and our young men!

The capital invested in our sailing-tonnage built for the foreign trade is now largely unproductive. A great deal of the tonnage is absolutely idle, and in danger of becoming a total loss to its owners. Ship proprietors have been losing money for several years. The coasting-trade continues to be regular and profitable. In the foreign trade, our sailing-ships are only made to pay to any extent when owned by merchants who trade in them on their own account. In the general carrying-trade they scarcely live, and, as stated before, many have been withdrawn from business altogether.

These are the principal facts in regard to depression in our navigation and the way it is affecting the country.

The political dangers arising from a feeble merchant marine ought not, however, to be overlooked; and there is another matter which may be mentioned to show what the United States is losing by its negligence to develop a steam marine for the foreign trade. The country is under the necessity of exporting its manufactures on a large scale. The home market is too small to keep our manufacturing population busy. The foreign markets in which a large sale of our goods can the most easily be created are in South America, Africa, and the Mediterranean countries. But the Europeans have an almost undisputed control of those markets at present, because they have abundant steam communication with them, a fact which enables them to land their goods more cheaply, and to take the quickest advantage of the state of the markets. The United States is under the need of extending its commerce, but is hampered by the insufficiency of its steam marine. We suffer from dull times and stagnation, when the starting of first-class steam lines to South America, Africa, and the Mediterranean, would quicken industry and agriculture in every part of the land.

This is the situation. The first question is, "What is the depression all due to, and is it likely to be permanent, or are the causes of depression under our control?" It is a question that should not be answered hastily. A time like this came once in the affairs of Italy, Spain, Portugal, and the Netherlands, and those countries never rose from the disasters which befell their merchant marine. Three of those powers were at different times, and for a long period, the common-carriers of almost the whole known world. Decay fell upon their marine, and they passed off the stage forever as great navigating peoples. Is this to be the fate of the United States? Or are our misfortunes merely the clouds of a day in the sky, and like clouds not likely long to remain?

II.

CAUSES OF MARITIME ACTIVITY.

IT will help us to understand the true state of the case in regard to our merchant marine by looking first at the general causes which affect maritime prosperity. The special causes which have affected our enterprise will be considered in other chapters.

There need be no uncertainty about the things which qualify a nation to become eminent in navigation, or which prevent it from becoming so. History is full of instances of the rise and fall of maritime nations, and of instances where nations never became maritime at all. It is not difficult to select from the conditions of national life the particular things which give rise to the impulse toward a navigation of the sea, and enable a people to gratify that impulse on a large scale ; or which create a disrelish for the sea, and guarantee that a race will remain landsmen for ages, if not for all time.

I. The first impulse toward maritime enterprise arises out of life in a region which will not support its inhabitants in agriculture. Original poverty of the soil, or limited extent of territory, almost rises to the rank of a necessary qualification to become a maritime people. The born navigators of the world always lived in little, half-barren countries situated in the midst of fruitful regions. Beginning with the Phœnicians, who lived in a contracted, sterile spot at the eastern end of the Mediterranean, no larger than a county in the Empire State, and coming along down to the Venetians, living on marshy islands in the sea, the Dutch, the Scots, the people of the north of Europe, the Icelanders, and the New-Englanders, who have been the only born navigators of the world, it will be seen that they occupied the comparatively unfertile lands. On the other hand, those who inhabited the fruitful regions never navigated to any extent until their population became so dense that agriculture would not support them. This was the case with the Carthaginians, the Greeks, the Latin races of Europe, the English, and peoples on various parts of the American Continent. As showing the influence of dense population, it is interesting to note a peculiar experience of Spain and Portugal. Before and at the time of the discovery of America, and of the ocean-route to the East Indies, both countries were very rich in shipping ; but both expelled the Saracens and Jews, and sent off a large number of their own people to colonize newly-discovered regions. Not only were both countries deprived of the whole of their surplus population, but they were left with an absolutely insufficient population. A decline in shipping immediately followed. Neither country ever recovered from the maritime decay which then set in. A people inhabiting a fertile territory which they have never been able to crowd with human beings have never yet actively navigated the sea. The Egyptians, in an experience of at least six thousand years, although living directly in the path of the East India trade, have never had ships, except during the reign of some king who built them mainly for military purposes. Superhuman efforts have been put forth to give Egypt a merchant marine. They all failed from the cause above stated. The passivity of the Brazilians is another illustration of the principle.

In the United States the original, and almost the only, navigators have been the New-Englanders and New-Yorkers. They occupied the poorer lands. In the South there was scarcely any shipping at all for a hundred years, and has been very little since. To-day not over one-ninth of the tonnage of the country is owned in that region. The rich lands prevented navigation. The ship-builders sent over to Virginia, by the company in England which planted the colony, themselves fell to planting tobacco. There was, however, great interest in the prosperity of our navigation in all parts of the country, even in the agricultural States, as long as our people lived on the coast, hedged in by the wilderness and the savage tribes of the interior. Interest in our navigation decayed when, by reason of the building of railroads and the employment of steam on the Western rivers, our population was enabled to spread itself over the vast agricultural regions of the interior. With the opening of the West to settlement, all pressure of population of preceding times passed away. A scarcity of population followed, and our foreign navigation began to decline. Coming down to 1879, we find now a pressure of population. Immigration has brought millions of people into the country. Natural increase has been doing its work. The country does not yet contain, perhaps, a fourth part of the population which may eventually gather here, but, under the circumstances of the times, the East is in a condition of over-population. The people cannot all live in farming; they cannot at present find full employment in the industries or mines; the country is crowded; it has reached the point where an active impulse to go into navigation on a large scale always makes itself felt.

It was when France reached this stage of development that Colbert and Richelieu at different periods found themselves forced to do something to create a national merchant marine. England, in a similar stage of its national life, adopted the Navigation Act. Is there not already visible in this country the workings of an impulse such as moved France and England, and such as one would expect to see under the same circumstances?

II. The genius of a people affects its maritime activity extremely. The case of the Egyptians above cited is in part an illustration of this. The easy life and profits of agriculture in a fertile region tend to keep a people away from navigation and industrial pursuits. This is because they can make more money with the same expenditure of labor. When, however, dazzling fortunes can be made in a commerce which sweeps past the doors of such a people, it is surprising not to find them leaving agriculture and going into active trade and navigation. The disadvantages of the Egyptians in reference to materials for boat-building were never greater than those of the Dutch, and there was every inducement for them to go into navigation. Yet they never could be induced to do it. The genius of the people was not favorable to it.

The dissimilarity of national traits has always had a marked influence. It has often been pointed out that an art-loving people cannot be expected to display energy in commerce and industry. The present eminence of the practical English is greatly due to the peculiar genius of the people. A roaming, restless disposition, a love of adventure, a jealousy of foreign participation in the affairs of the realm, and the spirit of traffic and industry, invariably impel in the direction of maritime enterprise. A people with such qualities will always demolish the obstacles to its navigation, and have its share of the carrying-trade of the world.

The Americans have inherited the best qualities of the English, and have made some improvements on the parent stock, we think, owing to the character of our political institutions, which stimulate greater personal effort and fruitfulness of mind. This may be expected to have an influence on the maritime destiny of the country.

III. Maritime activity is greatly affected by the possession of ocean-fisheries. A coast-people will always have boats if it has fisheries. It will also have able mariners. In every age the fisheries have been an original temptation to take to the sea, and an important qualification for engaging in general navigation on a comprehensive scale. The only races which have ever been eminent in shipping have fished from the beginning. In a national sense, the actual value of the cod, whales, herring, and other treasures taken from the bosom of the sea, has never been the principal source of blessing of large fisheries. Their chief utility has resided in the training of mariners, by teaching them to be constantly in their boats in stormy seas, and to voyage in all climates and in all parts of the world. They have always given a nation tars who could sail a ship well and make it last long, and were always ready to undertake the most daring and difficult enterprises. All other things being equal, that nation will be foremost on the sea which has the most abundant fisheries. Its progress will never be retarded by reason of the lack of competent seamen as long as it has whaling, cod, herring, and mackerel shipping. It may owe its progress entirely to the possession of a fleet of such vessels.

IV. Geographical location has always counted for something. To be in the centre, among a number of countries of widely-different productions, between which an exchange of commodities could be made to take place by establishing friendly relations, has been a characteristic of all the leading maritime nations. The flag of commercial empire has shifted from one place to another in the world, as the centre of civilization and settlement has shifted. To be in an out-of-the-way quarter of the earth is to be cut off from a great navigation. Iceland, Russia, Germany, and Canada, may have a considerable tonnage in the trade to adjoining coasts; no such nation can be first in the commerce of the world. It is only a region situated in the midst of great seas, and advantageously central in its age, that can in the long-run have the most ships and be supreme in commerce. While this has always been true in the past, it will be more so in the future, on account of the more general settlement of all parts of the earth. With respect to particular branches of commerce, nearness to important markets has an influence. Of two nations competing for trade and navigation to a great market, that one will in the end secure the larger share which is the nearest to it. In ancient days, Spain was one of the richest markets of the world. To the countries at the eastern end of the Mediterranean, it was a sort of Peru and United States in one. Phœnicia engrossed the extremely profitable trade to Spain at one time, but Carthage beat her entirely out of it in friendly competition, by reason of her greater nearness. There are many similar instances. This principle will probably be exemplified in time in the competition between the United States and Europe for the South American trade.

V. Another important point is the size of a country. The only permanent foundation upon which a merchant marine of any size can be built is a great population and a great surplus of native commodities. An extensive trade growing out of the wants and energies of a vast native population gives a country a superior position in navigation, if it chooses to take advantage of it. It is only necessary to secure that trade for native ships to create a vast marine. This is what made England the first maritime power of the world. Her large body of consumers and producers gave rise to an extensive trade. She simply diverted the larger part of this into vessels of her own nationality, in a characteristic manner, and gained the largest merchant-fleet in Europe, when before she almost had the smallest.

The sudden collapse of Italy, Portugal, and the Netherlands, in navigation, was precipitated by the lack of a home market sufficient to employ their shipping. Their carrying-trade was principally between other nations. A slight change in the currents of commerce left them utterly prostrate. There was nothing to fall back upon. When the distribution of East India products was taken away from the Dutch by the capture of their principal islands by the English, they had ten times as much shipping as they then had any employment for. The needs of their home market would not sustain it. Their maritime prosperity vanished like a dream. The experience of Italy and Portugal was the same.

In this age, given the largest territory and the largest population, and the largest native navigation can be made to follow it.

VI. Maritime activity is greatly influenced by the cost of operating a ship. In the foreign trade, ships enter in this age into free competition with those of all other nations. Cheapness of operation is, therefore, indispensable.

Now, to secure this several things are essential. Foremost of all is to have skillful ship-builders. Nothing will compensate for the lack of able ships. From antiquity down, through the several ages when oars, sails, and steam, were the principal means of propulsion, a perfect command of the art of construction has been necessary. There have been many interesting illustrations of this. A good and fast ship is the cheapest to operate in the long-run, and this cannot be had without good builders.

Then there must be economy in construction. Costly ships cannot be operated against cheaper ships of the same class. To build cheaply, the first thing necessary is an abundance of building-material at home. The disadvantages of a lack of it have never been overcome by more than one nation. The Dutch imported their timber and fabrics for cordage, etc., for centuries. They were enabled to do it only by their remarkable frugality. All other nations which have imported their building-material have lost ground in the trade with the nation from which the importation took place. It is the emphatic lesson of history that successful ship-building can only go on in an age of free competition in regions where there is an abundance of good materials. Moderate wages for labor are also necessary. Wages constitute three-quarters at least of the cost of a ship, and a comparatively inexpensive vessel can coexist only with a scale of wages not greatly in excess of that of a rival nation. In America our builders have not found it fatal to pay wages somewhat in excess of those paid in England and France. American labor is more efficient and goes further. Our builders would rather have it, even if they have to pay more for it. Besides, much labor is saved here by the use of machinery. Less labor is done by hand. The principal iron-ship yards of the United States, scattered along the banks of the river Delaware, are equipped with devices for the saving of labor to an extent which has often excited the surprise and admiration of English builders who have visited them. American builders can pay ten per cent. better wages, and not be placed at a disadvantage by it. A greater difference than that would be a drag upon national maritime enterprise.

2

Then there must be a moderate rate of interest. Low interest is a great help to a navigating country. This is the uniform experience of Europe and the United States.

The wages of sailors must not be greatly in excess of those of other nations. With an energetic and inventive people like the Americans, wages may be somewhat more generous than with their rivals, without affecting the total cost of operation, because their sailors are better men ; they make more voyages in the year; they wear a ship less ; a fewer number of them are needed to man a ship. With first-class sea-men, such as can be recruited from the fishing-towns of New England, a country can pay perhaps ten per cent. better wages and still hold its own. If the difference is twenty per cent., a people in this age might as well quit the sea. It will be driven off by competition if it does not go voluntarily.

It must not be forgotten that the predominant fact of navigation in this age is freedom. The sea has been cleared of pirates. Some of the merchant-ships sailing from New York Harbor for China still carry a few cannon as a measure of precaution, but the long battle against the freebooters has been substantially fought out, and ships are free to move about the world wheresoever they will. The old hamper-ing regulations of European nations have also been overcome. A vast number of these regulations were once in force, and no ship was free to sail about the world and get a cargo wherever it could find it, and carry it to any place where it could sell it. The United States broke down that ancient system by her example in making a reciprocity treaty with Holland in 1782, the first of the kind in history, and by her policy in subsequent years. The United States gave to progress and civilization the gift of maritime reciprocity. The old regulations have been re-pealed through her influence, and ships are now substantially free to go from one country to another anywhere in the world. Their limita-tion to direct trade has been abandoned. This brings against the ships of any nation the free competition of the vessels of all other nations, in foreign trade. The merchants of the world being free to choose the ships that shall carry their goods, naturally select the ones which will carry them the cheapest. It is this which now makes cheapness of op-eration an indispensable condition to maritime prosperity.

VII. The final reason is a favorable policy on the part of the gov-ernment.

This is a very important matter. If there were universal freedom of action throughout the world, and everything were left to private intelligence and enterprise, a governmental policy would not be needed by an energetic and happily-circumstanced people. But there is not now such freedom of action, and never has been. If one nation per-mits it, others do not and cannot be persuaded to permit it. The consequence is, that the citizens of a nation like America often have to contend not only with the private enterprise of older lands—itself a sufficient bar to their progress—but with the resources of wealthy foreign governments besides. In such cases private enterprise is powerless. Nothing can be done without a governmental policy to sustain the younger nation in the competition.

The above constitute the principal causes which affect maritime prosperity. If we look among them for the sources of the decay of American navigation, we will find that our decline cannot have been due to the lack of good seamen, to our geographical location, the genius of our people, or the lack of natural resources, good builders, and a commerce. The United States is well off in all these particulars. It may have been due to the ability of this country to employ its people profitably without building and navigating ships; to the high prices of labor, high interest, or foreign policy. As a matter of fact, it has been due to all four of these in varying degrees. The extent to which each of the four causes has operated, and is operative now, will be discussed in the following chapters.

III.

ENGLISH POLICY.

One of the most prolific sources of our maritime troubles is the course pursued by England for the benefit of her own marine. The study of it cannot fail to be profitable to Americans. A sketch of it is presented here. It will explain to us in great part our own misfortunes; and it will show how a people of the same race, language, and genius as ourselves, growing up under somewhat the same economic conditions, hampered by a too exclusive devotion to agriculture at home and by the powerful competition of rivals abroad, managed to make itself the first maritime power in the world. The policy of England cannot be imitated in all its details in this country, but a study of it will be extremely useful, for all that.

The story will be told from the English point of view.

The policy of England (to quote from David A. Wells) "is now, and always has been, framed solely and exclusively with reference to one object, viz., the promotion of supposed national self-interest—and has never had the slightest regard to the interest of any other nation, or to any arguments other than those based upon specific national wants and specific national experiences."

For the first six hundred years after the Conquest, England's maritime growth was slow. Agriculture was the principal interest. The population was scanty and poor. The island might have become densely settled early in its history, but the Government engaged in continual wars, leading to great destruction of life on land and sea, which the constant immigration from the mainland could not counteract. The lack of capital prevented the people from building ships to any extent. Encouraged by bounties and by trade, they did occasionally manage to create a little fleet, but this invariably proved a temptation to the king to go to war with somebody. The merchant-ships were impressed into the military service, and were not only thus diverted from legitimate navigation, but a large percentage of them were destroyed or captured by the enemy. Neutrals meantime gathered up the carrying-trade which the English neglected. So the kingdom was left both without ships and without the business by which it could secure the capital to build them. The Dutch, during the greater part of this period, engrossed nearly all the transportation of Europe, certainly nearly all in the north of it. They brought the bulky products of England and the north and south of Europe to their own ports, and then manufactured or warehoused them, and distributed them again all along the coasts from Russia to Egypt. Their only competitors were the Italians, but they steadily gained upon this ancient and active people, and, by the early part of the seventeenth century, had substantially beaten them out of the carrying-trade. They virtually monopolized all the important trade to England and to the English colonies in America. The English were only able to navigate at all by virtue of the creation of societies of merchants, to whom was given a monopoly of certain trades. The Dutch had 20,000 ships at sea, to 2,000 by the English.

The English had always deemed it proper to assert a political dominion of the sea. For two hundred years they had required the Dutch by treaty stipulation to strike the topsail and lower the flag in the presence of English men-of-war, a practice which they insisted upon down into the present century. In the seventeenth century it began to grow doubtful whether they could continue to enforce their claim. The Dutch had carried on for fifty years a war with the haughty empire of Spain, and had completely crushed its naval power. They now conceived the idea of making themselves masters of the colonies of that empire in America and Asia. In 1621 they incorporated a West India Company expressly to conquer Brazil and Peru ; and in fifteen years they had sent 800 ships to America, captured 545 Spanish and Portuguese vessels, and taken Brazil, and in Asia had taken possession of all the important spice and other islands in the Indies. The Dutch, during that period, built 1,000 ships a year, it is said, to 100 that were needed to carry the native commodities of the Netherlands.

The English were irritated by the overshadowing activity of the Dutch. They could not build up their own marine under the existing state of things. They could not even control the trade to the colonies, and they were in danger of being laughed at for their declaration of a right to rule the seas. They were at the same time under the necessity of extending their commerce and providing new fields of employment for their labor, owing to a recent increase in population. The whole force of English policy was now turned toward repressing the Dutch, and developing the shipping of the king's own subjects.

UNDER THE NAVIGATION ACTS.

The first step taken was very much in the direction of an old law of 1381, passed by Parliament under Richard II., in response to complaints that foreigners were monopolizing the whole navigation of the kingdom. That law provided that "for increasing the shipping of England, of late much diminished, none of the king's subjects shall hereafter ship any merchandise, either outward or homeward, but only in ships of the king's subjects, on forfeiture of ships and merchandise ; in which ships also the greater part of the crews shall be the king's subjects." This appeared to be a short and simple method of securing the whole trade of England to English ships. The law was a very inconsiderate one at the time, because there was both a lack of native shipping and of capital to build it. Trade was accordingly hampered by it, and it was virtually repealed the following year, by an enactment permitting merchants to employ foreign vessels if there were none of English nationality to be had. It was always disregarded. In the seventeenth century the kingdom was richer, had more shipping, and was better able to adopt some such aggressive policy. In 1650, accordingly, under Cromwell, a law was passed excluding foreigners from the trade to the English colonies in all parts of the world. In 1651, after a careful study of the whole field of commerce, the law of the previous year was superseded by the Navigation Act. In 1660 the act was confirmed by the royal Parliament under Charles II., and made more stringent.

The Navigation Acts established four rules :

1. None except Englishmen should engage in the trade and navigation to the colonies of the kingdom. The ships were to be English-built, and manned by a crew whereof at least three-fourths were Englishmen.

2. Europeans could trade to England only from their own ports.

3. Exportation should take place from the colonies only to the mother-country.

4. The coasting-trade was reserved to national vessels.

The object of this law was well understood in Europe. It was leveled directly at the Dutch, in favor of English shipping. When it was passed, nearly all the tobacco of Virginia and of other valuable produce of the colonies was being exported to the Netherlands from the colonies in Dutch ships, and was distributed to the rest of Europe from the Netherlandish ports. The Dutch were enjoying the long voyages from all parts of Europe to their own harbors, and were limiting the English substantially to the short voyage across the Channel. This law was intended to overturn all this; and, while crowding the Dutch out of the long voyages from America and the distant countries in Europe to England, to secure those voyages to English shipping. Moreover, it was an encouragement to the various countries of Europe, whose foreign navigation was being largely engrossed by the Dutch, to build ships for themselves. In the trade to England, they would only have to contend with the high-priced English ships, and not, as formerly, with the low-priced Netherlandish vessels. The law tended, therefore, to diffuse the shipping of the Continent more equally among the several powers and prevent its concentration in the hands of any one of them , and it did, in fact, have that effect. The export trade of England was left substantially free, except to the colonies. By giving native vessels a better position in the import trade, however, they were enabled to compete for and get their full share of the export trade, as was foreseen and intended.

England did not stop with passing the Navigation Act. She began a series of aggressions toward the Dutch, with the purpose of rendering their commerce at sea perilous and uncertain. In effect, she adopted the policy the Carthaginians pursued of capturing her rival's vessels and destroying them, and throwing the sailors into the sea, though she did not, in fact, throw the Dutchmen into the sea, but merely prevented large numbers of them from putting out to sea at all by her warfare and interferences. Two bloody wars took place in consequence of these aggressions. They were courted by England, and the Dutch were greatly weakened by them.

The policy of England was at first attended by some consequences which threatened to lessen its popularity. The cost of ships and freights advanced one-third. France in 1655 imposed a tax of fifty sols on all English shipping entering her ports. Other powers, before they saw what a benefit to them the Navigation Act would be, imposed similar taxes. By reason of the advance in freights, the kingdom was taxed hundreds of thousands of pounds annually, in order that a few English ship-owners might make a few thousand pounds of profit. The wars imposed a still heavier burden.

Parliament was sagacious enough to perceive that in a short time its policy would approve itself to the people. The policy was steadily persevered in. The end was as expected. In a few years, English merchants only asked that the law might be made more stringent. It had given them a vast advantage in trade theretofore engrossed by the Dutch. In the importations from Europe and America, the Dutch had so overshadowed the natives that the latter had a very limited quantity of tonnage. The trade could now be carried on only in English vessels, or in those of the country from which the importation took place. The English, by fitting out ships the most promptly for the several trades, got the largest share of them immediately into their hands. They obtained a position in the Mediterranean, Spanish, north of Europe, and colonial trade, such as they never had enjoyed, and almost at a word. Shipping increased rapidly in consequence, and found profitable employment. It doubled in ten years, and again in ten years more. The change which took place in the navigation of the kingdom will be illustrated by a few figures showing the tonnage which cleared from her ports at various periods; it being understood that, previous to 1651, the largest share of the tonnage was foreign. The figures are from Anderson's "History of Commerce," and begin in 1663, from which year certainty of statistics dates. They are as follows:

YEAR.		British.	Foreign.	Total Tonnage.
1663-'69	Average.........................	95,266	47,634	142,900
1668	....	190,533	95,267	285,800
1700-1702	Average.........................	273,693	43,635	317,328
1712	....	826,620	29,115	855,735
1726-'28	Average.........................	432,832	23,651	456,483
1760	....	471,241	102,737	573,978
1770	....	703,495	57,476	760,971
1774	....	798,964	65,192	864,156

There was a falling off of native shipping after 1774, owing to the independence of the American colonies. An enormous increase followed a little later, however, because England drove the Dutch out of the East Indies, in punishment for their aid to the United States during the war, and thereby secured a monopoly of that inexpressibly rich Eastern trade. In 1820 the United Kingdom owned 2,300,000 tons of shipping.

Macpherson says of the operations of the Navigation Act:

"We, by this Navigation Act, have gradually obtained a vast increase of shipping and mariners; for by patience and steadiness we have, in length of time, obtained the two ends of this ever-famous act, viz., the bringing our own people to build ships for carrying on such an extensive commerce as they did not have before. Sir Josiah Child was of the opinion that 'without this act we had not now (in 1668) been owners of one-half of the shipping or trade, nor should have employed one-half of the seamen we do at present;' so vast an alteration had this act brought about in a few years; insomuch that we are at length become, in a great measure, what the Dutch once were. i. e., the great carriers of Europe, more especially within the Mediterranean Sea. By this act we have absolutely excluded all other nations from any direct trade with our

American plantations; and were it not for this act, says that able author, we should see forty Dutch ships at our plantations for one of England. That before the passage of this act, and while our American colonies were but in childhood, the ships of other European nations, more especially the Dutch, resorted to our plantations both to lade and unlade; and their merchants and factors nestled themselves among our people there, which utterly frustrated the original intent of planting those colonies, viz., to be a benefit to their mother-country, to which they owed their being and protection; and it could not therefore be thought strange that when our planters were become able to stand on their own legs, and to supply considerable quantities of materials for exportation (as was now the case with Virginia for tobacco, and with Barbados for sugar, ginger, cotton, etc.), our Legislature thought it high time to secure to ourselves alone those increasing benefits, which had been produced at our sole charge and trouble. And in this respect Spain had long before set us a just and laudable example, since followed by other principal European nations who have planted in America. We may here also note that, till this act took place, the Dutch in a manner engrossed the whole trade of Sweden; whereas hereby our English ships have since got a share of the trade thither."

The first object of the law of 1650 was achieved in 100 years. After 1650, the Dutch ceased to carry several hundred cargoes a year to England, because those cargoes had previously been brought by them from regions which had little shipping of their own or none at all. The English instantly secured the carrying of the most of those cargoes because they had ships and shipyards, and the countries from which the cargoes were brought had not. The English drove the Dutch out of several important trades, and got the largest share of the business of which the Dutch were deprived themselves. The Dutch continually lost. Hundreds of their ships when worn out were not replaced. England continually gained. As commerce increased, protected by the operation of her law, she got the largest share of the new trade. She would not have had it without the law. By 1750 the Dutch had been crushed. Britannia was queen of the seas.

Up to the time of the independence of the American colonies, the act was of a good deal of service to the people in this country. It prevented freedom of trade with the Continent of Europe, but it protected them against the competition of Continental ships. They turned it to their advantage. They had an abundance of cheap building-materials. They were better off in this respect than the mother-country —a fact which is shown by the circumstance that, in 1703, England offered a bounty of £4 per ton of eight barrels of pitch and tar, £3 a ton for rosin and turpentine, £6 for hemp, and £1 for masts, yards, and bowsprits, imported to England from the American colonies, the bounty being designed primarily to give England cheap building-materials. The New-Englanders and New-Yorkers made good use of their abundant timber and the Navigation Act, and by the close of the Revolutionary War had created a considerable fleet of merchant-shipping, nearly enough for the trade of the country.

When the War for Independence was over, England foresaw the rise of a dangerous maritime rival in the New World. The objective point of her policy now changed from Europe to the new continent. From 1783 forward it was leveled steadily at a repression of the shipping of the American Republic. The Navigation Act was applied in all its rigor to the United States. The same policy exactly which had been pursued toward the Dutch was initiated in regard to America, only the result in the long-run was different, because the Americans were quite a different race of people. They were not tame-spirited. They were bold, daring, and aggressive, and when a national interest was attacked they were ready at a word to sacrifice life and ease to defend and uphold it.

English aggression began first by refusing to trade with the new republic. That was so clearly against the interests of the kingdom that the position was no sooner adopted than it was abandoned. A law was passed permitting trade, but putting it in the power of the king to suspend it at any moment, and for many years trade was legalized only by yearly proclamation of the king. Heavy taxes were levied on American vessels in the ports of the kingdom, and differential duties enforced against them. Americans were absolutely shut out of the ports of of the British West Indies and the Canadas at first. At sea, the ships sailing under the flag of the young republic were searched continually for contraband goods and British sailors, and sailors were taken from them in large numbers, and the ships and goods captured. Down to the War of 1812 over 1,600 American ships had been captured at sea while engaged in the peaceful missions of legitimate trade. In British ports American ships were detained and harassed. This policy was pursued against remonstrances and countervailing duties in America, until it had made of the commercial ventures of the young republic a species of gambling operations. There was no guarantee whatever that any of her ships once sent to sea would ever be heard of again. British policy was successful for a while in giving the ships of the kingdom a good position in the trade to the United States. For nearly ten years after independence they had at least half of the business, and part of the time more. There was too much energy in the character of the people of the New World to submit to these regulations and interferences. They demanded the utmost liberty and security for their commerce at sea, and the right to trade to any port in the world with the government of which they were at peace. After exhausting the resources of negotiation and legislation, they went to war in 1812 in behalf of their commerce. They beat the mother-country in this war, and then followed it up with a demand for reciprocity in trade to England and freedom of trade to her colonies.

This aggressive demand revealed to England that she had a very different antagonist from the Dutch to contend with, and brought her Government face to face with the question of the propriety of maintaining the integrity of the Navigation Acts and its warlike policy in view of the changed circumstances of the commerce and politics of the world. Open aggression was now abandoned, and England sought to gain her end by diplomacy. In regard to the question now before it, the Government was willing to agree to reciprocity in direct trade. No other course was left open, in fact, and it was believed that reciprocity would at least be attended with the employment of two sets of ships in the trade, and that Englishmen would have half of the trade, if they did not get it all. To admit the American Republic to the West India and Canada trade was a different matter. It could not be thought of under any circumstances if it would destroy the sale of British manufactures in those regions. If it would not affect the market for British goods, it still might be a dangerous precedent; and it would probably compel British ships to withdraw from the carrying-trade between the United States and the Canadas and Indies. The Government granted reciprocity at once in the treaty of peace of 1815, but hesitated long over the other branch of the subject. Finally, it was seen that British ships would be placed under disabilities in the United States unless the trade to the Canadas and Indies was opened to American goods. It was so opened in 1822. It was, however, immediately followed by a regulation which made it a grant of barren privileges. It was enacted that, if the goods imported to those colonies or to England should be brought from English warehouses in English ships, there should be a reduction of ten per cent. upon the duties, afterward twenty-five per cent. The object of this was quickly seen in its results. British ships loading in England with manufactures sailed with them to America, where they landed their goods and took on cargoes of American produce. Sailing thence to Canada, they put their cargoes into warehouses, actually sometimes, but more often nominally, and then went to the Indies or to England with their cargoes, where by reason of the differential duty they could dispose of them at rates which made it difficult if not impossible for the Americans to compete with them. Bounties were at the same time given for the exportation of English goods in English ships, which often more than paid the freight to America, and thus placed the vessels in a position to take return freights to England at an exceedingly low rate. The regulations of England in regard to the colonial trade were combated in the United States, and in 1825 England returned for a time to her rigidly exclusive policy, and forbade American vessels to enter her colonial ports on or near this continent under penalty of forfeiture of goods and vessels. As this again proved to be a disadvantage to the colonies, the regulation was repealed in 1830, and complete reciprocity of trade was granted.

After the Peace of 1815 there was a period of twenty years of extreme depression to British shipping. The world had been exhausted by wars, and commercial depression was universal. But the British ship-owners had something more to contend with than that. It was the enormous increase of the merchant-shipping of the world. The tonnage of England had grown from 1,500,000 in 1789 to over 2,000,000 in 1815, and the tonnage of the United States had sprung up from 280,000 to 1,100,000 in the same period. There had been an increase of 1,300,000 tons of shipping in these two countries alone, and the efficiency of the merchant-fleets of the two countries was so great, by reason of improvements in hulls and the greater ability of sailors, that the increase might reasonably be rated as amounting in fact to a quarter more. Besides this, there had been a vast production of merchant-vessels in the north of Europe. The Baltic trade in timber, naval stores, etc., had grown very large, and the exporting countries of the north had been able to build ships so cheap that they were taking the business into their own hands, and supplying the large fleets required to carry it on. The Italians, Russians, and Austrians, had built large fleets also in the Mediterranean. Shipping, in fact, had increased faster than commerce, and the world was flooded with it. The British ship-owner had to contend with a lack of cargoes, therefore, to begin with, and then with his brother ship-owner in England, and with the cheap ships of other countries in the matter of rates of freight. Freights fell very low in this period of depression. In 1827 it was found that the British ship-owners were nearly all losing money. A large proportion of merchant-vessels of the kingdom were heavily mortgaged. Owners were beginning to allow their property to be broken up rather than operate it at a continual loss. Building received a check, and the merchant-fleet of the kingdom ran down from 24,776 keels in 1824 to 23,195 in 1827.

The situation was remarkably similar to that existing in the United States after the war of 1861-'65 for the preservation of the Union. What rendered it more grievous to Englishmen was exactly the same thing which made the maritime depression in America after 1865 so intolerable to Americans. It was the continual growth and prosperity of the principal rival of the country in maritime enterprise, and the fact that that growth was a large part of the cause of the depression experienced at home. America had made wonderful strides since her independence, and was now sailing the sea in trades where Englishmen could not, and was gradually expelling Englishmen from the whole of the trade to the New World. Two sets of ships were still used in that trade, but the American set was very large, and the British set hardly

worth mentioning. In 1827 $145,000,000 of the commerce of the Unit-
ed States was carried on in American vessels, and only $14,000,000 in
all foreign vessels, the English only having a part of this very small
share. Besides that, the Americans had nearly driven the British shipping out of the carrying-trade to the East Indies, whose ports England
had been compelled to open to the vessels of the United States from
motives of interest. The feeling which this condition of things produced
in England can be understood from the following comments of the
London *Times* in May, 1827 :

" It is not our habit to sound the tocsin on light occasions, but we conceive
it to be impossible to view the existing state of things in this country without
more than apprehension and alarm. Twelve years of peace, and what is the
situation of Great Britain ? . . . . The shipping interest, the cradle of our navy,
is half ruined. Our commercial monopoly exists no longer; and thousands of
our manufacturers are starving or seeking redemption in distant lands. . . .
We have closed the Western Indies against America from feelings of commercial rivalry. Its active seamen have already engrossed an important branch of
our carrying-trade to the Eastern Indies. . . . Her starred flag is now conspicu-
ous on every sea, and will soon defy our thunder."

This state of things continued for many years. There were occasional symptoms of revival, but the depression continued with a per-
sistence which augured ill for the future of British navigation. Ship-
building was active in other countries, but in the United Kingdom it
decreased from 1,719 vessels, with a tonnage of 205,000, in 1826, to 1,039
vessels, with a tonnage of 103,031, in 1831. Trade began to expand
again, but the profits upon navigation continued to fall.

The situation became so serious that the British people awoke to
the necessity of taking some decided action to bring about a change,
to reorganize their whole commercial system if necessary. The first
step was taken in 1833, in response to a petition of between four and
five hundred ship-builders and merchants, praying that the Navigation
Acts might be so amended as to permit Englishmen to build or buy
ships in foreign countries. This proposed a startling innovation on
British policy. Still it came from a class of men who, more than any
others, were directly interested in the welfare of the national marine,
and it received prompt attention.

England has never framed or altered an important policy without a
mature consideration of all the facts of the case by men bred to public
affairs, and qualified by long years of service to judge accurately as to
the consequences of any special line of action. In the present instance
Parliament ordered a thorough investigation of the whole subject of
British trade, commerce, and navigation, as a necessary preliminary to
any action whatever. Only in the light of all the facts could it be
clearly seen what the needs of the national marine were, and what

change of policy would lift it once more to its feet and make it prosperous. Especial attention was given in this investigation, which was
long and able, to the state of the manufactures, shipping, and trade, in
other lands. The liveliest curiosity was manifested in regard to the
United States, and everybody who knew anything about that country
was impressed to give his testimony. From the testimony taken by
this committee it appeared that it was almost the unanimous opinion
among ship-owners that they had been injured by the acts of reciprocity of trade; and they gave their opinions on this subject with a mani-
festation of feeling which betrayed how they had suffered since 1815
better than the facts they recited. · It was stated that several other
countries enjoyed superior advantages with respect to ship-building.
They had an abundance of material, while England was obliged to
import. Vessels could be built for £8 a ton and less in Prussia, Denmark, and the north countries; for £11 a ton in France; and for from
£10 to £12 in the United States; while in England the cost was from
£15 to £18 a ton in the more favored localities, and £28 a ton in London. The operating expenses of other nations were also less. The ships
of the north countries and of the Mediterranean sailed regularly at less
than and sometimes at half the expense of English vessels, owing to
the lower wages of the sailors, and their contentment with a poorer
quality of provisions. Even the Americans, who paid their sailors first-
class wages, were able to navigate at less expense, because, their men
being more efficient, fewer of them were needed; and, besides that, the
Americans had many labor-saving devices for managing the topsail,
handling the anchor, etc., which also dispensed with men. These
cheaper ships were carrying on a large independent commerce which
interfered materially with the British ship-owners, and in the direct
intercourse with England were compelling them to sail at rates which did
not pay. In the trade to America, the ships of the United States now
had monopolized five-sixths of the business. They not only obtained
more freight but better prices for it, being paid $\frac{1}{16}$ of a penny more per
pound on cotton. They were better ships. They sailed faster than
English hulls, and were handled by men who could always make one
more voyage a year with them than Englishmen were in the habit of
making in the same class of vessels. They were insured better than
English ships in England. The low freights were by some considered
as not calculated entirely to be a disadvantage to England in the long-
run. Besides their effect in stimulating commerce, which certainly had
grown since freights broke down, they would be serviceable to England
in reducing the cost of her ship-building materials.

The general result of this investigation was, to convince Parliament
that the time had not yet come for any material alteration in the navigation laws, at least not for any of the sort described. If times were

dull in England, the proper remedy was not to take away more employment from the people by transferring the profitable and important
business of ship-building to other lands; and it was seen that even if,
by granting the petition of the builders and owners, cheaper ships
could be gained to England, still the matter of wages of sailors and
general expense of operating was left untouched thereby. The investigation opened the eyes of England more fully than ever before to the
dangerous rivalry growing up against her. But it was believed that the
state of British manufactures was such that the kingdom could yet hold
its own after a general revival of business. Steam had now been thoroughly utilized in English factories, and these establishments were turn-
ing out a prodigious quantity of serviceable and cheap goods, for which
there was already a world-wide distribution, and which would be sold in
increasing quantities as fast as trade improved. English ships would
certainly have a large share in this distribution. To South America,
they would have almost a monopoly of it. The clouds seemed to
scatter as Parliament studied the sky. At any rate, the emergency
was not considered sufficient to amend the laws and permit vessels of
foreign construction to fly the flag of England. An emergency would
have to be dire indeed to permit English ships to be built in the United
States. The owners and builders were left to work out their own salva-
tion with the aid of the cheap materials supplied by the cheap freights,
and of their own business skill and ability.

An expansion of trade taking place after the investigation of 1833,
the conservatism of Parliament was justified. Shipping again became
active, and building revived. In 1846 British tonnage had increased
from 2,271,000 in 1833 to 3,200,000. When 1846 arrived, important changes had taken place in naval art, and new phases of the commerce of the world began to attract the attention of British legislators.
The Navigation Acts were now felt by all to be a hinderance to British
enterprise. They had fulfilled the purpose for which they were framed,
and Britain had grown beyond them. An advantage could be gained
over the United States by repealing them. It was a period of great
agitation in England over the commercial laws. In 1847 another investigation was ordered of the state of British navigation. The committee that was appointed remained in session for a long time, and
laid hold of every British statesman, builder, and merchant, and of
every American trader and sea-captain, who knew anything that a
Briton ought to understand, about the subject in view. The committee
did not pay the slightest attention to the subject of steam-navigation
and iron ships, which every Englishman was thinking of at that time,
but devoted itself closely to discovering if British builders and owners
would be injured by repealing the laws. It was discovered that they
probably would not be, and the Navigation Acts were accordingly

repealed, as from the first day of January, 1850, the two hundredth year after the original enactment by the republicans under Cromwell, England let go of the registry, coasting-trade, and direct-trade laws, because she was virtually secure without them, and she wanted to grasp at something better. She herself now wanted to gain the very indirect trade against which she had been legislating for two centuries. She believed that she could drive the United States from the sea by securing it. She demanded at once of the United States and other countries the right to enter their ports in indirect trade, and, gaining this, at once put her shipping into fields of profitable employment, which had never been opened to it—particularly into that between the United States and South America. She was prepared also to push another policy, which might give her the absolute maritime supremacy of the whole world.

STEAM AND IRON.

Steamboats had been invented and employed early in the century, both in Europe and the United States. The Americans had made a marvelous use of the new agency; steamboats had been used on the Clyde since 1812. David Napier had in 1818 proved the practicability of using them in deep-sea navigation by building boats to run to Ireland. When the Savannah arrived in England from America in 1819, the kingdom received a great shock. The event was discussed in counting-rooms, clubs, and cabinet, and in the papers, and it was generally regarded as the most dangerous thing which had ever occurred in the history of British shipping. The Americans making no use of the new motive power on the Atlantic, however, the alarm subsided, but not the impression which it had produced. David Napier and others gave themselves up at once to studying the capacities of steam upon the sea. In 1824 four steamboats were established in the trade to Ireland from Liverpool. They were successful, and the British mind, quick as lightning to seize upon the new idea, at once took fire with the ambition to build steam-packets to run to every part of the globe. In 1825 there was a *furor* in England over the subject. In Liverpool a vast number of projects were formed, and companies organized, one of them having a capital of £600,000 to build and operate steamers in the ocean-service. This was fifteen years before the Americans or any other people had taken a practical step in the same direction. The minds of the projectors had, however, run in advance of the progress of invention. When a close calculation was made of the cost of steamers and the enormous quantities of coal the engines of that day would consume, there was a sudden cooling of enthusiasm. A reaction took place, during which it was confidently predicted that steam would never supersede sails upon the ocean; the largest vessel that could be built would not carry coal enough to get the steamer to any distant part of the world.

The change in the current of feeling affected neither the builders nor the Government. The former are a class of men who in England and America have repeatedly attempted the seemingly impossible, and succeeded. It is to their vigor and originality that the success either country has won upon the sea is prominently due. The builders gave themselves up to studying the problem before them. The Government aided them by large orders for steam-vessels for the navy, by means of which machine-shops, yards, and tools, were created for producing merchant-vessels. England has earned from the rest of the world a thousand times over the public money thus invested in aid of the ship-builders. The Government also resolved to try a few experiments. Calculations were made as to the cost of steam and the amount of money which would be required to enable a company operating a line of steamers in any particular trade to pay expenses and a dividend. Contracts were advertised for and awarded to steamboat companies to run to the Isle of Man at £850 per annum, in 1833; at £17,000 per annum, to run to Rotterdam and Hamburg twice a week, in 1834; at £30,000 per annum, to run to Gibraltar weekly, in 1836.

These experiments were satisfactory to the Government. The crossing of the Atlantic was now conceived, and this important work was undertaken at once. In November, 1836, the Government advertised for proposals for mail service to America. One tender was put in by the Great Western Steamship Company, which offered to run to Halifax once a month at £45,000 a year. The company proposed to put into the service one steamer of 2,900 tons, to cost £40,000 ; another of 1,700 tons, to cost £60,000 ; and a third of medium size. It refused absolutely to run to New York, because, as its vessels expected to use sails half the time, and would go heavily loaded with coal, it was not believed that they could compete with the beautiful clipper-ships of New York City, which then had a monopoly of the mail and passenger business to that port, and almost a monopoly of the freighting. Another set of merchants organized under the name of the St. George Steam-Packet Company, and offered to go to Halifax once a month for £45,000, and to New York for £65,000. Neither of these offers promised to secure the object for which the Government had deliberately planned this service.

While the two proposals were pending, Samuel Cunard, who had an idea of his own, went to the Government privately and presented it. He represented that, by going once a week to New York in swift steamers, he could get the whole of the letters and passengers which were being carried by the American packet-ships, and that they would cease to carry them. The Government entertained his proposal, but did not

at first wish to involve itself too deeply in what it regarded as in some
respects an experiment. Besides, to send the steamers to New York
would be to encourage the growth of New York; and England had,
from the foundation of the first colony in the New World, legislated
steadily against the building up of a great commercial foreign emporium
on the American Continent, of which she had a dread. It was arranged
that Cunard should have a contract to go twice a month to Halifax and
Boston, with an occasional steamer to Quebec. He was to have £60,000
for the service. Sir Charles Wood, then Chancellor of the Exchequer, and
Sir Francis Baring, afterward First Lord of the Admiralty, went into a
series of elaborate calculations with Cunard as to the expense of the
undertaking and the probabilities of success. The result was the offer
named. Cunard built his steamers, and began the service July 4, 1840.
His ships being larger than the contract required, the compensation was
soon increased to £90,000, £5,000 being taken off afterward on the dis-
continuance of the occasional voyage to Quebec. Thus England had
seized upon the American idea and turned it against her, backing it up
by a governmental policy as protective as was ever evolved from her
councils. Her example was not lost upon the United States. This
republic, which left so much to private enterprise in that age, and did
so little to help it, at length discovered the purpose of the British Government, and, under the spur of alarm, decided to act. Two companies
were formed in New York to send steamers to Europe, and the Government was solicited to give them a contract. Learning of this, Cunard immediately went to England and laid the facts before the Government. After a great deal of consultation it was agreed that the time
had come to carry out the original purpose of the contract. Cunard
was authorized to run once a week to Halifax, and thence alternately
to New York and Boston. A subsidy of £145,000 was voted to him
for the purpose, or more than double the amount of the original contract. The new plan went into operation immediately, and when the
rival American line finally started, and began to compete with Cunard,
the Government legislated in favor of the latter by taxing letters which
came by the American line twenty-four cents more postage apiece
than when sent by Cunard's steamers. This discrimination was abandoned upon the passage of a retaliatory law in America, but Cunard
was still left with the protection of a subsidy twice as large as that
enjoyed by Collins.

It having been fairly demonstrated by the Cunard line that steam
was available for the purpose of navigation to distant lands, England
entered at once upon colossal schemes for putting steamers into all
ocean-trades. The rest of the world seemed asleep on the subject.
France and America were the only countries in which there was anything doing ; but they did not act with vigor, and England was left to

3

pursue her schemes of maritime enterprise almost without a rival. In 1840 a subsidy of £37,000 was given for carrying the mails on from Gibraltar to Alexandria; in 1845 the service was extended to China and Japan, for £160,000. In 1840 the sum of £240,000 was voted to a company of responsible and eminent merchants in London to run steamers to the West Indies, Mexico, and the Isthmus; and in 1858 this company had twenty first-class steamers in the business, and was receiving £270,000 a year.

In 1849, and again in 1853, the Government directed thorough investigations of the steam-packet service, in order to determine how the new policy was working, and the amount of pay which steamers ought to receive. It went steadily ahead with its operations, which were proved to be working out marvelous results for the benefit of England. Money was advanced to merchants to build steamers, and a paying contract given to them when the ships were built. Old contracts were renewed as fast as they expired, with the same or larger pay, and to run ten years at a time. Every possible inducement was offered, to stimulate the building and operation of steam-vessels; and the result was that, in 1858, when the American competition broke down, and the United States was left with only seven steam-vessels in all its foreign trade, England had one hundred and twenty, plying to the extremities of the earth. She was at that time paying $5,000,000 a year in subsidies, and getting it nearly all back again in ocean-postages alone. Postages were high in those days, and the Government made several millions upon the Cunard contract alone. How frequently her expenditures came back to her in other ways we need hardly stop to say. England's ocean steam-tonnage of 1,470,000 in 1876 is the fruit of her policy in aiding her ship-builders and steamship companies to take advantage of the great opportunity which opened up before them forty years ago. England still pays $3,800,000 a year in subsidies.

Now, with reference to iron. In 1787 a canal-boat of 32 tons burden was built in England, with an iron hull and wooden frame. It was regarded as a great curiosity in mechanical art. The whole boat only weighed eight tons. Another boat was built soon after, and both were employed on the canal from Birmingham. This style of craft became very popular, and from 1800 to 1810 they were built in large numbers. They were not so expensive, compared with wood, when the art of making them had been mastered, because timber was dear in England, and coal and iron were cheap, and the boats outlived those of wood. In 1820 the principle was applied to the building of steamers, which class of vessels required a stiff frame and hull. Sir Charles Napier went into the business. The first boat was sent to France. Afterward others were built for English use. In 1834 John Laird was regularly building iron vessels, and in 1839 had launched two steamers of

570 and 660 tons burden, of iron, which afterward took part in the Chinese War in 1842.

The Government aided in the development of the means to build these vessels by ordering iron ships for the navy. It was seen that, if the new material should turn out to be as valuable as the first experiments with it gave promise, England would at last have gained a superior position in regard to building-materials. France and the Netherlands had no iron of any account. America had mines, but they were not developed, and finished iron was costly there. There was plenty of the metal in the north of Europe, but such were England's advantages in the way of development that, if iron was to be applied extensively to the construction of hulls, it only needed that the peculiar machinery for producing ship-iron should be created speedily in order to place England ahead of the world in the matter. The orders of the Government for navy-vessels enabled the principal builders to supply themselves with all the tools, machinery, and appliances, for building merchant-vessels of iron on a large scale. So judicious and timely was this aid that iron-ship building became at once a feature of the manufactures of England, and the business was practised there alone in Europe for many years. In the course of twenty-five years after Laird began, iron hulls had been thoroughly tested and found to be satisfactory in an eminent degree. They were stiffer than timber hulls, required less repairs, and accommodated so much more cargo, that an iron ship of 600 tons burden was scarcely larger than a 500-ton timber ship, and in 1857 were ten per cent. cheaper than the latter class of vessels. A remarkable incident in 1857 confirmed their value to the English. The Persia, of the Cunard line, encountered ice in mid-ocean while going at full speed. Her iron hull, stiff and sharp, split the ice and went through it unharmed. The Pacific, of the Collins line, a wooden steamer, meeting with ice on the same voyage, was broken up by it and went down. The ability and economy of the iron ships soon made them the favorite style of vessel among English merchants. A large proportion of the ship-owners have since 1840 supplied themselves with them.

France and the United States both began to build iron vessels, stimulated by the example of England. Both gave up the experiment after a short trial. England had the cheapest materials. After 1860 the whole business of constructing iron hulls returned to the British Isles, where for ten or twelve years a substantial monopoly of it was enjoyed.

The superior cheapness of iron vessels, and the preference they secured for a time in trade, owing to their speed and low expenses of operation, have been an advantage to the English merchant marine, and to-day it comprises one-third of the sailing-tonnage of the world. Surely, 20,300 ships, with a tonnage of 5,800,300, are something to boast of.

It has already been stated that the policy of England has been
* steadily directed to crushing out the competition of the United States.
The cap-stone of her efforts in this direction was her course during our
civil war. She did not dare to take an active part in our national
quarrel, as she would have done gladly had it been certain that she
would not have been molested by European powers ; but she had recourse to an almost equally effective plan, which will be described more
at length in the chapter on "American Annals." She fitted out powerful men-of-war to cruise against us, and she had the satisfaction of
seeing our supremacy receive a dreadful blow. It was the modern way
of serving us as she had served the Dutch in an earlier age. Its object
was gained by its removing the last obstacle to her temporary maritime
greatness.

IV.

THE POLICY OF OTHER GOVERNMENTS.

As far as it affects the navigation of the United States unfavorably,
the case may be summed up briefly:

France imitated the example of England in granting subsidies to
steamship companies to ply in the trade of the Mediterranean and the
American Continent. Her first company was the Messageries Impériales, formed to trade to the Levant and all Mediterranean countries.
It was liberally compensated by the Government, and in 1858 had fifty
steamships in the service. In 1858 contracts were offered as follows :
$620,000 a year for twenty-six voyages between Havre and New York, or
about $23,000 a voyage ; $940,000 a year for service to Brazil ; $1,300,-
000 for steamers to the West Indies and Mexico : in all, about $2,800,000.
The General Transatlantic Company was formed to undertake the
American service. The Messageries Impériales secured the Brazilian
contract. In 1870 France paid $4,732,267 to her ocean-mail lines, and
in 1876 was paying 23,388,892 francs, or something like $4,800,000.
Two of these lines are a direct obstacle to American navigation—the one
between New York and Havre, and the one to Brazil.

Austria and Italy both granted mail contracts to ocean-lines. These,
however, have not come into direct competition with American ships,
except in the Mediterranean. In that sea, the policy of those two
countries has been very much in the way of American enterprise.

Spain refused us reciprocity the longest of any country in the world,
and paid the Compagnie Gautier $25,000 a voyage to ply semi-monthly

between Cadiz and the West Indies. She has always interfered with our ships in the West Indian trade, and does so occasionally now.

Brazil did not grant us maritime reciprocity until 1867. She invites all nations to her coasting and river trades; but has subsidized a number of native and British steam lines for those trades, which virtually excludes us from them. She pays $1,706,000 in subsidies annually, $96,000 of it having until recently been paid to a British line running to New York. The policy of Brazil is at present friendly to the United States in intention, an exhibition of which is the grant of a subsidy of $100,000 to an American line to ply between Rio Janeiro and New York.

China is pursuing a policy of wonderful energy. Five years ago she resolved to take the carriage of commodities along her coasts into her own hands. Foreigners were then operating a large number of steamers in that immense trade ; and they had nearly ruined the owners of the native junks by depriving them of employment. Americans had steamers in the same trade. The Chinese Merchants' Steamship Company was organized, and the Government gave them 1,000,000 taels to build their vessels with, and then gave them a monopoly of the transportation of government grain on the rivers and along the coasts. The foreign companies were ruined by this new concern, and the Shanghai Steam Navigation Company, after a short fight, sold out to it bodily. The Chinese have finally secured the whole of the coasting trade of their great empire. The startling statement is now made that China has subsidized a line of steamers to run to the Sandwich Islands, and that the line is to be extended to the United States immediately. This looks like certain death to the China branch of the Pacific Mail Line, unless the United States shall sustain that line promptly.

There appears to be no prominent government in the world which, while legislating directly in favor of native shipping, does not give it financial support, except the United States.

V.

AMERICAN ANNALS.

THE history of American navigation can most profitably be considered by dividing it into periods. It is difficult to suggest an exact division of the subject, but the following will do for practical purposes : 1. The time down to 1815, comprehending the period of struggle to obtain security for our shipping on the high-seas ; 2. From 1815 to

1850, which formed the era of establishment of reciprocity ; 3. The
period of steam and iron.

During the first period our navigation was explicitly a national
question. During the second it gradually ceased to be. The third is
the period of decadence, our shipping having been left to its own resources, the regulation in regard to registry and the coasting-trade
being the only thing which saved it from extinction.

OUR EARLY NAVIGATION.

The first vessels built on our shores were for the fisheries and coasting-trade, but principally for the fisheries. The people were poor, and
had to pay for their vessels in grain, calicoes, and similar commodities.

The fisheries were very profitable. They had attracted attention in
Europe at a very early period, and large numbers of vessels went out to
America for no other purpose than to visit the fishing-banks. A voyage generally yielded from £3,000 to £4,000 profit. The consequence
was, that as early as 1660 there were often as many as six hundred sail
from Europe on the banks at one time. The New-Englanders went
into this business at once. Ship-builders were sent out to them from
London in 1631, and they fitted out a large number of vessels of very
respectable size for that age, some of them being of three hundred tons
burden, and put them at once into the fisheries, and subsequently into
trade.

The New England colonies had very little transatlantic trade of
their own until shortly before the Revolution, but they supplied the
principal part of the colonial shipping which went into the transatlantic commerce of the other portions of the coast. The Navigation Act
protected them against the Dutch, and their abundance of timber and
naval stores, and frugal habits, enabled them to compete for the carrying-trade with the mother-country. A very fair share of the fish, tobacco, rice, timber, and hides of this country, were sent to England in
our own shipping. At the time of the Revolution we owned nearly half
of the tonnage employed.

Besides this transatlantic trade, the shipping of the early colonies
was employed somewhat in trading to the Spanish West Indies. This
was against the law. It was in contravention both of English and
Spanish policy. It was, however, the principal resource of the colonists in obtaining a supply of silver for ready money, and they carried
it on in spite of its illegality and dangers. The enforcement of restric-
tions upon the freedom of our navigation to the Spanish colonies and
to the different ports of Europe was one cause of the Revolution.

During the Revolutionary War, navigation received a check, but
the building-art improved. Nearly all the ships built for the foreign

trade were privateers, made for strength and speed, and carrying an armament of guns. The loss of our shipping in that war was very great, for, able as were our sailors, the cannon of the English were superior to ours, and their ships generally larger and stronger as well as more numerous. Mr. Currier, the historian of ship-building on the Merrimac, tells how twenty-two gallant vessels sailed from Newburyport alone during that period, which, with the thousand men on board of them, were never heard of again. But this very superiority of the royal navy in weight of metal and size of ships was the most direct and powerful stimulus to our native builders, and they began to produce excellent vessels, which, before the war was over, attracted attention even in Europe.

· John Adams, in a letter to Senator Varnum, gave an illustration of this. He said: "In June, 1779, I dined with M. Thevenôt, intendant of the navy at l'Orient, certainly one of the most experienced, best read, and most scientific naval commanders in Europe. That excellent officer said to me in the hearing of the Chevalier de la Luzerne, M. Marbois, and twenty officers of the French Navy, 'Your country is about to become the first naval power in the world.' My answer was : 'It is impossible to foresee what may happen a hundred or two or three hundred years hence ; but there is at present no appearance or probability of any great maritime power in America for a long time to come.' 'Hundred years!' said Thevenôt; 'it will not be twenty years before you will be a match for any maritime power of Europe.' 'You surprise me, sir; I have no suspicion or conception of any such great things; will you allow me to ask your reasons for such an opinion?' 'My reasons,' said M. Thevenôt—'my reasons are very obvious ; you have all the materials, and the knowledge and skill to employ them. You have timber, hemp, tar, and iron ; seamen and naval architects equal to any in the world.' 'I know we have oak, and pine, and iron, and we may have hemp, but I did not know our shipwrights were equal to yours in Europe.' 'The frigate in which you came here,' said M. Thevenôt (the Alliance, Captain Landais), 'is equal to any in Europe. I have examined her, and I assure you there is not in the king's service, nor in the English Navy, a frigate more perfect and complete in materials and workmanship.'" Other incidents could be cited to show that, even before this country had obtained its independence, the building-art had so improved here as to make American ships respected everywhere for their speed, strength, and beauty, and to excite the liveliest anticipations as to the future of this republic in navigation. Building revived after the Revolution. It is not known what the tonnage was at that time. It could hardly have exceeded 100,000 tons, if it was as much as that. The facts do not appear in the colonial records, and the national Government had no control over the registry of shipping until after the

adoption of the Constitution. The prominent fact was the preponder-
ance of European bottoms in the foreign trade. In 1789 the registration was 123,893 tons in the foreign trade ; 68,607 in the coasting-
trade ; and 9,062 in the fisheries; and there were still 100,000 tons of
foreign shipping in the external commerce.

In the commercial intercourse of the world prior to the struggle for
American independence, there had been little in the nature of equitable
dealing by one nation toward the vessels of another trading to its ports.
The colonists in America had been made to feel the burdensomeness
of this, and one of the principles they fought to establish during
the war was the freedom of commerce and entire reciprocity in the
intercourse of nations. In 1778 Franklin negotiated a treaty with
Holland which gave expression to this principle, by providing for
putting the ships of both nations on a footing of exact reciprocity in
the ports of each other. It was with some difficulty that the treaty was
obtained, because, liberal-spirited as were the Dutchmen, political consequences were involved in it from which they shrank. It was consummated at length, however, and was signed by John Adams in 1782.
Holland lost a great deal by this act of friendliness to the American
Republic, because England went to war with her on account of it, took
from her the most valuable of her East India possessions, and crippled
her commerce, as a punishment for countenancing rebellious colonies.
The Americans gained little by it at the time, it may also be said, because, while it established a principle, England took care to interrupt
our commerce with the Netherlands, so that it should be of no practical
benefit to us for many years. It was useful afterward, but not then.
After the treaty of peace the United States proposed a treaty of reciprocity in commerce to England. Negotiations were delayed for several years, to enable the king's counselors to study the situation carefully. It was then refused. England believed that, by applying the
Navigation Act rigidly to the case of the United States, supplementing
it with discriminating tonnage duties, she could get the carrying-trade
to this continent entirely into her own hands. So far from conceding
to this young and poor republic what she had refused to the richest
monarchies of Europe, and which was obviously to her disadvantage,
she adopted a policy toward us even more severe than to the European
governments. Our representatives labored for some time in London to
bring about a favorable arrangement, but every negotiation ended in
failure. In 1785 John Adams wrote home indignantly to the Government : "This being the state of things, you may depend upon it the
commerce of America will have no relief at present, nor in my opinion
ever, until the United States shall have generally passed navigation
acts ; and, if this measure is not adopted, we shall be derided when
we suffer more and more, and our calamities be laughed at." Some

of the colonies immediately complied with this suggestion. They found, however, that this drove trade to the other colonies. The situation became embarrassing both to business interests and to national pride.

The first Congress under the Constitution met in April, 1789. It gave its attention immediately to shipping. Revenue was the uppermost object of legislation, but protection to navigation and industry was also explicitly aimed at. Within two days after the meeting of Congress, Mr. Madison had brought into the House bills for duties upon imports and tonnage, both of which legislated directly in behalf of American interests. Shipping at that time needed little if anything more, in the way of protection, than a law which would place it on a par with foreign vessels in transatlantic and coasting trade with reference to taxes and port charges. Our vessels were cheaper than those of England, France, and Spain. They were of equally good models, and were sailed by better seamen. Only an equality in regard to taxation was required to enable our shipping to play a creditable part in the operations of a rapidly-rising and valuable commerce. It did not have to wait for what it wanted. The spirit of the hour was protection to American interests against foreign policy, and it was resolved that there should be no half-way work about it. Mr. Madison, though a free-trader himself, proposed the protective legislation looking directly to the building up of our navigation. There was some debate on his bills, in which the general indifference of agricultural States to the shipping business was illustrated, though temperately, by the remarks of Southern representatives, who feared that their part of the Union would bear most of the burden of the new duties; but there was no opposition to the protective principle, and the third law of Congress was an act imposing discriminating duties in favor of American tonnage.

This law, signed July 20, 1789, provided that, on each entry from a foreign port, American ships should be taxed six cents a ton; vessels built upon our shores but owned abroad, thirty cents a ton; foreign ships fifty cents a ton. American ships in the coasting-trade and fisheries were to pay the tax of six cents per ton once a year only, while foreign ships were to pay a tax of fifty cents on each entry, which was virtually a prohibition of those trades to foreign flags. By the second law of the same Congress it was provided that, from the duties on all goods imported in American vessels, there should be a discount of ten per cent. A regulation in favor of the national flag was also made with reference to the China and India trade, which gave that valuable business entirely into our hands. A schedule of discriminating duties was fixed upon as follows:

IMPORTS.	U. S. Vessels coming direct.	U. S. Vessels from Europe.	Foreign Vessels.
Bohea, per pound........................	.06	.08	.15
Black teas, per pound....................	.10	.13	.22
Hyson teas.............................	.20	.26	.45
Other green teas, per pound..............	.12	.16	.27

On all other goods from India and China there was to be 12½ per cent. *ad valorem* if imported in foreign vessels, but no duty if imported in American vessels.

This legislation did not stop with putting a tax upon European bottoms in our ports equal to the charges imposed upon our ships in Europe. It went further than that, in fact and in intention. It proposed to give Americans a decided preference in their own commerce over foreigners, of whatever nationality, and to extend an inducement to Europeans to buy our ships ; thus giving explicit protection and encouragement to ship-building. The laws would have been made more stringent yet, had there been a sufficient supply of national tonnage to insure the rapid and convenient exportation of our rice, tobacco, grain, timber, and other produce, without recourse to the services of foreigners. A moderate effort was made to have the tax on foreign ships placed higher than fifty cents. The possibility of this being an inconvenience to Virginia, which had few ships, but did have a vast surplus of agricultural produce, deterred Congress from adopting the more radical policy until the effect of the experimental schedule of taxes could be observed.

It was not supposed in Europe that the United States would act with such vigor. With little wealth except the produce of her farms, and no means of obtaining an abundance of manufactured goods at moderate prices, except by exporting the surplus tobacco, rice, grain, and forestry produce of the country, the United States was depended upon to pursue a passive policy, and, at any rate, not to strike back in such spirited retaliation. The passage of the tonnage and duty acts imperiled the employment of 200,000 tons of foreign shipping, which, according to current estimates, was then trading to these shores. The laws which placed this tonnage under disabilities would probably compel its withdrawal in the course of two or three years, unless something was done to counteract their effect. The passage of the laws, therefore, created an extraordinary sensation in Europe, especially in the mother-country. There the policy of the United States was regarded simply in the light of retaliation. There was in consequence, at first, a truly British disposition to go on and adopt a harsher policy than ever toward the new republic. Our representatives abroad, however, found that on the whole prudence got the better of feeling, and it induced the powers to lend a more favorable ear to our applications for commercial treaties. Negotiation now became possible where before it was refused. It took several years to effect anything practical at any of the courts, but when it was finally observed that American vessels were being built in large numbers under the protection of the national laws, and that the new flag was beginning to crowd European shipping in European ports, the Old World yielded to our requests. A treaty was secured from England in November, 1794, from Spain in October, 1795, and from France in 1800. We already had a good one with the Netherlands, dated in 1782. Our first victory was won.

These treaties were not entirely satisfactory, however, because they did not guarantee full equality of tonnage and other duties between American ships and those of other foreign nations. They left room for the imposition of heavy discriminations against us. The treaty with England only opened the West India trade to a very limited extent, and to vessels of not over seventy tons burden, and it was expressly stipulated that this arrangement should end within two years after the war in which England was then engaged. The best that could be said of the negotiations was that they opened the East India trade fully, and secured some sort of recognition for our flag on the seas, and paved the way for future more equitable arrangements.

The Navigation Act was revised in 1790, and the discriminations therein contained made permanent. They continue in force to the present day, except where suspended by the operation of reciprocity laws and treaties. Their effect on this country after their enactment was remarkable. Ship-building revived spontaneously all along the coast. In less than five years, tonnage enough had been produced to enable us to carry on the larger part of our commerce in our own vessels. By 1800, enterprise had been so stimulated by protection that seven-eighths of the imports and exports of the country were being transported under the American flag. The China and India trade was ours exclusively. A large number of vessels were being built for foreigners, the sales from 1798 to 1812 being 197,000 tons, a large amount for those times. Our flag became the most aggressive in peaceful commerce. Secure in the protection of our laws, our merchants pushed their enterprises farther and farther, every year, against all opposition, and entered upon the present century a class of prosperous men, and full of confident anticipations for the future. Shipping had increased in tonnage as follows :

YEARS.	Registered for Foreign Trade.	Coasting-Trade.	Fisheries.
1789	123,893	68,607	9,062
1795	529,470	164,795	34,102
1800	669,921	245,295	30,078
1805	749,341	801,866	58,863

In March, 1804, Congress levied an additional tonnage duty of fifty cents on all foreign shipping for light money. A few Southern men had previously asked for a repeal of all tonnage duties. They were willing to abandon navigation, to secure a repeal of the duties on tobacco in Europe. Public policy was decidedly against giving up the profitable industries of ship-building and navigation, and an additional tax was levied as stated. Commerce was bringing to us capital and prosperity.

One of the annoyances to which our vessels were subjected in these times was the searching of them by English cruisers for the seamen of that nationality who had gone into our merchant-service. A large number of those mariners, seeking to better their condition, had engaged themselves to our captains. It was a maxim with England, "Once a subject always a subject." She asserted the right to impress a citizen-seaman, wherever found, for the purposes of the king's navy; and this was made a pretext for delaying American ships, and taking from them 6,257 of their men. This was a great injury to our commerce. Remonstrances were made against it, but were of no avail. One of the measures taken to guard against this interference was the arming of our merchant-vessels with cannon. In 1805, however, Congress forbade armed vessels to sail from our ports unless specially permitted, it being the desire of the Government to carry its point with England by peaceful negotiation.

In April, 1806, a non-importation act was passed in Congress by immense majorities designed to give weight to our applications for an abolition of this practice of search and impressment. England paid no attention to our demands. On the contrary, the fact that it annoyed and injured us was to her a reason for persisting in it. A further interference with our commerce took place by her blockade of the coast of France and the Netherlands, as a war measure against those powers. It will be recollected that France retaliated in 1806 in the Berlin Decree by forbidding all commerce with England; that the latter adopted orders in council forbidding commerce with France and the Netherlands; and that Napoleon then published the Milan Decree in 1807, in furtherance of his previous proclamation. Both of these jealous powers now began an active interference with American ships, while pursuing their peaceful voyages upon the high-seas, which continued for five years, with greater or less severity. Over 1,660 of our ships, worth millions of dollars, were captured, and either condemned with their cargoes or else compelled to suffer loss by detention. Others were thrown out of their course, and forced to run into neutral harbors for protection. They were delayed in port, searched at sea, and seized even at the mouths of our own harbors. Against this reckless aggression the United States protested in vain. The Embargo Act of December 22, 1807, was finally passed in retaliation; and another, January 10, 1809, to make the first more effectual. March 1, 1809, commerce with England and France was forbidden by the Non-intercourse Act. The quarrel in Europe was something we had nothing to do with, and we looked with impatience on the disastrous interferences with our commerce and navigation, for which it was made a pretext. There was only one sentiment in this country on this subject. In May, 1810, France announced the repeal of the Berlin and Milan Decrees, and a slight relief was granted to our shipping. Great Britain did nothing. The orders in council remained in force. It was denied that the French decrees were extinct, and they were made the excuse for a continuance of the exasperating policy, which, whatever the plausible explanation of it, aimed only at an extinction of the maritime power of America, and the maritime aggrandizement of England.

The War of 1812 was the consequence. This was purely a commercial war. Its object was liberty of navigation and the rights of citizenship. It proposed to protect an important national interest against a foreign policy which left no room for honorable competition, but employed only the arts of force and injustice. This costly war was a dreadful tax upon our young republic. It involved an expense of $150,000,000. It made double duties necessary. It cost us thousands of lives, and millions of property on land and sea. It left us with a business crisis and financial collapse upon our hands. Prof. Sumner, who scoffs at the idea of being governed in these matters by the sentiment of natiouality, speaks of this war as a piece of folly and imbecility. Without it, however, we should have been destroyed as a commercial power. Shipping had in two years declined 250,000 tons. Merchants were ruined by the losses of their property and goods at sea and in foreign ports. Working-men were out of employment. Agricultural production was checked. The discriminating duties of Europe were in force in all their rigor. Without a vigorous assertion of our rights and nationality we should have been left in the condition of a commercial and industrial vassal of England, and have been the laughing-stock of the world. With the war, American nationality gained the respect of the whole world, and our shipping a glorious prestige and leading position. The boast of England—

> " The winds and seas are Britain's wide domain,
> And not a sail but by *permission* spreads "—

which, though here expressed only in a poetical trifle, was the assertion of a claim which no other nation could endure with self-respect, was chastised. Dominion upon the seas was overthrown so effectually that England never again dared to reassert it. Reciprocity, and liberty, and security of navigation, within a few years were made sure by it, and the shackles with which England had sought to restrain our maritime expansion, for thirty-two years, were shattered to atoms. In July,

1815, England conceded to us a commercial treaty in which equality of
port charges and tonnage and other duties were provided for, and the
shipping of each power placed on a footing with the most favored
nations in each other's ports. Some sly attempts at evasion were afterward made by England, but they were promptly met by us, and reciprocity was soon carried out to the letter.

During the war ship-building was badly depressed. The yards were
not entirely deserted, it is true, for Congress having an inadequate
navy permitted private citizens to send out privateers. The construction of these gave considerable employment to the builders. A number
of armed merchant-vessels for regular trade were also built by those
who had the capital and were willing to risk it. Shipping decreased
steadily, however, until the declaration of peace. Our total tonnage
was 1,385,000 in 1810. On January 1, 1815, it was 1,028,000. The captures of the war, large as they were, did not check the decadence of our
tonnage. The captures in the three years amounted to more than
2,300 vessels, but our privateers destroyed many of these at sea, and
750 were retaken, and we in turn lost 1,407 of our own merchant-vessels and fishing-boats, so that the balance was only slightly in our favor.
The hostilities of the eight years following 1806 performed only one important service for our shipping. It improved the already fine models
of our vessels immensely. Speed became an important element. Special
study was given to that branch of the subject, and we came out of the
war in 1815 with a fleet of the ablest vessels in the world.

At the outbreak of hostilities, an additional tax of $1.50 was placed
upon foreign tonnage until the declaration of peace. This was continued until January 4, 1817. On that day a law was passed restoring
the duties of 1789.

THE ESTABLISHMENT OF RECIPROCITY.

We now enter upon a period extending down to 1850, which was
one of uninterrupted growth and prosperity. It is here designated as
the era of the establishment of reciprocity.

Absolute equality of duties in the direct trade was essential to the
growth of our merchant marine. We never obtained it until after the
War of 1812. Neither did we obtain the right to trade to any country
from countries other than our own until after the same point of time.
The United States demanded both of these things, and now devoted its
efforts to obtaining them. The first step was the law of March 3, 1815,
in regard to equalizing tonnage and import duties. This law enacted:

"That so much of the several acts, imposing duties on the tonnage of ships
and vessels, and on goods, wares, and merchandise, imported into the United
States, as impose a discriminating duty on tonnage, between foreign vessels and

vessels of the United States, and between goods imported into the United States in foreign vessels and vessels of the United States, be, and the same are hereby repealed, so far as the same respect the produce or manufacture of the nation to which such foreign ships or vessels may belong. Such repeal to take effect in favor of any foreign nation whenever the President of the United States shall be satisfied that the discriminating or countervailing duties of such foreign nation, so far as they operate to the disadvantage of the United States, have been abolished."

This was a warning and an invitation to all the nations of the world. It applied both to France and the Continental nations which conceded to us equality in theory but denied it in important respects in practice, and to England which until then denied it to us every way. The treaty with England of the following July was the first fruit of this enactment.

The next step was an important law passed in March, 1817, which substantially reënacted the navigation laws of England, and made various regulations for the promotion of our shipping. The law provided :

" That, after the thirtieth day of September next, no goods, wares, or merchandise, shall be imported into the United States from any foreign port or place except in vessels of the United States, or in such foreign vessels as truly and wholly belong to the citizens or subjects of that country of which the goods are the growth, production, or manufacture, or from which such goods can only be, or most usually are, first shipped for transportation. Provided, nevertheless, that this regulation shall not extend to the vessels of any foreign nation which has not adopted and which shall not adopt a similar regulation."

The coasting-trade was reserved exclusively to Americans. An encouragement to employ native mariners was given by a section taxing ships in the foreign trade fifty cents a ton unless two-thirds of the officers and crew were Americans. This law cut off England from the triangular trade to Brazil and the Indies, thence to the United States, and thence home, and reserved it to the United States, but offered to open it to England and the world upon the concession of general reciprocity to us. Another law was passed in May, 1828, offering still more explicitly to the nations of the world, to admit them to our ports on equal terms with our own citizens, provided that our citizens should be admitted to theirs on similar terms. It was a full, frank, fair offer of reciprocity. It proposed to put commerce upon the high plane of fraternity among nations, and leave all the victories within that field of action to the intelligence and enterprise of the different peoples of the world.

These offers were, however, fifty years in advance of the times, and the United States had many struggles to secure the object of them. England took about the same view of the matter, no doubt very properly for her, as we, very properly for us, have since then taken of her offer of free trade to all the world. However beneficial a free commerce might have been in quickening the civilization of the age, it would not have been at all advantageous to England, because the United States had such natural advantages that she would have beaten England out of her carrying-trade. The same was true in regard to France. Accordingly, those two nations tried to circumvent us and defeat our policy in many ways. England first closed the West India trade to us outright. Then, when by reason of a law we passed in 1818, forbidding British ships to enter our harbors from ports to which we were not allowed to trade, she was forced to permit us to enter her West India ports, she adopted regulations intended to injure us in another way. She ordained that goods of American production—naming the most important of them—if imported to England or her colonies from British warehouses, should pay a lower duty than when coming from the United States direct. The object was to secure the importation of our produce to England and the colonies from the Canadas in British ships, confining our ships to the short voyages to Canada. France conceded to us equality in tonnage-dues and light money, but she discriminated against us in another way. She had a large number of vessels trading to New Orleans and other Southern ports. She provided that, upon goods coming to France in those ships, the duty should be less than in other cases by 1½ cent a pound on tobacco, 1½ cent a pound on cotton, and $\frac{66}{100}$ of a cent per hundred-weight on potash. This actually more than paid the freight. An American ship of 300 tons tobacco-laden would have to pay $6,300 more duty than its French competitor.

The United States acted promptly in retaliation. In 1820 a duty of $18 a ton was levied on French vessels, and British ships were forbidden to enter our ports from any colony of England on or near this continent. In both cases our rivals were brought to reason. Matters were arranged with France by treaty in 1822, and the British orders in council were amended. In 1830 a permanent arrangement was made with England.

Our struggles were so successful that, within fifteen years after the Peace of 1815, reciprocity in direct trade had been secured with all the principal trading nations of the world. General reciprocity had been gained with Russia, Sweden, Norway, Prussia, Denmark, and Austria. England conceded general reciprocity in 1849. Since then every other nation of any account not theretofore in treaty with us has followed her example.

Our legislation in behalf of our shipping was timely, and attended with the happiest results. With the restoration of peace, commerce expanded in an extraordinary manner. From a total of $270,000,000 in 1815 it rose to $480,000,000 in 1836. Travel and immigration grew from 20,000 a year before the war to 75,000 within twenty years after it, and in twenty years more to 300,000. The mails became very heavy between this country and Europe. In 1850, the ocean traffic and travel of the United States gave employment to 2,335,000 tons of shipping. The total tonnage entering and clearing from our ports in 1850 was 8,000,000.

In this brilliant story of expansion the United States marine would probably have played a passive part except for our protective laws and aggressive policy.

The causes which operated to our advantage during this period may be briefly summed up as follows :

1. A widening field of commerce and equality of competition within it, owing to the operation of our reciprocity laws and treaties.

2. The United States ships cheaper and abler than those English-built. There was a constant difference in prices in favor of the United States. In 1824 a 300-ton ship would cost from £4,500 to £5,000 in this country, from £5,500 to £6,000 in Canada, and from £6,000 to £6,500 in England. In 1847 a 500-ton vessel would cost £7,500 here, against £8,750 in England, for the same grade of construction. In the north of Europe only were ships as cheap as in the United States, but those ships did not compete with ours. In twenty-five years after the peace, the United States sold 340,000 tons of shipping to foreigners. There was a good demand on account of the low cost and the excellence of the vessels. Our ships in that period made four voyages a year where the English and Dutch craft made three, and five where they made four. Our packet-ships were displaying a speed which toward the close of this period caused people to believe that they would never be superseded by steamers. They made from 200 to 275 miles a day in a fair wind. They have even made 300 miles a day, the average of transoceanic steamer speed. Our builders fixed their standard very high, and continually strove to excel it.

The testimony of all witnesses taken during this period by the committees of Parliament, who were appointed to ascertain what was the matter with British navigation, which was going into a decline, was unanimous in regard to the superiority of American ships. This testimony also went to show that high wages did not prevent the American ship from sailing more cheaply than its English competitor. A London ship-builder and owner, engaged in extensive trade to all parts of the world, made a statement of the facts, which the testimony of other witnesses corroborated, as follows :

VESSELS.	Cost of Ship.	Cost of a Year's Voyage.	Amount of Wages.
English ship of 500 tons..........................	£8,750	£2,623	£786
American ship of 500 tons.........................	7,250	2,191	669

3. American mariners were the best in the world. The larger proportion of these men received their training in the whale and other

4

fisheries. They were largely of New England origin. They combined with the discipline of long and rough voyages the energy and adaptability of the American character. They loved their art, and were proud of the exploits of their ships. The country was proud of them. Those who lived during the War of 1812 received a special education in the privateering of that period, and went back into the peaceful merchant-service at its close the most capable tars in the world. The country is indebted to them for the special maritime task which devolved upon our nautical world just after that war. England renewed the struggle for commercial superiority at once, and fitted out a large number of superior ships, manned by her best men, to go into the American trade. For one year she got one-third of the carrying-trade. We were not prepared to meet her prompt enterprise. But the United States replied to her movement by building a larger and better class of ships than we had ever employed before, and put upon them the flower of the mariners of 1812. In three years more, these able men had handled their vessels so well, making such flying trips across the Atlantic, delivering their cargoes in such admirable condition, and serving their masters so well, that they had reduced England's proportion of the trade to one-sixth. In 1850 England's proportion was still only one-fourth. This was as much due to the character of our mariners as to any other cause. They were well paid, temperate, ready, efficient men. They took good care of the ship ; they got it into and out of port with a surprising saving of time ; they saved it from wreck under circumstances which would have insured its destruction if it was in less capable hands ; and they served their masters and the public in a way that gave their flag the preference in all trade into which it could be lawfully put. Our sailors were very temperate, a point which was brought out in a report to Parliament in 1838 on temperance in the navy, from which it may not be inappropriate to quote. The committee said that " the happiest effects have resulted from the experiments tried in the American navy and merchant-service to do without spirituous liquors as an habitual article of daily use, there being at present more than 1,000 sail of American vessels traversing all the seas of the world in every climate, without the use of spirits by their officers and crews, and being, in consequence of this change, in so much greater a state of efficiency and safety than other vessels not adopting this regulation, that the public insurance companies in America make a return of five per cent. of the premium of insurance on vessels completing their voyages without the use of spirits, while the example of British ships, sailing from Liverpool on the same plan, has been productive of the greatest benefit to ship-owners, underwriters, merchants, officers, and crews."

4. The establishment of the packet-lines to Europe. Into these lines were put the finest and fastest of our ships. They were the mail

and passenger boats of those days, and they carried large quantities of freight besides. They made the run across the Atlantic in an average of less than twenty days, which was three or four days faster than the time of the English vessels in the same trade. The regularity of their departure was found to be an advantage by American buyers, who therefore insured the goods in this country, stipulating that they should come by packet. The packets accordingly soon came to monopolize all the valuable business between this country and the principal ports of Europe, and European ships were beaten out of it.

5. An exclusion of foreign flags from our coasting-trade and fisheries. After the war there was a great increase in the coasting-trade, especially about 1831. The productiveness of the South began to supply an enormous quantity of rice, tobacco, cotton, etc., for exportation. A large demand for these commodities for local consumption sprang up in the North, as in that part of the country the conveniences had been created both for their manufacture on a large scale for general home and for foreign consumption, and for dispatching them abroad, either in a raw or manufactured state. A heavy movement of Southern products accordingly took place along the coast, a return-current of domestic and foreign manufactures flowing back by the same route to pay for them. After 1830 the carrying-trade had grown so large that ships and brigs began to be put into it where before schooners and sloops only had been employed. After 1846 another increase of the trade took place consequent upon the settlement of California and the discovery of gold there. The greater part of this trade had to be carried on for several years by means of the long voyages around Cape Horn, and it gave employment accordingly to a class of vessels which soon came to rank in this country with the East Indiamen in England, being the largest and most powerful in the national marine. Such was the growth in this general department of our maritime activity that a trade which in 1812 found work for 500,000 tons of shipping only, employed in 1850 1,900,000 tons, and, to anticipate this story a little, 2,800,000 in 1871. Our ship-masters found the coasting-trade useful to them in their international voyages. It enabled them to make combinations of voyages in the intercourse with Europe and Asia. A foreign ship was compelled to sail from one part of our coast to another in search of a cargo empty. A national ship might carry a load of native goods, which placed it in a position to compete powerfully with foreign ships in the port of entry for the carrying-trade across the sea.

6. The aggressive policy of our Government. Aware of the superiority of our advantages for transacting the carrying-trade of the world, a constant effort was made to break down the foreign regulations that kept our shipping out of particular fields of employment. A jealous watch was kept upon the policy of other countries, and our

representatives abroad were continually pressing for an abandonment of all rules of intercourse which shackled in any way a general liberty of navigation. Interferences with our ships were promptly resented and chastised. In the last century the pirates of the Mediterranean and of the Chinese seas respected only one flag besides their own. That was the Cross of St. George, and British ships accordingly had a decided preference in the general trade to those seas. That preference was destroyed by the appearance of American ships in those seas. Several conflicts with pirates took place, and in every instance a severe lesson was taught to those who had interfered with our navigation. Our flag accordingly came to be respected in every part of the world, and the security of the commerce it protected guaranteed. The English complained after 1830 that they had lost their former preference in the Mediterranean on this account.

The result of all these causes was an increase of American shipping as follows :

DATE.	Registered for Foreign Trade.	Enrolled for Coasting-Trade, etc.	Licensed.
January 1, 1815...............................	674,632	338,198	16,453
July 1, 1850....................................	1,585,711	1,899,555	50,188

The proportion of the foreign trade of the country transacted in native and foreign vessels, in 1821, the earliest day when we have exact statistics, and in 1850 was as follows :

DATE.	American Vessels.	Foreign Vessels.
1821	$118,200,000	$14,358,000
1850	239,272,000	90,764,000

Three-fourths of the cotton export went in our vessels, and we got better pay for the service. All the mails and passengers, and a vast majority of the immigrants, were transported under our flag. The British whale-fisheries were almost extinct, while the Americans had over 700 ships and 17,000 seamen actively employed in that field. While ship-building stagnated in England, and owners were losing money, building was active here, and owners had many exceedingly prosperous years. From 1820 to 1850 this country built 3,900,000 tons of shipping. In 1831 $5,000 was often paid for a ship over and above the contract price when she was completed, property was increasing so rapidly in value. In 1840 many vessels repaid their original cost in freight-money. The interest was rich, prosperous, aggressive, and public expectation on both sides of the Atlantic would not have been disappointed had America become in twenty-five years the leading maritime nation of the world. It was already only second. Why it did not reach the first position will be explained by the events of the third period.

THE DECADENCE OF OUR MARINE.

Now for the period of the decadence of American navigation. Tracing things down to the bottom, the causes of the decline of our shipping may be stated to be as follows :

1. The temporary decline of national feeling in this country.
2. The policy of foreign nations—of England preëminently—but of other nations also who imitated her in an important respect.
3. The backwardness of the development of our iron-mines.
4. The high prices of the last fifteen years.
5. The discovery of petroleum.

The operation of these causes will be discovered in what took place in regard to the employment of steamships for the Atlantic and Pacific trades, the building of iron vessels, the decay of the whaling-fleet, and the destruction of our merchant-shipping during the War of 1861.

Before proceeding to a consideration of these subjects, it might be well to say that several things took place in and after 1850 which were of great advantage to our shipping for the time being, and would have contributed greatly to our attainment of maritime preëminence, had they not been offset by the greater influences above referred to. They were the repeal of the British Corn Laws, which increased the exports of this country enormously, they rising $50,000,000 in the single year from 1850 to 1851. Another was the Crimean War in 1854, which caused the withdrawal of a great deal of British steam and other shipping from the Atlantic trade. Another was the unprecedented immigration of 2,598,000 people in the ten years after 1850. It was by reason of the operation of these and the other favorable causes continuing from the preceding period that American tonnage increased from 1850 to 1861 from 3,530,000 to 5,350,000. It ought, however, to have grown more, to have kept pace with the age. It speedily became less.

The first check to our navigation arose out of the apathy of the people in regard to nourishing the employment of steam in transatlantic commerce. Steam was first applied in this country to the navigation of the rivers to which it was well adapted. A class of large and beautiful boats was constructed for river-service, and so rapidly did trade increase upon the great streams of the country that, as a result of it, the steam-tonnage of the Mississippi Valley in 1847 alone exceeded that of the whole British Empire. And, indeed, it is believed, and is so reported at Washington, that the steam-tonnage of the United States to-day still equals if it does not considerably exceed that of the empire referred to. The steamboat played a great part in the development of this country, and it was not only employed upon the rivers and lakes, but upon the coasts. By 1840, lines of serviceable boats were plying between all the principal commercial cities of the Atlantic seaboard. This country not only led the way in the utilization of steam for propulsion, but it was the first to attempt the passage of the Atlantic with paddle-wheels. The voyage of the Savannah in 1819 is famous. She ran from the port of that name to Liverpool in twenty-two days, steaming fourteen days, and advertised in Europe the mission of the American people, which is to conquer the elements of Nature and render them submissive to man. The electrical effect of this adventure upon the English mind has already been noted. It is surprising to observe how little was thought of it in this country. Twenty-two days—why, that was no faster than the American packet-ships! People dismissed the matter from their minds. They supposed that steamers would never be of particular value in deep-sea navigation. . The Savannah returned, landed her machinery, and went back to sails.

It was not until 1838 that popular interest in the subject revived to any extent. In that year two English steamers, the Sirius and the Great Western, enterprisingly attempted the crossing of the Atlantic, and steamed into the harbor of New York almost together. This event gave as great a shock to the public mind here as England had experienced in 1819. The subject of steam now secured the attention it deserved in commercial and political circles. A short examination of what England was doing sufficed to create a feeling of alarm among public men, who regarded the aggressive policy of our rival as a menace to our maritime prosperity, and saw the necessity of prompt action to counteract it. The subject came before Congress in 1841, and was a prominent feature in the debates of every succeeding session down to the outbreak of the civil war.

The idea of framing a policy in regard to ocean steam-navigation was taken up by Congress at first in the largest and most patriotic spirit. The ablest and most ardent advocates of it were Mr. King, of Georgia, and Mr. Rush, of Texas, whose section was purely agricultural, and which felt the least interest, therefore, in adopting any policy which would increase the taxation of the people. It was seen from the beginning that this Government could meet the new and dangerous competition which was springing up against its foreign navigation only by authorizing companies of merchants to build vessels to carry the mails to Europe, and by paying them a sum of money sufficient to enable them to meet their expenses and hold their own against the foreign lines. No part of the republic shrank from this at the time, particularly as it was seen that another important interest could be secured by encouraging private citizens to build able steamers, namely, national defense, for the steamers would at all times be available for the navy. Sentiment was generally favorable to it, and there was very little delay in making a practical reply to England's attack upon our maritime prosperity.

The plan proposed by Mr. King in 1841 was, to appropriate $1,000,-000 annually for the transportation of the foreign mails. For this sum of money, it was believed that there could be secured a line of four steamers from Boston to Havre to accommodate the growing commerce and immigration over that route ; a line of four steamers from New York to Liverpool to contest the ground with the Cunard steamers ; a line of three vessels from Norfolk to the West Indies; and another of three from New Orleans to the same islands. This plan was unfortunately not carried out. In 1845, however, the Postmaster-General was authorized to go ahead and contract for ocean-service in steamers wherever the public interests required it, leaving it to him to decide upon the routes and ports of the several lines. Under this law he contracted with Edward Mills for four ships and twenty trips a year from New York to Bremen and Havre, for $400,000 ; and with E. K. Collins & Co. for four ships and twenty trips from New York to Liverpool, for $385,-000. Contracts were also made for service from New York to New Orleans and the Isthmus of Panama, and from Panama to California and Oregon, for $489,600. Congress approved these contracts, and advanced part of the money upon them to assist in building the ships. It was stipulated that their hulls should be strong enough for war purposes. Service began on the Bremen line with one ship in July, 1847 ; on the line to California in 1848; and on the line to Liverpool in 1850 with two ships, two more being added within a year. By 1851 we had three steamships trading to Bremen and Havre, and four to Liverpool, under the pay of the Government—and our reply to England had been made.

The United States entered the field against the aristocratic Government of England with true republican deliberation, but her ships once put into the trade established their superiority within two years. The Bremen steamers were no better, perhaps, than those of the English lines, but the Collins ships were marvels of naval construction, and surpassed their competitors of the Cunard line in every point. Collins entered upon his contract with the distinct purpose of restoring the prestige of our navigation to Europe, which had been shaken by ten years of delay in utilizing the new motive power of steam. It had been said in England that we could not build ocean-steamers. His contract called for ships of 2,000 tons burden. This was larger than the Cunard ships, which averaged 1,200 and 1,500 tons; but, not content with fulfilling the letter of the contract, he built four ships of 3,250 tons burden, at a cost of $2,900,000, and in 1855 built one of 5,000 tons

burden, at a cost of $1,100,000. Speed, beauty, style, and excellence
of passenger accommodations, were aimed at, and the first four ships
each had besides cargo-room for 1,000 tons of freight. The exploits of
these ships amazed both our own countrymen and the merchants of
England. They made the run across the Atlantic in ten days (the average of trips at the present time), against thirteen days by the Cunard-
ers. The ships were without superiors in the world, and they gave
great strength for a time to the Government policy of a vigorous support to navigation. This policy had able and patriotic advocates in
Congress at that time from all parts of the country.

In 1850 lines from the Western coast to China, and from the Eastern
to Africa, were proposed, and a line was started to run from Charleston
to Havana, under a pay of $50,000 a year. Generous support was
given to Collins, whose pay was increased in 1852 to $858,000 a year.
In that year the Government was expending $1,840,000 in subsidies,
namely : For the service to Liverpool, $858,000 ; from New York to
Charleston, Havana, and New Orleans, $290,000 ; Panama and Oregon
service, $348,250 ; to Bremen and Havre, $294,000 ; Charleston and
Havana, $50,000.

Our policy, however, did not go far enough. Good such as it was, it
stopped short of the point where the greatest good would have been
gained. It never got beyond the preliminary stage of a few experiments. The English Government was doing better. It had begun
earlier, and was acting more energetically. It was paying a single line,
that to the West Indies and the Isthmus, nearly as much as we were
sustaining all our lines with. It gave that company $1,350,000 a year.
A great error was committed in not acting soon enough to save our
packet-business to England. The Cunard steamers had now secured
nearly all the valuable part of that business. We had only the share
of it which one small line of steamers could secure ; and as for our sail-
ing-packets they were being bankrupted and withdrawn. A worse
than the original error was, however, now about to be committed,
namely, the abandonment of all support to our rising steam-navigation
to Europe. Private enterprise was to be left unaided to meet the powerful competition of the capital and governmental backing of England.

The agricultural interests of the United States appeared in Congress
in 1853, and demanded a cancellation of the contracts. Debate began
in the session of 1853–'54, upon a proposition to reduce the compensation of Collins. It was continued through several succeeding years, the
whole policy of protection to steam-navigation undergoing a thorough
and protracted discussion, and being, at times, the leading topic before
Congress. The opposition to the subsidy system came chiefly from the
South. The politicians of that section had become predominant in

politics, and the interest they represented was dictating the whole policy of the Government on economical questions. An abolition of the protective tariff had been conceded to it years before, among other things. Jefferson Davis and Judah P. Benjamin were active advocates of an abandonment of the carrying-trade of the Atlantic to British hands, and hardly a voice was lifted in opposition to them from the agricultural States. Mr. Clingman, of North Carolina, proposed that an attempt should be made to induce England to abandon the subsidy system—a suggestion at the same time hopeless and absurd. The arguments of the Congressmen from the agricultural States were supplemented in 1855 by offers from the North-German Lloyd Company, which had begun to run steamers from Hamburg, and by Mr. Vanderbilt, who had two or three steamers for which he wished to find employment, to carry the mails at reduced rates. Whether political designs controlled in any degree the action of the representatives who proposed an abandonment of the American transatlantic marine to the severity of foreign competition, it would not be patriotic to attempt to say. But it is certain that the debates of that decade, on maritime and all other subjects, indicate that national sentiment had decayed in this republic, and that the agricultural interest cared far less for the glory and prosperity of the American people than for the promotion of its individual ends. There was nothing in this, perhaps, peculiar to the American agriculturists. The same phenomenon appears in the history of all the governments of the world. It was no less a fact, however, that the too exclusive devotion of the country in this period to agriculture caused an abandonment of the public-spirited policy of 1845 with reference to steam-navigation.

The compensation of Collins was reduced in 1856 to $385,000. The contract was canceled by failure of renewal in 1857. The steamers were then withdrawn and sold to the Pacific Mail Company for the coasting-trade. In 1857 the Bremen and Havre contracts also expired. The former service went into the hands of Mr. Vanderbilt. The latter was continued by Mr. Livingston, with his two splendid 2,600-ton ships, which he could not withdraw from the trade, for there was no other to put them into; which, however, he continued to operate after this at a loss. A policy conceived with the highest motives, in 1845, which had in ten years given us the finest steamers upon the sea, which we were abundantly able to carry on, and in which every laudable motive of public policy operated to induce us to persevere, was abandoned after a short and feeble trial. The worst of it was that our tardy and vacillating action had caused the Europeans to put into our trade the steamers which we refused to encourage the building of ourselves. Our withdrawal of support to Atlantic steam-navigation left us in 1858 with five steamers only, of 11,000 tons burden, trading to European ports.　The Europeans had thirty-one steamers, of 57,000 tons burden, trading to the United States, namely :

LINES.	SERVICE.	Number.	Tonnage.
Cunard..............................	Liverpool, New York, and Boston......	12	16,800
European and American Steamship Co..	Bremen, Antwerp, Southampton, N. Y.	4	10,000
Liverpool, Philadelphia, and New York.	Liverpool and New York..............	4	8,700
Glasgow and New York...............	Glasgow and New York..............	3	6,200
Belgian Transatlantic..	Antwerp and New York..............	4	8,800
Hamburg and American...............	Hamburg and New York..............	4	7,300

The United States had in all only 52 ocean-steamers afloat in all its foreign and coasting trade, of a tonnage of 71,000.　England had 156 steamers, of 210,000 tons burden, and the rest of Europe 130 steamers, of a tonnage of 150,000.　England was paying $5,330,000 in subsidies, and France had just offered $2,800,000 for the service to various parts of America alone.　It may be remembered that England still pays in subsidies to steamers the sum of $3,800,000 annually in gold.

Before any other effective cause came into play, the United States had abandoned the struggle for superiority upon the sea in the only class of vessels in which the bulk of the commerce of the world was thenceforward to be carried on.　It had made a present of its foreign carrying-trade to Europe.　The gift was accepted as fast as ships could be built to take advantage of it.　The change which took place immediately will be illustrated by comparing the proportion of the commerce of the country transacted in American and foreign ships before and after 1858, as follows :

YEARS.	IMPORTS.		EXPORTS.	
	American Vessels.	Foreign Vessels.	American Vessels.	Foreign Vessels.
1855......................	$202,234,000	$59,223,000	$203,250,000	$71,905,000
1856......................	249,972,000	64,667,000	232,295,000	94,688,000
1857..........	259,116,000	101,778,000	251,214,000	111,745,000
1859.................	203,700,000	78,918,000	243,490,000	81,144,000
1859......................	216,123,000	122,644,000	249,617,000	107,171,000
1860....	228,164,000	134,001,000	279,084,000	121,088,000

The increase in foreign vessels was from 24 per cent. of the whole to 33 per cent.　After the War of 1861 broke out a complete revolution took place.　The United States persisted in its passive policy, the rest of the world in an aggressive policy.　The results of all this, as far as the commerce of the United States is concerned, may be seen in the following statement for the year ending June 30, 1877 :

YEAR.	IMPORTS.		EXPORTS.	
	American Vessels.	Foreign Vessels.	American Vessels.	Foreign Vessels.
1877......................	$151,826,000	$329,565,000	$164,826,000	$520,354,000

Americans actually carried less than sixteen years ago, when the total commerce was only half as large, and they had only 27 per cent. of the whole !

The United States made no further efforts in behalf of its steam marine after 1858 until 1865, when a contract for $500,000 was given to the Pacific Mail Company for carrying the mails to China and Japan, and another to a New York line to carry the mails between that port and Brazil for $150,000. Both contracts were terminated at the end of ten years. The latter line being unable to maintain itself with the old-fashioned steamers it then had against those of more modern construction put by English merchants into the same trade, withdrew from the business. Five private efforts have since been made from Atlantic ports, but four were failures. The United States finds itself to-day without a policy in regard to foreign navigation ; with only three steam lines to transoceanic ports, two of which barely keep alive, and the third of which maintains itself only by reason of the Australian subsidy; with a marine diminished 1,000,000 tons since 1860 ; and with nothing in the world to preserve its shipping from total extinction, except the regulation in regard to registration and the coasting-trade and the efforts of a handful of able and enterprising ship-builders.

The United States lost in this matter of steam not only by failing to create a steam marine of her own, but by allowing another power to create an agency which took business away from American sailing-craft.

In order to save a paltry million or two to the public Treasury for the time being, it had subjected its shipping in the foreign trade to ruin, thrown thousands of its people out of employment, and brought upon the country a tax of more than $20,000,000 a year for freight and passenger-money paid to foreigners. It is fortunate for the United States that the agricultural South and West, which are responsible for these evils, are themselves now demanding a government policy for the revival of American shipping.

Before passing on from this branch of the subject, allusion may properly be made to the policy of England toward this country during the War of 1861. The unhappy conflict in this republic presented an important opportunity to commercial nations in the Old World, whose conduct was guided sufficiently by a regardless self-interest to permit them to take advantage of it. England actively promoted the attempt to bring about a division of the country with a view to secure an enlarged sale of her manufactures in the Southern States, and at the same time she put in operation the means of bringing about a great destruction of our shipping and a diversion of its carrying-trade. The war itself was a great calamity to navigation by reason of the fact that a republic like this, which does not care to support a large armed navy, can only engage in naval operations by making a draft upon its merchant-shipping; and in the present case there were 1,175,000 tons of our sailing-craft and steamers diverted from legitimate trade and employed in the service of the Government. This was not, however, so severe a blow to our shipping as the arming of Confederate cruisers in British ports, and the sending them out to prey upon our commerce. In the former case, at least a million of tonnage had been thrown out of employment in the coasting-trade by the prevalence of war. In the latter case, our shipping, engaged in profitable and peaceful navigation of the high-seas, was interfered with, captured, destroyed, and finally compelled to withdraw from trade, because there was too much insecurity in commerce under the American flag, and merchants gave their business in large part to the vessels of other nationalities. The cruisers destroyed only about 104,000 tons of shipping, but they threw hundreds of thousands more out of business. The English profited the most by this, as they intended to. They supplied nearly all the ships needed for our trade, doubling their ship-building from 208,000 tons in 1861 to 462,000 in 1864, and forcing themselves into our commerce against our own crippled and helpless navigation, until to-day the harbor of New York flutters with British flags, and little resembles the principal commercial emporium of a great independent republic. Philadelphia is to-day the only great port on our seaboard that even looks like an American possession, and even there the foreigner also predominates in trade.

The second great cause of our maritime decline is found in the facts in regard to the iron-industry. The United States is by Nature better qualified for the production of cheap iron of the best quality than England. It has an inexhaustible abundance of the metal and of coal, and the mines are more conveniently situated for getting out both materials with a minimum of labor. The lack of capital here prevented a general utilization of our iron-mines, however, for a long period, and, when they did begin to be productive to any extent, it became impossible to obtain the iron in a manufactured state as cheaply as the manufacturers in England could produce it, owing to a great variety of causes. The high tariff of 1842, the free-trade tariff of 1846, the demand for railway-material, and the high tariff of 1861, each operated to put this country for a time at a disadvantage in regard to iron-production.

Iron ship-building was practised to a considerable extent here before 1842. It began about 1825, when a steamboat called the Codorus was constructed, a light-draught affair, intended to run on the Susquehanna River. This boat was subsequently sent South to run on some of the rivers of that region. Several others were built in the North along through the next twenty years, some of them on the Hudson. One, launched in 1834, was employed on the Savannah River, where in 1843 five iron steamers were being actively employed. These boats sustained snagging wonderfully. In 1838 an iron steamboat called the Valley Forge was built at Pittsburg, to run as a packet between Nashville and New Orleans. She was a light, fast boat, and had other admirable qualities, among them being that of rigidity of hull which fitted her well for Western navigation. She was run until 1845, when, the trade of the West having grown beyond her capacity, she was dismantled and made up into nails and spikes. Iron steam lines began also to be used on the coast. One ran between Hartford and Philadelphia in 1842.

The rise in the price of iron at different periods, and the increase of trade which required the construction of a new and larger class of vessels, checked the use of iron hulls in this country. We had the skill to build them, but the disproportion between their cost and that of wooden vessels became too great.

After 1861 iron became so dear in this country that its use for anything except the armor of men-of-war was impossible ; and for more than ten years the construction of iron merchant-craft was entirely suspended. The tariff of 1861, however, brought about an extensive development of iron-mines. How well that tariff has done its work, and how much this country owes to it, need hardly be repeated. It gave us cheap iron among other things, and has put us in 1879 into a position to build iron vessels against any country in the world. While this development was taking place, however, England was actively building iron ships, sailers as well as steamers, which being cheaper than wooden ships, and being found to be, when well made, durable, needing little repair, and fleet, took the preference in many important trades over timber ships, and added another weight to the burden oppressing our navigation. It is yet doubtful whether the iron sailing-ship is destined to enjoy a permanent advantage over the timber ship. Sailors prefer the latter, and Americans are content to compete for trade in the same sort of craft with which they once had almost won the flag of maritime supremacy from England. There is no movement in this country toward the construction of iron sailing-craft, although our builders offer to manufacture them for the same prices for which they can be made in England. The building of wooden vessels still continues. If it were not for the rapid destruction of American forests now going on, it might be said still to be an unsettled question whether iron sailers would play any considerable part in the future commerce of the country. Whatever may be the case in the future, however, it does not affect the fact that, in the past, it has been a disadvantage to us not to be able to build of iron as cheaply as the English. The present state of the iron-building interest will be described in another chapter.

The high prices which prevailed during, and for ten years after, the

war were another cause of the decadence of our shipping. Labor con-
'stitutes so nearly the whole of the cost of a ship, that a small fluctua-
tion in its market value is sufficient to put a building country in the
van or in the rear of other nations.   It was always a chief cause of our
maritime growth that we could build cheaper than England.   The high
prices of the war immediately gave England the superiority over us,
even in the construction of timber ships.   It is only in the present year
that her superiority in these important particulars has been practically
destroyed, and the expense of construction somewhat equalized.   The
high prices also increased the cost of operating ships.   American sailors demanded higher wages in order to live.   That was a vast disadvantage, which, however, has now been remedied in great degree by
the return of more frugal times.

The discovery of petroleum had an important influence upon the
fleet engaged in the whale-fisheries.   We once had 700 sail in that
business, and 17,000 seamen.   The use of petroleum rendered the business unprofitable, and the tonnage ran down from 198,000 in 1858 to
39,000 in 1876.   The Americans still do about all the whale-fishing,
sea-elephanting, and sealing, that is carried on, but there are now only
about 170 vessels in the business.   Employment to shipping and valuable training for mariners are lost by this change.   The game itself is
scarcer than in old times, and part of the decline may be attributed to
that fact.   The use of mineral oils was, however, the principal cause.

Is it any wonder that American shipping declined?   Is it strange
that our total tonnage fell away from 5,353,868 in 1860 to 4,212,764 in
1878 ; and that part of it registered for the foreign trade from 2,546,-
237 in 1860 to 1,629,047 in 1878 ?   Is it likely that the decline will go
a step further except by reason of our subserviency to the ambitions
and designs of foreign powers, and a failure to do something for our
own legitimate interests ?   Is there anything in the present situation
which discourages in the slightest degree, except foreign policy ?   And
how are we to meet that ?

VI.

WHAT MAY BE DONE.

VARIOUS things may be done to meet the foreign competition against
our navigation.

One is a change of policy with respect to international trade.   A
revival of the law of 1817, which forbade any ship to bring a cargo to
the United States except from the ports of the country to which it be-

longs, would work out an interesting result in regard to the navigation to South America and Asia. There are few ships native to those countries trading to the United States. Less than twenty South American keels arrive in this country yearly out of a total of 1,100 entries from that part of the world. The vessels, not American, in the trade, are principally English. A law such as is referred to would instantly place in our hands the whole transportation between the United States and South America and Asia. We have all the steamers and sailing-craft needed to take advantage of it immediately. A law of that description would also assist us in the Mediterranean trade, in which field English steamers are now making triangular voyages, to the injury of our navigation. It would also work out a most important result in the trade from the whole Continent of Europe by confining the cheap sailing British, Italian, and Norwegian craft to the navigation from their own countries. This measure would secure an immediate extension of the operations of our shipping without costing the country a dollar. It would give employment at once to the tens of thousands of tons of sailing-craft lying idle in our harbors. It would enable the Government to refuse a subsidy to every existing line of steamers to a foreign land without injuring the line. It might, in fact, be a better thing for the line than a subsidy. It would assist us in the sale of manufactures. A regulation requiring direct trade would no doubt be responded to by England by an enactment depriving American ships of whatever general trade from foreign countries to English ports they now enjoy. Whether we should lose more by that than we should gain is extremely doubtful, and we can afford to abandon the lesser for the greater.

To adopt a policy of this sort would be to employ, in an age in which English public men are arguing that everything should be left as much as possible to private enterprise, the tactics of an age in which everything was seconded as much as possible by the efforts of the government. It would be characterized by every man of *laisser faire* sympathies as a step backward toward the barbarism of the middle ages, though, even if that were true, it would have nothing to do with the real question at issue, which is, Would it be useful ? Such a policy would also be exposed to the objection that it would be an open blow at British interests in every part of the world. But it seems to the writer that Americans should not be governed by too excessive a regard for our British rival, and that the only question to be considered is, What will be proper and beneficial for our own country ? Some better man may be able to see grave reasons why direct-trade laws should not be adopted by the United States which do not occur to the writer ; but, probably, no one will deny that the first effect of such a policy would be to give us a better position in the navigation to every part of the world immediately without cost to the country, thus giving employment to all our idle ships; and that in its further operation it would confer a favor and a benefit upon South America, with which we so much desire to cultivate close and friendly relations, and upon every other great nation of the world, England alone excepted, and that it would, therefore, be regarded in a friendly light by them; and that England would not have the shadow of a right to complain that it was either unjust or unfriendly to her, or founded upon anything except common-sense and legitimate business principles.

One change which has been suggested many times is in regard to the abolition of duties on ship-building material. There may have been a time when that would have benefited the foreign navigation of the United States. It would not be of the slightest advantage now.

Timber is as cheap here as anywhere in the world. Thirty years ago the north of Europe had cheaper timber than the United States. But the forests of the north of Europe are fast becoming exhausted, and timber has risen in consequence. In Canada, where they have cheap building-stuff, the wood is inferior in quality to that of American growth, and American ship-owners do not care to use it. Italy has enjoyed the advantage of cheap building-material in the past, but her situation is not superior to that of the United States, because her builders are obliged to import their masts and spars from America. Our position in regard to timber is as good as could be desired. No encouragement need be given to the importation of it. Advantage has never been taken of the law of 1872, which allows the importation of lumber for the construction and equipment of vessels for the foreign trade, more than to the extent of a few thousand dollars a year.

Under the law of 1872, copper, iron, and steel rods, bolts, spikes, nails, hemp, and manila, can be imported free of charge for shipping purposes. These things are all so cheap in the United States that the importation under the law is only about $100,000 worth a year.

The only material for ship-building which cannot now be imported free of duty is iron. Six years ago it might have been an important help to builders to be able to obtain their iron free of duty. The price was then $48 a ton. The duty was $7. To have permitted the free importation of iron for building might possibly have been a help. Since that time, however, the cost of iron has fallen, even going so low as $20 in 1878. It has risen this fall, but the rise is general all over the world. Besides, our builders do not need to have iron so cheap as formerly. No law abolishing the duty would put our builders in a much better position in regard to this class of raw material than they now enjoy. It may be mentioned that our builders do not at present ask for a repeal of the duty on iron. The demand for this does not come from them. On the contrary, it is believed they are generally opposed to it.

It does not clearly appear where the recent demand for a repeal of the duties on ship-building material comes from, or what those who propose it expect that we will gain by it. A brief consideration of the subject ought to convince an American, however, that nothing can be done in this direction which would be of any special value to American shipping.

A repeal of duties on all the supplies of a ship, so as to cheapen the expenses of operation, has been suggested by various ship-owners as of probable utility. Its value would be slight, but as far as the law would go it would probably be beneficial.

Would a change of the registry laws be of any avail? The free-traders are very active now in asserting that it would be. The question is, Would such an extraordinary change of our national policy secure a larger field for the employment of American ships? With reference to the coasting-trade, it is not clear how our ship-owners would gain by it. They enjoy an exclusive monopoly of that trade already. An abandonment of our policy in regard to the registration of vessels could only diminish the number of American ships in the business, if it had any effect at all. Would there be an increase of American tonnage in the foreign trade if Americans could buy their ships in other lands? That would appear to depend on the probability of obtaining ships at a materially reduced cost in foreign ship-yards. Eight years ago, when this subject was under discussion, Joseph Nimmo, Jr., chief of the tonnage division of the Treasury Department, collected a large amount of information in regard to the cost of ships. From his report it appears that the expense of building timber ships in the United States at that time was from $50 to $60 a ton in gold for oak ships, and from $40 to $50 a ton in Canada for spruce ships. The cost of iron sailing-vessels in England was $95 a ton in gold, and in the United States $125 a ton. A remarkable change in the expense of building has taken place since that time. It will be recollected that gold has fallen from 1.30 to 1.00; labor has depreciated thirty per cent.; and iron has fallen one-half. Interest has also been materially reduced. The result is, that the cost of building in this country does not now exceed the cost abroad by ten per cent. It is doubtful whether as great a difference as that exists. Our builders now offer to construct steam and sailing vessels, grade for grade, for the same prices as the builders abroad.

What fine point of advantage, then, would our ship-owners gain by buying their ships abroad? Do American ship-owners want to buy ships abroad? It is believed that they do not, and that the whole agitation of this subject originates outside of American shipping and mercantile circles. The principal effect of a repeal of the registry laws for the foreign trade would be the importation of old English hulls to America to be cut up as scrap-iron. It would afford no relief to American navigation.

5

There is one thing which may be done, which would have an important influence in increasing the amount of American tonnage in our foreign trade, and at the same time stimulate the industrial interests of the country in a useful manner. This is, to encourage our countrymen to build and operate lines of first-class steamships in our foreign trade. There can be no important revival of American navigation without a large and prosperous steam marine. Steam is superseding sails the world over. It is cheaper than the winds of heaven in certain trades, and more serviceable. No civilized nation of the earth dreams of maritime expansion in this age except in the direction of fleets of steam packet-ships. The day of the sailing-vessels for all regular and valuable trade is passing away, and the United States might as well equip its armies for the next foreign war with bows and arrows as expect to regain its maritime eminence with anything except iron steamships.

The present is a very interesting period in our national history. Our trade has grown to enormous proportions, yet we are under the necessity of expanding it still further. To employ our population, it is necessary to extend the sale of our manufactures in foreign lands. We can compete with our industrial rivals in the great markets of the South and West as far as excellence and prices of our goods are concerned, but we cannot get the goods to those markets rapidly and conveniently for lack of transportation facilities. A great opportunity opens before the country for maritime and industrial expansion. The Government would betray the people it has been created to aid and protect if it hesitates to discharge its duty in the matter.

The plan of encouraging our own citizens to build steamships, and to trade in them to Africa, South America, Europe, and other markets, by the grant of mail-contracts, is probably the best of those proposed for the revival of our navigation and the extension of our commerce. It will accomplish the end desired without sacrificing any other important national interest, and it is a simple and effective plan. The argument in behalf of mail-contracts is the old one, which has been regarded as valid in every age and every country, and is still influential with all the civilized governments of the world, our own included, that projects of vast public utility, of which individuals cannot bear the risk and expense, and which promise to promote the national wealth, and in time to be self-sustaining, may safely and prudently be treated as enterprises of public concern and directly encouraged by the Government. It was exactly this principle which led the State of New York to build the Erie Canal at its own expense—a work which repaid its whole cost of construction in ten years—reduced the cost of freight from Lake Erie to the Hudson from $100 to $7 a ton, and added $100,000,000 to the value of the farms of the State, to say nothing of what it did for the West. It is this principle which led the United

States to grant 183,000,000 acres of the public lands to aid in the construction of railroads, 38,000,000 of the grant having now been patented, a gift for which it has been fully reimbursed by the increased money-value of the other public lands in the neighborhood of the railroads, built by the aid of the land-grants, and which has proved of inestimable profit to private citizens by adding to the market-value of their lands, and reducing the cost of freight to one-tenth what it was before the roads were built, and often to less than one-tenth. The Government has been patriotic and liberal in its application of this principle to the benefit of the agricultural interest, and has been rewarded for it satisfactorily and completely.

It is now asked that the principle shall be applied for the benefit of the shipping and manufacturing interests of the country. The profit which will accrue to the people from taking this step will not be so palpable as in the case of Government aid to internal improvements, but it will be no less real and immediate. The expenditure of a few millions annually in compensation to steamship lines to enable them to meet the foreign competition, and get a foothold in trade, will save to the country $50,000,000 or more of tribute now paid to foreigners for freight and passenger-money. It will give employment on land and sea to American labor, and insure an enlarged sale of American manufactures abroad. It will secure to our countrymen the profits of their own vast commerce and its beneficial influence be felt in every part of the republic. This policy will be fully in accord, too, with the spirit of the age and the example of the older nations, whose example in other respects we regard as worthy of all imitation.

Senator Blaine recently wrote a letter on this subject to the merchants of New York. Having been present at the annual dinner of the Chamber of Commerce of that city, May 13, 1870, he responded by invitation to the toast, "Steam Mail Lines ; Keys with which Wise Statesmen open Foreign Ports to Maritime Commerce." His short speech was received with cordial signs of approval, and he was soon afterward invited to come to New York and speak at more length on "The Decay of American Commerce, and the Means of Promoting its Revival." The Senator could not comply in person, for Congress was then in session, and under the circumstances of the time it was difficult to get away ; but he wrote a letter, which fully expressed his views. It was dated at Washington, June 17, 1879, and was addressed to William E. Dodge, A. A. Low, James M. Brown, H. B. Claflin, Henry Hilton, B. G. Arnold, F. B. Thurber, Moses Taylor, John A. Stewart, and other members of the Chamber of Commerce. The letter was an analysis of causes, an eloquent plea for the construction of our ships in this country, and a suggestion as to the right policy to pursue in the future. The following is an extract :

"If I possessed the power to prescribe a policy for the revival of the American carrying-trade, I would make it very simple and very specific. I would continue the navigation laws as part of the very organic law of the land. For wooden sailing-ships no further aid is needed than these laws afford, if we will only seek in every way to lighten the burden of taxation on vessels. We can build wooden ships better than any other country, and we can build them as cheaply; but after they are launched and in trade they should not be worried and harried and burdened with every form of taxation, port-charge, and quarantine exaction at home; and maltreated and oppressed, as they too often are, by our consuls in foreign ports. They should have every facility for supply in our ports that England gives to her ships. Wooden ships will always be used so long as trees grow and winds blow, and they will form a large resource to our country. Indeed, it is almost the only resource we now have in foreign trade, and we should cherish the interest as one inwoven with our history and prosperity as a people. . . . My own State is more largely interested than any other in the Union in the building of wooden ships, and, if the specie basis can be firmly maintained, the United States and Canada will furnish the sailing-vessels for the world. Nothing but the inflation of the currency and the loss of the specie standard will prevent the steady growth of that valuable interest. Beyond all doubt that would prevent its revival and increase, and would ultimately result in its total destruction in our country.

"But, if we content ourselves with wooden sailing-vessels, we surrender the larger half of the world's commerce without a struggle. We must have iron steamships besides, and, with the start that other nations enjoy to-day, we shall never compete with them unless we use the same aids and the same instrumentalities that have built their steam fleets. And that aid I would give. And to give it effectively and wisely I would abandon all idea of granting subsidy to special lines as they apply to Congress for aid. That policy, however just and meritorious, will always be rendered abortive by prejudice, by jealousy, and by scandal, either actual or imputed. I would prefer a general law that should ignore individuals and enforce a policy. For instance, enact that any man or company of men who will build in an American yard, with American material by American mechanics, a steamship of three thousand tons and sail her from any port of the United States to any foreign port, he or they shall receive for a monthly line a mail allowance of $25 per mile per annum, for the sailing distance between the two ports; for a semi-monthly line, $45 per mile; for a weekly line, $75 per mile. Should the steamers exceed three thousand tons, a small advance on these rates might be allowed; if less than three thousand, a corresponding reduction; keeping three thousand tons as the average and the standard. Provide that the steamships shall be thoroughly inspected by a competent commission under the direction of the Secretary of the Treasury, the Secretary of the Navy, and the Postmaster-General, and thus insure the very first class of construction for safety and for speed both for passenger and cargo. . . . If the price I have named seems large for mail-pay, I beg to suggest that our Post-Office Department, without cavil or question, is paying a larger sum per mile for weekly, fortnightly, and monthly mails within our own territory—mails that carry fewer letters than these steamers would carry; mails that carry with them none of the incidental advantages which form the chief value of the steam lines under discussion.

"I know there is a large and influential class in the country who are utterly opposed to the policy thus imperfectly outlined. But suppose they should consent to make the experiment!"

The point which Mr. Blaine makes about the inland mail service is a forcible one. There were in the United States last winter about 9,920 mail routes, of which exactly 1,000 were railroad routes. The number is somewhat larger now. On the main railroad lines of the country the weight of mails carried is large. Eighty-six tons of mails a day are sent out from New York city alone, and the trunk lines between all the great cities run heavily burdened mail cars. The compensation of the principal railroad routes is from $375 to $1,155 per mile per annum, and that of the less important routes from $45 to $350 per mile per annum. Of the whole thousand of railroad routes, only two or three hundred earn the compensation the Government pays them. The postage on the mails carried by the other lines falls far short of reimbursing the Government for the cost of the service over them. It is also true that, of the 8,920 stage, steamboat, and railroad routes, the majority do not earn in postage enough to reimburse the Government for the mail pay of the routes. Now, no one has ever thought of calling the compensation of the non-paying lines the grant of a subsidy or gratuity, and it would be improper to call it so. It is compensation for a valuable public service performed. Besides, the system as a whole is substantially self-sustaining, and that is all that any one desires. It has been the misfortune of those suggesting mail pay to American steamers, however, to be met with the declaration that "the people are opposed to subsidies," meaning gratuities, and that it would not do at all to pay $75, $45, or even $25 per mile per annum for carrying the mails at sea. The Government is making a clear profit of about from $400,000 to $600,000 a year on the foreign mail service (charging five cents per half ounce on letters and paying the steamers only two cents thereon), and this sum of money would be sufficient to afford excellent mail pay to several American lines of steamers to foreign lands, and, if it were applied to that object, would lead to the establishment of such lines. But even this is not enough to satisfy the opponents of the welfare of American shipping, and they persist in calling the grant of mail pay to American steamships subsidies, meaning all the while gratuities. Mr. Blaine, by suggesting that the foreign mail service and the home service are entitled to be treated as parts of one system, has made a strong and just point in favor of a more intelligent policy toward American steamship lines.

A thorough-going congressional investigation of the whole subject of our commerce, manufactures, and navigation, would be of great service in enabling merchants and the Government to coöperate harmoniously and intelligently. It would bring about a better understanding between the agricultural, industrial, and mercantile classes, and would reveal the directions in which effort should be expended. It would tend to give us what we so greatly lack and so much need, a national policy with respect to our foreign navigation.

VII.

FREE SHIPS AND SUBSIDIES.

In the preceding chapters, an attempt has been made to explain the causes of the decline of American shipping. Various devices have also been adverted to for restoring American supremacy. It is proposed in this chapter to discuss the propriety of a resort to some of these devices, especially that of the policy of mail contracts. This is a question upon which a large part of the American public are in doubt. A great many owners and builders of merchant vessels are in doubt on the subject, not being sure that they are not unduly biased in their opinions by self-interest. The expediency of Government encouragement to navigation, of any sort, is denied, moreover, by many patriotic and intelligent citizens, who, convinced of the justice of their opinions, have been agitating for several years against the grant of subsidies and in favor of a repeal of the Navigation Laws, and who, though unsuccessful so far, intend in the truly American way to show their faith by their works at the coming session of Congress, and to make a renewed effort in behalf of their cause. If those of our countrymen who are of this way of thinking should succeed this winter, it is feared not only that the United States would be unable to regain its old time ascendancy in foreign commerce, but that a great deal of the navigation we now have would be absolutely destroyed, and that, our patriotic system of Navigation Laws being once shattered, that achievement would be made a precedent for moving to abolish the protection given by the laws to agriculture and manufactures, and the way would be opened for foreign nations to gain a complete triumph over us in all the fields of industrial and maritime activity. Considering the importance of the subject, the writer desires to submit a few suggestions on this general question of the expediency of maintaining our Navigation Laws in all their present integrity, and, further, of going on and promoting actively the enlargement of our navigation by the establishment of American steamship lines in the foreign trade.

It ought to be stated at the outset, in order to clear the way for a discussion of the real point in controversy, that this *is* a question of expediency simply. It is not a question of the province of government, as is sometimes claimed. The tendency of Anglo-Saxon thought in this age is to limit the province of government as much as possible ; and it is sometimes argued that governments should do nothing whatever in regard to their subjects except to protect them from force and fraud, that legislation should stop when that limit has been reached, and that all beyond that limit should be left to private and voluntary agency. John Stuart Mill committed himself at one time emphatically to this view (in his essay on " Liberty "), and a great many eminent public men both in Europe and America have lent their support to the doctrine. By the common consent of all who have written and spoken upon this subject, however, including Mr. Mill, it is impracticable to limit the activity of governments to the protection of their subjects against force and fraud, without sacrificing important public interests, and, as a matter of fact, no government does stop at that limit. Mr. Madison, who was in favor of giving trade " a free course under the impulse of individual interest and under the guidance of individual sagacity," said in a speech in Congress : "To allow trade to regulate itself is not, however, to be admitted as a maxim universally sound ; our own experience has taught us that it is in certain cases the same thing as allowing one nation to regulate it for another." Mr. Madison, in all his practice, showed that he believed that government should interfere actively in the affairs of the people and adopt positive and direct measures to promote their general welfare. Mr. Mill said in his " Political Economy," that " In the particular circumstances of a given age or nation, there is scarcely anything really important to the general interest, which it may not be desirable, or even necessary, that the government should take upon itself. . . . In these cases, the mode in which the government can most sincerely demonstrate the sincerity with which it intends the greatest good of its subjects, is by doing the things which are made incumbent upon it by the helplessness of the public, in such a manner as shall tend not to increase and perpetuate, but correct that helplessness." Mr. Mill enumerates a large number of things, which cannot be construed as measures of protection against force or fraud, which may be, and are, indeed, proper for governments to adopt. Every considerate writer and public man throughout the world, in fact, is compelled to admit that there is scarcely anything affecting the public welfare which is really and absolutely outside of the province of government. The only ground upon which a controversy can be maintained in any particular case is, the question whether the legislative authority is empowered by the laws of the land to act, and whether, if so empowered, it is expedient, all things considered, for the legislature to act.

Nor is this a question of the authority of Congress. The contro-

versy on that subject is past. It is now universally conceded that the
Constitution commits to Congress the absolute control of navigation
and intercourse, and the right to appropriate moneys liberally for the
carriage of the mails, if that object will promote the general welfare,
in the clauses which empower Congress to collect taxes "to provide
for the common defense and general welfare"; "to establish post-
offices and post-roads"; and "to regulate commerce." The grant of
power "to regulate commerce" is one of the most important in the
Constitution. Story in his "Commentaries" says: "The want of this
power (as has been already seen) was one of the leading defects of
the Confederation, and probably, as much as any one cause, conduced
to the establishment of the Constitution. It is a power vital to the
prosperity of the Union, and without it the Government would scarcely deserve the name of a national government; and would soon sink
into discredit and imbecility. It would stand, as a mere shadow of
sovereignty, to mock our hopes and involve us in a common ruin."
The right to regulate commerce gives Congress control of the whole
subject of navigation and intercourse, and even of manufactures so
far as they depend on navigation and intercourse. Under the grant of
power in regard to post-offices, the right to provide for carrying the
mails is held to be imparted, and under the clause about taxes and the
general welfare, the right to apply the public moneys to any object
which will promote any great public interest. The authority of Congress in these respects is not now seriously disputed. The whole practice of the Government, from the day of the meeting of the first
Congress down to the present time, is in conformity with the above
construction of the Constitution. The authority of Congress being
conceded, there remains open for discussion only the question of expediency in any particular case.

It might be said, further, on this general subject, that a grant of
power by the Constitution always implies not only the means of execu-
tion but the duty of employing the power whenever the public interests demand it. This is an important point. Congress is under the
expressly implied obligation to act whenever the exercise of authority
is necessary for the common defense or general welfare. This is the
constitutional doctrine on the subject. The language above used is
that of Story, Kent, and the other commentators on the Magna Charta
of our Republic. The conclusion is, that if the public welfare requires
it, it is not only within the province, but it is the duty of Congress to
pass and maintain navigation laws and appropriate moneys liberally
for the carriage of the ocean mails.

The inquiry then is, What do the public interests require? What
is it expedient for the Government to do? Those who differ from us
in opinion demand the repeal of the navigation laws, or a modification

equivalent to repeal, and incidentally oppose all grants of aid for the establishment of steamship lines to foreign lands. We, on our part, advocate the propriety of aiding the establishment of a large number of American steamship lines to foreign lands, by giving to them contracts and a just compensation for carrying the mails, favoring a rigid maintenance of the Navigation Laws of the United States as an incident of this policy. Which policy would best promote the public welfare ?

SHALL WE HAVE FREE SHIPS ?

I. First, with reference to the Navigation Laws. It is proposed to repeal them. It is claimed that they are antiquated and useless, and should be abolished. The propriety of maintaining these laws may be studied first in the light of the effect of their abolition on the coasting trade. What is the coasting trade of the United States ? It is the navigation from the harbors of one State to that of another along the ocean seaboards, the courses of the great rivers, and through the northern lakes. The power to reserve this navigation to the vessels of American citizens was one of the express objects for which the Constitution of the United States was ordained ; and one of the very first acts of Congress, after the Government had been formed, was, accordingly, to exclude from the trade of our rivers and coasts the vessels of all other nations. This was indispensable in order to prevent smuggling and in order to acquire the ships, seamen, and mechanics, necessary for our prosperity and defense. In the Southern States, where little shipping was owned, it was originally thought that this law would impose a tax upon that section, but those States were at the time willing to submit to some sacrifice for the sake of the general welfare, and in the end it was discovered that the law did not, after all, impose a tax upon that section. The law operated, on the other hand, to create a fleet of merchant vessels, so numerous and so eager in their competition with each other, that the South from the beginning enjoyed cheap transportation. The fleet engaged in the coasting trade, which, be it remembered, includes the rivers and great lakes of the country, now comprises about 19,000 vessels and 2,200 barges, employing 70,000 men, and the competition between them is so great that the charges for transportation have been reduced to a point never before known. Vessel-owners higgle with shippers for a difference of one sixteenth of one per cent. in the charges for freight. The public interests are subserved by this state of things, although vessel-owners grumble and declare that there are now so many ships and barges in the business that there is very little profit to be made by any of them. The value of these vessels and barges is at the least calculation $120,-

000,000. This enormous sum of money is invested by American citizens in vessels engaged in the coastwise and river transportation of the country.

Now, what would be the effect on this interest if the navigation laws were repealed? What would become of the Mississippi River steamers if a swarm of Italian, Norwegian, Spanish, and British ships, sailed by men who, it is said, can live on a greased rag, were allowed to enter the South Pass and roam at will up and down the great rivers of the Valley of the Mississippi? What would become of the large propellers and sailing-vessels now plying on the northern lakes in the produce and iron trade to the East? What would be the effect on the fleet trading along the Atlantic, Gulf, and Pacific coasts? There is not a vessel-owner in all those trades who would not reply with much feeling that it would be the last straw which would break the camel's back. Then, too, what would be the influence on agriculture were American sailors compelled to abandon the sea and seek their living on shore? Already there are complaints from the States in the vicinity of the Mississippi River. Farmers view the continued immigration to the West with alarm. It is said that, unless farmers have capital wherewith to work on a large scale, they suffer greatly now. It is only by the most economical management that they can make both ends meet. There is little profit in corn at six and ten cents a bushel, in wheat at from thirty to fifty cents, and pork and beef at from one to two cents a pound. What will it be when the already enormous production is doubled? Reflecting men among farmers in the West do not view with favor any proposition to deprive seamen and mechanics in the East of work; and, indeed, it is not for the interest of agriculture that anything should happen to precipitate upon that region a fresh avalanche of the unemployed, seeking homes and farms. Nor is it for the general welfare of the country.

The propriety of reserving the navigation of our coasts and rivers exclusively to our own citizens is so obvious that it is surprising that any intelligent man disputes it. The burden of proving that a different policy is desirable clearly belongs to our opponents. Does it not, in all fairness?

The same may be said with reference to the doctrine that the regulation ought to be repealed which entitles only those ships built in the United States to the protection of the United States Navy when engaged in foreign trade. It is incumbent on the advocates of that doctrine to show the practical advantages of the repeal. Every ship placed under the American flag must be protected by the armed vessels of the United States and the vigilant care of the civil officers of our Government, both at home and abroad. If foreign vessels are to be admitted to an American registry, and the vessels thus registered are not to be manned with American sailors, the United States will suffer loss all along the line of its native maritime resources. It will lose seamen, mechanics, and ship-yards, not to mention what it will suffer in respect to the profitable industry of building and repairing vessels. What will the country gain to compensate it for that loss? That must be clearly shown. The repeal of the Navigation Laws will, of course, be claimed to be a measure for the promotion of ship-owning in the foreign trade. That is all that can be claimed for it. Protectionists do not stop, however, with requiring their opponents to prove that that object will be promoted by repeal. They deny that it will be. Foreign ships are not so much cheaper as to tempt Americans to buy them, if the law were repealed. There is nothing, in fact, to prevent an American citizen now from buying a foreign ship, and sailing it in the foreign trade, if he wishes to. He would have to sail it under a foreign flag, perhaps, but if that flag were British he would gain the advantage of buying his supplies cheaper, and having the ship protected by a more powerful navy than that of his native country. Why does nobody do that now, if our Navigation Laws are an obstacle to the growth of our marine? The answer is, that no American is deterred from employing ships in the foreign trade of this country on account of the cost of the ships. As President Hayes has well said, in his recent speeches in the West, American ship-builders can now compete with their rivals on the Clyde, in excellence and cost of ships, successfully. Comparative cost and excellence have practically nothing to do with restraining the expansion of the ship-owning interest of this country. The real restraining cause—the subsidies paid by other countries, past and present, and the results flowing therefrom—would not be affected by a repeal of the American Navigation Laws.

Furthermore, look at the absurd position in which America might be placed, if the law should admit foreign vessels to the shelter of an American registry. The whole merchant fleet of Great Britain, and possibly that of some other country, could be placed under the American flag, in case of a European war. The most cogent reason Great Britain has for keeping the peace to-day is the danger to which her merchant ships would be exposed, if she should go to war. It is the opinion of most observers that England would have become involved in hostilities with Russia two years ago, except for fear of depredations on her commerce, and that this fear alone restrains her now. Suppose that Congress should repeal the Navigation Laws of the United States. Great Britain would then be able to place nearly her whole navigation under the protection of the American flag, and that, too, without letting go the ownership of the vessels, by the well-known process of "whitewashing" (a system of bills of sale and counter-mortgages). The American navy, not now large enough to 'protect our own commerce, would then be compelled to stand guard over the merchant fleet of our most powerful and most unscrupulous rival. What an inconvenient position for the navy to occupy! And, while the United States would be paying out millions to protect the ships of a foreign power, the warfare, which that power would be left free to carry on, would be the source of many an interference with our own proper merchant fleet, and of a serious disturbance of our own commerce. Why should the United States be placed in so anomalous a position? It is incumbent upon the advocates of repeal to explain, conclusively.

If ship-owning should be promoted by repeal, in the way claimed, namely, by permitting Americans to obtain cheaper ships by buying them abroad, then a disastrous blow would be administered to a profitable branch of American industry, that of ship-building. The sum of money spent in the United States for the building of new ships in 1855 was $27,700,000. With the decline of our navigation, this sum fell off to $6,800,000 in 1862. In 1878 it had revived to something like $11,000,000. What would happen if all our ships were to be built abroad?

The writer believes that the repeal of our Navigation Laws would be an unqualified evil. The world, indeed, has not quite stood still since the laws were enacted, but no changes have taken place which would justify so radical a change of policy as the one now proposed. Almost all the old reasons are in force yet. There are some new ones which did not exist in 1789. To abandon our historic policy would be disaster.

It is perfectly legitimate to call attention to the source where this agitation for repeal originates. It was explained by "The Boston Journal" in May, 1877, in a leading editorial on "What depresses American Shipping Interests." The "Journal" said :

"Within the past few months the Cobden Club has been unusually active in urging upon the friends of free trade in all parts of the world to make a fresh effort in behalf of their cause. English interests are suffering from the dullness which pervades commerce. Failures are twice as numerous in England as in other parts of the world, the United States especially, and there is scarcely a department of business that does not feel the stress of the times extremely. Among other incidental facts of the situation is this, that as many as 2,400 English ships of the various classes are out of employment. A fresh market in wealthy countries is therefore sought for English products, and fresh fields for the employment of English shipping. One response to the appeals of the Cobden Club is seen in the phenomenon of fresh agitation in the United States for free trade in ships."

These remarks were in strict conformity with the facts.

MAIL CONTRACTS TO AMERICAN STEAMERS.

II. Let us take up a more profitable branch of the subject. Let us consider not the effect of repeal, but the effect of maintaining the present system, and of going on and establishing a multitude of American steamship lines to trade to other continents. Let us see what advantages would be gained thereby.

At the threshold of the discussion we are met with a few objections. Let us consider them first.

It is said that to appropriate from $3,000,000 to $5,000,000 to encourage navigation would be to tax the people at large for the benefit of a single interest. It might be replied to this, first, that if it is wrong to tax the people in behalf of navigation, then the American Navy should be abolished at once. The navy costs the country $20,-000,000 a year, and its only practical purpose is to protect American ships when outside of the territorial jurisdiction of the United States. Twenty millions paid out in behalf of a single interest! Commerce would go on just the same if there were no American ships in which to transact any portion of it. It would also be wrong to extend our navigation at all, because, if navigation be extended, the navy would have to be enlarged too, to protect it, at an increased cost to the country. However, the argument against taxing the people at large in behalf of American navigation is a valid one. It has a direct bearing on the question of expediency. It will be fully met, further on, by showing the harvests of benefits which will accrue from the expenditure; but it may be said now, in passing, that those who oppose the appropriation of public money for ocean mail contracts, on the ground of the impropriety of taxation in behalf of a single interest, are inconsistent. Mr. Charles H. Marshall, of New York City, made the point as to taxation in an interesting address on "The Decline of American Shipping" to the Export Trade Convention, held at Washington on February 19, 1879. Mr. Marshall laid great stress on the injustice of a policy which would tax each one of our citizens to the extent of seven or eight cents a year, and advanced as his idea of the way to restore the prosperity of American shipping a return to the policy of pure free trade. In other words, he advocated a policy which would close a large proportion of the factories of the United States, and deluge agriculture with an inundation of unemployed men seeking homes and a living in the West; which would, in brief, lower the wages and income of every farmer and laborer in the land. This would be a far more startling form of taxation of the people at large for the benefit of a few than the one which protectionists propose.

Next, it is objected that the grant of mail contracts would establish

monopolies. This is *vox et præterea nihil.* The purpose of these contracts is to break down a monopoly, the foreign monopoly of the control of our commerce. Besides, if it were proper to say that a government contract for ocean mail service would establish a monopoly, it
would be equally proper to denounce the contracts with the one thousand railroad and the eight thousand nine hundred steamboat and
turnpike routes, which carry the domestic mails, for the same reason.
Every one of those routes is a monopoly. Yet no one objects to the
contracts with them. On the contrary, it is conceded that the public
welfare is promoted by them.

Lastly, it is objected that private enterprise is not helpless in the
matter of establishing all the steamship lines the country wants. This
is absurd. Manufacturers, anxious to extend their trade, have been
crying for years, after the fashion of Putnam at the siege of Boston,
" Oh, ye gods, give us American steamers ! " Lines have been needed
to run to both coasts of South America, to Africa, the Mediterranean,
India, China, and Japan, not to mention Europe, and to run exclusively in the interests of American trade. The matter has been brought
before the attention of ship-owners and wealthy men in commercial
cities repeatedly. All the facts have been repeatedly and carefully
canvassed. Companies and private firms have several times been
formed to run steamers to the lands named. One of them obtained a
charter from Congress. Ships have several times been dispatched, ex-
perimentally, to Chili, China, and elsewhere. If there had been any
confidence whatever that American lines would pay, twenty of them
would now be in active operation. But it is known that they would
not pay. The sea is covered with the steamships of England, France,
Spain, Germany, Italy, and Holland, almost all of them either being
now heavily subsidized by their respective governments, or having
been sustained with subsidies for a long period of years until they had
been able to expel every American steamer from competition with
them in the navigation of the world. In the North Atlantic trade
the English steamers now no longer receive subsidies, but they did
receive them until within five years ; and the enormous capital, the
skill in practical management, and the control of the trade, acquired
by means of those subsidies, now render it impracticable for American
steamers to enter into competition with them, unless backed by the
Government. There is also a difference in wages and cost of operation now against the American ship. In no direction now does an
American steamer ply on the high seas, unless it has a subsidy from a
foreign government, or a virtual monopoly of a small trade. As things
now stand, private enterprise is certainly helpless. The Government
must act, or nothing will be done.

But it is said that if the duty on wool and coffee and perhaps a very few other things were repealed, some of these lines would be started. Those who propose this must show that the sacrifice to important home interests would not be greater than the good gained. Perhaps they can demonstrate this. At any rate, it is for them to make the attempt.

Now we can go on with the argument. A general law to pay from $25 to $75 per mile per annum for the transportation of the United States mails in American ships to foreign lands, according as monthly or weekly trips are made, would cost the national treasury the sum of from $3,000,000 to $5,000,000 a year. The enlargement of our navigation would also require an expenditure for the enlargement of our Navy. What would the country gain from the expenditure? Let us offset the benefits against the cost and see in which direction falls the balance.

First, in regard to ship-owning. The imagination is kindled by a contemplation of the possibilities of enlargement of this interest. Refer to the table printed on page 7 of this pamphlet. Reflect for a moment that the almost incredible quantity of 11,150,000 gross tons of grain, oil, cotton, tobacco, provisions, metals, and other produce and manufactures was exported from the United States during the last fiscal year, and that this exportation is increasing at the rate of from 1,000,000 to 2,000,000 gross tons a year. Reflect that about 3,800,000 tons of goods are imported. About 15,000,000 tons of goods carried to and from the shores of the United States every year. If only one half of the business of carrying our enormous wealth of surplus commodities could be secured for American ships, sail and steam, the tonnage of the United States employed in the foreign trade would instantly be doubled, and would be larger than ever before in the history of the country. If all of the 15,000,000 tons of goods above referred to, not now carried by American vessels, could be secured, the United States would have a larger merchant fleet engaged in foreign trade than Great Britain herself. Such possibilities dazzle the mind. Yet they present themselves on the most cursory glance at the subject. It is not supposed that all of this carrying trade could be secured for American ships ; but the facts show that, with any sort of a favoring policy on the part of the American government, the ship-owning interest would be immensely expanded and would enter upon a period of prosperity such as has been never before known.

Hand in hand with the growth of our navigation would go the growth of the home ship-building interest. The effect of the new policy would be seen at once in the ship-yards of the United States and in the numerous industries to which the yards give employment. If judgment were exercised, as it ought to be, in the establishment of American steamship lines, no business would be taken away from

American sailing ships, but new transportation business would be
gained at the expense of foreign steamship lines and foreign sailing
ships. Timber ships would therefore continue to be built in America
as much as ever, and iron ships would be produced in vastly increased
numbers. The value of the iron building interest to a country was set
forth by "The New York Tribune," in its issue of April 7, 1877, in an
article on the growth of that industry. "The Tribune" said :

"It puts immense sums of money into circulation, very much larger than
people are generally aware, and it gives employment to more trades than any
other industry. Its benefits to a people continue after the expenditure of money
for labor and materials. A ship once set afloat upon the waters and actively
employed in commerce gives continued occupation to labor on land and sea.
Repairs and supplies are continually called for by it, and an amount of money
equal to 50 per cent. of its cost, if it is a steamship, and 30 per cent. if it is a
sailer, is expended upon it and by it annually during the whole of its active existence. It has to be replaced, too, in time, so that, when once set going in a
good trade, the employment it gives to labor and capital is permanent. . . .
Nowhere is this fact so well understood as in England. In that intelligent
country every possible encouragement has been given especially to the iron-ship-
building interest ; and this has been done not only to secure a commercial supremacy, but to secure the benefits at home of a steady and profitable employment of the labor of the country and the continued consumption of materials."

It is the continued employment of labor which constitutes in dollars and cents the greatest value of the ship-building interest to the country. How much labor is called for in the construction of vessels will
be seen from "The Tribune" explanation : "Labor constitutes fully 60
per cent. of the cost of a steamer and at least 50 per cent. the cost of a
sailing vessel. Going back to the raw materials, the iron and copper
ore, the coal, and the wood, it will be found that the labor is fully 95
per cent. of the cost of a steamship ; but, starting with the pig metal
and sawed lumber, about 80 per cent." It is substantially the same
thing, whether the ship be of wood or iron. About $11,000,000 is
now spent in the United States annually for new ships, wooden and
iron, and about $2,000,000 more for the repair of old ones. Of the to-
tal of $13,000,000, fully $10,000,000 pays for labor. The enormous proportion of labor to materials required and the high class of the labor
make this industry, by common consent of intelligent men, to rank as
of the highest importance to any country. Under a policy of government encouragement, expenditures for iron and wooden ships would
be increased at least to $40,000,000 a year. The record of the past
proves it. Concurrently, the expenditures for American labor and
supplies, in operating the ships, would be increased by $10,000,000 or
$15,000,000, perhaps considerably more. That is to say, there would
then be expended in the United States an immense sum of money not

now expended, which might be as large as $40,000,000, which would diffuse itself throughout the community and bless and quicken every department of human industry. Best of all, the money, thus spent, would be principally obtained from the foreigner. It would come from the earnings of the ships, which, in the export trade at least, are paid by consumers in foreign lands. In the import trade the money is paid by consumers here and is carried away from the country. The larger part of the money, therefore, would be a pure gain to the United States. The money is now earned by foreigners and they carry it abroad to be spent. They do not spend it here. Under a changed condition of things, it would be spent here.

Still a greater benefit would accrue from the stimulus to trade and domestic industry. It is often debated whether foreign trade grows up in consequence of the establishment of facilities for transportation, or whether ships are the offspring of a trade already in existence or of a strong desire to trade. There ought to be no dispute on that point, any more than there should be on the question as to which stands the best chance of getting married, a man or a woman ; and for the same reason—there is nothing to dispute about. On the one hand, if facilities are created, trade follows. Establish a canal through a farming region, a railroad into a new State or across the plains, or a steamship line to a populous foreign country with which we have little or no trade, or to some distant and unoccupied part of our own country, and a brisk and flourishing traffic soon springs up in its path. On the other hand, create trade and improved facilities follow. The history of the United States and of the world at large is full of remarkable illustrations of both these principles. Now, the point is that, if a number of companies could be formed to run swift and capacious steamers to different parts of South America, and to India, Africa, and the Mediterranean, in the interest of the trade of the United States, a large increase of foreign trade would follow. Even if history did not prove this, common sense would. Take South America alone. That region (including Mexico) imports about $290,000,000 worth of manufactured goods and articles of food yearly. Only one tenth of the amount is now imported from the United States. "The New York World" said, on May 28, 1877, in an article on "South American Trade":

"The United States are fitted to occupy the leading position in the trade with South America, both by nature and the energy and inventive genius of the people. South America produces only a fraction of the amount of the necessaries of life which her people consume. She finds profitable employment for her people in raising purely tropical products, cotton, coffee, India rubber, etc., and for generations to come there will be little or no temptation for her to employ them in anything except those occupations. South America accordingly does now and will for years go abroad to buy the greater part of her food, clothing,.

6

furniture, building materials, etc., which she would rather buy than produce. All these things, or nearly all, can now be bought in the United States as cheaply as anywhere in the world; but American merchants have simply neglected the market, and the consequence is that nine tenths of what the South Americans import is shipped to them by Europe from points 1,000 to 5,000 miles further away from them than the ports of the United States. Here is an illustration of the inferior position occupied at present by this country in that immense and profitable trade. No figures can be obtained later than 1874. In 1874 the United States, England, and France sold to South American countries the following amount of goods (the figures for England and France being for the calendar year):

	United States.	England.	France.
Peru	$2,621,906	$9,149,885	$6,498,610
United States of Columbia	5,859,344	12,960,780	4,705,695
Mexico	6,004,870	6,614,860	4,512,708
Argentine Republic	2,633,963	15,961,695	14,775,806
Chili	2,818,990	14,462,425	9,269,970
Uruguay	1,147,620	6,520,780	5,975,589
Brazil	7,778,676	40,280,750	16,656,215
Totals	$28,359,869	$105,900,695	$62,896,548

"The United States do not therefore now send to the whole continent of South America and to Mexico over $30,000,000 worth of goods in the course of a year, although they buy $75,000,000 worth from that region of the world annually. And yet the United States are now no longer beaten in the markets of the world in respect to the prices or the excellence of the things, which the peoples south of us buy in any quantity. . . . The secret of the supremacy of England and France in that commerce resides in the existence of their splendid steam lines. On an average, one steamer a day, of from 1,000 to 5,000 tons burden, leaves England for Brazil and the River Plata. There are three lines running to Pará at the mouth of the Amazon. There are two lines running direct to the west coast from Europe, having some of the best steamers afloat. They make a voyage of about fifteen thousand miles and carry freight for about $15 a ton, while from New York the facilities are so imperfect that freight costs $20 and upward a ton. It is useless to compete with Europe on a large scale, therefore, until the merchants of the United States take hold of the work of securing good steam communication to those countries, sincerely."

These remarks are perfectly true. If the United States had a number of steamship lines to South America, she could extend her trade with that region enormously. Indeed very little can be done until the lines are established. There is one line to Brazil now and trade has received a new impulse in consequence of its establishment, but there should be steamers to Buenos Ayres, to Chili, Peru, Venezuela, and other places. If there were, a few years' time would work wonders in the expansion of trade. It does not require any special reference to history to prove it. Nor does it require any argument to prove that all parts of the United States would be benefited by an expansion of our foreign trade.

"The World" might have mentioned one fact which it did not. The French, English, and German steamers running to South America were originally established, and are still maintained, by means of subsidies.

When the subject of subsidies was under discussion last winter, Mr. F. B. Thurber, of New York city, came forward among others as an advocate of proper compensation for ocean mail-service. In a short letter to "The Nation" in January, he said something which would be very appropriate here. Here it is:

"Divesting this question of all tariff, currency, and other sophistries, we must come down to the plain, business principle that, if we would compete for the trade of a certain country or locality, we must furnish equal facilities with other nations who are also catering for this trade. I recently had a practical illustration of the important bearing which transportation has upon business. Two retail grocers were competing for the trade of a certain outlying suburb, the people of which had for a long time, without solicitation from either grocer, purchased their supplies at whichever store they chose and taken them home the best way they could. One of the grocers conceived the idea of putting on a wagon, with a smart driver to solicit orders and deliver goods. As a natural consequence he soon absorbed a large part of the trade of the suburb, and his competitor found himself obliged to do the same thing in order to retain his portion of the trade. There is a strong analogy between this case and the present situation of the United States in regard to South American and other foreign markets. England, France, Spain, Italy, Holland, and other countries of minor commercial importance have all been sending out their steam messengers to the four quarters of the globe to solicit orders and deliver goods, while we in the United States have been attributing the paucity of our foreign orders principally to one cause, and, in my opinion, not the chief one."

There is a third reason why the United States should encourage the establishment of steamship lines. This is found in the relation of our ship-yards and merchant vessels to the United States Navy. If the Government of the United States were compelled to supply itself with the shops and mechanics indispensable for maintaining a navy, the cost to the people would be millions of money annually, over and above the $20,000,000 now spent every year for that purpose. It is almost without exception the rule that, whenever a government attempts to carry on a manufacturing business of any kind, the work is not so well done as it would have been in private establishments, or, if equally well done, then it is not done so cheaply. The extremely few exceptions prove the rule, and, indeed, the proposition is universally admitted to be sound. All governments act upon it by giving as much of their work as possible to private establishments, and the reasons for so doing are obvious. The machinery of shops is continually wearing out, as also the shops themselves; they have to be replaced. A certain number of men have to be kept employed, so that they may acquire and retain the skill for the proper construction of ships. The cost of the wear and tear of shops and of the keeping a certain number of men employed, if paid by a government, would add to the burdens of taxation heavily. It would add from $5,000,000 to $10,000,000 annually to the cost of our own navy. It is far better for the Government that there should be a large number of private ship-yards scattered throughout the country, fully equipped and manned, and having plenty to do. The Government, while thus spared the extravagant cost of maintaining expensive establishments, could at the same time always secure the construction and repair of ships as promptly as though it had its own shops and yards. In the late civil war the Government would have been helpless without the private establishments. What a spectacle the Brooklyn Navy Yard presented at that time! Seven thousand men employed there, and vessels standing at the wharves a hundred deep, waiting wearily for repairs. The same state of affairs existed at other government yards. The private shops were a more important resource in that hour of extreme peril than the whole array of government establishments. The experience of that four years of war and of the fifteen years since has established beyond question the importance of the private yards as a resource in war and a means of economy in times of peace.

Then, it is important to the navy that there should be among the merchant vessels of the United States a large number of iron steamships, swift, capacious, and stoutly built, to act as an auxiliary fleet in case of war. The type of war-ship now most gaining in favor throughout the world is the one known in England as the armed dispatch vessel and in France as the rapid type. The ship is unarmored, and is very fast, being capable of making 17 knots an hour, and having the strong frame and large coal-carrying capacity indispensable for maintaining a high speed for a considerable length of time. Now that Krupp and Armstrong are manufacturing 100 and 150 ton guns, armored ships are useless except for harbor defense. England has spent $80,000,000 upon armored ships within the last 15 years, and is now compelled to view with regret the fact that the vast majority of her fighting ships have been rendered obsolete or ineffective by the new guns. A large number of the costly ships of France, Germany, and other powers have been rendered antiquated by the same cause. There are already strong advocates of the idea of abandoning armor in Europe, and the popularity of swift unarmored war-ships is rapidly increasing. England, France, and Russia are now buying and building this class of vessels for cruisers. The cruising fleets of the world are to be reorganized on this principle. This outcome of the progress of invention makes the condition of the merchant steam marine of a country a matter of great importance. The absence of such a marine is now a source of weakness, to any country having a commerce to protect. Chief Engineer King, of the United States Navy, announced to Secretary Robeson in his report on "European Ships of War," in January, 1877,that the British mercantile marine possessed 419 steamers of above 1,200 tons and under 5,000 tons register, many of which would be relied on for 14 or 15 knots an hour in good weather, for seven or eight days consecutively. In the event of war any of those ships would be at the command of the Government ; and, with such a cruising fleet, England would be able to sweep the commerce of any nation from the high seas in three months time. The British Admiralty is now carefully considering the subject of utilizing those ships in case of war by arming them with light rifled guns and Whitehead torpedoes. Under the circumstances, a country like the United States, having a great coastwise and ocean commerce, which does not wish to maintain a large and costly navy, but which cannot afford to be left helpless in case of war, is bound by every consideration of duty and prudence, to provide itself with a large and efficient steam merchant marine, built, if possible, under the inspection of the Government, and convertible into cruisers in case of war. We could gain both the ships and the right of inspection, by offering to give mail contracts to those who would build and operate them. Ought we not to offer those contracts, then ? The prosperity of the people, farmers, artisans, and merchants alike, is intimately allied with the free and rapid export of the surplus commodities of the land. Can we afford not to be fully prepared to carry these commodities if the nations now carrying them should become involved in war, and to protect our commerce when that or any similar emergency shall arise ? And who that knows with what persistency all the powers of Europe maintain enormous armaments will venture to say that the emergency may not arise at any moment ?

The words of Jefferson in his famous " Report on Commerce " in 1794 are worth repeating, in connection with this subject. He said :

" Our navigation involves still higher considerations. As a branch of industry it is valuable; but as a resource of defense essential. The position and circumstances of the United States leave them nothing to fear from their landboard, and nothing to desire beyond their present rights. But on the seaboard they are open to injury, and they have there too a commerce which must be protected. This can only be done by possessing a respectable body of citizen seamen, and of artists and establishments in readiness for ship-building. If particular nations grasp at undue shares [of our commerce], and more especially if they seize on the means of the United States to convert them into aliment for their own strength and withdraw them entirely from the support of those to whom they belong, defensive and protecting measures become necessary on the part of the nation whose marine resources are thus invaded, or it will be disarmed of its defense, its productions will be at the mercy of the nation which has possessed itself ex-

clusively of the means of carrying them, and its politics may be influenced by
those who command its commerce. The carriage of our own commodities, if
once established in another channel, cannot be resumed in the moment we desire. If we lose the seamen and artists whom it now occupies we lose the present means of marine defense, and time will be requisite to raise up others, when
disgrace or losses shall bring home to our feelings the evils of having abandoned
them."   '

What would Jefferson have said, could he have foreseen that, a
century after his time, the foreign commerce of the United States
would be so wholly in the hands of foreign nations that the country
would not even have ships enough to transact and protect that commerce, if European nations should become involved in war?

A great many minor considerations can be advanced in favor of
the expediency of Government action. But these will suffice. Now
let us post up the account. Remember that foreign ships now carry
more than three-fourths of the commodities we exchange with foreign
nations. American ships carry less than one-fourth. It would cost
the country to change this state of affairs, by maintaining the Navigation Laws and establishing American steamship lines, perhaps $5,000,000
a year. It would cost perhaps $1,000,000 more a year for the Navy.
Now, first, these lines would save to the country at least one half of
the $50,000,000 of freight money now paid on imported goods, and they
would earn at least one half of the large sum paid by foreign nations
on the goods exported from this country. Then, they would give employment to tens of thousands more of American citizens, on land and
sea. They would also relieve agriculture, promote industry and trade,
and impart security to commerce. They would add enormously to the
resources, collective strength, and prestige of the American people.
What inexpressible benefits! How slight the cost! That cost, too,
to be cheapened by the increase of receipts from foreign mails. Is
there a shred of doubt left as to the expediency of Government action?
Ought we not, then, to go in for mail contracts to steamers?

Even if the balance had fallen on the wrong side in footing up the
account, it might still have been advisable to spend the money for the
sake of creating the means of defense, for use in case of need. John
Stuart Mill, speaking of the English Navigation Act, and the temporary rise in the cost of freights when the Act was passed, says: "I at
once admit that the object was worth the sacrifice; and that a country
exposed to invasion by sea, if it cannot otherwise have sufficient ships
and sailors of its own to secure the means of manning on an emergency
an adequate fleet, is quite right in obtaining those means, even at an
economical sacrifice in point of cheapness of transport." The United
States is exposed to invasion only from the sea. Her coast line is simply enormous, and it constitutes her one weakness, in the matter of

defense. It is her duty to guard that weak point even at "an economical sacrifice," and it would make no difference whether the sacrifice took money from the national treasury direct or from the pockets of the people in high freights. It would come to the same thing in the end.

If the American people could compete with their rivals in navigation on equal terms, the resource, genius, and enterprise of this country would soon restore the ascendancy of the American flag upon the high seas. But there is nothing like fair competition in navigation. Nearly all the Governments of the world have established systems of subsidies and regulations to promote the interests of their own shipping, and Americans when they attempt to go into steam navigation on the great oceans find themselves in competition, not with the individual business men of other lands simply, but with the collective strength and resources of the whole of some of the most wealthy nations in the world. The United States has nothing to hope from other nations in the way of equality of competition in navigation, unless the Government demands and fights for it. The United States has never gained any recognition of the rights of its merchant vessels, or any extension of its navigation, except by retaliatory laws of the most stringent character and by downright hard fighting with powder and ball. It never will, in the future, gain anything worth having except by the same pushing policy.

DISCRIMINATION AGAINST AMERICAN SHIPS.

III. In concluding, attention ought to be called to a strange anomaly in the postal laws of the United States. There is a discrimination in them against American vessels carrying the foreign mails. One phase of this matter was touched upon in the chapter preceding this, but a fuller notice of it is necessary. All the railroads and canals, and a majority of the plank-roads, turnpikes and rivers, and coastwise steam routes of the United States, are declared by law to be post routes of the United States. The Postmaster General is by the same authority empowered to provide for carrying the inland mails over these routes as many times per day or week as he may deem proper.

The law points out how he is to provide for carrying the mails, namely, "he may contract" with carriers on the different routes for the service. If he cannot induce the railroads to transport the mails for a compensation not exceeding the maximum rates allowed by law, he is expressly authorized to establish a system of fleet mail carriers on horseback for the dispatch of the lighter mails, and of wagons for the transportation of the heavier packages. He can resort to any other plan if he finds a better one. The Government once paid

$1,000,000 a year for a pony express, the one across the plains. The
point is that the Government constrains no carrier of the inland mails
to transport a single package of letters against its will, the few land-
grant railroads alone excepted. If the carrier does not think that the
compensation offered by the Government is sufficient to pay for the
trouble, it can decline to carry the mails, and there is no remedy. The
laws do not permit the Government to compel the carrier to perform
the service. This is, of course, simple justice to the citizen, whose
property and time cannot be taken without proper compensation.

But, now, how is it, on the other hand, with the carrier of the mails
on the high seas, if that carrier happen to be an American vessel? The
Government has no right to compel a foreign ship to carry a single
package of letters, but the merchant vessels of the United States are,
by law of Congress, compelled to carry all mails offered to the masters
thereof by the post-office authorities here, and by consuls abroad, and
to accept such compensation as Congress autocratically directs. This
compensation has at no time been in excess of the sea and inland postages combined on the mails carried. When the law was originally
enacted, this compensation was not so inadequate as now, because
inland postages were high, they being 25 and 12½ cents, being even
as high as 5 and 10 cents, according to distance, as late as 1845. In
1861 the postage to California was $1 per half ounce. The sea post-
ages were also very high. As late as only 10 years ago, the single
letter rate between this country and Europe was 24 cents. There was
some profit in carrying the mails at those rates. But now the postage
on all inland mails has been reduced to 3 cents ; the sea postage is 2
cents. Five cents per half-ounce letter, 2 cents for each postal card,
and 2 cents for each 4 ounce newspaper, is the utmost compensation
now. It is about one-tenth of what it used to be, and is an utterly
inadequate remuneration for the trouble and responsibility. The foreign ships receive only the sea postages. There is another point : The
necessity of delivering the mails committed to the master of a vessel
is frequently a source of delay and great expense to a ship, which may
have storms to fight, and whose plans, upon touching at some port for
telegraphic advices from home, may be changed by its owners. No
matter what the trouble, the ship is compelled to deliver the mails
assigned to its master, or forfeit all the rights and privileges of a vessel
of the United States. There is no opportunity for negotiation. There
is no appeal. This is a strange and unjust provision of the law. A
company of citizens who invest their capital at great risk to themselves
either in sailing ships or in a great steamship line to trade to a foreign
land are no less entitled to the protection of the laws and to fair treatment from the Government, than the company of men who put their
capital into a railroad. Yet the Government deals with them in an

entirely different manner. The Government would not dare treat railroad and local steam and wagon lines as it does ship-owners.

The stages and wagons carrying the inland mails under their contracts with the Post-Office Department, receive an average of $28 per mile of route per annum. The steamers on the rivers and along the coasts receive an average compensation of $43.50 per mile per annum. The railroads receive an average of $131 per mile per annum, the compensation to these lines ranging all the way from $35 on the less important roads to $538, $897, $922, $979, and $1,155 per mile of road per annum on the principal lines. On the vast majority of these routes, the postages collected do not repay the Government for the cost of the service. On only a few hundred out of the whole array of 9,900 routes, would the carrier consent to accept the postage as his compensation. Why should postages, then, be made the sole basis of compensation, especially when it happens, absurdly, that the merchant vessels of the United States, being compelled to accept the postages alone, can obtain only about $1 per mile of route per annum, for performing the valuable service of transporting the ocean mails? The American steamers from Philadelphia to Liverpool receive about 80 cents per mile per annum. The company sends off ships over a stormy ocean 3,100 miles wide, and receives less for carrying the mail than the stage-coach running up into some backwoods region in Maine, or the sleepy old sloop that carries a weekly mail out to the slumbering inhabitants of some little fishing island on the coast. And all the time the Government is making a handsome profit on the ocean mails. It does not attempt to make a profit on the inland mails.

The theory of our system is that the postages shall be rated so as merely to pay expenses. If we make a large profit on certain big lines, the money is employed to establish mails in new and non-paying regions. If an extension of the system is not needed, then the cost of postages is reduced. That is the historical theory of our system. The theory is utterly disregarded in the matter of the foreign mails. The treatment of our ships is "*L'indigne moitié d'une si belle histoire.*"

A private letter from Mr. Joseph H. Blackfan, United States Superintendent of Foreign Mails, says that the excess of postage receipts over expenditures for foreign mails in 1878 was $400,000. Mr. Blackfan did not mention it, but the writer knows that some years the profit has risen to $600,000, and this too under the cheap postages of the International Union. It would be appropriate to devote this money to extending the mail communications of the United States, and to a better compensation of the carriers.

Before closing, something might be said, perhaps, about the interoceanic canal. The whole world is excited now over the daring idea of building a canal across the American isthmus. De Lesseps 'has lent his great name to the scheme. General Grant is talked of as the executive head of the canal company, and the General has expressed his interest in the work. This canal will shorten the voyage from our North Atlantic seaports to points on the west coast of South America from 11,000 miles to a voyage of from 2,400 to 4,000 miles. It would shorten the voyage to San Francisco, now 15,300 miles, to 5,500 miles. What will that canal do for the shipping of the United States ? It will do much. It would give us an advantage in certain trades at once, unless England, France, and Germany should increase their present subsidies. But when are we to have that canal ? The new route from sea to sea can not be opened for travel in less than twelve years after the pick is first struck into the ground. This is the report of all engineers. It will be several years before the work is even begun. A route is not finally decided upon yet. De Lesseps does not expect to live to see the canal finished. He only wishes for the honor of seeing it begun. It will be 1895 or 1900 before a ship sails across the American isthmus from ocean to ocean. Meanwhile, what are we going to do about our shipping ? Wait for the canal ? What nonsense !

One thing more may be said, and the suggestion is of the utmost consequence. We may differ about the methods to be employed to restore our commercial supremacy upon the seas, but all must now admit that, if there is to be no change in our circumstances, supremacy will never come back to us, and ship-yards, ship-builders (for there are few learning the trade), and high-class ship-building will cease to exist in America. Builders have been waiting a number of years, paying taxes, taking care of their properties, and supporting the families of tens of thousands of mechanics, while making little money for themselves, hoping that Congress would do something for the shipping interest of the country ; and, unless wise heads do take hold of this matter, the present generation of builders and ship-mechanics will die out, and the country will be deprived of its most important resource in time of war, and its most profitable industry in time of peace.

Congress has a duty to perform in this matter. It has a duty to perform toward American labor as well as toward American capital. It should protect the American mechanic, the laboring-man, the farmer, the sea-captain, and the sailor from being ground down to the low standard of the working-man abroad. It is often said that American mechanics and farmers want books to read, pianos in their parlors, education for their children, and even pictures on the walls. The sea-captain expects to dine in a swallow-tail coat with the consignee, carry a gold watch, own ships, become a merchant, and go to Congress. The sailor has a home, and leaves the ship the moment it arrives in port to greet his family. These things all tell against us, it is said, because it prevents us from producing and operating ships as cheaply as our rivals. Give us free trade. Grind down the mechanic and all who live by his work, and the sea-captain and the sailor, and then we can get along without subsidies. But it is a good thing in every point of view that American mechanics and seamen live as they do. They are better men, and make better citizens, because they live well and desire the enjoyments of the mind. We want them to live well. Their mode of life makes them a tower of strength to the country. Ask the working-men and seamen of America what they think of the duty of Congress in this matter. What does Congress itself think about the idea of oppressing American labor?

THE END.

THE MERCANTILE AGENCY.

R. G. DUN & CO., **DUN, BARLOW & CO.,**
DUN, WIMAN & CO., **E. RUSSELL & CO.**

The object of THE MERCANTILE AGENCY is to supply information as to the Capital, Capacity, and Character of parties engaged in trade. Established forty years ago, this concern was the first organized effort to relieve the merchants, manufacturers, and bankers of this country from the uncertainty of credit operations. It sought to substitute for the tardy, expensive, and unsatisfactory results of individual investigation, a *system* that should be alike prompt, economical, and reliable. How far that system has been successfully applied, we leave it for the public to judge, after an uninterrupted existence of nearly half a century, during which time our business relations with mercantile circles have so increased as to necessitate the establishment of a branch office in every city of any prominence whatever in this country, in Canada, and in several leading capitals of Europe.

ADVANTAGES OF EIGHTY-ONE BRANCH OFFICES.

The advantage enjoyed by the subscribers to an agency having eighty-one branch offices, over those connected with an institution having less than half that number, ought to be very apparent, but it is sometimes not sufficiently appreciated. If these branches are, for a long period of years, sustained by local revenue, it implies that the information in each locality must be gleaned in a manner satisfactory to those who, being on the spot, are the best judges of its reliability and completeness. If on these reports local transactions are constantly consummated, the information is as constantly tested and confirmed, or revised and amended ; so that the result, so far as the locality is concerned, is a photograph of the local impression faithfully gathered. These photographic reports are transmitted and interchanged between each of the eighty-one branches needing them. The subscriber has whatever benefit arises from this large expenditure, in the fullest details regarding his customers in their respective localities. The difference is between having on the spot a well-trained staff of agency men, devoting their whole time to the work, spending a large local revenue, and constantly under the surveillance of local patrons, as compared with the opinions of a single unknown correspondent, constantly underpaid, if paid at all, who will have his own purposes to serve, and will certainly make the most—honestly if he can—out of the connection. The division of the country into eighty small compact districts, each under the supervision of persons entirely familiar with the work, it is submitted, ought to result more satisfactorily to subscribers than if the country were divided into thirty large departments, remote portions of which it is impossible to report except by relying on the most slender kind of local material. If merchants themselves can not thus see the advantage of employing the agency with the largest revenue, employing the largest number of trained men, and with the largest number of subscribers to criticise reports, they are less obtuse in other matters than in this.

CHEAP OR SECOND-RATE AGENCIES.

The difference in price for the use of the various agencies is rarely less than $25. Now, to save this paltry sum, spread over an entire year (or this percentage, if the use is large), some are disposed to content themselves with a second-rate agency. A moment's reflection ought to convince those who so decide that the saving thus made is most unwise, for the following reasons : Presuming that an agency, to be worth anything, must have at least 5,000 subscribers, by accepting the low rate it voluntarily relinquishes an income of $125,000, which, if received and judiciously spent, would make a very great difference in the quality of its information. The subscriber, by saving his $25 a year, thus deprives himself of the advantage of an expenditure of $125,000 per year. But a really first-class agency, that has, say 10,000 subscribers, by its insistence on the payment of even this additional $25 as a remunerative rate, thereby adds to its revenue $250,000. If the subscriber can, by the payment of $25, secure all the advantages of a judicious expenditure of a quarter of a million of dollars, by persons in whom he has confidence, directed by long years of experience, and with machinery in perfect working order, is there in the whole course of his business an expenditure that will pay him a better return than this $25 additional ?

R. G. DUN & CO.,

Albany, Allentown, Atlanta, Baltimore, Binghamton, Buffalo, Burlington, Charleston, Chicago, Cincinnati, Cleveland, Columbus, Dallas, Davenport, Dayton, Denver, Des Moines, Detroit, Dubuque, East Saginaw, Elmira, Erie, Evansville, Galveston, Gloversville, Grand Rapids, Hartford, Houston, Indianapolis, Kansas City, Keokuk, La Crosse, Leavenworth, Little Rock, Louisville, Memphis, Milwaukee, Minneapolis, Mobile, Nashville, Newark, New Haven, New Orleans, Norfolk, Omaha, Oswego, Peoria, Philadelphia, Pittsburg, Portland (Ore.), Providence, Quincy, Richmond, Rochester, St. Joseph, St. Louis, St. Paul, San Francisco, Savannah, Scranton, Springfield, Syracuse, Toledo, Troy, Utica, Williamsport, London and Manchester (England), Glasgow (Scotland), Paris (France), and Leipzig (Germany).

DUN, BARLOW & CO., 314 and 316 Broadway and 60 Wall Street, New York.
DUN, WIMAN & CO., Montreal, Toronto, Hamilton, London, Halifax, and St. John, N. B.
E. RUSSELL & CO., Boston, Worcester, and Portland.

LIGHT.

RELIABLE, SAFE, ECONOMICAL.

ELECTRIC LIGHT, as so far developed, has a comparatively limited field of usefulness, but in that field has no equal. The phenomenal success of the now famous BRUSH ELECTRIC LIGHT has attracted general attention to the subject, and owners and managers of industrial establishments throughout this and foreign countries are beginning to realize the great advantages, both in economy and in more effective light, which this new and wonderful illuminator offers. Over *six hundred Brush Electric Lights* have been sold for actual use during the past year (1879), and they have gone into manufactories, mills, mines, hotels, stores, parks, steamers, seaside resorts, and places of similar character throughout the country, from Maine to California, and also in foreign countries. The following are mentioned as a few of the most prominent users of the Brush light in this country.

66 lights	in	Grand Depot of John Wanamaker, Philadelphia, Pa.
2	" "	Reading Railway Company's steamer Harrisburgh, Philadelphia, Pa.
4	" "	Edgmoor Iron Company. Edgmoor, Del.
12	" "	Phœnix Iron Company, Phœnixville, Pa.
10	" "	Pennsylvania Steel Company, Baldwin Station, Pa.
16	" "	Pottstown Iron Company, Pottstown, Pa.
16	" "	Park Bros., Black Diamond Steel Works, Pittsburgh, Pa.
80	" "	Riverside Worsted Mills, Providence, R. I.
6	" "	Willimantic Linen Company, Willimantic, Conn.
36	" "	Conant Thread Company, Pawtucket, R. I.
6	" "	Continental Clothing House, Washington Street, Boston, Mass.
6	" "	Nantasket Beach, Boston Harbor, Boston, Mass.
54	" "	Oswego Falls Woolen Mills, Fulton, N. Y.
4	" "	Washburn & Moen Manufacturing Company Wire Mills, Worcester, Mass.
23	" "	Iron Pier at Coney Island, New York.
6	" "	Loeser & Company, Dry Goods Store, Brooklyn, N. Y.
17	" "	Prospect Park and American Falls, Niagara Falls, N. Y.
16	" "	Chautauqua Lake Sunday School Assembly, Fairpoint, N. Y.
16	" "	Chicago Times Establishment, Chicago, Ill.
16	" "	Grand Pacific Hotel, "
2	" "	Otis Iron and Steel Company Rolling Mill, Cleveland, O.
12	" "	Monumental Park, Cleveland, O.
13	" "	Cooper, Bailey & Company, Circus, "On the road."
4	" "	Deer Creek Mine, near Smartsville, Cala.
4	" "	Lake Superior Iron Company Mine, Ishpeming, Mich:
10	" "	Palace Hotel, San Francisco, Cala.
16	" "	Mechanics' Pavilion, "
6	" "	Pacific Coast Line steamer State of California, San Francisco, Cala.
18	" "	Atlantic Mills, Providence, R. I.
18	" "	Globe Mill, Pawtucket, R. I.
6	" "	Passaic Rolling Mill, Paterson, N. J.

In all of these places the *Brush Electric Light* is used because it is the cheapest and best light for the purpose, and not solely because of its great beauty and attractiveness. The case of the Riverside Mill at Providence, R. I., an enormous factory of worsted goods, well illustrates the advantages offered by this light. They first ordered a sixteen-light Brush machine for use in their weaving shed, and, as it proved entirely successful, ordered more until now they have arranged for no less than five of these large machines, yielding in all eighty powerful lights of two thousand candle power each, and with them light their entire establishment, thereby saving enough over their former expenditure for gas to *pay for the entire cost of the apparatus inside of two years*. In many other places equal success has been attained, and the factory of the Telegraph Supply Co. where the machines are made is driven to its utmost capacity day and night to supply the demand. In all cases where power is already in use, and enough can be spared to run the Brush machine, the cost of the light is reduced to the mere consumption of the carbon points in the light, which amount to just *one cent per hour* for each light; and each light will displace from ten to fifty gas burners, varying according to the situation.

The Brush Electric Light is therefore offered as the best and most economical light now known for use in factories, mills, parks, large stores, hotels, seaside resorts, wharves, docks, steamers and ferry boats, mines, newspaper establishments, and large spaces generally. Inquiries regarding the apparatus will be answered and more detailed information furnished by the

TELEGRAPH SUPPLY CO., *Sole Manufacturers,*
Cleveland, O., U. S. A.

M. D. LEGGETT, *President*   GEO. W. STOCKLY, *Vice-Pres. and Manager.*
(Formerly Com. of Patents).

THE DAILY GRAPHIC.

The Field of Illustrated Journalism.

The circulation of the "Daily Graphic" is national in its extent. Since the beginning of 1877, its number of subscribers has increased more than three-fold. The paper is sold on the stands of newsdealers in nearly every city in the United States. It has regular subscribers in important towns in every state and territory. Its regular circulation outside the city undoubtedly exceeds the combined country circulation of all the other evening papers, and is larger than the country circulation of most of the morning papers.

The origin of illustrated journalism was very simple. A London newsdealer observed that whenever a paper contained a diagram, wood-cut, or map of any kind, it attracted attention and had an increased sale. He reflected on the fact, and the "Illustrated London News" was the result of his cogitations. It met with an unexpected success, and led to a number of imitations.

The idea of the old newsdealer was sound. People love to grasp situations at a glance of the eye. They love to take in a landscape at a look, and find more joy in a cheap print which represents a real scene than in any amount of elegant verbal description. The eye is the window of the mind, the telescope of the imagination. The picture tells a whole story at once. It photographs itself in the memory. It delights the fancy. It informs without weariness. It pleases without dissipation. The child begins to learn by picture-seeing. The first writing in the world was hieroglyphic; and the stories told by the old Egyptians in those rude figures cut in the walls of temples and of tombs convey whole volumes of information. Illustrated journalism is the application of the simplest principle to the diffusion of intelligence. It supplements words, that make dim images on the mind, with pictures, that give form, and body, and character to the objects described, and transfers a whole scene instantaneously to the imagination. We are fast learning that pictures are something more than objects to lazily enjoy, over which one may spend an idle hour. They are a language. They are the best possible vehicle of communicating intelligence to mind and imagination. They are poetry reduced to form. They can be made, as we have abundantly shown, the means of telling the news more effectually, easily and completely than any words yet invented. The recognition of this principle has given "The Graphic" its wide circulation and made its name the synonym of enterprise.

"The Graphic" has the best, fullest, and latest financial and mining intelligence of any paper in New York.

Terms, postpaid, per year, $12.00.

Address,

THE DAILY GRAPHIC,

39 and 41 Park Place, N. Y.

Anonymous

Area and Product of Cereals Grown in 1879

Anonymous

Area and Product of Cereals Grown in 1879

ISBN/EAN: 9783337411800

Printed in Europe, USA, Canada, Australia, Japan

Cover: Foto ©Andreas Hilbeck / pixelio.de

More available books at **www.hansebooks.com**

OF

CEREALS

GROWN IN 1879,

AS RETURNED BY THE

CENSUS OF 1880.

———•◆•———

WASHINGTON:
GOVERNMENT PRINTING OFFICE.
1883.

THE CEREALS OF 1879.

The Census has never returned area cultivated, or other areas except improved and unimproved land in farms, until 1880. The progress of production of corn, wheat, and oats, which together constitute more than 97 per cent. of the cereals of the United States, is shown by the figures below. This reproduction of revised census returns of cereals is made by the Department of Agriculture for the information of its corps of correspondents, as a basis for their annual estimates, which should be made in form for each county, and kept as a permanent record for their guidance.

3

QUANTITY OF CORN, WHEAT, AND OATS PRODUCED IN 1860, 1870, 1880.

States and Territories.	Corn 1860.	Corn 1870.	Corn 1880.	Wheat 1860.	Wheat 1870.	Wheat 1880.	Oats 1860.	Oats 1870.	Oats 1880.
	Bushels.	Bushels.	Bushels.	Bushels.	Bushels.	Bushels.	Bushels.	Bushels.	Bushels.
Maine	1,546,071	1,089,888	960,633	233,876	278,783	665,714	2,948,939	2,351,354	2,265,575
New Hampshire	1,414,628	1,277,768	1,150,248	238,965	193,621	169,316	1,329,233	1,146,451	1,017,620
Vermont	1,525,411	1,689,682	2,014,271	437,037	454,703	337,257	3,630,267	3,602,430	3,742,282
Massachusetts	2,157,063	1,397,807	1,797,768	119,783	34,648	15,768	1,180,075	707,664	645,159
Rhode Island	461,497	311,957	372,967	1,131	784	340	344,453	157,010	159,389
Connecticut	2,059,835	1,570,361	1,880,421	52,401	38,114	38,742	1,522,218	1,114,586	1,009,706
New York	20,061,049	16,462,825	25,690,156	8,681,105	12,178,462	11,587,766	35,175,134	35,293,625	37,575,506
New Jersey	9,723,336	8,745,361	11,150,218	1,763,218	2,301,433	1,901,739	4,589,132	4,069,890	3,710,573
Pennsylvania	28,196,821	34,702,006	45,821,531	13,042,165	19,672,967	19,462,405	27,387,147	36,478,585	33,841,430
Delaware	3,892,337	3,010,390	3,894,264	912,941	895,477	1,175,272	1,046,910	554,388	378,504
Maryland	13,444,922	11,701,817	15,968,533	6,103,480	5,774,503	8,004,864	3,959,208	3,221,643	1,794,872
Virginia	38,319,999	17,649,304	29,119,761	13,130,977	7,394,787	7,826,174	10,186,720	6,867,555	5,333,181
North Carolina	30,078,564	18,454,215	28,019,839	4,743,706	2,859,879	3,397,393	2,781,860	3,220,105	3,836,068
South Carolina	15,065,606	7,614,207	11,767,099	1,285,631	783,610	962,358	936,974	613,593	2,715,505
Georgia	30,776,293	17,646,459	23,202,018	2,544,913	2,127,017	3,159,771	1,231,817	1,904,601	5,548,743
Florida	2,834,391	2,225,056	3,171,231	2,808	9,906	422	16,899	114,204	468,112
Alabama	33,226,282	16,977,948	25,451,278	1,218,444	1,055,068	1,529,657	682,179	770,966	3,039,639
Mississippi	29,057,682	15,637,316	21,310,800	587,925	254,479	218,890	221,215	111,586	1,959,620
Louisiana	16,853,745	7,596,628	9,889,689	32,208	9,906	5,034	89,377	17,782	220,840
Texas	16,500,702	20,554,538	29,065,172	1,478,345	415,112	2,567,737	985,889	762,063	4,893,459
Arkansas	17,823,588	13,382,145	24,156,417	957,601	711,706	1,269,715	475,268	528,777	2,210,822
Tennessee	52,080,926	41,343,614	62,764,429	5,459,268	6,188,916	7,411,353	2,267,814	4,513,315	4,722,190
West Virginia		8,197,865	14,090,609		2,463,513	4,004,711		2,413,749	1,908,505
Kentucky	64,043,633	50,091,006	72,852,263	7,394,809	5,728,701	11,356,113	4,617,029	6,620,163	4,580,738
Ohio	73,543,190	67,501,144	111,877,121	15,119,047	27,882,159	46,014,869	15,409,234	25,347,549	28,664,505
Michigan	12,444,676	14,086,238	32,461,452	8,336,368	16,265,773	35,532,543	4,036,980	8,954,466	18,190,783
Indiana	71,588,919	51,094,538	115,482,300	16,848,267	27,747,222	47,284,853	5,317,831	8,590,409	15,389,518

Illinois	115,154,777	129,921,385	325,792,481	21,857,023	30,128,465	51,110,502	15,220,029	42,780,851	63,189,200
Wisconsin	7,517,300	15,033,198	34,230,579	15,657,454	24,606,344	24,884,689	11,059,260	29,180,016	32,905,320
Minnesota	2,941,952	4,733,117	14,831,741	2,186,951	18,866,073	34,601,030	2,176,002	10,678,364	23,382,158
Iowa	12,410,646	68,535,065	275,014,247	8,449,463	29,425,422	31,151,205	5,887,645	21,905,142	59,610,591
Missouri	72,892,157	66,034,675	292,414,413	4,227,586	14,315,926	24,966,627	3,640,470	16,578,313	29,670,958
Kansas	6,140,727	17,025,525	105,729,325	191,173	2,301,198	17,324,141	88,325	4,097,925	8,140,385
Nebraska	1,482,040	4,736,710	65,450,135	117,867	2,125,086	13,847,007	74,502	1,477,562	6,555,875
California	510,708	1,221,222	1,993,325	5,928,470	16,676,702	29,017,707	1,043,006	1,757,507	1,341,571
Oregon	76,122	72,138	126,862	856,776	2,340,746	7,480,010	885,673	2,029,909	4,365,650
Nevada	480	9,640	12,891	3,611	228,866	69,298	1,082	55,016	186,660
Colorado		231,903	456,968		258,474	1,425,014		332,940	640,903
Arizona		32,041	34,746		27,052	136,427		25	564
Dakota	20,293	133,140	2,000,864	915	170,662	2,830,289	2,540	114,327	2,217,132
District of Columbia	80,840	28,020	29,750	12,760	3,782	6,402	29,544	8,500	7,440
Idaho	5,750		16,408		75,050	540,589		100,119	462,296
Indian Territory									
Montana	320		5,649		181,184	469,688		149,367	960,915
New Mexico	709,304	640,823	633,780	434,309	352,822	706,641	7,246	67,660	156,527
Utah	90,482	95,567	163,312	381,882	558,174	1,169,199	63,211	65,650	418,082
Washington	4,712	21,781	39,183	846,219	217,043	1,921,322	134,334	255,169	1,551,766
Wyoming						4,674		100	22,512
Total	838,792,742	760,914,549	1,754,591,676	173,104,924	287,745,626	439,483,137	172,613,185	282,107,157	407,858,989

SUMMARY BY STATES.

States.	BARLEY.		BUCKWHEAT.		RYE.	
	Acres.	Bushels.	Acres.	Bushels.	Acres.	Bushels.
United States.........	1,907,727	43,907,495	848,389	11,817,327	1,842,233	10,831,595
Alabama	511	5,281	42	363	5,764	28,402
Arizona	12,404	239,051	....	....	....	.....
Arkansas..................	157	1,952	92	548	3,290	22,387
California.................	586,350	12,463,561	1,012	22,307	20,281	181,681
Colorado...................	4,112	107,116	8	110	1,294	19,465
Connecticut	575	12,286	11,231	137,563	29,794	370,733
Dakota	16,156	277,424	321	2,521	2,385	24,339
Delaware..................	19	523	397	5,857	773	5,953
District of Columbia.......	....	....	....	....	301	3,704
Florida	21	210	....	....	601	2,965
Georgia....................	1,439	18,662	58	402	25,854	101,716
Idaho......................	8,291	274,750	....	....	354	4,341
Illinois	55,267	1,220,523	16,457	178,859	192,138	3,121,785
Indiana	16,399	382,835	8,846	89,707	25,400	303,105
Iowa	198,861	4,022,348	10,010	166,805	102,607	1,518,605
Kansas	23,993	300,273	2,458	24,421	34,621	413,181
Kentucky	20,069	486,326	1,024	9,942	89,417	668,050
Louisiana..................	....	....	....	....	201	1,013
Maine......................	11,106	242,185	20,135	382,701	2,161	26,398
Maryland..................	226	6,097	10,294	136,667	32,405	288,067
Massachusetts.............	3,171	80,128	5,617	67,117	21,666	213,716
Michigan	54,506	1,204,316	33,948	413,062	22,815	294,918
Minnesota.................	116,020	2,972,965	3,677	41,750	13,614	215,245
Mississippi................	44	348	....	....	806	5,134
Missouri...................	6,472	123,031	5,463	57,640	46,484	535,426
Montana...................	1,323	39,970	34	437	15	430
Nebraska..................	115,201	1,744,686	1,666	17,562	34,297	424,348
Nevada....................	19,390	513,470	....	....	....	.....
New Hampshire...........	3,461	77,877	4,535	94,090	3,218	34,658
New Jersey................	240	4,091	35,373	466,414	106,025	949,064
New Mexico...............	2,548	50,053	....	....	17	240
New York..................	356,629	7,792,062	291,228	4,461,200	244,923	2,634,690
North Carolina	230	2,421	5,725	44,668	61,953	285,160
Ohio	57,482	1,707,129	22,130	280,229	29,409	389,221
Oregon	29,311	920,977	372	6,215	841	13,305
Pennsylvania	23,592	438,100	246,199	3,593,326	398,465	3,683,621
Rhode Island	715	17,783	105	1,254	1,270	12,997
South Carolina	1,162	16,257	....	....	7,152	27,049
Tennessee	2,600	30,019	4,907	33,434	32,403	156,419
Texas	5,527	72,786	48	535	3,326	25,399
Utah	11,268	217,140	....	....	1,153	9,605
Vermont...................	10,552	267,625	17,649	356,618	6,310	71,733
Virginia	859	14,223	16,403	136,004	48,746	324,431
Washington	14,080	566,537	106	2,498	518	7,124
West Virginia	424	9,740	30,334	283,298	17,279	113,181
Wisconsin	204,335	5,013,118	34,117	299,107	169,692	2,298,513
Wyoming	....	....	....	....	6	78

SUMMARY BY STATES.

States.	INDIAN CORN. Acres.	Bushels.	OATS. Acres.	Bushels.	WHEAT. Acres.	Bushels.
United States	62,368,504	1,754,591,676	16,144,593	407,858,999	35,430,333	459,483,137
Alabama	2,055,929	25,451,278	324,628	3,039,639	264,971	1,529,657
Arizona	1,818	34,746	29	564	9,026	136,427
Arkansas	1,298,310	24,156,417	166,513	2,219,822	204,084	1,269,715
California	71,781	1,993,325	40,947	1,341,271	1,832,429	29,017,707
Colorado	22,991	455,968	23,023	640,900	64,693	1,425,014
Connecticut	55,796	1,880,421	36,691	1,009,706	2,198	38,742
Dakota	90,852	2,000,864	78,226	2,217,132	265,298	2,830,289
Delaware	202,120	3,894,264	17,158	378,508	87,539	1,175,272
District of Columbia	1,032	29,750	267	7,440	284	6,402
Florida	360,294	3,174,234	47,962	468,112	81	422
Georgia	2,538,733	23,202,018	612,778	5,548,743	475,684	3,159,771
Idaho	569	16,408	13,197	462,236	22,066	540,589
Illinois	9,019,381	325,792,481	1,959,889	63,189,200	3,218,542	51,110,502
Indiana	3,678,420	115,482,300	623,531	15,599,518	2,619,695	47,284,853
Iowa	6,616,144	275,014,247	1,507,577	50,610,591	3,049,288	31,154,265
Kansas	3,417,817	105,729,325	435,859	8,180,385	1,861,402	17,324,141
Kentucky	3,021,176	72,852,263	403,416	4,560,738	1,160,108	11,356,113
Louisiana	742,728	9,889,089	26,861	229,840	1,501	5,034
Maine	30,997	960,633	78,785	2,265,575	43,829	665,714
Maryland	664,928	15,968,533	101,127	1,794,872	569,296	8,004,864
Massachusetts	52,555	1,797,768	20,659	645,159	963	15,768
Michigan	919,656	32,461,452	536,187	18,190,793	1,822,749	35,532,543
Minnesota	438,737	14,831,741	617,469	23,382,158	3,044,670	34,601,030
Mississippi	1,570,550	21,340,800	198,497	1,959,620	43,524	218,890
Missouri	5,588,265	202,414,413	968,473	20,670,958	2,074,394	24,966,627
Montana	197	5,649	24,691	900,915	17,665	469,088
Nebraska	1,630,660	65,450,135	250,457	6,555,875	1,469,865	13,847,007
Nevada	487	12,891	5,937	186,860	3,674	69,298
New Hampshire	36,612	1,350,248	29,485	1,017,620	11,248	169,316
New Jersey	344,555	11,150,705	137,422	3,710,573	149,760	1,901,739
New Mexico	41,449	633,786	9,237	156,527	51,230	706,641
New York	779,272	25,690,156	1,261,171	37,575,306	736,611	11,587,766
North Carolina	2,305,419	28,019,839	500,415	3,838,068	646,829	3,397,393
Ohio	3,281,923	111,877,124	910,388	28,664,505	2,556,134	46,014,809
Oregon	5,646	126,862	151,624	4,385,650	445,077	7,480,010
Pennsylvania	1,373,270	45,821,531	1,237,593	33,841,439	1,445,384	19,462,405
Rhode Island	11,893	372,907	5,575	159,339	17	240
South Carolina	1,303,404	11,767,099	201,445	2,715,505	170,902	962,356
Tennessee	2,904,873	62,764,429	468,566	4,722,190	1,196,563	7,331,353
Texas	2,468,587	29,065,172	238,010	4,893,359	373,570	2,567,737
Utah	12,007	163,342	19,525	418,082	72,542	1,169,199
Vermont	55,249	2,014,271	99,548	3,742,282	20,748	337,257
Virginia	1,768,127	29,119,761	563,443	5,333,181	901,177	7,826,174
Washington	2,117	39,183	37,962	1,571,706	81,554	1,921,322
West Virginia	565,785	14,090,609	126,931	1,908,505	393,068	4,001,711
Wisconsin	1,015,393	34,230,579	955,597	32,905,320	1,948,160	24,884,689
Wyoming			822	22,512	241	4,674

ALABAMA.

Counties.	BARLEY.		BUCKWHEAT.		RYE.	
	Acres.	Bushels.	Acres.	Bushels.	Acres.	Bushels.
The State	511	5, 281	42	363	5, 764	28, 402
Autauga........					63	282
Baldwin						
Barbour					112	473
Bibb					151	501
Blount					98	444
Bullock........					68	506
Butler						
Calhoun					287	1, 700
Chambers......	39	327			123	637
Cherokee					163	1, 020
Chilton	22	179			60	268
Choctaw.......					5	29
Clarke					24	163
Clay	25	151			142	737
Cleburne					91	556
Coffee.........					31	115
Colbert	10	350			69	415
Conecuh					32	270
Coosa	10	68			14	72
Covington					0	50
Crenshaw......					18	102
Cullman	7	104	24	155	480	2, 513
Dale					24	87
Dallas	9	133			20	210
DeKalb........					383	1, 182
Elmore	15	157			27	116
Escambia......						
Etowah........					72	224
Fayette					46	172
Franklin.......					39	121
Geneva						
Greene					25	133
Hale	33	360			56	463
Henry	13	65			263	844
Jackson	9	50			347	1, 613
Jefferson......	12	34			83	359
Lamar	20	100			75	320
Lauderdale					262	1, 133
Lawrence......					117	612
Lee	12	166			85	655
Limestone					234	1, 378
Lowndes.......						
Macon					45	246
Madison	25	396			174	898
Marengo.......						
Marion					113	370
Marshall.......	3	50			150	691
Mobile........						
Monroe	4	20				
Montgomery....			11	155	15	115
Morgan	68	902	7	53	136	805
Perry	7	34			70	261
Pickens.......	4	28			36	223
Pike					23	134
Randolph	79	736			179	922
Russell					28	103
Saint Clair....					43	181
Shelby					76	445
Sumter					25	162
Talladega	36	315			143	842
Tallapoosa.....	30	348			24	114
Tuscaloosa	20	173			130	689
Walker	8	35			81	344
Washington						
Wilcox........					22	146
Winston......					31	137

ALABAMA.

Counties.	INDIAN CORN.		OATS.		WHEAT.	
	Acres.	Bushels.	Acres.	Bushels.	Acres.	Bushels.
The State	2.055,929	25,451,278	324,628	3,039,639	264,971	1,529,657
Autauga	20,417	184,393	2,153	22,044	700	3,459
Baldwin	2,041	28,428	350	5,108		
Barbour	61,822	437,415	10,264	90,295	131	530
Bibb	18,816	236,086	2,935	21,926	3,125	16,700
Blount	29,161	422,048	4,551	44,194	10,087	60,856
Bullock	47,441	379,876	6,177	43,028	111	455
Butler	24,648	274,668	7,494	71,109	10	150
Calhoun	33,714	469,598	8,852	93,368	10,745	67,660
Chambers	49,306	458,286	9,258	80,592	11,520	73,945
Cherokee	33,373	509,381	7,477	66,215	10,085	66,956
Chilton	18,185	183,975	2,255	18,300	4,507	20,661
Choctaw	25,613	272,213	3,338	28,432		
Clarke	28,220	312,718	5,065	47,737	7	30
Clay	24,503	292,870	4,834	39,308	9,785	54,603
Cleburne	21,552	362,335	5,672	58,084	7,504	48,904
Coffee	18,068	155,014	2,370	15,025	22	85
Colbert	31,575	500,701	3,846	43,914	1,704	10,923
Conecuh	20,118	181,277	3,173	25,136		
Coosa	29,990	364,399	5,325	41,758	9,735	55,028
Covington	10,558	81,907	2,114	16,266		
Crenshaw	28,090	254,050	5,208	36,480	26	139
Cullman	10,343	102,982	1,179	8,198	2,560	12,452
Dale	31,867	221,497	5,114	28,894	59	336
Dallas	46,542	707,139	8,260	111,213	71	487
DeKalb	23,920	322,259	5,113	34,843	6,846	37,382
Elmore	20,000	211,688	5,153	49,849	3,883	20,779
Escambia	3,699	34,336	809	8,979		
Etowah	24,801	382,788	5,025	44,734	7,063	40,192
Fayette	24,950	342,520	3,627	27,302	4,826	22,745
Franklin	21,038	348,897	3,020	23,143	1,660	7,331
Geneva	9,476	58,887	1,705	10,004		
Greene	31,826	402,992	2,163	22,464	314	1,803
Hale	43,254	595,185	3,671	45,075	1,437	15,273
Henry	46,661	325,846	7,002	63,402	193	906
Jackson	60,285	1,099,486	8,241	90,962	10,051	58,335
Jefferson	30,928	420,660	4,708	43,414	10,589	60,038
Lamar	28,303	352,474	4,139	32,440	5,627	24,221
Lauderdale	42,890	721,039	4,609	39,233	8,475	36,376
Lawrence	54,643	708,931	5,691	56,352	5,919	34,024
Lee	30,137	244,903	11,918	101,911	8,697	50,225
Limestone	44,612	710,928	4,134	40,380	7,561	41,638
Lowndes	41,169	611,184	3,630	43,922		
Macon	23,893	173,969	6,195	53,336	1,916	9,094
Madison	69,246	1,033,223	6,877	81,161	12,578	80,716
Marengo	43,876	608,009	6,574	83,234		
Marion	21,835	272,481	2,321	15,680	3,925	15,136
Marshall	27,113	465,582	3,471	31,873	5,797	30,084
Mobile	1,639	25,272	139	1,440		
Monroe	24,135	251,068	4,597	44,024		
Montgomery	62,303	767,427	4,895	62,292	58	393
Morgan	35,610	580,687	4,704	40,533	7,005	39,829
Perry	48,132	628,248	6,003	63,710	440	2,974
Pickens	43,104	491,496	8,053	76,044	2,220	11,985
Pike	42,207	374,170	5,424	38,698	72	408
Randolph	29,595	332,466	4,850	43,558	10,155	58,379
Russell	34,335	215,555	9,789	91,141	1,099	6,771
Saint Clair	25,465	341,703	4,603	41,291	9,841	54,853
Shelby	26,159	312,830	4,764	39,348	6,204	34,324
Sumter	51,402	699,883	2,706	31,380	24	225
Talladega	40,376	454,873	9,278	92,356	13,233	80,868
Tallapoosa	41,415	461,960	9,106	78,084	14,572	99,061
Tuscaloosa	38,638	480,784	6,974	63,013	2,689	12,388
Walker	21,798	263,123	2,570	21,687	5,420	26,149
Washington	4,259	58,105	404	3,547		
Wilcox	40,053	573,385	7,011	92,933	22	179
Winston	8,098	88,781	579	4,043	1,967	8,314

ARIZONA.

Counties.	BARLEY.		BUCKWHEAT.		RYE.	
	Acres.	Bushels.	Acres.	Bushels.	Acres.	Bushels.
The Territory	12, 404	239, 051				
Apache	692	20, 751				
Maricopa	6, 039	125, 138				
Mohave	274	5, 817				
Pima	2, 212	33, 511				
Pinal	2, 311	33, 890				
Yavapai	726	16, 944				
Yuma	150	3, 000				

ARKANSAS.

	BARLEY.		BUCKWHEAT.		RYE.	
	Acres.	Bushels.	Acres.	Bushels.	Acres.	Bushels.
The State	157	1, 952	92	548	3, 290	22, 387
Arkansas						
Ashley					8	66
Baxter					45	304
Benton	6	200	22	183	177	1, 360
Boone	14	346			276	1, 939
Bradley	8	65				
Calhoun					15	100
Carroll					582	4, 820
Chicot						
Clark	8	62			48	290
Clay					6	34
Columbia	6	94			44	159
Conway					12	63
Craighead						
Crawford	13	117			8	55
Crittenden					5	60
Cross					16	166
Dallas					44	244
Desha						
Dorsey						
Drew						
Faulkner	15	113			9	74
Franklin					21	229
Fulton					51	368
Garland					32	237
Grant					7	40
Greene					13	80
Hempstead	13	95			17	118
Hot Spring					61	504
Howard	9	63			36	93
Independence	22	300			54	371
Izard					227	1, 098
Jackson						
Jefferson					14	180
Johnson					21	131
La Fayette						
Lawrence					41	360
Lee						
Lincoln					11	99
Little River						
Logan					37	254
Lonoke					18	125
Madison	10	50			167	1, 226
Marion					134	1, 185
Miller						
Mississippi						
Monroe						
Montgomery					15	77
Nevada					45	168
Newton					88	666

ARIZONA.

Counties.	INDIAN CORN.		OATS.		WHEAT.	
	Acres.	Bushels.	Acres.	Bushels.	Acres.	Bushels.
The Territory	1,818	34,746	29	564	9,026	136,427
Apache	294	4,368	29	564	642	11,075
Maricopa	76	2,165			4,721	87,315
Mohave	28	430			23	320
Pima	474	9,486			833	9,890
Pinal	176	2,205			2,302	22,357
Yavapai	725	14,841			290	5,070
Yuma	45	1,251			215	400

ARKANSAS.

	INDIAN CORN.		OATS.		WHEAT.	
The State	1,298,310	24,156,417	166,513	2,219,822	204,084	1,269,715
Arkansas	10,248	136,232	685	10,354	48	539
Ashley	15,335	152,289	1,411	12,218	14	85
Baxter	10,804	261,337	2,024	21,678	1,776	9,995
Benton	49,135	1,119,834	13,912	245,382	21,461	156,087
Boone	26,713	653,945	5,752	92,372	8,499	56,581
Bradley	12,330	97,241	1,073	8,316	336	1,309
Calhoun	12,910	100,688	873	5,838	128	652
Carroll	22,979	582,734	4,626	64,451	7,343	51,992
Chicot	7,309	117,391	80	372		
Clark	27,005	470,352	2,121	25,069	2,515	11,953
Clay	13,979	343,836	977	12,406	2,240	13,408
Columbia	28,868	235,376	3,241	22,545	1,019	3,542
Conway	15,950	349,294	1,685	24,674	1,778	9,346
Craighead	15,023	367,451	1,374	20,260	2,734	15,552
Crawford	19,777	465,356	2,369	33,216	5,347	31,040
Crittenden	9,810	216,194	73	1,128	20	200
Cross	6,985	138,614	835	11,121	471	2,643
Dallas	13,330	136,760	894	5,749	443	2,010
Desha	9,819	180,177	169	3,139	18	171
Dorsey	14,737	113,630	1,777	13,967	660	3,319
Drew	20,005	145,401	1,488	11,522	280	1,214
Faulkner	19,647	347,062	2,793	30,247	3,300	18,197
Franklin	23,024	547,723	3,383	52,509	6,017	31,803
Fulton	11,686	299,030	1,602	20,827	1,602	10,394
Garland	8,785	153,434	1,281	17,656	1,445	7,442
Grant	12,765	149,854	1,244	10,408	573	2,616
Greene	14,068	347,926	1,802	20,110	1,702	10,475
Hempstead	30,284	418,837	3,489	42,676	1,289	6,702
Hot Spring	13,602	268,650	910	11,191	1,377	7,384
Howard	17,671	272,635	2,486	20,409	3,357	13,618
Independence	31,114	691,188	5,100	61,209	8,055	57,104
Izard	21,728	431,904	4,913	40,593	4,830	25,902
Jackson	17,861	384,398	500	6,399	910	7,415
Jefferson	16,639	290,508	398	6,596	32	278
Johnson	20,003	463,488	2,763	34,693	3,509	18,496
La Fayette	8,366	97,371	140	1,362	13	77
Lawrence	19,902	522,720	3,256	40,851	2,591	18,662
Lee	16,124	271,650	806	12,047	83	620
Lincoln	12,547	144,068	1,400	15,210	185	1,021
Little River	9,141	166,819	582	9,523	113	774
Logan	24,136	491,526	3,543	46,918	4,376	20,211
Lonoke	17,502	249,764	3,310	49,674	1,131	5,563
Madison	29,514	720,428	4,368	75,068	12,318	85,414
Marion	13,034	330,305	1,985	26,704	2,494	13,816
Miller	16,672	223,728	601	6,798		
Mississippi	9,858	314,116	181	4,240	68	655
Monroe	12,945	208,667	764	13,995	60	200
Montgomery	9,629	187,991	825	9,000	3,023	16,790
Nevada	23,173	253,222	1,329	11,851	635	2,807
Newton	12,217	287,869	1,906	23,810	2,241	14,302

ARKANSAS—Continued.

Counties.	BARLEY.		BUCKWHEAT.		RYE.	
	Acres.	Bushels.	Acres.	Bushels.	Acres.	Bushels.
Ouachita					72	154
Perry						
Phillips					43	740
Pike					38	208
Poinsett			6	28		
Polk					13	52
Pope	9	151			47	223
Prairie					10	94
Pulaski					27	245
Randolph					22	117
Saint Francis					14	230
Saline			11	44	28	136
Scott	5	24			6	15
Searcy					87	433
Sebastian					9	55
Sevier	19	272			16	45
Sharp					40	269
Stone					17	110
Union					165	309
Van Buren					62	241
Washington			53	293	106	900
White					45	399
Woodruff						
Yell					9	49

CALIFORNIA.

	Acres.	Bushels.	Acres.	Bushels.	Acres.	Bushels.
The State	586, 350	12, 463, 561	1, 012	22, 307	20, 281	181, 681
Alameda	39, 075	1, 213, 820	228	4, 027	82	1, 020
Alpine	113	3, 410				
Amador	3, 291	101, 054			17	270
Butte	23, 288	516, 474	5	325	326	4, 904
Calaveras	1, 926	47, 294				
Colusa	39, 939	899, 558			172	5, 050
Contra Costa	19, 674	501, 880			66	1, 250
Del Norte	54	1, 530			17	200
El Dorado	1, 137	22, 911			174	2, 568
Fresno	9, 504	118, 527				
Humboldt	2, 629	94, 848	8	177	43	1, 047
Inyo	1, 686	35, 845				
Kern	6, 151	119, 571				
Lake	4, 551	124, 300	12	400	14	140
Lassen	1, 950	37, 073			102	1, 140
Los Angeles	38, 823	405, 708	6	130	272	1, 855
Marin	1, 499	37, 554				
Mariposa	1, 314	26, 239			134	1, 701
Mendocino	3, 544	101, 829	13	330	158	2, 220
Merced	10, 181	88, 036			2, 378	8, 932
Modoc	3, 956	91, 325			101	1, 065
Mono	295	3, 925				
Monterey	35, 426	825, 550	88	1, 215	41	590
Napa	5, 753	130, 844	28	754	26	460
Nevada	543	10, 632			224	1, 735
Placer	5, 504	68, 275			260	3, 003
Plumas	16	535			74	857
Sacramento	30, 547	650, 448	264	7, 958	19	235
San Benito	10, 469	192, 462			12	245
San Bernardino	4, 076	82, 563			48	1, 045
San Diego	3, 573	45, 330				
San Francisco	349	3, 500			37	183
San Joaquin	32, 669	796, 409	25	130	8, 334	76, 438
San Luis Obispo	9, 658	205, 869	20	100	1, 023	23, 300
San Mateo	16, 705	349, 644	7	160		

ARKANSAS—Continued.

Counties.	INDIAN CORN.		OATS.		WHEAT.	
	Acres.	Bushels.	Acres.	Bushels.	Acres.	Bushels.
Ouachita	21,924	155,655	567	2,921	164	693
Perry	6,469	134,935	842	11,119	561	2,881
Phillips	19,685	332,585	834	13,410	36	367
Pike	11,604	188,256	1,232	11,043	2,032	8,893
Poinsett	3,907	87,133	258	3,490	237	1,529
Polk	10,616	179,400	1,416	15,816	2,424	13,096
Pope	24,736	494,773	2,688	30,741	7,772	34,439
Prairie	10,113	135,462	2,191	31,944	457	2,214
Pulaski	20,843	369,911	2,199	32,976	1,076	5,623
Randolph	27,312	728,403	2,903	33,137	4,016	31,244
Saint Francis	9,934	197,061	706	8,849	354	1,835
Saline	15,821	292,628	2,802	38,046	1,454	7,589
Scott	15,435	279,533	2,345	29,661	1,956	7,957
Searcy	14,399	362,828	1,901	24,776	3,085	19,179
Sebastian	28,283	553,513	4,378	53,976	6,095	32,157
Sevier	10,557	156,839	1,045	12,693	1,012	4,740
Sharp	18,508	432,570	4,411	52,241	3,178	18,908
Stone	9,156	209,375	1,429	19,297	2,006	13,537
Union	27,795	171,779	1,249	6,405	103	243
Van Buren	17,548	345,315	2,627	31,666	3,325	15,233
Washington	53,083	1,225,557	13,103	220,617	28,507	224,669
White	29,148	444,893	6,957	95,359	3,509	17,220
Woodruff	11,146	229,962	497	9,908	307	1,867
Yell	22,791	495,138	2,634	42,480	5,954	32,678

CALIFORNIA.

	Acres.	Bushels.	Acres.	Bushels.	Acres.	Bushels.
The State	71,781	1,993,325	49,947	1,341,271	1,832,429	29,017,707
Alameda	1,139	37,573	1,458	32,766	36,032	620,758
Alpine	8	235	236	5,985	179	2,936
Amador	1,191	40,695	31	822	2,386	48,323
Butte	1,325	31,210	418	13,700	127,189	2,244,770
Calaveras	206	7,295	13	330	807	16,256
Colusa	851	15,735	176	3,600	261,381	4,537,504
Contra Costa	55	1,360	1,280	37,455	71,870	1,267,016
Del Norte	42	1,710	200	4,830	56	995
El Dorado	13	414	57	1,168	1,360	20,777
Fresno	414	10,053	9	205	20,474	190,923
Humboldt	624	16,313	8,817	354,785	3,437	84,532
Inyo	1,682	33,213	791	22,538	1,525	30,004
Kern	1,694	35,046	80	2,400	6,887	85,682
Lake	735	19,277	352	10,243	8,296	173,842
Lassen	15	330	1,465	33,126	4,773	75,361
Los Angeles	22,771	752,104	78	1,470	29,349	316,042
Marin			1,031	26,937	2,603	55,520
Mariposa	30	720	12	255	337	4,476
Mendocino	884	20,526	2,843	80,288	8,899	166,666
Merced	574	15,715	25	30	67,975	296,308
Modoc	18	440	774	20,883	4,301	78,335
Mono			12	250	11	200
Monterey	488	14,978	3,363	88,362	69,022	779,286
Napa	1,664	41,722	1,014	22,250	33,653	611,445
Nevada	32	665	1,165	26,871	304	3,235
Placer	160	4,879	873	14,524	11,751	183,547
Plumas			2,574	87,797	1,129	21,217
Sacramento	3,928	149,550	871	22,745	44,123	804,631
San Benito	299	6,720	41	846	32,223	837,271
San Bernardino	774	23,136			2,558	45,582
San Diego	440	8,017	77	958	8,929	60,650
San Francisco			44	440		
San Joaquin	2,333	68,890	130	2,820	201,461	3,529,511
San Luis Obispo	458	13,503	937	13,405	10,618	173,531
San Mateo	118	1,380	7,376	132,473	10,767	219,084

14

CALIFORNIA—Continued.

Counties.	BARLEY.		BUCKWHEAT.		RYE.	
	Acres.	Bushels.	Acres.	Bushels.	Acres.	Bushels.
Santa Barbara	13,598	245,667	17	300		
Santa Clara	29,613	716,860			224	2,740
Santa Cruz	5,945	176,804	106	2,280	50	1,110
Shasta	6,762	87,303			437	7,363
Sierra	391	1,172			129	248
Siskiyou	3,598	114,013	12	460	69	720
Solano	32,222	571,403	15	300	30	400
Sonoma	11,126	256,007	11	152	207	4,058
Stanislaus	19,559	312,682			4,646	22,619
Sutter	14,830	365,086	119	2,703	27	450
Tehama	14,967	261,838			55	1,031
Trinity	14	220	8	110		
Tulare	3,661	69,200	5	117		
Tuolumne	2,558	41,018			47	486
Ventura	28,171	551,289			53	300
Yolo	18,320	519,479	15	119	63	901
Yuba	11,057	218,458				

COLORADO.

	Acres.	Bushels.	Acres.	Bushels.	Acres.	Bushels.
The State	4,112	107,116	8	110	1,294	19,465
Arapahoe	884	21,578			68	881
Bent	15	209				
Boulder	586	15,783			253	4,276
Chaffee						
Clear Creek						
Conejos	14	470				
Costilla						
Custer	136	3,893			13	373
Douglas	500	14,914			567	7,788
Elbert	131	4,466			18	240
El Paso	31	604			237	3,356
Fremont	8	345			6	100
Gilpin						
Grand						
Gunnison						
Hinsdale						
Huerfano	41	1,333				
Jefferson	302	12,009	8	110	73	1,734
Lake						
La Plata	49	1,282				
Larimer	544	12,504			6	95
Las Animas	64	805			19	467
Ouray	8	140				
Park	5	100			6	100
Pueblo	86	2,489				
Rio Grande	77	2,125				
Routt						
Saguache	11	264			8	55
San Juan						
Summit						
Weld	558	11,702				

CONNECTICUT.

	Acres.	Bushels.	Acres.	Bushels.	Acres.	Bushels.
The State	575	12,286	11,231	137,563	29,794	370,733
Fairfield	23	444	1,285	16,697	5,083	63,656
Hartford	9	128	1,914	20,447	7,620	86,578
Litchfield	155	2,940	2,284	30,128	5,128	58,200
Middlesex	6	149	547	7,691	1,722	30,743
New Haven	61	1,348	1,071	13,549	4,905	78,256
New London	103	1,987	1,042	12,201	1,410	15,587
Tolland	34	803	1,232	15,915	2,126	18,434
Windham	184	4,457	1,856	20,935	1,800	17,279

CALIFORNIA—Continued.

Counties.	INDIAN CORN.		OATS.		WHEAT.	
	Acres.	Bushels.	Acres.	Bushels.	Acres.	Bushels.
Santa Barbara	3,167	123,795	24	330	16,492	265,955
Santa Clara	261	10,391	260	4,771	38,623	648,055
Santa Cruz	1,768	43,873	934	21,513	12,060	291,049
Shasta	59	1,590	677	22,039	6,267	90,010
Sierra			1,082	2,320	308	689
Siskiyou	112	3,015	3,208	106,350	6,330	98,370
Solano	443	16,685	127	2,015	107,588	2,042,533
Sonoma	5,961	158,820	2,615	68,685	39,820	742,123
Stanislaus	378	13,655			172,445	1,642,892
Sutter	1,596	28,935	243	5,916	74,338	1,205,883
Tehama	24	750	298	9,114	84,254	1,386,228
Trinity	30	980	165	3,626	1,071	14,185
Tulare	2,535	46,255	6	100	28,131	371,081
Tuolumne	24	373	69	1,885	4,055	62,824
Ventura	9,121	148,485	40	300	8,470	113,497
Yolo	714	10,090	55	1,480	115,369	2,086,550
Yuba	603	12,220	1,461	23,210	28,134	359,967

COLORADO.

	Acres.	Bushels.	Acres.	Bushels.	Acres.	Bushels.
The State	22,991	455,968	23,023	640,900	64,693	1,425,014
Arapahoe	909	16,835	997	36,618	2,684	70,231
Bent	120	2,105	178	4,545	65	543
Boulder	4,262	72,192	3,640	112,095	16,879	422,056
Chaffee			502	15,707	71	1,025
Clear Creek			58	1,260		
Conejos	5	46	145	2,800	93	1,007
Costilla	79	1,346	95	2,360	140	4,018
Custer			707	21,708	41	958
Douglas	578	12,842	1,038	28,434	886	22,051
Elbert	177	4,243	356	12,006	83	1,861
El Paso	935	16,665	1,236	29,629	675	11,634
Fremont	1,366	34,480	566	14,892	554	9,924
Gilpin						
Grand						
Gunnison						
Hinsdale			35	650		
Huerfano	493	5,985	349	6,658	416	6,886
Jefferson	1,539	35,750	2,240	65,505	10,137	213,855
Lake						
La Plata	45	839	578	15,367	371	7,078
Larimer	2,669	73,143	2,287	77,106	9,027	193,154
Las Animas	3,527	62,900	1,659	29,258	6,836	126,381
Ouray			139	4,030	20	497
Park			31	1,002		
Pueblo	1,397	20,709	1,062	24,750	507	7,928
Rio Grande			265	7,715	105	1,630
Routt			31	1,208		
Saguache			1,387	32,539	355	5,613
San Juan						
Summit						
Weld	4,890	95,930	3,382	92,449	14,748	314,884

CONNECTICUT.

	Acres.	Bushels.	Acres.	Bushels.	Acres.	Bushels.
The State	55,796	1,580,421	36,691	1,009,706	2,198	38,742
Fairfield	10,059	353,493	7,004	194,893	721	13,338
Hartford	11,526	337,109	3,566	83,261	271	5,233
Litchfield	8,709	301,425	9,350	281,028	536	6,580
Middlesex	2,677	111,777	1,131	30,634	355	7,734
New Haven	5,899	232,379	2,926	76,164	249	4,650
New London	7,273	244,943	5,131	146,321	23	430
Tolland	3,878	117,472	2,277	53,562	27	542
Windham	5,775	181,823	5,216	141,843	16	226

DAKOTA.

Counties.	BARLEY.		BUCKWHEAT.		RYE.	
	Acres.	Bushels.	Acres.	Bushels.	Acres.	Bushels.
The Territory	16,156	277,424	321	2,521	2,385	24,359
Aurora						
Barnes	75	2,821				
Beadle						
Billings						
Bonhomme	1,801	22,542			341	2,449
Boreman						
Bottineau						
Brookings	400	9,672	43	533	11	110
Brown						
Brule						
Buffalo						
Burleigh			10	55		
Campbell						
Cass	703	22,640	10	219		
Cavilier						
Charles Mix	35	900				
Cheyenne						
Clark						
Clay	529	5,008	30	223	42	103
Codington	17	522				
Custer	8	153				
Davison	68	1,185				
Day						
Delano						
De Smet						
Denel	90	2,310				
Douglas						
Edmonds						
Emmons						
Faulk						
Forsyth						
Foster						
Gingras						
Grand Forks	57	2,001				
Grant	39	585				
Gregory						
Hamlin	57	1,700	12	100		
Hand						
Hanson	11	156				
Howard						
Hughes						
Hutchinson	1,187	18,478	7	40	74	950
Hyde						
Kidder						
Kingsbury						
Lake	478	10,482			122	1,808
La Moure						
Lawrence	401	9,811	70	442	19	387
Lincoln	1,492	13.397	41	244	481	3,743
Logan						

Counties.	INDIAN CORN.		OATS.		WHEAT.	
	Acres.	Bushels.	Acres.	Bushels.	Acres.	Bushels.
The Territory	90,852	2,000,864	78,226	2,217,132	265,298	2,830,289
Aurora	10	395				
Barnes	13	617	283	11,351	1,327	25,237
Beadle	27	350				
Billings						
Bonhomme	7,217	140,079	5,163	123,777	21,131	122,048
Boreman	15	450	14	500		
Bottineau						
Brookings	565	13,625	1,907	75,456	6,213	77,646
Brown	18	100			5	21
Brule	107	3,370				
Buffalo	52	430	30	600	40	240
Burleigh	334	9,334	1,814	66,124		
Campbell						
Cass	306	8,198	7,152	310,086	51,727	1,012,565
Cavilier						
Charles Mix	407	9,695			12	66
Cheyenne						
Clark						
Clay	14,307	375,837	4,663	50,645	5,211	8,335
Codington	169	5,455	798	35,386	1,484	22,660
Custer	13	268	69	2,758	8	128
Davison	269	3,675	184	4,724	305	2,020
Day						
Delano						
De Smet						
Deuel	257	4,807	879	29,294	3,550	39,785
Douglas						
Edmonds						
Emmons	35	900	6	160		
Faulk						
Forsyth						
Foster			50	2,500	10	306
Gingras						
Grand Forks	20	511	1,893	72,043	4,978	98,352
Grant	622	18,285	452	11,566	1,730	17,804
Gregory						
Hamlin	139	1,885	267	10,043	889	9,499
Hand						
Hanson	229	3,625	220	6,615	384	3,674
Howard						
Hughes	92	1,160				
Hutchinson	3,646	53,256	3,287	65,768	19,260	135,304
Hyde			585	18,040		
Kidder						
Kingsbury	8	160	29	985	25	180
Lake	1,351	33,216	2,391	94,546	5,881	60,467
La Moure						
Lawrence	607	12,848	3,001	120,968	869	18,000
Lincoln	15,765	368,241	6,104	155,112	12,107	24,547
Logan						
Lugenbeel						
Lyman	10	650				
McCook	730	10,862	354	9,166	1,052	11,013
McHenry						
McPherson						
Mandan	31	615	40	800		
Meyer						
Mercer						
Miner	265	8,070	95	2,509	312	1,633
Minnehaha	6,948	151,282	9,021	270,204	41,426	245,019
Moody	1,761	49,847	3,026	114,011	12,631	110,735
Morton						
Monutraille						
Pembina	15	582	727	29,609	2,398	63,676
Pennington	26	710	324	10,509	126	1,423

DAKOTA—Continued.

Counties.	BARLEY.		BUCKWHEAT.		RYE.	
	Acres.	Bushels.	Acres.	Bushels.	Acres.	Bushels.
Potter						
Pratt						
Presho....................						
Ramsey...................						
Ransom	64	1,520				
Renville..................						
Richland	522	15,330				
Rolette						
Rusk						
Shannon..................						
Sheridan..................						
Sisseton (Indian reservation)						
Spink						
Stanley...................						
Stark.....................						
Stevens....................						
Stutsman..................	47	1,075	13	80		
Sully						
Todd						
Traill....................	513	13,339				
Tripp.....................						
Turner	1,614	24,986	14	63	289	2,896
Union	355	2,344	23	97	253	1,626
Wallette..................						
Walworth..................						
White River...............						
Williams						
Yankton...................	1,383	11,127	17	61	85	590
Ziebach...................						

DELAWARE.

	Acres.	Bushels.	Acres.	Bushels.	Acres.	Bushels.
The State.............	19	523	397	5,857	773	5,953
Kent.....................			317	5,072	528	3,809
New Castle................	19	523	40	466	76	1,270
Sussex....................			40	319	169	874

DISTRICT OF COLUMBIA.

	Acres.	Bushels.	Acres.	Bushels.	Acres.	Bushels.
Washington					301	3,704

FLORIDA.

DAKOTA—Continued.

Counties.	INDIAN CORN.		OATS.		WHEAT.	
	Acres.	Bushels.	Acres.	Bushels.	Acres.	Bushels.
Potter	15	400	16	600		
Pratt						
Presho						
Ramsay			5	60		
Ransom	54	1,375	68	4,290	463	8,000
Renville						
Richland	25	845	1,274	63,243	9,086	184,753
Rolette						
Rusk						
Shannon	6	250			10	200
Sheridan						
Sisseton (Indian reservation)					45	430
Spink						
Stanley						
Stark						
Stevens			45	2,000		
Stutsman	39	705	1,852	34,730	1,158	10,985
Sully						
Todd						
Traill	57	1,916	3,057	114,575	13,707	333,409
Tripp						
Turner	6,155	173,971	5,533	140,463	15,430	90,236
Union	18,739	305,189	2,624	30,672	5,026	13,023
Wallette						
Walworth	61	1,850				
White River						
Williams						
Yankton	9,315	220,953	6,824	120,644	25,282	76,741
Ziebach						

NOTE.—Area in wheat, with total failure of crop, mainly from grasshopper devastation, is reported as follows: 15,610 acres in Clay County; 17,081 acres in Lincoln County, and 24,266 acres in Union County. Smaller areas in other crops are also reported without production, in these and other counties.

DELAWARE.

The State	202,120	3,894,264	17,158	378,508	87,539	1,175,272
Kent	60,135	1,289,285	4,682	65,924	35,375	446,542
New Castle	36,543	1,180,948	9,682	281,490	35,736	575,134
Sussex	105,442	1,424,031	2,794	31,094	16,428	153,596

DISTRICT OF COLUMBIA.

Washington	1,032	29,750	267	7,440	284	6,402

FLORIDA.

The State	360,294	3,174,234	47,962	468,112	81	422
Alachua	19,246	221,869	1,006	10,787		
Baker	2,388	22,838	484	2,584		
Bradford	9,511	91,305	2,119	17,829		
Brevard	555	6,186	5	100		
Calhoun	1,643	17,303	391	4,340		
Clay	1,885	16,850	214	2,509		
Columbia	18,685	172,795	4,616	38,389	8	30
Dade						
Duval	1,939	17,030	46	617		
Escambia	602	6,423	132	1,541		

FLORIDA—Continued.

Counties.	BARLEY.		BUCKWHEAT.		RYE.	
	Acres.	Bushels.	Acres.	Bushels.	Acres.	Bushels.
Franklin						
Gadsden						
Hamilton					42	164
Hernando						
Hillsborough						
Holmes					8	34
Jackson						
Jefferson					5	28
La Fayette					5	30
Leon					42	262
Levy						
Liberty						
Madison					204	1,125
Manatee	6	60				
Marion	9	90			8	21
Monroe						
Nassau						
Orange					31	100
Polk						
Putnam					23	132
Saint John's					20	25
Santa Rosa					5	21
Sumter					14	55
Suwannee	6	60			72	311
Taylor					9	50
Volusia					10	10
Wakulla						
Walton					6	62
Washington						

GEORGIA.

	BARLEY.		BUCKWHEAT.		RYE.	
	Acres.	Bushels.	Acres.	Bushels.	Acres.	Bushels.
The State	1,439	18,662	58	402	25,854	101,716
Appling					8	38
Baker					54	53
Baldwin	6	106			73	296
Banks					24	147
Bartow	47	868			164	952
Berrien						
Bibb					44	200
Brooks					161	879
Bryan					6	23
Bulloch						
Burke					29	307
Butts					37	253
Calhoun					12	44
Camden						
Campbell					31	188
Carroll					134	491
Catoosa	13	172	9	42	62	201
Charlton						
Chatham					7	50
Chattahoochee					396	759
Chattooga					95	389
Cherokee					416	1,919
Clarke	10	101			36	176
Clay					29	78
Clayton					24	291
Clinch						
Cobb	9	70			85	589
Coffee					5	20
Colquitt					12	30
Columbia	62	300				

FLORIDA—Continued.

Counties.	INDIAN CORN.		OATS.		WHEAT.	
	Acres.	Bushels.	Acres.	Bushels.	Acres.	Bushels.
Franklin	145	1,761				
Gadsden	25,753	183,539	2,853	26,286	5	75
Hamilton	14,991	110,503	2,570	21,413	36	180
Hernando	10,883	146,008	1,371	15,960		
Hillsborough	4,908	48,719	98	775		
Holmes	4,273	31,479	761	5,780		
Jackson	33,780	234,425	6,174	50,621		
Jefferson	39,059	350,148	3,949	48,357		
La Fayette	3,420	33,420	351	2,969		
Leon	43,745	345,381	3,193	45,768		
Levy	7,250	73,899	2,096	19,782		
Liberty	2,202	16,285	621	5,756		
Madison	33,493	285,281	5,894	64,130	25	109
Manatee	2,668	19,978				
Marion	16,641	186,917	1,793	15,629		
Monroe	64	645				
Nassau	2,550	23,449	204	2,535		
Orange	2,763	26,727	140	1,412		
Polk	5,593	52,073	269	1,556		
Putnam	2,075	29,019	566	5,757		
Saint John's	1,282	13,997	52	481		
Santa Rosa	1,135	9,850	60	435		
Sumter	6,909	68,972	627	5,572		
Suwannee	12,410	99,855	2,132	18,634	7	28
Taylor	5,224	49,051	835	6,940		
Volusia	1,250	12,072	40	375		
Wakulla	6,871	50,140	554	6,207		
Walton	6,025	50,275	1,091	9,703		
Washington	5,809	47,167	565	6,574		

GEORGIA.

	INDIAN CORN.		OATS.		WHEAT.	
The State	2,538,733	23,202,018	612,778	5,548,743	475,684	3,159,77
Appling	6,816	56,573	4,097	31,594		
Baker	20,606	100,501	5,614	39,345	68	440
Baldwin	17,599	125,572	1,858	23,954	1,607	10,160
Banks	11,789	147,981	2,022	18,638	3,036	21,935
Bartow	26,874	358,161	9,852	81,801	15,265	131,935
Berrien	8,429	80,681	8,190	80,166	15	128
Bibb	14,325	137,720	4,101	32,588	748	4,974
Brooks	23,027	173,530	14,087	163,802	46	315
Bryan	5,000	38,248	1,786	14,409		
Bulloch	15,394	134,222	7,661	71,880	15	65
Burke	68,131	505,290	4,457	52,860	406	1,778
Butts	15,880	149,838	2,254	18,876	4,135	30,138
Calhoun	19,642	91,323	5,526	41,968	108	1,035
Camden	3,195	29,792	138	1,343		
Campbell	14,056	209,789	5,269	44,797	5,774	46,315
Carroll	28,964	370,892	7,729	78,735	10,414	74,826
Catoosa	10,783	151,767	1,503	9,440	5,911	34,613
Charlton	1,980	16,763	684	3,597		
Chatham	2,224	26,763	619	9,128	20	300
Chattahoochee	11,618	75,441	1,774	15,020	740	2,482
Chattooga	20,078	287,611	6,044	48,111	7,930	46,969
Cherokee	20,330	396,018	5,172	35,998	10,283	65,909
Clarke	7,394	67,940	1,755	16,098	1,387	11,104
Clay	14,898	73,467	2,844	25,108	150	928
Clayton	11,458	132,446	3,496	32,355	3,849	20,161
Clinch	5,524	48,995	3,350	26,623		
Cobb	29,699	406,730	6,789	57,621	10,147	80,617
Coffee	6,925	58,408	5,450	44,760		
Colquitt	4,375	24,110	2,198	18,080	8	36
Columbia	15,632	93,191	3,804	50,105	1,005	7,151

GEORGIA—Continued.

Counties.	BARLEY. Acres.	BARLEY. Bushels.	BUCKWHEAT. Acres.	BUCKWHEAT. Bushels.	RYE. Acres.	RYE. Bushels
Coweta	15	203			76	417
Crawford					46	150
Dade	30	248			54	173
Dawson					186	879
Decatur					8	63
De Kalb	21	197			36	193
Dodge						
Dooly					122	652
Dougherty					19	63
Douglas						
Early						
Echols					46	157
Effingham					11	124
Elbert	12	195			50	280
Emanuel					33	159
Fannin			13	94	2,099	8,050
Fayette	6	77			16	116
Floyd	12	169	5	25	52	304
Forsyth					74	347
Franklin					15	102
Fulton	30	202			24	291
Gilmer					950	3,729
Glascock					54	123
Glynn						
Gordon	22	453			169	1,005
Greene	149	1,974			92	516
Gwinnett	9	100			98	452
Habersham					602	2,153
Hall					369	1,698
Hancock	11	155			120	454
Haralson					88	190
Harris	102	1,551			23	231
Hart					10	35
Heard	18	107			40	247
Henry					44	163
Houston					223	1,040
Irwin						
Jackson					34	111
Jasper	17	411			33	189
Jefferson					307	941
Johnson					107	270
Jones	62	700			147	686
Laurens					498	1,397
Lee					149	523
Liberty					5	38
Lincoln					13	125
Lowndes					32	154
Lumpkin			5	35	582	2,513
McDuffie	7	115			10	66
McIntosh						
Macon					284	1,160
Madison	5	65			28	141
Marion					1,121	2,980
Meriwether	74	1,132			209	991
Miller					10	10
Milton					113	601
Mitchell					17	75
Monroe	36	503			246	993
Montgomery	43	140			9	47
Morgan	95	1,755			111	861
Murray	5	34			128	633
Muscogee					31	179
Newton	37	370			36	341
Oconee	16	266			29	181
Oglethorpe	78	1,114			19	172

Counties.	INDIAN CORN.		OATS.		WHEAT.	
	Acres.	Bushels.	Acres.	Bushels.	Acres.	Bushels.
Coweta	28,960	336,342	10,385	106,331	9,392	77,075
Crawford	16,737	144,351	2,688	26,928	2,040	13,080
Dade	6,336	140,264	2,299	20,064	3,996	24,712
Dawson	14,906	191,006	882	7,068	4,649	26,554
Decatur	30,847	201,872	9,282	84,482	22	146
DeKalb	21,034	263,448	5,974	52,842	5,866	49,579
Dodge	9,132	72,038	2,054	15,581	23	48
Dooly	40,304	302,649	9,522	87,699	1,509	7,838
Dougherty	23,263	141,029	6,052	48,797	116	695
Douglas	10,586	140,966	3,189	29,620	3,521	27,754
Early	17,624	110,682	4,750	39,604	39	230
Echols	5,159	30,873	1,650	11,918		
Effingham	9,337	72,619	2,096	18,930		
Elbert	20,360	212,058	5,552	46,883	7,688	48,883
Emanuel	24,300	195,694	3,957	32,110	950	4,033
Fannin	14,220	189,655	1,005	6,281	3,649	15,363
Fayette	14,195	137,545	3,477	29,730	4,259	31,705
Floyd	29,872	405,290	8,413	69,435	9,251	65,766
Forsyth	20,324	285,610	6,040	47,925	7,797	50,805
Franklin	20,523	229,779	4,627	31,634	6,520	39,434
Fulton	13,988	184,630	3,069	32,764	2,836	24,914
Gilmer	16,178	233,348	582	3,050	5,903	25,209
Glascock	10,742	64,701	1,076	15,851	4,257	14,197
Glynn	1,565	17,546	241	2,415		
Gordon	22,661	345,800	6,069	48,434	14,239	113,222
Greene	25,827	188,909	6,674	77,269	6,473	44,581
Gwinnett	36,568	470,409	8,526	61,814	11,138	74,795
Habersham	14,797	172,806	1,921	15,036	2,458	12,923
Hall	26,632	354,329	4,798	35,424	8,771	54,876
Hancock	33,328	233,608	6,503	74,810	5,913	34,142
Haralson	13,048	174,011	2,736	25,144	4,909	34,163
Harris	26,871	238,452	5,438	48,220	5,549	32,503
Hart	14,312	126,958	4,876	28,453	4,646	24,977
Heard	17,209	195,161	3,092	25,315	4,900	35,439
Henry	21,903	109,132	5,321	30,861	7,406	56,513
Houston	48,785	354,229	10,570	121,261	3,289	19,909
Irwin	4,049	38,391	3,319	29,114		
Jackson	27,675	295,641	7,355	54,649	7,485	56,359
Jasper	23,303	163,152	2,687	30,122	4,649	37,760
Jefferson	42,335	296,551	6,146	59,037	5,783	23,767
Johnson	14,288	87,413	1,826	15,084	404	1,616
Jones	22,464	181,777	3,010	31,392	2,685	17,374
Laurens	25,563	196,486	4,745	40,123	478	1,624
Lee	24,045	161,574	6,721	56,912	367	2,660
Liberty	8,565	74,041	3,597	27,178		
Lincoln	11,029	87,317	7,035	73,380	2,125	15,431
Lowndes	20,016	138,671	9,945	102,276	64	488
Lumpkin	11,232	134,747	1,554	12,059	2,781	13,229
McDuffie	13,935	87,614	5,616	57,864	2,779	17,367
McIntosh	2,825	34,463	354	4,197		
Macon	23,910	154,238	4,313	40,712	2,702	11,105
Madison	14,471	145,422	4,631	32,423	6,168	42,150
Marion	21,053	141,145	1,889	16,800	3,481	13,132
Meriwether	35,842	310,428	7,340	57,913	8,026	53,965
Miller	9,229	55,809	4,188	33,647		
Milton	13,039	197,188	3,025	25,486	4,187	31,100
Mitchell	23,806	127,161	8,721	67,835	51	373
Monroe	20,884	238,776	6,765	76,543	6,742	54,998
Montgomery	10,231	84,375	4,904	36,218	142	495
Morgan	22,510	105,358	4,017	32,198	4,980	39,884
Murray	14,338	211,059	2,168	14,361	8,178	51,502
Muscogee	8,263	60,059	2,071	22,649	310	1,577
Newton	17,112	140,808	4,999	49,465	4,892	40,657
Oconee	9,930	97,566	2,215	18,454	2,136	17,415
Oglethorpe	22,019	200,584	6,310	59,832	7,184	57,713

GEORGIA—Continued.

Counties.	BARLEY.		BUCKWHEAT.		RYE.	
	Acres.	Bushels.	Acres.	Bushels.	Acres.	Bushels.
Paulding					116	591
Pickens					357	1,633
Pierce						
Pike	30	378			136	1,069
Polk					28	161
Pulaski					120	531
Putnam	40	826			93	467
Quitman					29	114
Rabun					1,675	6,811
Randolph					637	1,535
Richmond					12	74
Rockdale					25	203
Schley					444	1,254
Screven					7	24
Spalding	17	119			18	97
Stewart					206	804
Sumter					443	1,348
Talbot	28	525			82	338
Taliaferro	17	168			34	261
Tattnall					19	107
Taylor					246	602
Telfair						
Terrell					246	626
Thomas					19	81
Towns					1,339	6,669
Troup	30	448			87	816
Twiggs	35	250			502	1,378
Union			26	206	1,934	9,132
Upson					23	210
Walker	25	267			166	738
Walton	11	106			97	414
Ware					8	28
Warren	11	178			6	21
Washington					1,966	5,456
Wayne						
Webster					463	1,492
White					489	1,903
Whitfield	35	324			193	772
Wilcox						
Wilkes	101	1,220			77	460
Wilkinson					1,404	3,790
Worth					7	39

IDAHO.

	BARLEY.		BUCKWHEAT.		RYE.	
	Acres.	Bushels.	Acres.	Bushels.	Acres.	Bushels.
The Territory	8,201	274,750			354	4,341
Ada	3,264	97,633			222	2,479
Alturas	87	1,600				
Bear Lake	113	2,536				
Boise	432	16,132				
Cassia	815	22,993				
Idaho	104	3,915				
Kootenai	33	580				
Lemhi	8	205				
Nez Perce	1,200	51,644			40	25
Oneida	101	1,639			70	1,377
Owyhee	581	18,220				
Shoshone						
Washington	1,553	57,653			22	460

GEORGIA—Continued.

Counties.	INDIAN CORN.		OATS.		WHEAT.	
	Acres.	Bushels.	Acres.	Bushels.	Acres.	Bushels.
Paulding	21,953	318,520	6,101	53,613	6,372	48,240
Pickens	12,774	189,245	1,619	12,542	5,992	33,995
Pierce	4,105	39,026	2,209	21,786		
Pike	29,243	244,674	5,596	48,976	7,510	52,880
Polk	16,331	241,382	6,114	67,515	6,538	50,010
Pulaski	28,505	242,814	3,370	29,604	208	1,326
Putnam	23,175	141,172	2,881	35,234	2,855	24,591
Quitman	7,506	40,220	2,202	22,398	560	2,419
Rabun	8,810	115,456	455	2,823	457	1,870
Randolph	27,484	130,258	6,770	46,612	2,790	12,653
Richmond	11,793	102,619	4,209	73,155	1,549	13,553
Rockdale	9,951	91,552	2,401	23,349	3,268	27,128
Schley	15,845	99,186	1,447	12,408	1,944	7,986
Screven	24,154	180,215	3,502	35,347	60	452
Spalding	15,560	140,142	3,132	22,355	4,084	29,574
Stewart	31,979	182,948	5,284	61,370	2,652	12,922
Sumter	37,495	272,238	8,742	83,868	1,984	9,650
Talbot	25,696	234,545	3,652	36,834	3,882	26,411
Taliaferro	9,901	83,239	4,305	38,769	3,086	20,647
Tattnall	10,991	96,189	4,802	36,954	8	67
Taylor	16,426	115,400	2,108	19,177	3,079	14,739
Telfair	6,302	49,942	2,032	15,658		
Terrell	21,719	137,882	6,210	42,830	1,928	9,710
Thomas	35,839	245,531	18,281	158,467	34	160
Towns	7,001	87,895	830	4,465	2,055	8,559
Troup	38,077	341,963	6,075	69,672	7,342	55,572
Twiggs	23,732	168,044	1,176	9,202	374	1,876
Union	14,347	198,531	2,139	12,697	4,612	20,743
Upson	23,143	193,694	3,205	30,140	6,751	52,258
Walker	26,033	369,298	5,915	36,861	15,115	96,344
Walton	26,769	288,761	6,454	50,633	9,418	65,385
Ware	3,388	29,184	1,953	14,376		
Warren	16,450	89,770	4,885	48,915	3,649	19,229
Washington	58,653	411,499	7,566	88,184	7,464	30,460
Wayne	4,243	39,112	2,188	15,506		
Webster	16,121	96,105	2,809	20,039	2,236	8,834
White	11,097	148,120	2,228	19,225	2,319	12,843
Whitfield	19,992	255,923	5,443	36,085	8,168	40,267
Wilcox	7,604	61,511	3,086	20,711	6	32
Wilkes	21,493	191,218	11,855	133,277	4,287	32,732
Wilkinson	32,394	224,305	4,967	37,665	4,872	19,805
Worth	13,671	86,222	4,687	33,466	101	607

IDAHO.

	INDIAN CORN.		OATS.		WHEAT.	
The Territory	569	16,408	13,197	462,236	22,066	540,589
Ada	388	9,936	2,701	97,681	7,081	163,298
Alturas			63	1,950	11	215
Bear Lake			1,143	30,840	1,402	34,859
Boise	13	645	893	33,719	699	21,739
Cassia	11	330	361	11,617	394	7,767
Idaho	82	3,150	1,238	53,968	1,870	47,233
Kootenai			55	800	28	475
Lemhi			901	38,628	883	33,504
Nez Perce	29	768	3,224	133,897	5,394	148,422
Oneida	21	504	2,180	41,781	3,149	44,160
Owyhee	16	640	213	6,960	53	1,413
Shoshone			28	1,300		
Washington	9	435	197	9,095	1,102	37,444

Counties.	BARLEY.		BUCKWHEAT.		RYE.	
	Acres.	Bushels.	Acres.	Bushels.	Acres.	Bushels.
The State	55,267	1,229,523	16,457	178,859	192,138	3,121,785
Adams	143	3,928	190	1,131	1,008	13,904
Alexander					24	248
Bond			6	52	128	1,871
Boone	504	11,110	703	8,997	1,581	24,879
Brown			20	144	333	4,069
Bureau	1,950	41,907	137	1,316	2,207	41,140
Calhoun	7	124	5	70	37	351
Carroll	5,369	127,452	137	1,424	5,127	73,330
Cass	35	545	10	133	624	6,610
Champaign	10	350	315	3,773	4,089	67,742
Christian	380	7,867	51	560	1,041	17,556
Clark			220	2,908	253	2,731
Clay			138	1,490	365	2,742
Clinton	14	260	17	155	116	1,560
Coles	165	2,119	98	1,397	181	8,857
Cook	228	4,706	74	498	1,173	20,623
Crawford			214	2,923	266	1,967
Cumberland			233	3,310	484	3,953
DeKalb	2,823	64,478	731	8,450	995	18,506
De Witt	30	500	52	916	3,061	52,933
Douglas	6	196	130	1,632	1,227	16,082
Du Page	149	3,662	58	507	1,725	38,875
Edgar	148	1,322	33	464	612	8,653
Edwards			6	125	7	70
Effingham			121	1,455	557	4,657
Fayette	15	150	101	1,019	576	5,053
Ford	15	217	69	550	1,171	18,110
Franklin	17	294			12	163
Fulton	107	1,661	506	4,097	10,957	182,822
Gallatin					22	224
Greene	19	325	44	504	86	1,384
Grundy	117	2,141	112	956	1,829	27,030
Hamilton			7	143	78	1,378
Hancock	26	304	277	2,587	3,298	50,320
Hardin			6	73	33	374
Henderson	5	60	133	1,888	3,948	53,194
Henry	848	17,938	186	2,071	4,941	90,318
Iroquois	191	3,056	690	6,705	4,251	61,886
Jackson	84	1,922	39	541	147	2,149
Jasper			241	2,627	448	4,078
Jefferson	30	580	10	131	93	902
Jersey			7	73	20	289
Jo Daviess	1,073	23,087	327	4,181	2,286	32,549
Johnson					121	822
Kane	541	13,537	590	6,028	2,154	48,913
Kankakee	161	3,396	166	1,374	3,856	63,465
Kendall	38	550	106	1,120	366	6,026
Knox	48	1,390	417	3,981	4,916	79,370
Lake	315	7,704	311	2,154	499	8,406
La Salle	1,060	22,934	320	3,310	3,183	60,643
Lawrence	159	6,000	141	2,035	130	1,358
Lee	5,507	121,410	541	7,604	2,583	47,534
Livingston	43	532	431	3,954	6,743	112,057
Logan	281	7,590	56	577	3,001	54,905
McDonough	55	910	263	2,471	6,045	104,047
McHenry	954	21,788	1,308	14,601	1,271	22,109
McLean	304	6,187	167	1,883	9,151	174,998
Macon	95	1,008	41	634	1,011	27,042
Macoupin	16	194	25	314	401	7,473
Madison	5	54	9	80	161	2,299
Marion			252	2,835	719	7,306
Marshall			57	588	3,006	51,262
Mason	74	958	83	887	4,452	48,260
Massac					5	47
Menard	34	532	28	129	399	5,715

ILLINOIS—Continued.

Counties.	INDIAN CORN.		OATS.		WHEAT.	
	Acres.	Bushels.	Acres.	Bushels.	Acres.	Bushels.
The State............	9, 019, 361	325, 792, 481	1, 959, 889	63, 189, 200	3, 218, 542	51, 110, 502
Adams................	105, 243	3, 840, 525	27, 335	756, 901	82, 720	1, 505, 036
Alexander	14, 159	454, 705	632	12, 816	8, 025	129, 478
Bond	47, 378	1, 470, 940	11, 278	223, 141	44, 523	725, 474
Boone................	31, 761	1, 119, 383	24, 906	805, 601	3, 914	52, 895
Brown	35, 898	1, 104, 074	4, 917	89, 036	22, 520	362, 219
Bureau...............	208, 814	8, 425, 683	31, 587	1, 188, 234	22, 206	264, 626
Calhoun..............	19, 036	637, 532	1, 500	32, 498	22, 085	330, 106
Carroll...............	69, 565	2, 913, 111	26, 114	977, 871	16, 823	252, 068
Cass	72, 041	2, 532, 842	9, 609	220, 814	23, 788	462, 959
Champaign	263, 178	10, 132, 525	40, 480	1, 327, 055	18, 833	433, 849
Christian	160, 295	6, 143, 469	22, 562	749, 479	59, 321	1, 456, 544
Clark	51, 363	1, 384, 571	9, 562	208, 681	43, 285	504, 419
Clay	42, 885	1, 058, 186	9, 210	157, 063	20, 376	223, 520
Clinton	54, 474	1, 582, 886	18, 267	416, 320	83, 617	1, 315, 138
Coles................	97, 943	3, 857, 893	14, 913	474, 511	25, 356	444, 381
Cook.................	54, 713	1, 619, 528	60, 509	2, 223, 052	3, 652	37, 043
Crawford	44, 250	1, 195, 290	6, 661	151, 355	44, 966	549, 476
Cumberland	37, 619	1, 186, 633	9, 401	216, 020	27, 349	303, 819
De Kalb	112, 432	4, 357, 761	43, 331	1, 818, 381	8, 445	75, 630
De Witt	97, 691	3, 998, 701	17, 376	663, 062	9, 706	190, 337
Douglas	87, 783	3, 335, 008	13, 382	464, 278	9, 924	215, 307
Du Page.............	28, 631	907, 451	26, 185	1, 063, 608	3, 508	45, 994
Edgar	112, 321	4, 116, 096	12, 462	392, 799	37, 311	729, 023
Edwards	19, 760	620, 193	3, 036	54, 909	24, 440	364, 743
Effingham	47, 899	1, 436, 646	17, 337	307, 918	44, 141	372, 554
Fayette	70, 578	1, 992, 603	15, 289	308, 157	60, 065	741, 806
Ford	134, 005	4, 527, 164	14, 353	476, 068	997	16, 644
Franklin	38, 278	1, 049, 554	6, 883	130, 702	43, 223	453, 922
Fulton	130, 895	4, 618, 903	22, 635	587, 256	37, 862	671, 334
Gallatin.............	33, 185	1, 069, 405	1, 126	22, 314	23, 754	328, 101
Greene...............	64, 273	2, 605, 641	3, 721	95, 830	60, 198	1, 138, 854
Grundy..............	106, 660	3, 670, 009	12, 810	440, 588	838	7, 985
Hamilton	39, 545	1, 131, 195	5, 082	96, 533	41, 113	437, 675
Hancock.............	146, 512	5, 259, 059	38, 072	1, 196, 529	34, 685	596, 319
Hardin...............	13, 134	306, 960	1, 859	21, 454	5, 154	42, 997
Henderson...........	73, 502	2, 856, 035	12, 515	401, 372	14, 381	218, 217
Henry	211, 905	8, 774, 002	30, 371	1, 103, 842	12, 804	121, 315
Iroquois	262, 354	8, 394, 776	36, 749	1, 190, 750	6, 243	121, 335
Jackson..............	34, 029	1, 068, 557	4, 321	72, 622	55, 191	755, 019
Jasper	42, 452	1, 185, 016	9, 935	211, 541	30, 055	231, 103
Jefferson	43, 618	1, 202, 026	11, 091	201, 468	38, 125	687, 068
Jersey	38, 100	1, 485, 494	4, 073	112, 974	53, 241	908, 658
Jo Daviess...........	61, 113	2, 567, 588	34, 012	1, 118, 375	10, 442	165, 984
Johnson..............	27, 206	706, 888	1, 727	23, 940	21, 342	195, 356
Kane	60, 412	2, 315, 126	30, 687	1, 267, 133	3, 842	41, 780
Kankakee	134, 650	4, 076, 888	31, 298	1, 117, 451	3, 412	56, 818
Kendall..............	75, 295	2, 484, 200	19, 553	835, 190	2, 131	23, 781
Knox	152, 795	6, 015, 818	32, 085	1, 024, 648	13, 237	155, 645
Lake.................	26, 621	882, 249	24, 328	872, 929	3, 443	45, 729
La Salle..............	280, 866	11, 148, 779	55, 328	2, 110, 752	16, 430	197, 152
Lawrence.............	36, 444	958, 013	4, 511	65, 077	44, 695	619, 075
Lee	147, 384	5, 742, 335	42, 492	1, 704, 103	20, 543	244, 713
Livingston...........	309, 315	11, 094, 043	49, 807	1, 555, 536	5, 634	61, 490
Logan...............	189, 001	6, 740, 175	20, 024	619, 579	14, 753	350, 113
McDonough	117, 718	4, 571, 804	24, 763	745, 443	24, 855	355, 153
McHenry.............	61, 504	2, 154, 530	38, 347	1, 455, 051	8, 802	114, 101
McLean	297, 191	11, 976, 581	37, 990	2, 110, 790	14, 599	239, 890
Macon	150, 838	5, 517, 110	23, 624	946, 288	20, 359	434, 226
Macoupin............	113, 997	4, 323, 732	19, 836	532, 974	107, 691	1, 999, 387
Madison.............	98, 780	4, 058, 156	13, 905	351, 505	129, 861	2, 607, 969
Marion	52, 356	1, 385, 747	14, 582	351, 057	44, 881	462, 372
Marshall.............	92, 842	3, 624, 024	22, 128	742, 026	5, 619	61, 587
Mason	115, 839	3, 555, 516	18, 344	342, 144	24, 773	449, 097
Massac	16, 155	450, 010	1, 276	20, 606	20, 362	202, 095
Menard..............	66, 689	1, 964, 837	9, 469	228, 618	14, 827	290, 990

ILLINOIS—Continued.

Counties.	BARLEY.		BUCKWHEAT.		RYE.	
	Acres.	Bushels.	Acres.	Bushels.	Acres.	Bushels.
Mercer	12	142	243	1,944	3,237	46,435
Monroe	93	3,025	5	110	63	1,381
Montgomery	33	835	93	643	989	16,598
Morgan	16	93	35	823	444	7,364
Moultrie	82	1,600	59	573	874	12,305
Ogle	11,581	248,083	528	6,058	4,465	75,062
Peoria	36	350	317	3,377	8,280	123,941
Perry			7	59	40	376
Piatt	22	553	137	1,670	1,921	34,274
Pike			48	425	245	3,080
Pope	20	600	6	51	39	322
Pulaski	8	182			7	107
Putnam	16	280	21	251	792	14,102
Randolph	40	1,303	16	87	42	764
Richland			177	2,338	96	754
Rock Island	710	11,230	286	2,609	3,512	55,413
Saint Clair	513	15,286	14	229	26	423
Saline			6	67	52	774
Sangamon	317	5,497	18	225	1,946	32,656
Schuyler			128	1,025	750	8,157
Scott			7	10	277	2,544
Shelby	8	125	205	2,625	1,593	21,210
Stark	41	629	114	1,020	1,418	25,231
Stephenson	12,810	289,076	334	4,597	11,577	211,061
Tazewell	163	1,929	183	2,626	6,048	89,718
Union	7	151	22	127	6	65
Vermillion	86	1,739	312	3,091	1,823	27,125
Wabash			18	239	42	526
Warren	33	472	151	1,384	1,798	2,855
Washington					62	544
Wayne			113	1,544	60	500
White			6	56	47	580
Whiteside	2,837	63,841	363	3,618	6,650	116,382
Will	121	2,647	161	1,362	1,774	33,463
Williamson					35	254
Winnebago	1,289	32,211	368	3,339	9,547	137,503
Woodford	169	3,210	169	2,023	4,975	85,759

INDIANA.

The State	16,399	382,835	8,846	89,707	25,400	303,105
Adams			75	745	69	998
Allen	97	1,421	203	2,606	289	3,830
Bartholomew	117	2,694	73	943	155	2,102
Benton	425	7,733	156	1,343	560	8,180
Blackford			52	496	69	798
Boone	113	2,801	73	812	234	3,309
Brown	5	110	59	356	60	468
Carroll	13	529	38	284	53	677
Cass	62	1,349	93	721	109	1,267
Clark	22	296	19	210	335	2,234
Clay	63	1,708	42	551	71	789
Clinton	71	1,455	75	839	145	1,040
Crawford	11	23	6	78	69	318
Daviess	22	400	70	961	121	1,346
Dearborn	3,827	79,800	124	1,601	678	6,608
Decatur	160	3,211	42	541	238	1,907
Ke Kalb	14	312	195	2,632	129	2,181
Delaware	16	425	101	915	192	2,617
Dubois	240	3,714	11	87	28	215
Elkhart			336	3,440	504	6,324

ILLINOIS—Continued.

Counties.	INDIAN CORN.		OATS.		WHEAT.	
	Acres.	Bushels.	Acres.	Bushels.	Acres.	Bushels.
Mercer	116,759	5,100,895	18,780	621,814	16,362	157,146
Monroe	19,767	703,778	5,984	121,682	58,753	1,116,979
Montgomery	107,072	4,241,288	22,263	505,083	86,088	1,858,343
Morgan	101,932	3,913,267	8,733	237,808	37,083	741,144
Moultrie	81,347	2,896,737	13,975	489,903	16,242	322,218
Ogle	134,361	5,408,462	61,570	2,297,359	17,662	238,609
Peoria	116,662	4,109,589	28,050	733,407	9,475	147,438
Perry	22,365	633,227	8,817	153,913	58,915	729,430
Piatt	106,769	4,170,041	16,152	630,064	8,600	176,515
Pike	92,288	3,598,216	7,189	172,397	112,135	2,181,987
Pope	32,926	884,620	1,039	94,177	21,691	181,478
Pulaski	12,343	320,552	971	19,124	10,188	116,592
Putnam	34,334	1,400,487	5,049	186,054	3,664	42,546
Randolph	33,267	1,122,186	12,399	247,861	99,666	1,628,631
Richland	31,725	783,703	7,646	111,734	40,247	412,020
Rock Island	68,858	3,073,109	12,608	414,540	9,300	96,837
Saint Clair	52,862	2,154,129	14,309	342,729	147,712	2,959,444
Saline	35,651	982,635	3,852	59,385	27,761	273,407
Sangamon	186,207	6,813,714	16,497	470,535	48,419	1,017,260
Schuyler	48,499	1,554,725	7,116	151,806	25,908	440,654
Scott	36,387	1,312,135	1,084	25,105	27,855	585,613
Shelby	120,774	4,118,740	24,506	655,764	57,630	909,946
Stark	78,482	3,232,541	15,290	525,565	4,598	43,905
Stephenson	86,467	3,538,288	39,849	1,438,823	22,414	347,376
Tazewell	132,574	4,847,331	30,245	916,228	21,118	421,954
Union	26,549	806,830	5,131	106,972	30,917	371,620
Vermillion	184,555	6,385,086	23,330	777,484	34,491	761,788
Wabash	19,299	629,680	1,615	28,748	28,733	472,164
Warren	130,719	5,489,684	25,375	847,495	11,400	132,114
Washington	41,171	1,155,590	22,724	582,289	107,078	1,594,721
Wayne	51,699	1,445,019	10,323	187,317	43,925	484,013
White	53,968	1,819,538	3,679	63,541	58,503	773,653
Whiteside	138,613	5,220,329	31,268	1,107,273	16,763	195,890
Will	143,815	4,072,806	72,308	2,701,670	4,023	50,826
Williamson	41,461	1,058,661	6,563	78,639	37,594	339,942
Winnebago	82,737	2,935,384	47,664	1,633,640	7,638	100,313
Woodford	122,738	4,913,307	36,404	1,237,484	11,875	147,818

INDIANA.

	INDIAN CORN.		OATS.		WHEAT.	
	Acres.	Bushels.	Acres.	Bushels.	Acres.	Bushels.
The State	3,678,420	115,482,300	623,531	15,599,518	2,619,695	47,284,853
Adams	21,763	627,070	8,994	282,881	20,667	407,972
Allen	41,695	1,331,237	17,536	586,733	47,653	917,824
Bartholomew	57,170	1,842,869	5,925	98,715	38,448	672,947
Benton	98,455	3,315,387	12,962	476,642	3,528	71,161
Blackford	14,211	417,079	1,614	45,093	8,950	152,879
Boone	63,087	2,280,742	4,285	117,070	33,679	623,289
Brown	15,436	314,124	4,940	71,313	7,875	67,380
Carroll	41,852	1,439,184	6,046	170,729	39,794	892,458
Cass	39,224	1,235,849	6,321	183,601	36,135	796,820
Clark	29,761	619,002	7,369	77,425	16,112	188,777
Clay	31,917	964,658	6,367	134,304	28,174	403,652
Clinton	55,813	2,042,485	6,345	196,908	37,956	863,631
Crawford	20,390	311,464	6,659	64,826	9,138	70,040
Daviess	39,330	1,115,060	5,655	101,027	45,388	659,570
Dearborn	29,067	921,031	7,879	152,376	23,991	314,848
Decatur	45,693	1,415,660	6,194	134,984	28,481	485,117
DeKalb	23,905	762,918	12,791	460,632	32,487	644,723
Delaware	47,688	1,680,883	2,762	85,353	31,180	639,900
Dubois	28,118	558,703	10,629	122,397	23,804	205,410
Elkhart	30,589	1,153,286	10,585	363,872	50,716	1,005,995

INDIANA—Continued.

Counties.	BARLEY.		BUCKWHEAT.		RYE.	
	Acres.	Bushels.	Acres.	Bushels.	Acres.	Bushels.
Fayette	68	2,431	50	465	129	1,579
Floyd	23	627			100	946
Fountain			47	530	149	2,299
Franklin	2,374	61,609	187	2,262	466	4,128
Fulton	48	1,205	94	723	143	1,916
Gibson	80	1,716	28	418	59	870
Grant	42	842	101	1,875	184	2,048
Greene	36	354	102	1,043	143	774
Hamilton	26	548	236	1,692	88	1,535
Hancock	267	7,995	54	688	62	861
Harrison	45	1,313			260	1,963
Hendricks			17	224	342	4,465
Henry	25	565	48	837	56	1,695
Howard	22	308	18	128	37	682
Huntington	99	2,818	58	504	97	1,564
Jackson	55	450	34	289	391	3,761
Jasper	212	3,621	193	1,425	1,021	12,150
Jay	80	1,583	133	1,457	122	1,544
Jefferson	1,013	20,230	102	1,306	194	1,352
Jennings	8	213	126	1,280	198	1,722
Johnson	30	900	28	416	95	1,652
Knox					46	559
Kosciusko	37	736	195	2,329	167	2,822
Lagrange			193	2,032	207	3,444
Lake	5	98	332	2,675	933	14,494
La Porte	185	3,810	628	4,622	627	6,903
Lawrence			12	103	1,453	21,489
Madison	58	1,781	85	950	75	1,266
Marion	278	10,027	56	965	115	1,790
Marshall	27	721	155	2,358	204	2,392
Martin	37	718	64	783	93	728
Miami	179	5,514	47	425	74	830
Monroe	9	246	16	124	235	2,060
Montgomery	92	1,915	82	898	303	4,077
Morgan	120	2,850	10	106	363	4,177
Newton	9	240	166	1,452	1,041	15,711
Noble	36	723	190	2,007	77	1,115
Ohio	395	8,431	37	470	284	2,244
Orange			10	124	243	1,641
Owen	6	245	68	650	292	3,553
Parke	15	120	48	391	304	3,765
Perry	154	3,290	10	92	56	368
Pike					51	442
Porter	63	1,347	303	2,519	1,213	14,828
Posey	111	2,937	10	129	6	83
Pulaski	38	754	256	1,525	1,171	12,333
Putnam			30	240	773	8,378
Randolph	103	3,266	77	915	119	1,042
Ripley	54	1,404	78	729	478	4,350
Rush	400	10,821	17	190	70	803
Saint Joseph	724	12,781	156	1,537	261	2,892
Scott			18	127	22	136
Shelby	1,343	41,034	53	741	68	975
Spencer	467	10,538	23	305	100	1,056
Starke			179	996	1,003	8,782
Steuben	62	1,655	290	3,253	89	1,232
Sullivan			31	416	114	1,243
Switzerland	272	4,280	147	1,966	1,302	12,368
Tippecanoe	64	672	116	1,297	363	6,242
Tipton			57	306	166	2,172
Union	416	11,596	43	393	57	620
Vanderburgh	40	820	8	153	24	1,009
Vermillion			30	389	39	948
Vigo			15	199	86	936
Wabash	64	1,547	97	1,233	39	677
Warren	20	400	65	525	345	4,910
Warrick	26	442	13	221	113	775
Washington	7	188			250	1,899
Wayne	454	14,162	69	1,075	111	941
Wells	45	906	110	950	255	4,269
White	141	2,451	558	5,093	934	11,621
Whitley			90	997	32	502

INDIANA—Continued.

Counties.	INDIAN CORN. Acres.	Bushels.	OATS. Acres.	Bushels.	WHEAT. Acres.	Bushels.
Fayette	31,053	1,131,623	3,206	97,372	19,214	420,472
Floyd	8,585	170,758	2,942	25,304	7,200	96,201
Fountain	54,876	1,882,341	6,836	190,127	40,646	904,378
Franklin	39,756	1,230,806	8,747	176,528	27,951	419,566
Fulton	28,977	824,197	4,697	118,856	27,554	358,472
Gibson	42,732	1,428,574	1,325	20,622	65,240	1,100,782
Grant	47,871	1,534,538	3,311	104,501	30,753	617,000
Greene	48,303	1,274,368	9,127	152,639	28,778	339,590
Hamilton	60,479	2,233,158	5,499	161,854	30,988	762,665
Hancock	41,780	1,390,291	1,957	50,855	28,914	604,887
Harrison	32,108	553,098	10,279	84,641	32,465	350,671
Hendricks	54,114	2,016,351	4,699	138,917	31,523	553,506
Henry	54,572	2,003,625	4,564	143,001	36,908	876,582
Howard	37,774	1,250,153	2,016	63,821	26,519	577,356
Huntington	36,373	1,114,429	5,052	154,614	31,094	643,978
Jackson	46,436	1,174,081	11,552	167,716	23,171	259,202
Jasper	42,531	1,188,509	7,681	235,832	5,147	92,901
Jay	36,895	1,068,523	9,402	279,744	24,183	418,674
Jefferson	28,932	627,208	5,727	73,447	21,019	246,002
Jennings	28,698	651,119	5,808	67,904	15,515	159,358
Johnson	51,743	1,987,379	1,834	48,289	35,052	649,937
Knox	54,232	1,691,010	2,603	54,427	59,442	1,018,998
Kosciusko	37,702	1,256,807	10,047	324,475	43,725	895,125
Lagrange	24,044	895,892	5,976	194,604	42,429	884,131
Lake	36,269	833,288	18,619	615,962	2,864	51,478
La Porte	43,481	1,208,227	11,668	356,524	42,211	936,249
Lawrence	37,112	912,215	14,406	251,876	15,036	138,051
Madison	61,719	2,106,768	2,524	79,254	40,742	875,580
Marion	60,937	2,227,537	6,275	202,362	34,527	729,332
Marshall	32,984	1,088,734	8,090	259,386	39,692	837,196
Martin	25,483	534,434	6,425	90,576	17,470	159,803
Miami	40,402	1,321,740	4,885	153,088	37,490	835,425
Monroe	25,758	608,987	9,046	160,637	10,980	111,356
Montgomery	69,673	2,619,457	8,245	228,570	48,124	983,550
Morgan	51,954	1,720,269	4,678	92,568	26,940	449,355
Newton	57,097	1,842,754	11,170	394,955	4,356	92,877
Noble	26,848	936,079	9,096	327,711	40,158	877,215
Ohio	9,756	292,167	484	7,837	8,044	94,441
Orange	30,897	595,078	13,549	172,880	14,176	114,424
Owen	27,434	740,052	7,838	146,530	18,106	214,401
Parke	49,608	1,737,472	5,464	133,481	38,725	739,848
Perry	19,971	449,831	4,458	52,659	13,399	124,402
Pike	35,102	913,473	3,936	61,581	30,730	376,893
Porter	33,650	838,331	13,450	412,625	13,091	290,858
Posey	49,377	1,941,310	1,327	22,837	58,132	1,013,716
Pulaski	20,277	416,421	3,980	94,009	11,633	231,733
Putnam	47,513	1,646,470	6,465	145,011	24,571	385,256
Randolph	61,034	2,091,377	9,812	319,793	35,296	688,862
Ripley	32,695	703,963	11,384	196,571	22,703	269,405
Rush	60,872	2,265,928	3,185	100,443	42,777	930,738
Saint Joseph	27,746	954,615	8,048	271,767	41,765	952,327
Scott	15,611	294,712	3,774	33,223	7,669	70,963
Shelby	72,454	2,678,681	2,403	60,452	51,831	976,209
Spencer	30,522	913,120	7,045	102,635	28,542	306,777
Starke	7,555	133,310	1,259	21,953	3,954	49,102
Steuben	22,288	890,719	6,021	208,335	28,251	522,879
Sullivan	47,832	1,347,855	5,501	102,035	56,888	807,614
Switzerland	22,109	555,203	1,988	28,545	16,371	194,759
Tippecanoe	92,793	3,276,795	13,708	414,109	43,589	981,937
Tipton	33,914	1,115,816	1,539	45,333	14,855	273,212
Union	23,398	862,689	2,268	70,755	14,247	291,401
Vanderburgh	24,890	806,896	1,314	23,528	29,218	467,026
Vermillion	36,523	1,348,321	3,791	101,820	31,611	666,854
Vigo	60,303	1,917,103	5,471	124,188	52,891	896,846
Wabash	45,288	1,531,075	4,693	117,538	39,696	898,489
Warren	62,952	2,134,441	10,587	355,666	15,862	363,651
Warrick	35,775	869,741	4,610	64,399	29,024	316,711
Washington	36,852	680,222	16,763	183,245	17,848	147,877
Wayne	59,040	2,082,914	9,800	298,051	31,434	681,939
Wells	30,604	878,085	4,508	140,639	24,493	461,065
White	60,792	1,754,277	13,628	389,563	16,052	311,007
Whitley	25,847	875,819	7,518	260,042	25,136	494,928

Counties.	BARLEY.		BUCKWHEAT.		RYE.	
	Acres.	Bushels.	Acres.	Bushels.	Acres.	Bushels.
The State............	198,861	4,022,588	16,318	166,895	102,607	1,518,605
Adair......................	597	11,166	93	645	641	9,785
Adams.....................	418	4,610	141	1,295	690	11,257
Allamakee.................	4,776	100,769	374	4,192	1,372	19,677
Appanoose.................			213	2,444	1,545	14,864
Audubon	584	13,008	37	211	104	1,338
Benton	8,829	186,618	316	3,328	754	13,098
Black Hawk................	1,100	20,742	238	2,013	2,967	41,375
Boone.....................	1,203	22,031	76	799	485	8,684
Bremer....................	1,431	26,149	147	1,364	446	5,925
Buchanan..................	1,047	12,860	340	3,489	374	4,498
Buena Vista	1,149	21,097	150	1,799	429	7,155
Butler	1,040	20,614	335	2,576	1,249	20,871
Calhoun	399	7,555	58	382	304	4,089
Carroll...................	4,811	110,137	95	549	398	7,314
Cass	877	15,405	20	155	385	6,124
Cedar	10,219	216,687	403	4,790	1,317	23,541
Cerro Gordo	2,718	52,873	118	1,314	41	810
Cherokee	2,130	36,310	112	889	416	7,215
Chickasaw.................	3,027	63,722	466	4,762	226	2,802
Clarke....................	29	680	168	1,714	538	6,821
Clay	1,837	32,683	126	759	169	2,765
Clayton	5,275	106,169	295	3,447	1,244	17,460
Clinton	11,830	241,771	462	5,898	1,653	32,615
Crawford	2,489	58,402	116	831	603	10,773
Dallas	137	2,373	41	353	735	12,325
Davis.....................	8	105	192	1,463	3,481	39,198
Decatur	7	20	127	1,243	1,682	18,391
Delaware	973	16,052	394	4,746	1,324	16,874
Des Moines	93	1,655	181	2,260	915	13,429
Dickinson	323	5,220	32	240	262	2,925
Dubuque	2,741	51,613	93	881	1,071	14,342
Emmett	433	8,219	22	239	14	264
Fayette...................	3,340	56,718	686	7,065	333	3,652
Floyd.....................	1,318	28,103	262	2,592	120	1,773
Franklin..................	1,141	24,033	119	919	430	5,748
Fremont...................	4,173	79,258	55	515	1,320	24,298
Greene....................	714	14,218	128	1,106	620	10,360
Grundy....................	5,230	109,674	258	2,210	436	7,350
Guthrie...................	344	5,453	88	666	257	4,098
Hamilton	342	7,329	77	828	166	3,344
Hancock...................	584	12,513	62	945	53	1,148
Hardin	457	10,268	120	1,268	403	7,615
Harrison..................	227	3,910	56	803	525	8,271
Henry	93	1,476	94	999	2,000	29,537
Howard....................	4,835	103,579	255	2,507	113	1,703
Humboldt	740	13,478	79	776	634	12,308
Ida.......................	1,051	17,036	43	158	163	3,021
Iowa......................	2,049	40,751	216	2,025	1,454	30,308
Jackson...................	1,149	20,623	493	5,147	2,590	34,412
Jasper....................	2,539	48,801	239	2,370	2,003	34,176
Jefferson			88	755	3,763	48,725
Johnson	1,532	28,646	300	3,614	4,705	73,026
Jones.....................	1,444	21,366	508	6,747	2,000	32,450
Keokuk....................	364	7,480	145	1,281	2,115	30,379
Kossuth...................	832	14,746	126	1,471	274	4,462
Lee.......................	283	5,162	172	1,440	5,028	66,055
Linn	589	9,095	351	3,602	1,772	26,051
Louisa....................	56	1,679	201	2,011	2,242	32,334
Lucas.....................	25	437	212	2,094	1,459	19,753
Lyon	1,263	8,522	95	921	120	618
Madison	328	6,206	68	522	702	11,695
Mahaska..................	107	2,302	110	1,300	1,712	28,996
Marion	58	959	131	1,341	1,636	29,678
Marshall..................	1,467	30,987	248	2,748	757	13,680
Mills.....................	1,853	32,156	50	528	307	4,417

Counties.	INDIAN CORN.		OATS.		WHEAT.	
	Acres.	Bushels.	Acres.	Bushels.	Acres.	Bushels.
The State	6, 616, 144	275, 014, 247	1, 507, 577	50, 610, 591	3, 049, 288	31, 154, 205
Adair	80, 068	3, 151, 003	9, 430	296, 341	32, 915	330, 245
Adams	72, 139	2, 843, 272	8, 845	255, 079	25, 510	231, 422
Allamakee	38, 997	1, 510, 394	18, 747	628, 387	57, 505	535, 074
Appanoose	63, 232	2, 410, 620	18, 598	643, 704	6, 750	65, 793
Audubon	36, 985	1, 512, 702	2, 871	93, 996	20, 406	285, 851
Benton	127, 752	5, 871, 574	24, 420	892, 835	56, 928	609, 550
Black Hawk	90, 444	3, 903, 944	27, 560	992, 762	50, 720	521, 039
Boone	94, 109	3, 916, 693	16, 884	604, 235	18, 055	182, 580
Bremer	48, 979	1, 873, 813	22, 805	764, 797	40, 851	301, 629
Buchanan	82, 326	3, 158, 505	32, 570	1, 125, 471	21, 688	109, 532
Buena Vista	39, 248	1, 462, 936	9, 458	303, 287	23, 641	246, 239
Butler	73, 748	2, 920, 920	20, 046	683, 227	55, 202	505, 021
Calhoun	27, 019	981, 698	5, 540	168, 416	8, 619	106, 399
Carroll	67, 328	2, 671, 169	9, 736	302, 478	47, 230	680, 086
Cass	105, 299	4, 604, 482	8, 209	262, 880	51, 485	549, 369
Cedar	107, 035	5, 180, 808	23, 657	874, 524	22, 925	156, 169
Cerro Gordo	33, 090	1, 276, 922	15, 511	528, 445	65, 642	650, 998
Cherokee	54, 960	2, 306, 301	9, 274	243, 995	36, 102	306, 828
Chickasaw	31, 384	1, 208, 201	20, 332	708, 098	68, 984	505, 424
Clarke	61, 359	2, 370, 160	18, 192	578, 707	10, 082	80, 596
Clay	21, 795	753, 600	6, 195	164, 295	6, 029	33, 861
Clayton	62, 247	2, 618, 851	26, 920	885, 368	78, 462	735, 780
Clinton	129, 544	5, 885, 760	34, 158	1, 279, 070	38, 372	411, 522
Crawford	73, 920	3, 047, 849	7, 095	234, 810	46, 461	704, 020
Dallas	105, 381	4, 392, 193	14, 576	519, 379	22, 695	219, 388
Davis	64, 551	2, 084, 715	19, 629	577, 166	10, 609	133, 493
Decatur	65, 757	2, 535, 481	16, 284	550, 664	7, 785	78, 109
Delaware	88, 370	3, 654, 947	33, 099	1, 194, 034	16, 779	106, 065
Des Moines	67, 228	2, 812, 975	12, 710	431, 874	18, 113	263, 697
Dickinson	4, 903	148, 042	2, 997	85, 305	3, 257	17, 098
Dubuque	77, 673	3, 319, 826	35, 159	1, 133, 818	27, 196	254, 544
Emmet	3, 587	135, 581	1, 642	52, 577	2, 049	17, 264
Fayette	66, 663	2, 442, 680	35, 543	1, 216, 081	50, 485	341, 932
Floyd	42, 948	1, 801, 836	19, 197	695, 235	90, 374	896, 006
Franklin	56, 136	2, 117, 940	17, 397	600, 039	43, 159	507, 482
Fremont	121, 918	5, 875, 156	6, 053	206, 150	21, 915	299, 503
Greene	71, 986	2, 975, 538	12, 463	427, 678	16, 587	177, 876
Grundy	87, 508	3, 742, 904	23, 492	846, 878	57, 622	683, 387
Guthrie	72, 599	2, 985, 347	8, 855	281, 710	27, 736	290, 515
Hamilton	48, 625	1, 940, 770	11, 076	402, 207	20, 697	259, 926
Hancock	7, 501	255, 598	4, 419	140, 371	18, 614	168, 782
Hardin	71, 067	2, 742, 057	19, 346	687, 798	29, 487	346, 929
Harrison	93, 377	4, 363, 991	4, 941	156, 725	18, 879	240, 093
Henry	68, 057	2, 598, 693	16, 542	521, 268	20, 594	261, 869
Howard	18, 652	618, 133	19, 887	667, 911	80, 231	612, 100
Humboldt	25, 270	928, 605	5, 827	201, 982	9, 539	125, 915
Ida	24, 205	977, 208	3, 381	111, 636	17, 844	250, 407
Iowa	93, 765	4, 094, 205	14, 642	550, 359	44, 071	456, 265
Jackson	74, 591	3, 360, 568	33, 396	1, 032, 181	25, 008	316, 367
Jasper	136, 333	5, 917, 671	26, 824	979, 559	48, 966	554, 927
Jefferson	61, 138	1, 782, 128	18, 320	555, 308	20, 109	242, 137
Johnson	108, 417	4, 951, 472	22, 238	736, 649	30, 250	242, 229
Jones	95, 825	4, 207, 611	25, 253	867, 095	11, 988	74, 636
Keokuk	89, 606	3, 520, 690	18, 946	642, 355	29, 594	323, 917
Kossuth	21, 058	635, 631	6, 934	214, 343	8, 529	88, 906
Lee	71, 086	2, 723, 829	18, 003	570, 478	20, 879	332, 721
Linn	120, 872	5, 022, 699	33, 959	1, 135, 004	20, 516	148, 246
Louisa	63, 253	2, 810, 850	9, 302	317, 819	16, 624	189, 553
Lucas	61, 190	2, 412, 069	15, 743	518, 731	6, 846	50, 728
Lyon	6, 410	213, 648	4, 036	67, 194	12, 338	23, 741
Madison	95, 217	3, 882, 063	11, 725	396, 847	42, 145	426, 310
Mahaska	90, 457	3, 846, 572	22, 501	874, 214	31, 028	393, 938
Marion	93, 527	3, 990, 241	14, 631	461, 573	39, 077	429, 805
Marshall	103, 187	4, 538, 136	20, 113	759, 424	44, 489	559, 656
Mills	93, 621	4, 192, 319	7, 079	230, 171	21, 742	232, 884

IOWA—Continued.

Counties.	BARLEY. Acres.	BARLEY. Bushels.	BUCKWHEAT. Acres.	BUCKWHEAT. Bushels.	RYE. Acres.	RYE. Bushels.
Mitchell	4,673	113,800	164	1,686	58	1,129
Monona	151	3,395	22	207	126	2,431
Monroe	42	496	157	1,807	1,288	15,805
Montgomery	472	6,586	43	463	1,004	17,718
Muscatine	5,702	117,615	509	6,220	3,538	49,896
O'Brien	1,083	10,871	76	376	354	4,390
Osceola	831	6,828	25	291	218	954
Page	3,064	54,405	68	682	3,093	55,864
Palo Alto	826	13,919	39	275	177	3,128
Plymouth	2,737	10,305	190	1,467	290	1,772
Pocahontas	209	4,070	13	123	325	5,135
Polk	259	5,162	71	624	948	19,679
Pottawattamie	3,762	73,325	132	1,391	950	13,984
Poweshiek	2,185	40,256	215	2,380	1,026	17,662
Ringgold	53	860	210	1,447	937	11,490
Sac	1,272	26,076	98	846	570	10,708
Scott	34,717	848,306	156	1,715	607	9,636
Shelby	2,561	57,975	31	353	283	6,024
Sioux	3,219	25,416	65	436	433	3,409
Story	176	3,131	136	1,127	1,117	19,550
Tama	6,484	132,405	248	3,067	910	17,144
Taylor	916	14,996	119	1,164	1,442	19,334
Union	163	3,654	100	1,189	685	10,729
Van Buren	17	203	253	1,765	3,019	36,478
Wapello	169	2,853	103	827	2,696	34,986
Warren	242	3,957	174	1,338	945	15,088
Washington	403	8,317	166	1,736	2,519	38,435
Wayne	17	123	270	2,992	1,836	19,277
Webster	630	13,141	22	202	606	11,313
Winnebago	602	13,484	9	123	8	185
Winneshiek	5,396	117,351	188	2,275	273	3,866
Woodbury	460	3,115	35	250	34	371
Worth	1,807	41,499	37	461	44	808
Wright	461	9,626	55	637	70	1,211

KANSAS.

Counties.	BARLEY. Acres.	BARLEY. Bushels.	BUCKWHEAT. Acres.	BUCKWHEAT. Bushels.	RYE. Acres.	RYE. Bushels.
The State	23,993	300,273	2,458	24,421	34,621	413,181
Allen			101	1,073	265	2,388
Anderson	13	350	57	618	222	2,718
Arrapahoe						
Atchison	311	4,280	25	279	459	6,868
Barbour	11	20			80	385
Barton	334	1,541	17	82	267	1,026
Bourbon	10	50	157	1,491	212	2,277
Brown	5,332	98,435	29	398	1,857	29,023
Buffalo						
Butler	53	1,691	16	95	102	1,035
Chase	49	50	21	136	263	2,735
Chautauqua	5	84	8	24	45	509
Cherokee	42	1,240	45	519	143	1,482
Cheyenne						
Clark						
Clay	216	2,297	30	224	1,161	13,428
Cloud	293	3,458	28	345	908	10,623
Coffey	5	109	36	297	327	4,598
Comanche						
Cowley	27	480	52	439	58	710
Crawford	7	207	114	1,474	113	1,622
Davis	60	183			180	1,858
Decatur	78	451	22	346	202	2,794
Dickinson	245	2,104	29	212	538	6,753
Doniphan	2,098	37,526	8	58	664	10,536

IOWA—Continued.

| Counties. | INDIAN CORN. | | OATS. | | WHEAT. | |
	Acres.	Bushels.	Acres.	Bushels.	Acres.	Bushels.
Mitchell	22,031	885,044	19,851	815,439	107,124	1,155,142
Monona	49,593	2,320,332	3,297	101,967	10,259	126,307
Monroe	47,691	1,754,539	14,128	462,304	9,494	101,261
Montgomery	98,161	4,314,280	8,503	260,705	30,733	285,308
Muscatine	77,653	3,453,186	15,688	552,044	16,642	141,818
O'Brien	17,322	651,095	5,329	116,864	8,472	35,990
Osceola	7,912	239,676	4,083	68,646	9,746	15,507
Page	133,631	6,297,632	12,015	390,066	28,203	351,299
Palo Alto	16,505	540,504	4,403	148,215	4,019	37,646
Plymouth	41,310	968,032	11,035	52,463	37,195	67,268
Pocahontas	20,390	686,602	4,765	154,023	3,913	40,383
Polk	106,932	4,860,898	18,459	709,603	28,888	350,729
Pottawattamie	157,334	7,350,176	11,293	370,788	59,073	699,324
Poweshiek	104,500	4,228,057	23,416	875,859	41,980	435,425
Ringgold	68,857	2,689,549	13,836	411,840	10,179	86,115
Sac	52,649	1,931,335	9,972	317,602	34,325	438,152
Scott	76,164	3,904,552	18,341	691,336	32,869	361,083
Shelby	89,300	4,039,100	7,045	253,774	45,954	690,659
Sioux	23,554	767,156	9,640	133,273	37,850	86,790
Story	90,556	3,579,260	15,742	557,037	19,406	197,613
Tama	107,904	4,629,361	18,367	657,016	77,950	944,565
Taylor	105,095	4,510,116	16,907	510,953	24,245	228,197
Union	60,813	2,267,508	12,753	406,342	16,523	160,308
Van Buren	56,128	1,907,680	17,212	508,927	14,441	192,231
Wapello	57,897	1,918,179	16,667	533,437	15,692	183,621
Warren	100,080	4,419,556	13,730	452,417	38,512	404,809
Washington	96,236	4,194,499	21,753	735,633	31,833	316,922
Wayne	88,081	3,479,724	23,173	838,041	8,220	67,124
Webster	61,362	2,386,552	12,837	440,745	18,169	217,403
Winnebago	4,774	165,907	3,654	134,920	19,964	207,356
Winneshiek	42,641	1,790,061	29,548	1,107,294	117,753	1,036,113
Woodbury	39,925	1,458,939	4,706	41,286	10,330	57,469
Worth	11,048	403,203	10,686	404,086	65,056	658,996
Wright	25,263	997,750	8,010	262,639	16,858	204,289

KANSAS.

| | INDIAN CORN. | | OATS. | | WHEAT. | |
	Acres.	Bushels.	Acres.	Bushels.	Acres.	Bushels.
The State	3,417,817	105,729,325	435,859	8,180,385	1,861,402	17,324,141
Allen	45,800	1,418,563	4,960	61,428	4,886	59,465
Anderson	37,581	1,201,323	5,028	79,681	4,465	66,088
Arrapahoe						
Atchison	57,531	2,129,689	6,206	182,372	24,710	362,078
Barbour	1,379	5,996	733	2,784	996	2,659
Barton	36,657	593,835	7,287	56,194	60,619	286,521
Bourbon	73,964	2,307,528	8,170	112,070	9,823	95,829
Brown	93,812	3,912,865	7,688	268,406	27,930	424,884
Buffalo						
Butler	72,411	2,099,604	9,277	146,879	43,612	368,258
Chase	19,701	693,622	2,815	42,422	9,595	92,133
Chautauqua	30,612	1,048,485	1,552	20,912	7,429	81,893
Cherokee	75,679	2,335,175	12,934	242,751	16,058	216,760
Cheyenne						
Clark						
Clay	57,762	1,876,262	6,286	141,317	39,977	325,184
Cloud	60,724	2,064,376	4,627	115,819	35,331	246,031
Coffey	42,981	1,513,209	4,897	85,928	5,439	82,823
Comanche	18	100				
Cowley	70,694	2,274,855	7,884	136,471	53,179	624,535
Crawford	81,347	2,797,340	11,534	258,056	13,380	198,493
Davis	16,879	481,218	1,709	28,743	13,595	132,882
Decatur	3,662	54,017	79	1,242	1,182	9,997
Dickinson	52,858	1,528,282	6,975	95,417	85,309	698,426
Doniphan	60,091	2,475,986	7,198	209,185	35,409	518,140

KANSAS—Continued.

Counties.	BARLEY.		BUCKWHEAT.		RYE.	
	Acres.	Bushels.	Acres.	Bushels.	Acres.	Bushels.
Douglas	9	136	21	222	278	4,650
Edwards	1,210	1,158	11	36	76	165
Elk	26	948	36	453	25	222
Ellis	47	185			132	695
Ellsworth	142	1,082	18	133	279	3,108
Foote						
Ford	437	1,493			33	39
Franklin	7	70	59	554	139	1,974
Gove						
Graham	14	145			63	761
Grant						
Greeley						
Greenwood	17	70	56	687	125	1,691
Hamilton						
Harper			17	123	48	60
Harvey	314	2,805	12	74	265	2,985
Hodgeman	392	117			73	130
Jackson	145	2,286	5	110	729	10,113
Jefferson	89	963	10	88	325	5,113
Jewell	577	5,232	43	286	1,058	10,181
Johnson	60	1,112	33	331	308	4,770
Kansas						
Kearney						
Kingman					16	151
Labette	46	870	54	368	269	2,938
Lane						
Leavenworth	149	1,747	13	117	85	1,604
Lincoln	150	1,181			191	1,832
Linn			104	1,218	230	2,480
Lyon	38	543	72	560	496	4,242
McPherson	411	3,495			183	1,945
Marion	292	2,484	7	39	506	4,094
Marshall	440	6,004	58	432	2,288	32,510
Meade						
Miami	13	212	23	130	344	5,218
Mitchell	45	456	7	26	514	4,486
Montgomery	92	1,687	93	706	38	582
Morris	123	1,819	15	95	191	2,223
Nemaha	321	4,248	79	743	684	7,389
Neosho			72	510	137	1,615
Ness	5	10			104	143
Norton	277	2,975	7	61	765	7,427
Osage	16	206	91	2,057	313	3,783
Osborne	147	1,940	5	48	551	5,526
Ottawa	114	1,166	30	220	500	5,277
Pawnee	289	961	19	113	260	958
Phillips	557	6,929			1,377	12,570
Pottawatomie	908	10,670	57	644	1,104	14,771
Pratt	24	121			100	649
Rawlings					11	20
Reno	196	447	16	78	536	1,875
Republic	3,059	43,322	52	491	2,184	28,249
Rice	347	1,504	17	103	212	1,471
Riley	229	2,192	20	216	933	12,921
Rooks	297	5,492	38	396	497	6,034
Rush	230	599	16	46	169	478
Russell	22	121			243	2,471
Saline	546	3,992	11	80	165	1,180
Scott						
Sedgwick	104	1,363	62	612	369	4,363
Sequoyah						
Seward						
Shawnee	87	1,038	28	249	682	11,564
Sheridan	24	140			9	86
Sherman						

| Counties. | INDIAN CORN. | | OATS. | | WHEAT. | |
	Acres.	Bushels.	Acres.	Bushels.	Acres.	Bushels.
Douglas	66,986	2,398,574	8,531	226,583	23,871	403,133
Edwards	3,416	9,080	2,059	5,728	12,629	27,468
Elk	35,676	1,009,521	1,796	26,524	6,507	83,345
Ellis	10,214	106,665	931	9,008	17,083	116,062
Ellsworth	24,408	625,143	2,376	39,653	22,389	222,803
Foote					107	185
Ford	1,013	3,895	670	2,333	2,749	4,493
Franklin	63,803	2,202,778	5,397	138,896	7,460	104,575
Gove	223	2,385			59	259
Graham	4,925	42,260	60	1,575	1,013	8,194
Grant						
Greeley						
Greenwood	37,254	1,305,067	3,070	45,340	7,762	103,005
Hamilton						
Harper	10,565	159,570	1,264	11,480	3,607	25,288
Harvey	43,794	1,122,916	13,422	176,517	37,100	313,957
Hodgeman	1,458	8,750	769	1,814	4,782	6,015
Jackson	50,614	1,715,828	4,947	118,150	12,517	177,981
Jefferson	73,155	2,436,016	7,822	220,354	32,844	516,258
Jewell	74,067	2,386,624	5,652	143,067	49,916	347,684
Johnson	76,922	3,209,213	9,095	270,357	23,959	390,714
Kansas						
Kearney						
Kingman	9,931	102,842	1,222	6,468	6,097	27,836
Labette	82,	2,460,220	11,404	188,434	27,759	340,411
Lane	1,102	6,151	48	820	760	2,968
Leavenworth	53,910	1,785,976	6,637	188,816	27,786	418,211
Lincoln	23,021	398,864	2,194	34,530	29,981	263,860
Linn	84,518	2,736,540	7,625	116,124	10,045	104,312
Lyon	53,538	1,891,370	5,231	98,948	9,235	92,551
McPherson	59,584	1,670,101	18,786	297,696	89,340	932,037
Marion	35,392	992,748	8,799	96,698	37,390	377,917
Marshall	58,568	2,112,421	9,840	297,455	39,237	346,561
Meade						
Miami	99,199	3,592,607	8,998	238,566	13,245	181,560
Mitchell	50,601	1,255,180	3,403	61,676	35,892	268,726
Montgomery	72,018	2,043,882	7,696	120,733	26,172	350,520
Morris	26,601	812,151	4,277	73,267	17,115	157,108
Nemaha	56,276	2,109,444	7,440	105,686	7,254	62,735
Neosho	66,890	1,920,159	6,758	117,988	12,000	149,450
Ness	1,928	8,092	21	150	1,437	3,194
Norton	12,718	256,280	660	13,679	7,889	74,449
Osage	62,313	2,101,517	4,909	123,154	11,495	170,354
Osborne	33,126	638,897	2,007	38,266	30,529	269,003
Ottawa	33,976	971,805	4,924	93,114	41,267	360,785
Pawnee	7,703	66,765	2,003	8,106	21,259	51,051
Phillips	26,928	710,396	1,763	39,416	26,004	238,447
Pottawatomie	59,179	2,137,162	9,037	218,405	16,048	195,185
Pratt	6,577	72,064	1,505	9,933	4,927	20,456
Rawlings	180	3,760	20	900	86	252
Reno	55,488	724,408	16,815	102,715	65,724	204,010
Republic	58,388	2,012,116	6,121	180,622	41,479	279,055
Rice	37,549	824,780	6,857	87,185	28,083	147,536
Riley	33,934	1,204,122	3,504	85,959	12,706	117,312
Rooks	18,017	350,566	708	16,515	9,964	98,121
Rush	11,636	82,342	1,725	6,589	19,895	58,810
Russell	19,512	361,752	1,481	26,113	19,922	185,235
Saline	41,894	1,321,171	8,910	115,594	71,643	610,763
Scott						
Sedgwick	84,234	2,347,080	19,435	301,192	72,163	574,741
Sequoyah						
Seward						
Shawnee	62,020	2,339,645	4,558	123,726	12,863	183,564
Sheridan	1,139	15,300	53	898	320	1,986
Sherman						

KANSAS—Continued.

Counties.	BARLEY.		BUCKWHEAT.		RYE.	
	Acres.	Bushels.	Acres.	Bushels.	Acres.	Bushels.
Smith	340	3,817	18	182	748	7,855
Stafford	263	494			129	422
Stanton						
Stevens						
Sumner	349	3,737	44	520	254	2,071
Thomas						
Trego	7	25			24	115
Wabaunsee	198	2,171	50	440	300	4,250
Wallace						
Washington	527	7,286	53	551	3,417	47,345
Wichita						
Wilson	7	142	72	843	122	1,497
Woodson			32	250	269	3,087
Wyandotte	11	300	7	70	80	1,500

KENTUCKY.

	BARLEY.		BUCKWHEAT.		RYE.	
	Acres.	Bushels.	Acres.	Bushels.	Acres.	Bushels.
The State	20,089	486,326	1,024	9,942	89,417	668,050
Adair					651	3,459
Allen			7	32	151	675
Anderson					1,424	9,079
Ballard					281	1,902
Barren			9	144	1,485	8,320
Bath					1,050	9,160
Bell					307	1,342
Boone	57	1,432			2,537	26,956
Bourbon	232	6,142	6	100	1,048	15,515
Boyd	11	100			125	965
Boyle	150	3,433	143	1,170	973	11,930
Bracken	12	187	5	60	894	7,578
Breathitt					411	2,124
Breckinridge	43	937			459	3,213
Bullitt			22	94	466	3,246
Butler					37	208
Caldwell					231	1,096
Calloway			5	45	304	1,158
Campbell	1,809	37,032	29	303	883	9,195
Carroll	38	270			684	7,019
Carter	10	50	22	153	496	2,851
Casey			5	44	1,730	9,678
Christian					379	2,544
Clark	370	9,559			1,557	15,465
Clay			12	73	741	3,362
Clinton					217	875
Crittenden	6	25			40	374
Cumberland					477	2,880
Daviess	151	3,535	9	67	1,466	10,694
Edmonson					121	661
Elliott			20	226	1,110	4,987
Estill					1,012	5,612
Fayette	4,231	93,897	52	674	1,645	18,000
Fleming	10	131	6	65	608	6,223
Floyd			16	137	608	3,320
Franklin	665	13,599	25	229	1,173	8,093
Fulton					167	1,655
Gallatin	12	200			934	10,425
Garrard	36	1,030	6	95	2,297	18,423
Grant	24	644			1,592	16,224
Graves					308	2,128
Grayson					242	1,482
Green					615	2,851
Greenup	341	6,598	47	224	197	1,909
Hancock	5	75			269	2,107

KANSAS—Continued.

Counties.	INDIAN CORN.		OATS.		WHEAT.	
	Acres.	Bushels.	Acres.	Bushels.	Acres.	Bushels.
Smith	51,936	1,381,448	1,880	32,799	38,462	268,980
Stafford	20,542	159,724	3,863	10,862	20,444	37,498
Stanton						
Stevens						
Sumner	70,082	1,602,794	12,009	143,324	59,467	410,730
Thomas	185	4,175	20	380	78	500
Trego	1,727	15,005	114	999	1,874	11,577
Wabaunsee	26,977	1,008,990	2,092	48,484	14,003	217,911
Wallace	107	2,129			30	100
Washington	64,199	2,279,596	8,942	270,084	31,758	280,553
Wichita						
Wilson	57,525	1,848,119	6,014	93,611	16,342	212,327
Woodson	25,909	809,399	4,049	61,748	2,992	39,136
Wyandotte	16,567	620,640	1,096	57,493	11,663	178,599

KENTUCKY.

	INDIAN CORN.		OATS.		WHEAT.	
	Acres.	Bushels.	Acres.	Bushels.	Acres.	Bushels.
The State	3,021,176	72,852,263	403,416	4,580,738	1,160,108	11,356,113
Adair	29,230	492,413	2,231	16,482	11,303	68,424
Allen	31,578	401,279	6,369	56,821	10,505	46,848
Anderson	19,482	527,680	1,945	20,936	7,492	58,265
Ballard	36,851	951,357	1,626	20,982	21,166	161,843
Barren	50,291	850,338	13,887	150,904	17,819	119,775
Bath	27,061	830,986	3,816	50,257	8,619	124,603
Bell	11,558	201,777	1,521	11,091	518	2,784
Boone	25,881	897,292	3,380	59,545	6,800	94,954
Bourbon	28,196	1,135,572	2,326	47,199	17,776	370,247
Boyd	7,377	149,797	1,364	13,721	3,205	24,967
Boyle	15,386	570,943	1,815	26,245	10,407	140,541
Bracken	21,025	502,550	705	9,715	13,435	179,979
Breathitt	15,472	291,217	2,005	15,279	1,420	8,913
Breckinridge	43,854	864,772	13,533	152,033	13,331	113,423
Bullitt	22,227	520,157	4,170	43,899	7,267	55,389
Butler	34,579	651,593	7,271	88,583	5,860	32,513
Caldwell	31,580	707,609	3,394	34,776	6,821	51,468
Calloway	35,209	780,839	3,420	33,050	8,076	47,890
Campbell	14,025	346,095	3,233	57,900	7,921	104,650
Carroll	13,971	400,785	932	10,628	4,126	50,021
Carter	18,248	281,371	5,010	40,148	3,792	25,880
Casey	22,736	491,243	786	7,064	5,535	39,087
Christian	60,724	1,430,154	4,981	64,341	40,247	437,668
Clark	20,452	791,292	1,146	14,836	7,931	129,943
Clay	21,475	401,457	2,299	13,905	3,498	18,703
Clinton	16,311	281,808	1,465	10,115	6,687	33,375
Crittenden	37,706	848,900	3,608	37,022	7,295	48,221
Cumberland	15,248	315,602	1,256	12,396	5,529	37,221
Daviess	53,321	1,392,599	5,678	79,946	13,813	147,303
Edmonson	19,682	328,159	1,733	13,057	4,649	22,858
Elliott	15,528	201,445	3,353	24,330	2,934	19,444
Estill	19,459	397,932	1,340	10,827	3,400	22,617
Fayette	28,839	1,080,029	3,659	68,896	21,402	380,474
Fleming	26,552	711,669	4,583	60,433	16,819	207,625
Floyd	21,351	429,298	2,501	15,072	2,750	18,356
Franklin	19,464	543,749	2,542	31,894	9,505	103,475
Fulton	19,755	617,202	631	10,835	10,978	93,795
Gallatin	11,886	401,996	1,139	18,844	2,910	38,216
Garrard	24,446	828,173	1,733	21,356	14,064	143,960
Grant	28,491	952,678	1,685	23,258	10,419	130,893
Graves	59,359	1,540,245	4,546	52,876	23,379	147,925
Grayson	39,391	597,346	9,026	82,531	10,757	64,545
Green	20,065	411,278	3,279	24,843	8,672	57,557
Greenup	18,404	379,276	3,601	44,439	6,419	63,429
Hancock	17,983	389,305	2,112	23,522	4,000	39,868

Counties.	BARLEY.		BUCKWHEAT.		RYE.	
	Acres.	Bushels.	Acres.	Bushels.	Acres.	Bushels.
Hardin					712	3,951
Harlan					258	1,342
Harrison	115	3,250	28	2-2	1,137	10,805
Hart			22	254	2,381	12,100
Henderson	16	300			350	3,577
Henry	10	100			2,964	19,725
Hickman					18	151
Hopkins					90	662
Jackson			6	22	230	966
Jefferson	914	21,643	10	106	1,101	10,413
Jessamine	1,023	23,775	13	170	745	5,662
Johnson			14	126	354	2,063
Kenton	20	626			1,246	12,515
Knox					819	3,277
La Rue					561	2,774
Laurel			21	106	265	965
Lawrence			10	96	779	3,461
Lee					257	1,658
Leslie					217	802
Letcher			6	30	408	2,284
Lewis	76	1,440	14	145	232	3,041
Lincoln			9	74	1,113	7,792
Livingston					164	928
Logan	10	150			109	829
Lyon					55	408
McCracken			16	110	482	1,455
McLean					74	725
Madison			5	42	5,679	44,590
Magoffin					449	2,392
Marion			12	225	1,733	12,851
Marshall					68	716
Martin					43	227
Mason	740	20,525			769	10,734
Meade			7	74	795	4,777
Menifee			25	231	126	701
Mercer	25	400	17	140	1,224	9,205
Metcalfe			8	59	1,005	4,016
Monroe					292	776
Montgomery					1,050	11,282
Morgan			30	273	699	3,192
Muhlenburgh					59	214
Nelson			11	103	1,377	10,434
Nicholas			7	159	695	7,553
Ohio					161	906
Oldham	30	960			581	4,800
Owen			11	134	2,683	10,814
Owsley			7	52	337	1,618
Pendleton	94	2,319	35	522	1,324	12,514
Perry			5	40	163	573
Pike			29	241	390	2,021
Powell					445	2,766
Pulaski			37	365	1,408	5,805
Robertson					546	3,907
Rock Castle			6	33	437	1,886
Rowan			12	140	70	426
Russell					141	810
Scott	2,223	61,138	56	681	727	7,503
Shelby	212	5,028	13	149	4,256	35,244
Simpson					50	201
Spencer	93	858			1,172	6,789
Taylor					453	2,025
Todd			6	42	260	1,896
Trigg					214	1,134
Trimble					322	2,784
Union	24	600			165	1,280

KENTUCKY—Continued.

| Counties. | INDIAN CORN. | | OATS. | | WHEAT. | |
	Acres.	Bushels.	Acres.	Bushels.	Acres.	Bushels.
Hardin	56, 699	1, 131, 070	6, 539	62, 435	36, 041	259, 781
Harlan	11, 633	208, 365	741	5, 643	405	2, 385
Harrison	30, 413	982, 202	2, 787	33, 996	19, 137	240, 045
Hart	38, 361	760, 489	4, 366	41, 994	14, 387	99, 672
Henderson...............	55, 038	1, 080, 007	1, 781	27, 589	9, 832	124, 991
Henry	28, 009	889, 831	3, 330	48, 968	7, 923	95, 162
Hickman	28, 208	784, 828	889	13, 857	14, 296	107, 006
Hopkins.................	44, 726	925, 188	5, 889	70, 173	10, 713	75, 509
Jackson	13, 775	244, 191	2, 496	15, 067	2, 085	10, 905
Jefferson	38, 757	1, 056, 209	8, 056	114, 793	15, 825	186, 212
Jessamine	15, 816	521, 412	1, 688	28, 589	16, 692	223, 605
Johnson	17, 711	372, 073	3, 543	21, 892	2, 589	17, 267
Kenton	14, 997	428, 102	1, 680	29, 405	4, 230	55, 049
Knox	23, 199	405, 140	3, 736	26, 183	4, 894	23, 468
La Rue	28, 048	556, 184	6, 447	67, 575	13, 795	96, 848
Laurel..................	17, 982	278, 074	3, 933	26, 378	4, 559	22, 525
Lawrence................	26, 179	472, 071	4, 930	35, 188	4, 858	32, 083
Lee	8, 269	146, 725	1, 441	10, 547	1, 181	8, 152
Leslie	6, 916	111, 255	284	1, 328	316	1, 490
Letcher.................	11, 175	213, 547	1, 141	8, 804	1, 640	10, 622
Lewis	21, 117	584, 939	4, 536	84, 551	7, 690	100, 342
Lincoln	22, 139	628, 807	1, 263	13, 942	10, 746	98, 946
Livingston..............	29, 661	740, 746	2, 469	29, 072	7, 298	62, 465
Logan	54, 988	1, 181, 699	8, 932	130, 659	36, 893	340, 262
Lyon	18, 657	405, 802	1, 166	12, 116	3, 608	26, 485
McCracken	20, 542	483, 776	2, 856	30, 677	8, 814	64, 549
McLean	22, 456	542, 349	3, 539	45, 752	8, 248	69, 643
Madison	39, 351	1, 192, 350	3, 711	33, 601	12, 638	129, 652
Magoffin	13, 751	267, 726	3, 004	20, 643	2, 186	14, 801
Marion	27, 275	745, 464	5, 021	56, 920	8, 466	77, 852
Marshall	28, 379	602, 013	3, 410	32, 014	9, 766	47, 755
Martin	5, 339	104, 527	712	3, 847	248	1, 434
Mason	25, 619	1, 011, 105	1, 055	20, 706	19, 361	385, 347
Meade	26, 325	562, 493	4, 015	44, 482	16, 142	140, 870
Menifee	7, 932	179, 528	1, 104	6, 656	716	4, 873
Mercer	26, 992	856, 933	2, 216	28, 481	17, 891	168, 936
Metcalfe................	21, 812	286, 280	3, 917	32, 100	8, 265	45, 614
Monroe	27, 540	463, 600	6, 404	44, 846	10, 441	45, 034
Montgomery.............	16, 920	575, 091	1, 495	18, 624	5, 303	81, 393
Morgan	19, 298	364, 205	3, 438	25, 318	3, 968	25, 680
Muhlenburgh	35, 798	652, 279	7, 814	100, 340	9, 688	63, 874
Nelson..................	34, 163	987, 007	5, 003	59, 783	17, 387	177, 020
Nicholas................	20, 047	688, 329	2, 134	37, 188	11, 941	159, 945
Ohio	46, 526	935, 515	10, 477	125, 244	12, 441	85, 954
Oldham	15, 863	445, 053	3, 861	49, 747	3, 902	47, 931
Owen	36, 649	1, 016, 362	2, 014	18, 479	10, 788	104, 764
Owsley	9, 566	183, 687	2, 350	15, 909	2, 264	12, 208
Pendleton	28, 813	792, 695	1, 636	20, 696	14, 740	181, 845
Perry	10, 086	170, 191	596	3, 173	991	5, 508
Pike	26, 505	543, 463	3, 402	24, 186	3, 059	18, 207
Powell..................	8, 175	189, 788	523	4, 314	1, 045	6, 929
Pulaski.................	42, 355	612, 388	11, 136	76, 159	16, 267	80, 636
Robertson	11, 155	269, 109	498	5, 553	6, 774	76, 821
Rock Castle	17, 387	298, 693	3, 158	19, 421	2, 977	16, 202
Rowan	8, 879	168, 010	1, 752	14, 699	1, 130	7, 893
Russell	18, 123	280, 488	1, 308	9, 363	6, 545	38, 218
Scott	26, 605	919, 757	2, 848	43, 707	20, 939	322, 173
Shelby	40, 939	1, 493, 101	4, 868	86, 488	21, 627	282, 672
Simpson	29, 778	579, 055	6, 132	86, 709	18, 267	117, 010
Spencer	17, 473	528, 987	1, 296	18, 743	11, 705	116, 006
Taylor..................	20, 993	363, 207	3, 208	39, 511	6, 201	43, 920
Todd	33, 515	749, 789	3, 731	54, 407	22, 897	259, 984
Trigg	32, 919	796, 954	1, 319	14, 879	9, 789	94, 516
Trimble	13, 135	281, 183	2, 199	25, 399	5, 505	66, 027
Union	47, 818	1, 663, 957	2, 957	53, 375	21, 684	256, 697

Counties.	BARLEY.		BUCKWHEAT.		RYE.	
	Acres.	Bushels.	Acres.	Bushels.	Acres.	Bushels.
Warren			8	100	839	5, 123
Washington			9	90	2, 634	18, 832
Wayne			16	149	329	1, 468
Webster					86	604
Whitley					756	2, 663
Wolfe			13	94	592	3, 284
Woodford	6, 251	164, 338	15	258	522	4, 430

LOUISIANA.

The State					201	1, 013
PARISHES.						
Ascension						
Assumption						
Avoyelles						
Bienville					41	104
Bossier						
Caddo						
Calcasieu						
Caldwell						
Cameron						
Catahoula						
Claiborne					28	88
Concordia						
De Soto						
East Baton Rouge						
East Carroll						
East Feliciana						
Franklin						
Grant						
Iberia						
Iberville						
Jackson						
Jefferson						
La Fayette						
Lafourche						
Lincoln					40	244
Livingston						
Madison						
Morehouse						
Natchitoches					9	30
Orleans						
Ouachita						
Plaquemines						
Pointe Coupée						
Rapides						
Red River						
Richland						
Sabine						
Saint Bernard						
Saint Charles						
Saint Helena						
Saint James						
Saint John Baptist						
Saint Landry						
Saint Martin						
Saint Mary						
Saint Tammany						
Tangipahoa						
Tensas						
Terrebonne						
Union					83	547

KENTUCKY—Continued.

Counties.	INDIAN CORN. Acres.	Bushels.	OATS. Acres.	Bushels.	WHEAT. Acres.	Bushels.
Warren	67,177	1,495,419	14,448	204,000	21,173	150,750
Washington	31,205	987,576	3,948	53,942	15,309	135,099
Wayne	27,774	462,894	3,285	24,127	10,943	59,574
Webster	33,968	847,233	4,257	57,446	10,961	86,401
Whitley	24,802	390,429	3,001	20,417	4,472	17,954
Wolfe	12,756	261,896	2,745	18,518	2,514	16,935
Woodford	16,706	601,196	2,857	58,773	18,791	289,795

LOUISIANA.

	INDIAN CORN. Acres.	Bushels.	OATS. Acres.	Bushels.	WHEAT. Acres.	Bushels.
The State	742,728	9,889,689	26,861	229,840	1,501	5,034

PARISHES.

	Acres.	Bushels.	Acres.	Bushels.	Acres.	Bushels.
Ascension	6,112	110,137	38	380		
Assumption	14,055	356,995	6	40		
Avoyelles	21,403	456,039	18	340		
Bienville	19,255	117,523	2,004	13,913	59	267
Bossier	20,153	176,630	1,041	12,725	26	78
Caddo	23,169	156,118	446	4,100		
Calcasieu	7,995	98,317	337	3,057		
Caldwell	5,717	53,312	188	1,616		
Cameron	2,766	43,255				
Catahoula	11,094	134,053	35	509		
Claiborne	42,920	332,158	4,394	28,175	898	2,974
Concordia	6,114	109,333	7	75		
De Soto	31,080	158,665	616	5,200		
East Baton Rouge	11,735	211,449	218	3,453		
East Carroll	7,115	126,691	15	350		
East Feliciana	16,522	206,307	501	7,752		
Franklin	7,235	100,708	94	1,280		
Grant	8,177	95,179				
Iberia	23,740	508,430	165	1,270		
Iberville	11,991	231,596	16	320		
Jackson	9,572	63,049	1,648	10,615	66	335
Jefferson	2,065	30,210				
La Fayette	21,713	350,604				
Lafourche	16,018	292,668				
Lincoln	21,602	150,165	2,684	17,071	117	590
Livingston	3,936	52,911	91	975		
Madison	7,797	127,459	15	250		
Morehouse	17,846	286,294	301	3,568		
Natchitoches	17,871	151,545	362	3,211		
Orleans	35	310				
Ouachita	13,143	130,993	143	1,158	80	340
Plaquemines	1,767	30,469				
Pointe Coupée	14,817	305,470	5	75		
Rapides	29,366	488,370	168	2,481		
Red River	10,566	82,250	88	1,065		
Richland	9,378	140,855	19	195		
Sabine	7,971	60,897	487	4,355		
Saint Bernard	395	6,945				
Saint Charles	1,287	11,915				
Saint Helena	10,540	113,855	1,115	11,053		
Saint James	11,303	189,700				
Saint John Baptist	2,888	89,906				
Saint Landry	57,411	831,181	81	1,725		
Saint Martin	11,283	211,995				
Saint Mary	11,302	210,074				
Saint Tammany	1,224	16,086	108	1,370		
Tangipahoa	6,617	82,268	2,256	24,844		
Tensas	11,427	205,797			195	157
Terrebonne	14,338	291,833				
Union	25,551	197,302	1,097	7,661	38	191

44

LOUISIANA—Continued.

Parishes.	BARLEY.		BUCKWHEAT.		RYE.	
	Acres.	Bushels.	Acres.	Bushels.	Acres.	Bushels.
Vermillion						
Vernon						
Washington						
Webster						
West Baton Rouge						
West Carroll						
West Feliciana						
Winn						

MAINE.

	Acres.	Bushels.	Acres.	Bushels.	Acres.	Bushels.
The State	11,106	242,185	20,135	382,701	2,161	26,308
COUNTIES.						
Androscoggin	409	9,057	152	2,074	118	1,152
Aroostook	771	15,777	15,009	296,793	696	10,804
Cumberland	859	17,624	81	809	173	1,512
Franklin	340	7,331	185	3,382	49	556
Hancock	338	6,737	23	302		
Kennebec	1,713	39,389	184	2,708	140	1,586
Knox	243	5,348	20	456	43	542
Lincoln	1,026	22,147	11	157	37	515
Oxford	113	2,392	904	14,832	441	3,935
Penobscot	1,299	29,367	1,658	28,394	177	2,583
Piscataquis	385	9,515	292	4,821		
Sagadahoc	443	9,961	7	81	14	161
Somerset	1,475	33,991	796	13,469	117	1,226
Waldo	454	9,340	177	2,623	79	895
Washington	341	6,827	587	10,941		
York	897	17,382	49	769	77	841

MARYLAND.

	Acres.	Bushels.	Acres.	Bushels.	Acres.	Bushels.
The State	226	6,007	10,294	136,667	32,405	288,067
Alleghany			1,130	11,368	2,832	19,165
Anne Arundel			20	402	2,138	16,394
Baltimore City						
Baltimore County	17	448	720	9,467	4,990	49,821
Calvert	6	23			148	941
Caroline			44	343	1,600	6,096
Carroll	133	3,724	972	12,543	5,209	54,879
Cecil			315	4,082	109	1,333
Charles			5	36	284	1,330
Dorchester			7	53	123	630
Frederick	51	1,723	216	2,328	4,013	42,592
Garrett			4,980	72,333	2,746	21,552
Harford			975	13,586	418	3,694
Howard	14	154	302	3,451	732	7,488
Kent			17	68		
Montgomery			260	3,057	1,785	17,109
Prince George's			125	1,764	2,522	17,041
Queen Anne			10	187	638	4,408
Saint Mary's					64	241
Somerset			8	93	51	230
Talbot					15	104
Washington			183	1,506	1,818	21,750
Wicomico					74	349
Worcester	5	25			36	242

LOUISIANA—Continued.

Parishes.	INDIAN CORN.		OATS.		WHEAT.	
	Acres.	Bushels.	Acres.	Bushels.	Acres.	Bushels.
Vermillion....................	13,554	166,709	7	66	....	....
Vernon	8,320	74,234	682	5,083	....	....
Washington	7,974	85,306	1,733	15,936	....	....
Webster.....................	14,824	126,270	2,556	22,617	22	102
West Baton Rouge	7,263	170,591	17	340	....	....
West Carroll	3,868	58,062	9	215	....	....
West Felicinua	9,000	140,595	64	1,425	....	....
Winn........................	8,588	81,651	986	7,931	....	....

MAINE.

The State...............	30,997	960,633	78,785	2,265,575	43,829	665,714
COUNTIES.						
Androscoggin	2,409	79,778	3,262	99,523	1,069	14,795
Aroostook	30	382	20,101	628,435	8,286	138,236
Cumberland	2,866	93,619	3,019	87,940	1,459	20,531
Franklin...................	1,768	51,754	4,650	133,549	2,679	38,704
Hancock...................	237	5,468	1,113	29,893	1,778	32,718
Kennebec..................	3,664	121,394	6,210	186,547	3,293	47,006
Knox	524	17,457	508	14,328	1,273	23,396
Lincoln...................	1,051	32,359	1,222	35,126	836	13,075
Oxford....................	4,899	149,572	5,392	152,924	3,572	48,306
Penobscot	2,456	71,137	12,110	320,174	7,108	107,351
Piscataquis	1,130	30,402	3,096	98,544	2,069	29,186
Sagadahoc.................	494	15,962	680	19,936	477	6,964
Somerset	3,304	92,545	9,479	273,438	3,463	46,846
Waldo	1,592	45,496	3,967	104,263	3,692	54,394
Washington	30	675	1,563	46,091	1,615	28,736
York	4,543	152,633	1,453	34,864	1,160	15,470

MARYLAND.

The State...............	664,928	15,968,533	101,127	1,794,872	569,296	8,004,864
Alleghany	8,661	206,949	3,772	52,570	7,549	67,458
Anne Arundel..............	29,674	692,611	5,108	60,798	10,854	98,147
Baltimore City.............	5	200	....	....	10	350
Baltimore County...........	39,433	1,204,698	16,264	314,060	28,629	393,402
Calvert	10,848	211,534	865	7,664	6,581	50,170
Caroline	30,500	512,930	956	8,854	18,336	187,581
Carroll....................	31,983	911,379	11,972	262,458	40,077	579,333
Cecil	25,764	847,754	7,043	190,790	29,875	471,045
Charles	25,922	412,146	2,423	18,230	15,042	108,133
Dorchester................	39,380	844,957	1,107	10,194	25,979	197,905
Frederick..................	52,002	1,774,256	5,051	94,267	83,767	1,418,542
Garrett...................	3,714	87,295	8,657	171,723	4,122	44,399
Harford...................	26,506	1,015,762	10,189	232,339	25,143	420,850
Howard....................	17,925	505,864	2,586	46,594	18,445	305,555
Kent......................	29,937	800,005	1,388	19,503	37,581	556,947
Montgomery................	35,287	1,020,573	3,126	59,537	35,673	615,702
Prince George's	28,897	656,888	2,798	37,395	14,181	129,946
Queen Anne................	38,653	934,831	1,614	22,944	41,223	558,353
Saint Mary's..............	23,388	360,756	1,356	11,387	18,554	155,677
Somerset	22,594	389,896	3,776	49,152	8,082	83,812
Talbot	26,053	691,919	794	12,257	33,129	468,316
Washington	31,910	1,069,802	2,874	52,497	56,923	1,024,769
Wicomico..................	41,214	447,519	1,363	10,641	3,720	27,034
Worcester.................	44,588	568,009	6,045	49,018	5,821	41,438

MASSACHUSETTS.

Counties.	BARLEY.		BUCKWHEAT.		RYE.	
	Acres.	Bushels.	Acres.	Bushels.	Acres.	Bushels.
The State............	3,171	80,128	5,617	67,117	21,666	213,716
Barnstable.................	36	730	....	....	430	4,003
Berkshire.................	478	12,418	2,737	35,459	4,190	45,896
Bristol...................	127	3,227	16	157	470	5,916
Dukes	9	126	....	....	32	252
Essex....................	225	5,009	9	125	252	3,248
Franklin..................	262	7,473	289	3,761	2,309	22,853
Hampden.................	121	2,967	1,464	13,582	6,945	55,226
Hampshire	83	1,988	553	6,338	3,871	33,584
Middlesex	297	6,334	116	1,532	940	12,472
Nantucket................	....	....	....	....	....	....
Norfolk..................	44	861	17	202	197	3,516
Plymouth.	44	1,018	8	78	463	5,013
Suffolk..................	....	....	....	....	50	1,255
Worcester	1,445	37,977	408	5,883	1,517	20,482

MICHIGAN.

	BARLEY.		BUCKWHEAT.		RYE.	
The State............	54,506	1,204,316	33,948	413,062	22,815	294,918
Alcona	25	581	16	165	28	332
Allegan..................	1,310	28,323	1,066	12,762	1,793	21,706
Alpena..................	50	989	17	336	38	566
Antrim..................	147	2,437	175	2,867	286	4,413
Baraga	7	190	....	....	....	....
Barry....................	278	6,348	654	8,238	825	9,684
Bay.....................	99	2,484	183	2,699	153	2,006
Benzie...................	32	598	204	2,247	259	2,863
Berrien	133	3,216	702	5,439	522	5,923
Branch..................	62	1,604	951	13,228	113	1,591
Calhoun	941	23,103	884	12,334	190	2,484
Cass	26	532	593	5,893	114	1,136
Charlevoix	40	952	74	1,270	168	2,700
Cheboygan	19	337	17	320	68	966
Chippewa	24	558	9	195	....	....
Clare	....	....	31	353	94	697
Clinton	944	20,370	165	1,641	25	403
Crawford	....	....	40	420	197	1,421
Delta	28	537	8	193	15	330
Eaton...................	417	9,754	680	10,626	72	1,190
Emmet	60	1,342	73	1,442	37	716
Genesee	1,470	30,859	569	5,807	101	982
Gladwin	....	....	5	101	....	....
Grand Traverse	131	2,421	228	3,196	408	5,327
Gratiot	346	6,813	218	2,336	59	924
Hillsdale	448	9,364	905	11,546	179	2,371
Houghton	116	1,197	....	....	6	135
Huron...................	410	7,901	254	4,065	111	1,736
Ingham..................	748	17,917	803	8,866	97	1,645
Ionia	2,107	44,255	338	3,618	100	1,039
Iosco	10	136	57	906	72	1,492
Isabella.................	145	2,395	71	625	57	718
Isle Royale	....	....	....	....	....	....
Jackson	888	22,179	1,111	13,721	167	2,422
Kalamazoo...............	556	13,542	886	11,102	643	7,949
Kalkaska	....	....	134	2,481	92	1,146
Kent....................	1,377	27,985	966	9,486	803	8,468
Keweenaw................	....	....	....	....	....	....
Lake....................	59	1,061	180	1,531	297	2,440
Lapeer	2,406	50,030	599	6,888	110	1,324
Leelanaw................	57	1,045	259	4,269	757	10,092
Lenawee.................	1,360	33,786	811	11,841	525	10,461
Livingston	1,862	39,738	794	7,483	313	3,413
Mackinac................	....	....	....	....	....	....
Macomb.................	2,714	60,877	1,783	21,633	573	7,771

MASSACHUSETTS.

Counties.	INDIAN CORN. Acres.	Bushels.	OATS. Acres.	Bushels.	WHEAT. Acres.	Bushels.
The State	52,555	1,797,768	20,059	645,159	963	15,768
Barnstable	1,329	31,457	199	4,656		
Berkshire	6,182	202,221	8,545	288,937	136	2,284
Bristol	3,274	117,294	909	28,030	13	170
Dukes	323	8,317	146	2,571		
Essex	2,552	104,528	263	7,612	43	717
Franklin	5,815	216,230	1,869	57,783	349	6,015
Hampden	7,190	205,142	1,997	51,772	52	671
Hampshire	7,175	220,232	1,749	49,263	84	1,756
Middlesex	5,272	194,831	633	14,875	44	616
Nantucket	214	3,108	11	216		
Norfolk	1,332	55,056	116	2,452	9	159
Plymouth	2,500	80,402	338	9,094	19	263
Suffolk	11	280				
Worcester	9,386	358,670	3,884	127,904	212	3,117

MICHIGAN.

The State	INDIAN CORN. Acres.	Bushels.	OATS. Acres.	Bushels.	WHEAT. Acres.	Bushels.
The State	919,656	32,461,452	536,187	18,190,793	1,822,749	35,532,543
Alcona	29	877	378	11,115	356	7,632
Allegan	35,410	1,368,851	11,511	360,334	57,675	1,116,778
Alpena	59	1,901	741	23,218	662	12,581
Antrim	1,316	48,382	749	21,616	3,147	42,844
Baraga			44	850	15	230
Barry	27,838	987,897	10,221	331,636	60,853	1,170,496
Bay	2,648	94,755	3,065	96,815	5,624	120,606
Benzie	1,436	29,315	479	11,367	1,879	19,123
Berrien	35,557	1,077,146	13,276	410,754	43,700	890,780
Branch	35,146	1,475,626	13,316	475,288	48,963	933,573
Calhoun	34,818	1,402,013	15,877	579,852	82,775	1,709,769
Cass	39,360	1,393,481	12,459	369,914	56,581	1,104,171
Charlevoix	875	23,144	983	25,477	2,149	32,037
Cheboygan	83	3,079	859	21,545	941	14,651
Chippewa	15	390	692	16,295	962	13,190
Clare	324	7,123	274	5,707	754	9,961
Clinton	20,420	693,972	14,587	529,549	70,165	1,669,723
Crawford	144	2,160	105	1,555	52	375
Delta	48	1,146	839	25,143	424	7,215
Eaton	26,628	1,009,121	13,414	493,523	55,109	1,026,241
Emmet	948	27,515	478	14,746	1,378	20,938
Genesee	22,088	721,101	21,101	768,563	55,724	1,099,027
Gladwin	120	3,553	209	5,677	405	6,234
Grand Traverse	3,302	95,983	2,087	54,751	6,413	85,982
Gratiot	12,853	390,899	8,099	256,535	30,296	601,941
Hillsdale	37,171	1,390,481	17,286	647,248	56,442	1,122,288
Houghton			260	5,407	50	697
Huron	1,580	53,314	5,715	156,803	22,099	380,608
Ingham	22,969	776,777	11,245	416,011	49,257	922,864
Ionia	22,356	744,577	12,513	399,099	68,160	1,608,230
Iosco	111	3,702	294	9,264	317	5,224
Isabella	4,539	138,391	3,805	91,495	12,837	231,802
Isle Royale						
Jackson	33,093	1,237,914	13,002	469,033	76,533	1,580,102
Kalamazoo	37,123	1,467,269	10,968	373,629	72,692	1,451,381
Kalkaska	877	27,226	360	9,641	1,225	14,394
Kent	30,498	941,916	16,446	447,489	67,119	1,432,558
Keweenaw			17	480	21	265
Lake	636	13,866	382	8,854	1,381	16,565
Lapeer	14,844	435,759	13,868	460,054	45,984	847,400
Leelanaw	2,250	54,370	1,822	38,673	5,148	67,621
Lenawee	46,646	1,759,467	24,671	952,933	57,281	1,251,479
Livingston	22,002	723,927	10,756	393,846	54,353	948,420
Mackinac			32	985		
Macomb	21,284	696,151	24,352	935,474	33,875	598,559

MICHIGAN—Continued.

Counties.	BARLEY.		BUCKWHEAT.		RYE.	
	Acres.	Bushels.	Acres.	Bushels.	Acres.	Bushels.
Manistee	188	2,902	144	1,300	349	5,247
Manitou	20	460			120	2,240
Marquette	9	244			16	320
Mason	244	3,741	130	1,226	339	4,448
Mecosta	274	3,407	237	2,410	316	3,630
Menominee	27	456			13	210
Midland	21	290	185	712	71	856
Missaukee	46	1,083	12	183	14	265
Monroe	2,189	54,907	2,164	30,247	396	4,969
Montcalm	513	9,736	336	4,076	218	2,634
Montmorency						
Muskegon	246	4,780	300	2,659	460	5,170
Newaygo	161	2,527	293	3,376	332	3,098
Oakland	4,510	104,613	2,008	20,460	505	5,679
Oceana	521	9,329	484	5,046	755	9,393
Ogemaw	10	163	72	644	11	92
Ontonagon	33	759				
Osceola	124	1,903	156	2,016	409	5,716
Oscoda						
Otsego	15	261	14	221	7	97
Ottawa	1,104	25,621	696	8,439	1,242	14,978
Presque Isle	196	3,323	16	442	793	12,986
Roscommon						
Saginaw	905	21,398	483	5,347	434	6,644
Saint Clair	9,028	192,571	1,166	14,259	581	7,470
Saint Joseph	145	3,159	868	10,525	157	2,213
Sanilac	3,954	82,157	441	5,448	239	2,793
Schoolcraft					43	275
Shiawassee	1,447	32,132	286	2,651	29	434
Tuscola	306	9,598	785	9,782	236	3,170
Van Buren	445	9,288	1,475	14,111	1,971	22,494
Washtenaw	3,814	94,259	758	11,048	458	6,540
Wayne	1,923	49,083	2,860	41,548	1,028	24,298
Wexford	137	2,384	66	717	236	3,287

MINNESOTA.

	BARLEY.		BUCKWHEAT.		RYE.	
	Acres.	Bushels.	Acres.	Bushels.	Acres.	Bushels.
The State	116,020	2,972,965	3,677	41,756	13,614	215,245
Aitkin						
Anoka	97	1,370	126	1,193	872	10,624
Becker	454	12,454	7	211	35	795
Beltrami						
Benton	53	1,102	8	122	260	4,066
Big Stone	240	5,496	12	140	89	761
Blue Earth	3,029	56,398	53	544	244	4,959
Brown	1,367	29,047	12	82	269	4,850
Carlton					37	650
Carver	1,479	48,084	12	390	116	2,610
Cass						
Chippewa	521	12,527	25	335	6	128
Chisago	201	6,311	5	62	267	3,957
Clay	405	13,606				
Cook						
Cottonwood	2,088	38,972	123	607	175	2,811
Crow Wing					28	645
Dakota	2,583	67,892	63	635	201	2,906
Dodge	5,771	153,873	188	1,756	35	578
Douglas	812	20,761	81	1,276	178	3,609
Faribault	2,686	59,238	55	646	62	1,003
Fillmore	6,684	176,037	312	2,630	183	2,603
Freeborn	3,015	72,647	77	1,430	181	3,107
Goodhue	11,062	324,059	91	1,687	183	3,309
Grant	304	8,805	6	88		

MICHIGAN—Continued.

Counties.	INDIAN CORN.		OATS.		[WHEAT.	
	Acres.	Bushels.	Acres.	Bushels.	Acres.	Bushels.
Manistee	1, 330	28, 346	947	21, 509	1, 878	23, 472
Manitou	81	1, 976	220	4, 118	497	7, 487
Marquette			427	13, 604	18	367
Mason	1, 103	42, 259	936	21, 548	3, 092	35, 767
Mecosta	3, 839	84, 289	3, 201	56, 219	9, 537	134, 423
Menominee	82	1, 802	364	9, 636	95	1, 939
Midland	1, 564	42, 603	1, 349	38, 101	2, 882	50, 810
Missauker	363	9, 075	872	18, 668	759	10, 930
Monroe	32, 118	1, 114, 570	19, 629	745, 143	31, 390	658, 561
Montcalm	9, 985	278, 567	6, 171	155, 191	25, 471	518, 413
Montmorency						
Muskegon	4, 082	141, 871	2, 448	65, 026	6, 905	117, 089
Newaygo	5, 934	163, 506	2, 848	66, 776	9, 229	136, 288
Oakland	39, 547	1, 311, 190	26, 397	909, 048	78, 255	1, 254, 583
Oceana	4, 682	129, 718	1, 877	46, 346	9, 630	131, 779
Ogemaw	125	4, 622	197	6, 045	343	5, 555
Ontonagon	7	393	461	14, 817	43	847
Osceola	1, 838	62, 869	1, 811	41, 666	5, 413	79. 463
Oscoda						
Otsego	108	6, 002	93	2, 440	319	4, 083
Ottawa	18, 830	610, 442	10, 030	317, 935	31, 054	657, 750
Presque Isle	272	11, 889	1, 054	25, 424	785	13, 492
Roscommon	9	100	64	1, 512		
Saginaw	11, 859	376, 295	14, 246	461, 296	26, 808	537, 826
Saint Clair	11, 168	360, 092	27, 637	903, 611	37, 886	622, 934
Saint Joseph	35, 275	1, 358, 318	9, 858	310, 042	66, 669	1, 263, 661
Sanilac	2, 650	79, 007	12, 201	344, 121	34, 692	541, 612
Schoolcraft	6	184	130	4, 995	6	93
Shiawassee	18, 004	602, 974	12, 852	456, 860	51, 118	1, 071, 090
Tuscola	10, 759	431, 473	9, 445	299, 411	32, 893	638, 860
Van Buren	37, 755	1, 402, 368	10, 767	324, 319	44, 085	721, 327
Washtenaw	33, 220	1, 187, 756	18, 201	754, 484	72, 084	1, 004, 857
Wayne	32, 001	1, 198, 684	24, 659	937, 092	23, 233	465, 476
Wexford	1, 052	33, 025	1, 116	25, 547	1, 904	25, 152

MINNESOTA.

	INDIAN CORN.		OATS.		WHEAT.	
The State	438, 737	14, 831. 741	617, 469	23, 382, 158	3, 044, 670	34, 601, 030
Aitkin	17	515	13	490		
Anoka	4, 496	121, 995	1, 862	54, 876	7, 754	94, 058
Becker	228	9, 353	3, 158	122, 377	16, 004	212, 629
Beltrami						
Benton	1, 081	29, 573	1, 571	52, 214	5, 161	74, 739
Big Stone	746	13, 203	1, 995	77, 882	9, 346	110, 659
Blue Earth	21, 636	689, 835	21, 766	699, 426	96, 410	858, 647
Brown	9, 874	335, 055	12, 004	453, 274	54, 766	424, 051
Carlton	50	2, 281	152	5, 395	60	1, 157
Carver	7, 405	298, 772	6, 498	291, 460	33, 730	595, 058
Cass					7	60
Chippewa	2, 080	65, 853	5, 874	240, 275	30, 245	354, 421
Chisago	1, 738	45, 435	2, 980	109, 112	9, 912	153, 709
Clay	70	1, 784	4, 932	191, 154	24, 341	370, 239
Cook						
Cottonwood	4, 181	103, 297	5, 857	205, 155	30, 860	127, 228
Crow Wing	145	5, 002	208	5, 899	148	2, 103
Dakota	14, 673	467, 135	19, 735	731, 897	123, 958	1, 323, 975
Dodge	8, 105	294, 624	17, 114	666, 081	90, 400	884, 839
Douglas	1, 278	50, 991	6, 748	277, 996	27, 602	459, 877
Faribault	21, 277	733, 330	19, 012	664, 894	61, 366	645, 618
Fillmore	27, 724	970, 818	36, 681	1, 370, 309	165, 904	1, 626, 367
Freeborn	14, 537	532, 514	20, 443	747, 030	103, 783	1, 143, 839
Goodhue	16, 846	586, 798	29, 794	1, 275, 772	199, 142	2, 415, 891
Grant	155	5, 847	3, 047	137, 952	15, 857	226, 467

MINNESOTA—Continued.

Counties.	BARLEY.		BUCKWHEAT.		RYE.	
	Acres.	Bushels.	Acres.	Bushels.	Acres.	Bushels.
Hennepin	317	9,168	51	623	402	6.603
Houston	2,556	60,141	83	1,198	658	9,733
Isanti	35	823	33	314	716	10,325
Itaska						
Jackson	1,479	22,150	43	387	141	1,945
Kanabec	15	319				
Kandiyohi	703	18,068			71	1,217
Kittson	10	240				
Lac-qui-parle	470	11,735	70	907	14	274
Lake						
Le Sueur	452	11,910	9	122	146	3,234
Lincoln	279	6,925	14	100		
Lyon	1,346	50,569	41	374	16	224
McLeod	772	21,322	30	206	131	3,410
Marshall	5	56				
Martin	1,455	28,689	230	2,027	65	947
Meeker	886	24,968			131	2,632
Mille Lacs	42	850	18	195	172	1,850
Morrison	243	8,464	24	253	461	4,903
Mower	9,382	257,342	196	1,500	185	2,471
Murray	1,049	20,539	31	250	18	214
Nicollet	1,754	50,624	20	607	219	5,822
Nobles	1,116	12,762	63	575	186	1,501
Olmstead	12,603	344,962	191	3,404	35	496
Otter Tail	946	23,568	82	1,168	581	10,560
Pine						
Pipe Stone	116	2,660	22	203	55	603
Polk	582	15,544	56	741	63	1,424
Pope	423	11,670	29	415	100	2,318
Ramsey	203	4,505	19	161	89	1,490
Redwood	1,559	29,337	54	489	222	1,333
Renville	1,353	33,541	73	800	50	628
Rice	890	22,789	102	1,316	65	1,240
Rock	1,762	28,804	12	30	662	8,309
Saint Louis	115	2,287			190	4,069
Scott	360	9,846	23	347	332	5,484
Sherburne	43	1,102	89	1,162	1,283	15,829
Sibley	1,599	47,743	38	361	103	3,361
Stearns	1,518	39,259	93	1,156	892	15,987
Steele	869	21,585	37	518	31	763
Stevens	693	21,135				
Swift	885	19,177	8	147	88	1,738
Todd	132	3,170	72	888	743	12,464
Traverse	74	2,045				
Wabashaw	10,343	282,962	69	1,184	162	3,520
Wadena	52	1,699	22	320	56	1,296
Waseca	912	20,106	32	347	15	307
Washington	2,506	67,693	8	77	136	2,454
Watonwan	819	13,927	20	62	54	788
Wilkin	110	3,006			15	191
Winona	6,368	168,662	280	2,619	171	2,626
Wright	470	14,434	20	299	252	4,448
Yellow Medicine	378	9,375	5	70	16	117

MISSISSIPPI.

MINNESOTA—Continued.

Counties.	INDIAN CORN.		OATS.		WHEAT.	
	Acres.	Bushels.	Acres.	Bushels.	Acres.	Bushels.
Hennepin	16,488	594,159	10,594	414,664	49,020	671,015
Houston	22,692	822,763	14,699	514,076	62,161	654,336
Isanti	2,078	58,877	1,919	64,604	9,505	140,546
Itaska						
Jackson	4,040	105,279	6,069	202,634	15,952	81,680
Kanabec	30	896	49	1,585	193	2,445
Kandiyohi	2,313	91,671	10,390	426,642	60,326	800,753
Kittson			65	1,870	146	2,110
Lac-qui-parle	2,233	57,445	3,765	165,205	22,937	274,085
Lake			21	558		
Le Sueur	15,035	595,588	6,535	267,553	37,430	580,793
Lincoln	1,055	10,199	1,998	78,589	9,047	94,880
Lyon	4,091	103,464	7,706	278,914	35,785	323,044
McLeod	5,802	209,739	9,201	401,934	40,592	537,447
Marshall	17	540	108	2,638	173	3,594
Martin	10,181	312,235	9,643	332,225	13,161	100,924
Meeker	4,459	166,625	10,132	398,071	55,008	665,269
Mille Lacs	658	23,663	563	18,571	1,192	16,440
Morrison	1,318	37,350	3,298	157,546	11,992	199,931
Mower	13,145	423,113	27,443	1,044,943	138,023	1,370,160
Murray	2,439	56,867	3,317	111,417	12,587	77,970
Nicollet	8,628	325,918	14,899	491,304	59,094	704,290
Nobles	5,894	160,334	6,978	141,862	22,353	60,698
Olmstead	15,449	568,150	28,377	1,093,924	152,204	1,656,286
Otter Tail	2,234	62,568	12,030	437,748	56,189	860,905
Pine	28	1,150	86	2,824	122	1,554
Pipe Stone	928	16,914	1,711	52,192	5,673	37,547
Polk	117	3,627	6,678	226,221	30,061	529,692
Pope	1,009	36,785	6,815	288,337	32,233	381,977
Ramsey	1,675	58,360	2,258	80,204	8,460	122,466
Redwood	4,660	122,527	6,614	212,647	34,014	207,535
Renville	6,532	233,371	12,212	503,299	57,784	605,404
Rice	11,524	405,990	12,726	507,522	74,873	907,514
Rock	5,551	173,158	7,974	246,994	36,018	118,378
Saint Louis			349	11,856	209	3,878
Scott	8,593	303,475	6,014	266,166	40,863	697,261
Sherburne	5,365	143,408	1,618	49,380	8,527	115,388
Sibley	7,226	247,617	10,541	459,239	46,393	598,956
Stearns	8,883	274,770	19,559	728,996	79,193	1,135,704
Steele	9,461	329,460	13,044	512,287	76,772	846,219
Stevens	338	11,632	7,682	304,007	31,517	417,076
Swift	1,809	46,768	8,037	304,302	44,396	492,763
Todd	1,191	38,025	3,396	113,854	13,433	190,074
Traverse	404	6,730	1,016	38,446	3,448	45,668
Wabashaw	13,949	488,236	18,194	744,653	118,435	1,461,674
Wadena	232	6,685	480	17,924	2,976	47,634
Waseca	9,183	292,790	11,151	405,653	68,827	693,861
Washington	7,388	255,110	8,928	343,392	52,208	657,569
Watonwan	5,595	131,999	6,327	191,548	23,854	121,613
Wilkin	52	1,707	1,109	39,147	5,141	72,500
Winona	15,289	546,767	19,947	795,624	113,962	1,216,872
Wright	10,871	371,235	7,436	292,303	38,792	603,240
Yellow Medicine	2,293	62,986	4,262	193,124	24,504	285,672

MISSISSIPPI.

The State	1,570,550	21,340,800	198,497	1,959,620	43,524	218,800
Adams	9,037	128,647	57	909		
Alcorn	22,589	381,385	3,358	31,939	1,078	5,070
Amite	22,589	262,352	3,184	27,160		
Attala	33,784	413,532	6,888	66,106	1,400	6,031
Benton	22,877	330,688	1,735	16,846	1,285	6,073

MISSISSIPPI—Continued.

Counties.	BARLEY.		BUCKWHEAT.		RYE.	
	Acres.	Bushels.	Acres.	Bushels.	Acres.	Bushels.
Bolivar						
Calhoun					19	100
Carroll						
Chickasaw	9	44			14	86
Choctaw					9	37
Claiborne						
Clarke					6	53
Clay					7	7
Coahoma						
Copiah						
Covington						
De Soto					5	71
Franklin						
Greene						
Grenada					10	50
Hancock						
Harrison						
Hinds						
Holmes						
Issaquena						
Itawamba					28	181
Jackson						
Jasper					12	71
Jefferson						
Jones						
Kemper					11	65
La Fayette					13	79
Lauderdale					32	209
Lawrence					37	442
Leake					25	157
Lee	5	10			41	400
Le Flore						
Lincoln						
Lowndes					57	409
Madison						
Marion						
Marshall					59	182
Monroe	8	64			100	744
Montgomery					13	89
Neshoba					10	44
Newton					17	82
Noxubee					16	129
Oktibbeha						
Panola					27	268
Perry						
Pike						
Pontotoc					17	83
Prentiss					25	102
Quitman						
Rankin						
Scott						
Sharkey						
Simpson						
Smith	7	53			7	41
Sumner	15	177				
Sun Flower						
Tallahatchee						
Tate					25	50
Tippah					9	77
Tishomingo					14	94
Tunica						
Union					9	68
Warren						
Washington						
Wayne					9	39

Counties.	INDIAN CORN.		OATS.		WHEAT.	
	Acres.	Bushels.	Acres.	Bushels.	Acres.	Bushels.
Bolivar	16,624	383,466	187	3,254		
Calhoun	22,414	353,919	4,464	44,009	908	4,753
Carroll	30,019	315,722	1,877	22,154	337	1,973
Chickasaw	34,258	512,005	3,735	49,627	1,415	9,033
Choctaw	18,139	243,287	3,931	38,709	2,215	9,413
Claiborne	15,744	197,568	82	1,290		
Clarke	17,338	174,712	3,193	30,101		
Clay	26,295	400,397	3,117	35,592	431	2,137
Coahoma	14,297	338,054	138	2,340	76	832
Copiah	38,292	447,197	5,320	59,021		
Covington	10,682	115,088	3,553	32,215		
De Soto	37,452	581,272	1,688	18,008	1,236	7,283
Franklin	12,045	145,581	1,012	9,021		
Greene	3,563	27,271	891	5,790		
Grenada	15,906	163,580	568	6,223	6	63
Hancock	41	410	29	5,300		
Harrison	1,064	15,130	142	2,110		
Hinds	47,510	532,636	1,962	26,380	16	130
Holmes	37,355	463,614	1,237	17,441	59	483
Issaquena	3,849	89,630	17	260		
Itawamba	22,055	304,652	3,134	21,772	1,918	8,580
Jackson	138	1,826	5	80		
Jasper	19,934	202,643	5,467	56,380	5	100
Jefferson	16,365	251,586	312	3,195		
Jones	5,664	47,269	3,481	30,992		
Kemper	23,246	347,258	3,706	37,599	56	255
La Fayette	35,809	492,614	4,091	36,375	2,052	9,222
Lauderdale	23,345	254,798	5,967	57,843	5	50
Lawrence	20,758	217,041	4,845	41,809	6	25
Leake	21,390	256,331	4,749	44,070	204	1,527
Lee	36,073	590,899	4,676	48,047	1,400	7,387
Le Flore	10,965	144,273	76	1,231		
Lincoln	19,843	209,747	5,704	49,924		
Lowndes	42,855	582,736	3,784	41,230	1,618	8,009
Madison	37,989	381,297	1,490	21,107	22	221
Marion	9,087	99,941	1,348	12,202		
Marshall	50,140	686,062	3,130	26,646	3,094	14,605
Monroe	53,431	700,957	7,278	76,270	4,114	18,296
Montgomery	17,768	200,650	3,178	31,275	148	630
Neshoba	16,752	207,784	3,512	26,810	223	1,215
Newton	20,638	261,207	6,716	58,336	127	653
Noxubee	50,904	741,542	5,429	74,165	39	158
Oktibbeha	25,251	395,553	3,288	39,063	1,088	6,078
Panola	43,091	521,193	2,119	22,016	1,603	9,351
Perry	4,466	38,446	2,615	20,208		
Pike	19,218	206,810	6,003	55,909	8	60
Pontotoc	26,586	414,335	2,169	18,826	2,751	14,692
Prentiss	23,018	368,777	3,806	35,534	993	4,798
Quitman	1,477	34,510	24	660		
Rankin	23,450	271,996	5,781	59,450	4	45
Scott	15,664	193,013	5,129	50,370	111	729
Sharkey	7,540	169,130	35	350		
Simpson	14,165	147,672	4,211	34,817	5	40
Smith	14,614	156,952	5,009	46,959	78	478
Sumner	18,900	287,362	3,269	29,544	1,874	8,379
Sun Flower	3,730	61,393	80	1,515		
Tallahatchee	16,169	205,719	772	9,288	108	670
Tate	33,321	467,144	1,763	17,028	1,100	6,495
Tippah	23,388	385,623	3,814	36,435	3,587	17,941
Tishomingo	15,965	280,054	3,237	25,282	702	3,094
Tunica	9,447	198,252	137	2,820		
Union	25,834	429,040	2,695	26,413	2,426	13,255
Warren	10,371	188,567	69	1,945		
Washington	16,515	400,418	65	830		
Wayne	10,411	93,890	1,408	12,044	7	42

MISSISSIPPI—Continued.

Counties.	BARLEY.		BUCKWHEAT.		RYE.	
	Acres.	Bushels.	Acres.	Bushels.	Acres.	Bushels.
Wilkinson						
Winston					5	24
Yalabusha					33	308
Yazoo					7	70

MISSOURI.

Counties.	BARLEY.		BUCKWHEAT.		RYE.	
	Acres.	Bushels.	Acres.	Bushels.	Acres.	Bushels.
The State	6,472	123,031	3,463	57,640	46,484	535,426
Adair			262	3,661	559	6,355
Andrew	6	106	20	184	550	8,487
Atchison	3,295	62,589	16	261	1,477	22,082
Audrain			90	497	483	5,171
Barry			54	425	243	2,447
Barton	9	115	19	160	62	736
Bates			45	427	195	2,209
Benton			21	71	57	391
Bollinger	84	1,515	9	97	48	272
Boone			10	43	951	12,431
Buchanan	22	513	5	65	259	3,311
Butler					26	105
Caldwell	5	100	195	1,673	251	2,253
Callaway			13	61	551	4,738
Camden			10	48	37	364
Cape Girardeau	209	4,552	9	97	86	1,133
Carroll			67	828	1,150	12,926
Carter						
Cass			24	203	63	725
Cedar			42	295	138	1,024
Chariton	19	435	140	1,518	1,054	11,814
Christian					34	317
Clark	66	1,202	202	1,728	2,814	32,232
Clay					551	7,688
Clinton			13	130	190	2,109
Cole	18	232	10	130	226	2,379
Cooper	6	50	20	313	316	4,225
Crawford			24	281	121	973
Dade			62	465	211	1,905
Dallas			15	142	114	877
Daviess	5	60	62	526	934	10,292
De Kalb	19	319	47	403	602	6,638
Dent			11	195	105	829
Douglas			21	145	47	437
Dunklin	10	400			59	537
Franklin	50	1,232	8	76	83	1,012
Gasconade	64	1,642	7	55	51	387
Gentry			12	117	448	4,137
Greene			15	103	107	1,521
Grundy			35	271	835	11,434
Harrison	10	100	77	719	2,780	39,154
Henry	15	80	19	130	106	1,171
Hickory					70	604
Holt	639	8,888			1,301	19,260
Howard			69	1,039	917	12,016
Howell			5	88	120	936
Iron			7	80	49	289
Jackson	13	150	6	38	227	4,159
Jasper	9	51	35	629	170	1,728
Jefferson	58	1,035			35	221
Johnson	15	538	21	156	409	5,184
Knox			572	7,033	527	5,619
Laclede	7	25	50	419	58	560
La Fayette	94	1,240	7	93	217	2,781
Lawrence	6	84	31	202	98	876

MISSISSIPPI—Continued.

Counties.	INDIAN CORN.		OATS.		WHEAT.	
	Acres.	Bushels.	Acres.	Bushels.	Acres.	Bushels.
Wilkinson	15,068	206,985	204	3,035		
Winston	17,131	217,786	4,170	37,075	902	4,560
Yalabusha	23,609	275,309	1,728	17,479	594	2,981
Yazoo	38,207	524,615	454	5,824		

MISSOURI.

	Acres.	Bushels.	Acres.	Bushels.	Acres.	Bushels.
The State	5,588,265	202,414,413	968,473	20,670,958	2,074,304	24,966,627
Adair	51,890	1,881,493	10,266	291,147	2,763	37,105
Andrew	64,779	2,723,745	9,888	254,728	29,603	291,717
Atchison	113,589	4,977,476	5,792	176,833	25,855	329,810
Audrain	106,165	3,961,290	15,827	352,031	5,470	76,314
Barry	30,803	819,580	5,773	80,807	19,432	172,693
Barton	41,677	1,189,672	8,195	157,910	13,174	143,648
Bates	130,783	5,441,503	14,086	326,431	23,824	277,703
Benton	47,303	1,505,440	7,335	102,631	13,007	120,733
Bollinger	23,304	577,095	7,098	75,059	17,862	135,335
Boone	75,931	2,537,859	15,832	291,453	27,903	337,021
Buchanan	60,603	2,289,204	7,742	188,642	38,828	443,178
Butler	11,825	281,770	1,695	23,283	1,604	10,925
Caldwell	77,317	3,147,148	8,397	182,688	5,339	38,417
Callaway	67,503	2,219,588	20,994	438,992	21,232	234,296
Camden	16,487	448,411	1,961	27,151	7,972	69,171
Cape Girardeau	32,084	964,998	8,967	124,523	45,736	535,893
Carroll	121,749	5,290,581	17,680	455,826	25,960	309,628
Carter	4,245	100,836	515	4,202	874	6,546
Cass	110,046	4,581,775	12,076	273,424	37,910	519,526
Cedar	35,314	1,105,775	8,467	157,196	10,337	96,031
Chariton	86,812	3,565,473	12,832	298,011	17,303	229,061
Christian	20,067	635,549	3,574	75,223	14,804	145,513
Clark	61,536	2,168,222	16,697	484,078	6,932	97,253
Clay	52,359	2,204,376	5,058	104,311	22,443	257,887
Clinton	76,788	3,455,610	10,323	299,186	10,859	121,598
Cole	21,324	586,157	6,092	110,296	24,744	288,193
Cooper	63,988	2,389,965	12,479	253,289	40,374	516,138
Crawford	19,120	466,616	4,477	60,359	12,762	121,496
Dade	44,806	1,373,896	9,025	178,978	11,055	110,157
Dallas	25,892	726,040	7,235	116,914	10,368	82,696
Daviess	78,335	3,079,861	12,657	319,199	17,268	161,874
De Kalb	71,848	3,113,160	9,570	257,003	11,128	167,034
Dent	16,489	447,749	4,676	62,149	11,185	99,319
Douglas	15,130	385,358	2,910	53,547	5,783	41,236
Dunklin	20,121	603,909	1,066	19,869	2,905	24,160
Franklin	42,285	1,342,997	14,111	262,375	58,685	796,726
Gasconade	17,903	530,732	7,594	171,163	27,625	343,224
Gentry	68,557	2,677,047	9,753	256,398	10,357	103,466
Greene	59,055	1,619,253	12,135	191,664	48,199	553,670
Grundy	53,677	1,941,023	10,375	302,856	10,329	138,440
Harrison	92,383	3,513,186	16,714	506,126	12,055	147,273
Henry	131,368	5,002,216	13,730	279,911	17,982	191,457
Hickory	21,389	594,278	4,578	52,193	7,495	68,944
Holt	75,614	3,308,326	6,085	174,108	23,955	297,907
Howard	46,960	1,770,520	8,242	164,155	27,945	308,934
Howell	21,486	576,332	3,846	48,220	5,441	37,667
Iron	9,695	224,761	2,200	22,156	5,526	49,521
Jackson	85,745	3,760,259	7,311	178,435	34,115	449,335
Jasper	74,023	1,942,296	11,088	160,691	39,840	501,557
Jefferson	27,711	827,969	3,494	57,974	33,174	423,788
Johnson	127,861	5,350,265	15,420	352,603	56,614	791,674
Knox	68,261	2,643,890	12,784	357,336	3,556	49,258
Laclede	22,793	736,111	5,225	98,800	15,132	128,152
La Fayette	84,356	3,812,887	9,805	244,092	71,450	857,668
Lawrence	45,628	1,361,545	8,992	140,106	28,208	305,173

MISSOURI—Continued.

Counties.	BARLEY.		BUCKWHEAT.		RYE.	
	Acres.	Bushels.	Acres.	Bushels.	Acres.	Bushels.
Lewis	10	30	94	836	748	6,442
Lincoln					264	2,749
Linn			181	2,046	1,023	11,809
Livingston			88	872	721	8,461
McDonald			18	176	73	488
Macon			336	3,348	1,336	13,792
Madison	44	992			123	885
Maries					69	549
Marion			36	328	768	8,977
Mercer			39	443	2,016	20,680
Miller	10	58	10	78	126	905
Mississippi					8	114
Moniteau	23	93	10	36	127	908
Monroe			106	908	1,185	12,160
Montgomery	9	65	83	363	309	3,361
Morgan			16	135	58	302
New Madrid					39	345
Newton	21	83	52	379	95	963
Nodaway	467	7,162	58	306	1,964	25,657
Oregon					19	185
Osage	12	108	8	117	45	533
Ozark					55	434
Pemiscot	12	200			30	150
Perry	337	8,133	7	65	16	154
Pettis			5	40	521	5,902
Phelps			58	553	136	1,332
Pike			30	238	217	2,557
Platte	8	40	20	750	303	4,544
Polk			28	353	89	1,218
Pulaski			0	87	67	651
Putnam			145	1,234	1,771	17,659
Ralls	10	120	25	291	458	4,504
Randolph			85	833	1,271	12,055
Ray			6	40	574	6,883
Reynolds					70	616
Ripley			9	73	23	188
Saint Charles	199	5,010			124	2,084
Saint Clair			17	210	94	957
Saint Francois	64	1,500	6	53	81	776
Saint Genevieve	149	3,887			45	332
Saint Louis City					7	210
Saint Louis	154	2,678	16	166	519	6,643
Saline			7	86	438	7,716
Schuyler			179	1,083	1,136	10,674
Scotland			549	5,999	1,348	15,366
Scott	68	2,582			17	162
Shannon			9	76	70	614
Shelby	6	130	403	4,052	456	4,174
Stoddard	5	24			36	311
Stone					33	258
Sullivan			70	906	1,013	11,748
Taney					17	164
Texas			21	104	172	1,392
Vernon			27	146	74	986
Warren	68	1,362	8	105	78	760
Washington	25	423			70	378
Wayne					20	108
Webster			43	764	75	452
Worth	18	138	14	112	401	4,088
Wright			16	227	262	3,928

MISSOURI—Continued.

Counties.	INDIAN CORN.		OATS.		WHEAT.	
	Acres.	Bushels.	Acres.	Bushels.	Acres.	Bushels.
Lewis	56,340	1,857,423	13,546	293,501	10,696	143,126
Lincoln	54,454	1,563,356	16,764	319,008	37,413	424,119
Linn	72,901	3,006,850	13,747	340,206	6,650	96,776
Livingston	64,511	2,558,490	10,721	267,201	18,079	206,330
McDonald	17,856	467,554	3,761	46,176	9,135	95,309
Macon	87,471	3,222,855	13,025	272,902	5,108	64,270
Madison	15,555	388,931	4,219	54,004	9,153	73,691
Maries	18,331	502,687	6,525	113,374	11,222	106,132
Marion	45,299	1,779,972	7,557	123,190	22,253	353,617
Mercer	54,676	1,761,648	13,211	380,329	6,885	82,653
Miller	23,612	747,412	4,579	97,014	14,589	150,092
Mississippi	42,298	1,509,055	1,130	24,420	8,276	110,448
Moniteau	45,065	1,355,512	11,186	182,098	22,140	222,339
Monroe	87,840	3,379,539	13,586	217,664	10,716	132,705
Montgomery	60,107	1,927,103	23,397	551,506	15,507	193,085
Morgan	39,651	1,215,783	8,542	126,358	9,019	79,231
New Madrid	37,463	1,116,696	601	11,345	4,326	49,273
Newton	40,613	966,619	10,742	132,379	21,947	231,434
Nodaway	159,598	6,961,556	18,029	562,077	33,290	374,085
Oregon	12,749	338,339	1,118	13,027	2,053	16,295
Osage	23,211	598,479	5,930	94,530	27,350	336,879
Ozark	10,445	236,572	1,547	19,919	2,133	13,008
Pemiscot	11,936	406,999	80	1,613	208	3,020
Perry	18,428	519,143	5,081	65,375	36,148	472,435
Pettis	102,215	3,847,619	19,537	412,044	22,977	268,748
Phelps	20,009	571,103	6,577	102,043	15,795	144,442
Pike	68,389	2,564,430	16,841	409,219	45,260	669,523
Platte	53,211	2,038,870	5,478	128,410	45,604	600,654
Polk	49,740	1,482,281	13,089	244,237	18,348	148,840
Pulaski	15,535	478,652	2,632	39,920	7,500	37,573
Putnam	48,551	1,695,441	13,801	423,011	3,188	32,885
Ralls	53,035	2,140,276	9,723	168,601	22,394	355,056
Randolph	53,555	1,861,667	9,805	167,625	6,116	70,724
Ray	80,209	3,490,332	9,729	224,116	17,651	181,646
Reynolds	13,390	347,295	2,217	23,980	4,310	33,033
Ripley	13,140	317,140	1,709	14,984	1,745	12,196
Saint Charles	47,291	1,614,960	11,483	249,554	61,099	1,124,518
Saint Clair	50,202	1,614,817	5,305	77,132	13,207	121,961
Saint Francois	19,889	506,627	5,739	86,342	16,116	163,350
Saint Genevieve	15,610	429,529	3,850	52,432	27,019	337,592
Saint Louis City	1,930	64,627	512	15,815	469	11,295
Saint Louis	47,062	1,893,425	8,037	177,773	47,883	908,838
Saline	101,800	4,836,829	13,107	344,695	60,152	858,105
Schuyler	33,063	1,087,370	8,332	230,508	3,098	38,058
Scotland	58,367	1,788,675	15,977	481,066	5,718	60,725
Scott	24,453	721,376	1,119	19,639	16,227	200,376
Shannon	7,288	168,842	945	11,099	1,732	13,107
Shelby	63,883	2,603,962	8,909	157,016	4,782	61,045
Stoddard	28,815	917,694	3,135	48,724	11,875	97,811
Stone	9,043	254,663	976	14,492	3,737	38,264
Sullivan	59,733	2,064,933	12,024	330,203	3,705	50,933
Taney	11,627	294,602	1,729	29,678	3,196	19,943
Texas	22,491	640,352	5,962	88,812	10,970	84,661
Vernon	83,201	2,732,906	11,568	168,446	22,265	240,370
Warren	28,081	819,500	13,171	270,085	23,465	306,925
Washington	20,320	498,739	4,600	55,200	12,620	118,894
Wayne	20,291	524,126	4,614	50,293	6,619	52,562
Webster	22,518	555,657	6,062	89,218	15,665	120,064
Worth	34,230	1,199,160	5,969	159,796	6,199	60,783
Wright	20,044	554,094	4,707	93,192	8,952	68,296

MONTANA.

Counties.	BARLEY. Acres.	BARLEY. Bushels.	BUCKWHEAT. Acres.	BUCKWHEAT. Bushels.	RYE. Acres.	RYE. Bushels.
The Territory	1, 323	39, 970	34	437	15	430
Beaver Head	34	1, 204				
Choteau	5	244				
Custer						
Dawson						
Deer Lodge	224	5, 844			5	230
Gallatin	245	8, 586	14	230		
Jefferson	219	5, 696				
Lewis and Clarke	157	5, 958	8	107		
Madison	126	3, 997			10	200
Meagher	241	6, 166	5	40		
Missoula	72	2, 275	7	60		

NEBRASKA.

Counties.	BARLEY. Acres.	BARLEY. Bushels.	BUCKWHEAT. Acres.	BUCKWHEAT. Bushels.	RYE. Acres.	RYE. Bushels.
The State	115, 201	1, 744, 686	1, 666	17, 562	34, 297	424, 348
Adams	3, 778	75, 132	14	152	352	4, 383
Antelope	419	6, 878	19	143	316	4, 132
Boone	625	10, 835			565	8, 876
Buffalo	1, 048	22, 878	11	66	489	6, 706
Burt	210	2, 968	22	207	349	6, 314
Butler	1, 762	32, 579	27	380	491	5, 011
Case	7, 810	108, 631	85	768	1, 216	17, 759
Cedar	656	8, 605	42	297	10	61
Chase						
Cheyenne						
Clay	11, 704	244, 992	82	513	912	13, 625
Colfax	873	4, 305	51	681	830	4, 936
Cuming	628	7, 494			1, 161	14, 018
Custer	89	1, 464			19	373
Dakota	81	1, 357			10	137
Dawson	1, 173	14, 157	6	32	154	1, 882
Dixon	502	3, 197	17	162	200	1, 094
Dodge	1, 731	24, 143	29	395	1, 253	16, 678
Douglas	1, 662	29, 809	61	687	572	9, 690
Dundy						
Fillmore	8, 627	153, 632	76	1, 079	1, 362	17, 478
Franklin	322	4, 755	19	180	325	3, 639
Frontier	36	333			33	274
Furnas	794	10, 323	21	780	950	11, 077
Gage	1, 335	9, 766	73	572	982	9, 253
Gosper	171	1, 234			232	1, 435
Greeley	157	2, 587			114	1, 843
Hall	1, 618	28, 912	16	248	1, 294	17, 151
Hamilton	5, 153	71, 020	19	178	981	11, 182
Harlan	1, 045	11, 149	12	102	995	9, 422
Hayes						
Hitchcock						
Holt	295	3, 836	13	134	184	2, 270
Howard	761	13, 555			325	4, 809
Jefferson	3, 094	28, 903	39	335	858	9, 622
Johnson	2, 103	21, 095	23	274	507	6, 622
Kearney	668	14, 547			452	5, 572
Keith						
Knox	368	5, 620			88	1, 283
Lancaster	2, 886	38, 776	76	1, 023	921	10, 855
Lincoln					10	200
Madison	376	5, 903			768	7, 609
Merrick	907	17, 018	38	298	1, 114	14, 230
Nance					22	130
Nemaha	2, 530	35, 412	50	525	756	11, 245

MONTANA.

Counties.	INDIAN CORN.		OATS,		WHEAT.	
	Acres.	Bushels.	Acres.	Bushels.	Acres.	Bushels.
The Territory	197	5,649	24,691	900,915	17,665	469,688
Beaver Head			291	8,746	231	5,851
Choteau			1,298	38,541	137	2,401
Custer	26	440	826	16,330	11	354
Dawson						
Deer Lodge			4,622	147,874	497	14,193
Gallatin			4,730	222,888	5,301	151,513
Jefferson	5	135	675	26,988	577	15,437
Lewis and Clarke	45	1,210	1,480	53,803	1,184	30,531
Madison			3,556	116,460	3,376	81,551
Meagher	10	120	3,910	137,523	3,017	79,502
Missoula	111	3,744	3,294	131,762	3,334	88,355

NEBRASKA.

The State	1,630,660	65,450,135	250,457	6,555,875	1,469,865	13,847,007
Adams	29,397	900,866	5,023	137,771	64,074	685,084
Antelope	7,081	228,360	1,625	50,716	6,354	54,581
Boone	7,385	248,715	2,598	81,242	14,670	163,873
Buffalo	15,578	369,907	2,481	62,968	29,040	257,914
Burt	36,759	1,655,484	4,929	175,356	16,961	209,362
Butler	38,250	1,640,046	7,097	195,959	51,461	529,921
Cass	97,901	4,312,032	8,907	228,877	39,443	394,701
Cedar	6,524	217,161	3,212	59,722	7,183	20,217
Chase						
Cheyenne						
Clay	40,226	1,533,821	7,050	204,235	86,411	892,035
Colfax	24,224	816,977	5,718	76,153	28,944	118,173
Cuming	24,409	880,413	6,532	143,149	25,143	214,991
Custer	1,370	34,315	207	5,116	1,006	10,780
Dakota	11,820	496,465	1,350	35,964	9,019	83,468
Dawson	4,572	143,361	1,119	24,841	3,827	37,269
Dixon	9,456	320,608	2,451	30,706	9,583	34,317
Dodge	53,095	2,374,942	10,262	311,410	45,584	518,434
Douglas	37,533	1,696,825	6,972	213,485	9,006	108,730
Dundy						
Fillmore	47,537	1,893,944	7,018	206,575	75,025	785,809
Franklin	17,913	511,347	1,481	30,766	15,780	136,272
Frontier	419	5,165	8	110	94	355
Furnas	8,994	236,495	882	18,634	7,047	64,619
Gage	53,711	1,990,835	7,571	170,964	34,902	230,861
Gosper	2,364	32,325	270	3,370	2,431	9,157
Greeley	2,716	70,830	737	19,308	3,664	39,405
Hall	19,408	644,864	6,019	156,904	41,609	413,498
Hamilton	28,296	1,041,003	5,812	119,197	64,994	601,287
Harlan	15,507	392,649	985	16,027	16,284	120,594
Hayes	29	545				
Hitchcock	145	2,150				
Holt	5,554	88,121	1,119	25,262	2,796	18,318
Howard	8,590	300,860	3,433	93,076	19,023	217,838
Jefferson	24,692	853,210	3,681	81,898	28,711	239,403
Johnson	48,354	2,166,868	5,466	123,151	18,814	147,461
Kearney	14,032	342,760	2,032	55,631	21,078	225,382
Keith						
Knox	4,431	106,496	1,403	40,805	5,195	38,580
Lancaster	92,350	4,128,866	12,482	349,155	55,191	487,463
Lincoln	53	1,195	52	850	19	75
Madison	18,309	646,105	5,514	158,540	14,768	111,332
Merrick	16,632	583,731	5,179	129,225	21,758	176,547
Nance	1,223	30,600	197	3,570	1,045	9,807
Nemaha	66,962	2,942,770	4,259	118,606	25,694	273,708

NFBRASKA—Continued.

Counties.	BARLEY.		BUCKWHEAT.		RYE.	
	Acres.	Bushels.	Acres.	Bushels.	Acres.	Bushels.
Nuckolls	950	17,066	10	126	198	3,259
Otoe	8,311	113,980	28	238	1,172	14,000
Pawnee	510	3,873	47	413	521	6,403
Phelps	271	5,054	....	....	124	1,045
Pierce	64	587	....	....	231	1,279
Platte	702	10,518	84	848	675	7,031
Polk	1,173	18,519	11	92	755	9,924
Red Willow	16	298	....	....	231	2,321
Richardson	3,428	50,737	101	944	1,370	23,377
Saline	9,304	118,016	46	414	1,071	12,048
Sarpy	1,241	21,796	27	252	212	3,124
Saunders	2,524	36,703	72	713	890	11,711
Seward	4,589	64,788	94	1,190	513	6,046
Sherman	237	4,383	....	....	201	2,277
Sioux	....	....	....	....	....	....
Stanton	530	1,680	26	48	300	742
Thayer	4,399	71,731	10	128	724	10,147
Unorganized territory	44	643	....	....	....	....
Valley	367	6,220	....	....	26	386
Washington	807	13,682	114	1,294	1,129	19,754
Wayne	46	423	....	....	127	1,246
Webster	1,461	13,960	24	276	234	2,009
Wheeler	39	1,170	....	....	36	588
York	6,171	90,159	31	366	1,388	13,055

NEVADA.

	BARLEY.		BUCKWHEAT.		RYE.	
The State	19,399	513,470	....	....	....	....
Churchill	1,261	36,208	....	....	....	....
Douglas	2,948	69,374	....	....	....	....
Elko	5,993	160,978	....	....	....	....
Esmeralda	2,994	80,549	....	....	....	....
Eureka	6	25	....	....	....	....
Humboldt	1,068	37,591	....	....	....	....
Lander	732	24,377	....	....	....	....
Lincoln	792	19,904	....	....	....	....
Lyon	302	7,417	....	....	....	....
Nye	1,314	28,906	....	....	....	....
Ormsby	40	600	....	....	....	....
Roop	145	2,973	....	....	....	....
Storey	....	....	....	....	....	....
Washoe	641	15,785	....	....	....	....
White Pine	1,163	28,783	....	....	....	....

NEW HAMPSHIRE.

	BARLEY.		BUCKWHEAT.		RYE.	
The State	3,461	77,877	4,535	94,090	3,218	34,638
Belknap	121	2,087	52	687	135	1,543
Carroll	43	733	71	1,046	161	1,337
Cheshire	549	14,165	147	2,416	368	3,958
Coos	82	1,893	1,701	43,431	65	923
Grafton	370	8,981	1,581	32,961	475	5,813
Hillsborough	500	11,911	191	1,980	652	6,588
Merrimack	330	6,279	251	2,976	523	4,932
Rockingham	423	8,531	63	1,067	414	4,987
Strafford	311	5,786	18	204	128	1,412
Sullivan	723	17,511	400	7,322	297	3,145

NEBRASKA—Continued.

Counties.	INDIAN CORN.		OATS.		WHEAT.	
	Acres.	Bushels.	Acres.	Bushels.	Acres.	Bushels.
Nuckolls	14,145	499,698	1,576	46,703	14,759	116,382
Otoe	86,315	3,591,019	7,814	197,394	26,605	248,364
Pawnee	38,572	1,516,879	5,628	118,331	9,779	62,422
Phelps	7,556	122,496	557	11,371	8,289	61,865
Pierce	2,776	84,610	1,107	24,655	3,261	10,864
Platte	26,101	920,140	7,270	155,717	37,537	228,671
Polk	27,671	1,276,956	4,864	135,776	41,815	392,946
Red Willow	2,200	54,412	51	1,284	717	6,443
Richardson	86,766	3,931,837	6,171	188,220	31,579	372,725
Saline	57,480	2,310,851	8,714	252,486	57,619	569,511
Sarpy	33,942	1,584,880	6,024	208,692	9,507	105,281
Saunders	87,501	4,108,655	12,727	374,120	75,676	784,829
Seward	56,242	2,499,888	7,601	214,494	57,226	573,951
Sherman	4,432	107,013	910	26,743	4,271	46,154
Sioux	16	575	......	......	......	......
Stanton	7,234	143,715	2,143	18,815	9,084	13,203
Thayer	14,845	493,608	2,069	60,028	18,537	178,071
Unorganized territory	690	13,275	133	2,863	406	4,084
Valley	2,714	87,656	1,273	27,411	4,381	43,442
Washington	50,858	2,326,329	8,329	259,416	26,514	319,969
Wayne	2,341	86,205	560	11,555	1,684	10,845
Webster	26,415	711,273	2,765	50,030	28,454	216,748
Wheeler	757	18,890	176	4,310	715	8,807
York	48,421	2,075,243	7,868	205,267	77,720	789,183

NEVADA.

The State	487	12,891	5,937	186,860	3,674	60,298
Churchill	......	......	19	120	......	......
Douglas	6	119	2,942	84,589	496	8,355
Elko	......	......	1,933	74,596	955	18,574
Esmeralda	46	1,074	134	2,270	486	9,406
Eureka	......	......	......	......	......	......
Humboldt	......	......	40	500	163	5,096
Lander	......	......	......	......	20	515
Lincoln	324	8,415	42	790	148	3,425
Lyon	61	1,930	52	1,090	68	1,516
Nye	29	920	56	2,675	43	671
Ormsby	......	......	......	......	......	......
Roop	......	......	......	......	7	190
Storey	......	......	......	......	......	......
Washoe	13	158	664	19,021	1,230	20,289
White Pine	8	275	55	1,209	58	1,261

NEW HAMPSHIRE.

The State	36,612	1,350,248	29,485	1,017,620	11,248	169,316
Belknap	2,282	86,024	1,149	33,941	1,205	17,477
Carroll	2,830	86,445	1,381	35,227	1,202	14,713
Cheshire	2,834	150,788	2,535	90,774	176	2,666
Coos	350	10,129	5,666	228,698	1,565	31,464
Grafton	5,438	206,323	9,719	360,902	2,749	43,318
Hillsborough	5,092	192,580	1,772	49,441	648	9,070
Merrimack	6,379	229,877	2,092	75,039	1,956	25,403
Rockingham	4,690	175,705	1,155	26,572	445	5,634
Strafford	2,285	76,690	520	12,546	380	5,126
Sullivan	3,432	135,677	2,896	104,480	922	14,443

NEW JERSEY.

Counties.	BARLEY.		BUCKWHEAT.		RYE.	
	Acres.	Bushels.	Acres.	Bushels.	Acres.	Bushels.
The State.............	240	4, 091	35, 373	466, 414	106, 025	949, 064
Atlantic................			103	777	616	4, 075
Bergen.................			1, 204	17, 135	3, 228	40, 372
Burlington..........			674	9, 039	13, 495	135, 149
Camden..............			111	1, 007	2, 688	23, 198
Cape May............			16	174	39	269
Cumberland..............	9	128	281	3, 102	629	4, 131
Essex...................	5	50	215	2, 741	616	9, 707
Gloucester..............			445	4, 666	3, 568	27, 473
Hudson.................						
Hunterdon.............	137	2, 225	5, 741	82, 099	11, 057	87, 418
Mercer.................			913	9, 373	5, 107	54, 284
Middlesex	7	08	1, 051	10, 536	4, 749	52, 233
Monmouth..............	10	240	515	5, 389	12, 489	133, 560
Morris.................	35	844	5, 281	57, 937	4, 818	41, 723
Ocean.................			229	2, 249	2, 348	17, 807
Passaic			1, 318	17, 643	1, 767	21, 825
Salem..................			321	3, 785	601	3, 716
Somerset	13	181	1, 079	12, 485	6, 572	56, 429
Sussex.................	9	181	8, 016	119, 809	13, 498	98, 300
Union..................			335	4, 442	527	6, 897
Warren................	15	174	7, 525	101, 856	17, 613	129, 898

NEW MEXICO.

The Territory	2, 548	50, 053			17	240
Bernalillo...............	57	2, 420				
Colfax.................						
Dona Aña	847	8, 001				
Grant.................	389	14, 937				
Lincoln.................	10	114				
Mora.................	311	6, 681				
Rio Arriba	75	889			10	120
San Miguel..............	5	20			7	120
Santa Fé..............						
Socorro	813	15, 975				
Taos..................	41	926				
Valencia...............						

NEW YORK.

The State.............	356, 629	7, 792, 062	291, 228	4, 461, 200	244, 923	2, 634, 690
Albany	1, 077	17, 952	14, 774	211, 225	14, 710	158, 600
Allegany	2, 875	60, 674	5, 570	105, 857	408	5, 468
Broome.................	265	5, 439	8, 804	126, 910	993	9, 837
Cattaraugus	1, 421	33, 534	2, 091	38, 228	167	2, 322
Cayuga.................	23, 516	576, 813	4, 158	72, 480	437	5, 490
Chautauqua	3, 124	61, 356	1, 735	30, 803	154	2, 192
Chemung...............	3, 260	63, 926	8, 182	105, 112	697	6, 606
Chenango...............	419	9, 883	2, 507	38, 397	406	4, 873
Clinton	1, 124	20, 560	11, 445	164, 404	2, 677	26, 057
Columbia...............	284	5, 865	8, 624	128, 878	42, 493	408, 584
Cortland...............	717	18, 514	1, 510	22, 493	11	105
Delaware...............	538	12, 981	11, 106	198, 374	2, 022	20, 332
Duchess................	405	8, 541	4, 292	56, 813	18, 367	189, 558
Erie	13, 419	255, 505	4, 143	72, 842	2, 342	36, 975
Essex...................	532	9, 772	4, 806	53, 277	1, 467	11, 175

NEW JERSEY.

Counties.	INDIAN CORN.		OATS.		WHEAT.	
	Acres.	Bushels.	Acres.	Bushels.	Acres.	Bushels.
The State............	344, 555	11, 150, 705	137, 422	3, 710, 573	149, 760	1, 901, 739
Atlantic....................	4, 519	98, 173	90	1, 569	872	10, 519
Bergen	6, 074	178, 002	2, 250	49, 587	584	9, 189
Burlington	34, 030	1, 256, 523	4, 237	131, 663	15, 072	241, 412
Camden	8, 250	284, 555	438	12, 558	3, 949	67, 604
Cape May	4, 996	110, 428	335	5, 080	1, 343	18, 196
Cumberland	20, 330	602, 546	2, 445	63, 324	8, 744	157, 952
Essex	2, 211	92, 664	324	28, 010	427	8, 461
Gloucester..................	19, 156	675, 653	1, 349	29, 299	11, 233	108, 154
Hudson.....	65	2, 656	....	....	....	....
Hunterdon	42, 343	1, 252, 598	29, 584	854, 852	21, 365	234, 795
Mercer .... ,..	21, 673	702, 937	12, 899	396, 570	11, 085	158, 417
Middlesex	19, 738	397, 491	9, 651	247, 080	8, 197	112, 973
Monmouth.................	30, 385	1, 048, 940	5, 314	149, 769	12, 369	179, 421
Morris.....................	18, 579	651, 352	13, 634	377, 576	4, 889	53, 257
Ocean.....................	4, 626	137, 277	443	10, 629	1, 151	12, 149
Passaic	3, 169	97, 427	1, 573	36, 209	350	5, 538
Salem......................	30, 460	1, 064, 227	5, 315	142, 729	20, 256	269, 670
Somerset...................	25, 655	727, 683	20, 711	547, 220	13, 974	137, 619
Sussex....	17, 354	571, 484	10, 641	229, 537	3, 138	30, 560
Union......................	3, 256	122, 166	1, 424	38, 690	334	4, 962
Warren.....................	27, 677	869, 923	14, 165	358, 622	9, 328	80, 891

NEW MEXICO.

	Acres.	Bushels.	Acres.	Bushels.	Acres.	Bushels.
The Territory	41, 449	633, 786	9, 237	156, 527	51, 230	706, 641
Bernalillo.................	1, 233	35, 185	61	1, 215	790	21, 245
Colfax	376	8, 230	510	10, 578	92	1, 533
Dona Aña	5, 710	41, 738	8	135	6, 205	62, 982
Grant.....................	1, 443	49, 665	35	995	458	10, 615
Lincoln...................	2, 623	41, 597	129	1, 703	841	9, 806
Mora......................	4, 363	72, 210	1, 902	38, 484	4, 964	97, 305
Rio Arriba.................	3, 808	42, 862	1, 096	10, 188	4, 673	53, 323
San Miguel................	7, 032	108, 490	587	18, 670	7, 813	87, 041
Santa Fé..................	1, 588	23, 161	....	....	863	12, 371
Socorro	3, 329	51, 300	10	170	4, 590	93, 853
Taos......................	7, 874	115, 044	4, 890	74, 389	18, 002	226, 715
Valencia...................	2, 064	44, 304	....	....	1, 939	29, 852

NEW YORK.

	Acres.	Bushels.	Acres.	Bushels.	Acres.	Bushels.
The State............	779, 272	25, 690, 156	1, 261, 171	37, 575, 506	736, 611	11, 587, 766
Albany	11, 845	296, 145	30, 160	787, 529	1, 652	23, 128
Allegany	6, 716	241, 364	32, 821	985, 938	11, 425	158, 128
Broome....................	9, 673	281, 955	22, 485	728, 242	6, 116	77, 335
Cattaraugus	8, 930	305, 193	29, 064	933, 579	4, 589	64, 978
Cayuga	29, 225	1, 086, 061	29, 724	1, 041, 403	45, 055	692, 028
Chautauqua	16, 806	542, 889	24, 645	912, 679	7, 223	119, 171
Chemung	8, 352	205, 446	16, 796	505, 528	10, 056	118, 034
Chenango..............	9, 727	323, 244	18, 368	639, 487	3, 323	44, 119
Clinton	8, 701	232, 041	22, 547	521, 130	5, 237	45, 007
Columbia	22, 211	537, 196	29, 070	724, 719	1, 043	13, 141
Cortland	5, 373	185, 979	12, 430	416, 175	2, 400	30, 315
Delaware.................	6, 175	189, 373	27, 048	780, 024	1, 882	23, 897
Duchess	29, 003	730, 513	20, 719	756, 375	8, 727	96, 149
Erie	22, 610	775, 761	49, 353	1, 518, 615	29, 417	557, 367
Essex	5, 626	132, 379	13, 878	281, 903	2, 523	19, 372

Counties.	BARLEY.		BUCKWHEAT.		RYE.	
	Acres.	Bushels.	Acres.	Bushels.	Acres.	Bushels.
Franklin	1,264	23,370	2,772	35,510	3,216	28,941
Fulton	264	5,434	4,750	79,797	1,221	11,271
Genesee	15,341	338,992	1,075	18,649	268	3,643
Greene	195	3,533	9,246	131,181	8,269	71,430
Hamilton	10	199	658	12,295	25	305
Herkimer	1,705	43,561	2,693	49,585	83	1,169
Jefferson	20,429	393,024	2,097	33,556	4,785	57,312
Kings			7	142	88	2,052
Lewis	1,868	45,612	1,302	20,743	1,029	11,359
Livingston	17,080	358,729	3,259	57,553	813	8,124
Madison	4,241	95,074	2,248	34,647	231	1,655
Monroe	22,925	560,528	951	15,590	2,010	30,298
Montgomery	1,775	34,942	5,523	86,538	685	9,109
New York						
Niagara	22,732	495,541	971	12,653	501	7,496
Oneida	2,741	65,908	4,125	57,662	1,446	12,492
Onondaga	16,735	399,075	4,336	60,870	1,340	10,307
Ontario	25,136	587,713	1,790	29,489	459	5,497
Orange	22	500	2,521	40,940	9,524	106,981
Orleans	17,286	389,376	831	12,638	226	3,352
Oswego	1,587	37,109	6,008	86,313	3,116	35,771
Otsego	1,822	35,402	7,781	132,774	1,293	12,436
Putnam			929	11,255	1,368	14,769
Queens	95	1,863	1,714	25,167	4,294	69,926
Rensselaer	340	6,853	3,899	52,062	20,099	240,059
Richmond			46	773	159	2,420
Rockland			1,045	13,170	2,066	26,124
Saint Lawrence	11,302	196,172	3,085	38,481	3,919	48,116
Saratoga	126	2,666	10,914	147,360	15,695	133,897
Schenectady	1,407	22,892	4,263	68,152	6,348	52,152
Schoharie	1,559	30,157	18,583	293,443	5,041	76,628
Schuyler	16,420	313,419	6,879	102,439	1,229	12,389
Seneca	17,768	421,012	1,238	22,014	96	1,396
Steuben	16,984	332,515	22,724	401,761	5,117	52,376
Suffolk	199	5,459	1,449	17,656	3,931	47,471
Sullivan	12	201	10,864	183,879	8,339	73,648
Tioga	467	8,397	9,579	129,131	937	9,236
Tompkins	9,404	204,979	8,680	116,168	782	8,368
Ulster	13	222	10,893	153,924	18,710	191,246
Warren	6	53	4,393	62,649	2,362	14,864
Washington	259	4,414	3,800	52,660	9,851	100,981
Wayne	20,275	453,635	3,162	58,234	713	9,876
Westchester	84	2,094	1,101	13,364	4,038	55,130
Wyoming	9,814	203,711	1,890	34,168	207	2,389
Yates	21,961	506,351	1,311	22,072	717	5,995

NORTH CAROLINA.

	BARLEY.		BUCKWHEAT.		RYE.	
	Acres.	Bushels.	Acres.	Bushels.	Acres.	Bushels.
The State	230	2,421	5,725	44,668	61,953	285,160
Alamance					149	619
Alexander					760	2,445
Alleghany			755	6,254	3,121	17,638
Anson					179	574
Ashe			818	6,131	4,685	33,809
Beaufort					16	94
Bertie					33	191
Bladen					261	756
Brunswick			16	50	127	616
Buncombe			575	3,981	2,966	12,707
Burke			7	46	1,054	4,009
Cabarrus					75	355
Caldwell			35	304	684	2,855
Camden					5	30
Carteret					85	264

NEW YORK—Continued.

Counties.	INDIAN CORN.		OATS.		WHEAT.	
	Acres.	Bushels.	Acres.	Bushels.	Acres.	Bushels.
Franklin	6,739	134,211	17,094	401,342	7,061	62,439
Fulton	6,661	195,316	12,258	345,672	558	9,287
Genesee	16,896	712,449	15,582	551,696	34,387	715,108
Greene	9,543	253,049	14,195	370,615	762	10,251
Hamilton	563	10,797	1,102	29,920	5	72
Herkimer	6,331	222,420	19,759	677,400	1,280	23,129
Jefferson	11,398	357,964	46,731	1,256,468	22,356	189,322
Kings	1,256	52,990	68	3,158	139	3,240
Lewis	2,837	71,625	16,748	493,704	2,078	26,739
Livingston	18,084	744,961	21,032	696,194	45,388	706,029
Madison	12,569	466,326	22,885	755,189	8,379	115,059
Monroe	29,132	1,269,480	28,016	1,070,779	54,831	1,140,907
Montgomery	9,922	312,396	26,568	791,269	4,899	85,414
New York	78	2,490	18	1,110		
Niagara	22,606	833,226	21,389	751,549	46,644	866,531
Oneida	19,622	630,432	31,664	1,092,675	5,406	89,958
Onondaga	29,565	1,026,713	36,937	1,292,677	37,332	554,045
Ontario	24,650	1,022,226	24,975	905,346	48,918	835,531
Orange	19,427	619,753	15,815	424,772	5,849	75,156
Orleans	12,446	511,277	12,409	438,039	28,666	551,063
Oswego	20,620	615,105	22,907	702,706	7,004	88,691
Otsego	11,785	373,047	35,152	952,047	3,974	50,629
Putnam	3,944	132,906	3,456	89,326	252	3,756
Queens	15,741	598,923	5,069	148,166	5,854	115,945
Rensselaer	14,246	365,189	24,952	697,610	433	6,073
Richmond	1,173	46,433	638	17,358	153	2,906
Rockland	3,840	102,890	2,264	50,917	561	6,792
Saint Lawrence	12,249	295,466	54,654	1,356,239	17,974	175,102
Saratoga	25,035	612,222	25,401	726,036	1,892	24,150
Schenectady	5,667	152,552	11,547	310,664	823	12,263
Schoharie	7,602	217,506	32,804	727,690	5,789	80,467
Schuyler	7,826	275,194	11,853	311,254	13,039	149,779
Seneca	13,155	542,412	12,525	470,201	31,941	483,612
Steuben	17,373	641,235	59,164	1,596,530	33,022	385,672
Suffolk	18,097	624,407	9,556	311,581	9,660	182,537
Sullivan	7,426	222,737	11,470	298,742	242	2,529
Tioga	10,562	313,087	21,584	652,918	7,047	83,367
Tompkins	15,159	498,466	22,907	750,627	17,669	241,910
Ulster	19,237	548,575	17,027	426,609	3,194	36,254
Warren	6,444	136,777	5,905	128,788	371	2,868
Washington	18,995	537,060	31,321	889,834	1,242	16,809
Wayne	30,840	1,172,374	24,512	855,629	39,018	714,181
Westchester	11,131	377,357	9,004	238,509	1,582	22,698
Wyoming	8,051	282,318	20,259	601,211	12,991	209,029
Yates	11,765	490,278	11,159	381,992	24,649	347,250

NORTH CAROLINA.

	Acres.	Bushels.	Acres.	Bushels.	Acres.	Bushels.
The State	2,305,419	28,019,839	500,415	3,838,068	646,829	3,397,393
Alamance	24,628	305,874	9,618	48,809	18,661	82,163
Alexander	16,789	272,382	7,503	51,752	6,376	35,338
Alleghany	7,201	122,587	1,933	19,365	1,760	10,291
Anson	29,121	305,139	8,999	72,454	5,069	25,846
Ashe	15,616	277,027	3,357	37,955	5,473	39,407
Beaufort	20,225	286,211	1,395	18,436	374	2,736
Bertie	37,735	345,691	2,403	20,517	309	2,189
Bladen	21,556	188,208	302	3,795	109	521
Brunswick	4,915	46,329	240	2,262	8	70
Buncombe	29,108	490,544	6,967	62,079	17,501	84,974
Burke	22,613	325,656	3,455	21,762	10,016	49,538
Cabarrus	26,841	381,321	7,592	54,519	17,550	84,656
Caldwell	17,915	274,495	3,886	30,592	8,271	42,513
Camden	23,663	295,447	1,008	8,854	461	4,428
Carteret	5,156	41,458	107	1,122	418	2,090

2062 AGRI——5

NORTH CAROLINA—Continued.

Counties	BARLEY.		BUCKWHEAT.		RYE.	
	Acres.	Bushels.	Acres.	Bushels.	Acres.	Bushels.
Caswell					53	346
Catawba					181	783
Chatham					63	328
Cherokee			12	77	1,126	4,781
Chowan						
Clay			23	157	834	3,562
Cleveland					210	875
Columbus					128	301
Craven					79	847
Cumberland					1,513	4,343
Currituck					15	75
Dare						
Davidson	35	364			277	1,414
Davie					444	1,986
Duplin					422	1,931
Edgecombe	9	54			139	711
Forsyth					402	1,366
Franklin					229	961
Gaston					64	265
Gates						
Graham			5	25	566	2,126
Granville					64	360
Greene					394	1,909
Guilford	87	1,068	14	62	354	1,725
Halifax	9	76			123	520
Harnett					489	1,257
Haywood			633	4,684	757	4,383
Henderson			107	637	3,734	16,351
Hertford					112	334
Hyde					14	133
Iredell			9	85	350	1,581
Jackson			175	1,100	1,583	7,878
Johnston					324	1,032
Jones					245	1,210
Lenoir					685	2,460
Lincoln					28	155
McDowell			31	202	1,360	5,016
Macon	6	50	75	701	1,823	8,734
Madison	7	70	319	2,809	816	4,641
Martin					25	115
Mecklenburg	9	138			78	403
Mitchell			378	3,468	1,358	9,021
Montgomery					130	425
Moore					1,512	3,954
Nash					85	336
New Hanover						
Northampton					55	448
Onslow					31	65
Orange					39	208
Pamlico						
Pasquotank					13	98
Pender	8	20			14	46
Perquimans					30	259
Person					13	86
Pitt			10	10	284	1,394
Polk					606	2,680
Randolph	35	467			148	729
Richmond					942	2,328
Robeson					1,548	3,952
Rockingham	6	60	18	126	301	1,363
Rowan			8	43	254	1,134
Rutherford					6,9	2,438
Sampson					499	2,086
Stanly					89	497
Stokes			6	40	1,195	5,023

NORTH CAROLINA—Continued.

Counties.	INDIAN CORN.		OATS.		WHEAT.	
	Acres.	Bushels.	Acres.	Bushels.	Acres.	Bushels.
Caswell	25,663	361,641	14,441	101,398	10,841	58,137
Catawba	21,248	358,210	7,566	64,236	15,054	104,770
Chatham	43,087	558,281	19,861	120,341	28,930	122,760
Cherokee	14,507	227,650	1,534	11,657	4,317	17,898
Chowan	13,877	143,156	791	6,888	622	4,357
Clay	7,810	113,462	1,230	7,607	3,282	13,093
Cleveland	31,339	390,281	10,939	62,211	11,116	55,983
Columbus	15,723	136,546	267	2,517	38	223
Craven	19,001	218,256	333	4,426	235	1,533
Cumberland	32,677	282,423	1,500	13,791	1,141	7,494
Currituck	23,310	324,819	267	2,734	101	892
Dare	956	11,205	17	230	25	107
Davidson	36,983	549,906	16,924	122,063	32,195	174,671
Davie	22,125	438,595	13,366	139,126	13,244	71,127
Duplin	36,813	330,437	433	6,132	1,031	6,292
Edgecombe	46,235	433,214	9,589	94,021	2,422	16,712
Forsyth	20,920	335,164	11,780	95,304	13,590	77,082
Franklin	32,642	338,239	5,560	45,812	8,362	45,504
Gaston	24,678	373,472	6,699	50,244	11,566	62,860
Gates	21,946	170,642	1,210	10,016	708	4,187
Graham	4,222	66,092	628	3,914	718	2,919
Granville	42,608	515,159	14,344	110,690	14,428	90,764
Greene	25,148	173,421	1,738	16,772	3,638	19,392
Guilford	39,790	519,185	20,774	129,723	27,743	127,214
Halifax	44,790	437,321	4,497	41,771	1,300	9,235
Harnett	21,244	180,458	1,202	7,640	2,393	10,957
Haywood	17,254	314,446	4,099	35,834	10,054	56,587
Henderson	16,407	227,411	2,908	23,087	2,598	12,295
Hertford	25,521	236,088	1,800	14,512	817	6,891
Hyde	21,632	243,623	1,354	18,400	1,079	8,949
Iredell	39,264	588,220	17,488	126,429	17,476	88,056
Jackson	12,793	188,521	1,521	9,440	4,217	21,801
Johnston	45,045	428,996	3,176	29,958	3,711	25,111
Jones	19,425	186,954	455	5,426	429	2,588
Lenoir	29,838	274,010	1,060	12,217	5,007	32,800
Lincoln	19,338	313,907	6,313	44,939	10,159	65,949
McDowell	17,675	265,924	1,690	13,111	6,397	32,903
Macon	14,423	222,855	1,621	12,209	5,505	27,038
Madison	17,816	348,858	4,238	38,816	7,702	40,192
Martin	24,209	227,445	1,447	11,229	940	6,254
Mecklenburg	41,285	539,385	12,949	94,356	12,295	66,767
Mitchell	11,894	209,131	3,990	40,845	3,374	19,725
Montgomery	18,090	210,521	7,852	50,248	9,197	39,702
Moore	27,934	302,196	7,924	48,744	11,242	45,413
Nash	32,490	295,610	3,875	30,135	3,787	27,560
New Hanover	2,008	15,937	86	606		
Northampton	45,224	431,581	4,805	45,769	1,725	14,193
Onslow	23,250	185,019	96	1,280		
Orange	28,542	366,640	12,243	86,208	18,358	96,006
Pamlico	6,381	107,959	378	4,845	285	2,101
Pasquotank	28,525	348,119	1,930	17,438	3,300	22,453
Pender	16,550	159,064	183	2,269	7	28
Perquimans	21,910	202,850	1,222	13,921	2,957	25,514
Person	19,372	241,523	9,821	56,926	8,974	51,935
Pitt	46,482	458,166	3,301	29,406	3,787	22,664
Polk	10,632	139,315	877	5,786	1,896	9,516
Randolph	35,338	477,168	13,524	88,360	29,443	137,104
Richmond	29,502	277,974	3,571	32,279	3,751	19,994
Robeson	49,961	360,128	2,814	22,845	875	6,153
Rockingham	25,175	392,767	15,200	133,266	11,298	71,187
Rowan	38,963	597,519	17,751	142,121	24,195	138,278
Rutherford	32,783	394,062	6,166	31,971	8,683	39,085
Sampson	53,951	486,768	654	6,297	1,240	7,970
Stanly	22,426	271,877	10,975	72,223	16,465	70,070
Stokes	19,969	338,781	8,408	72,391	9,374	55,281

NORTH CAROLINA—Continued.

Counties.	BARLEY.		BUCKWHEAT.		RYE.	
	Acres.	Bushels.	Acres.	Bushels.	Acres.	Bushels.
Surry			71	505	3,027	10,482
Swain			18	146	515	2,259
Transylvania			60	395	3,289	16,043
Tyrrell						
Union					12	67
Wake					211	1,100
Warren					39	189
Washington	5	50			68	380
Watauga			951	7,937	2,387	18,850
Wayne					819	2,922
Wilkes			218	1,530	5,236	17,569
Wilson					73	522
Yadkin			27	188	821	3,723
Yancey	14	64	351	2,915	1,290	7,647

OHIO.

The State	57,482	1,707,129	22,130	280,229	29,499	389,221
Adams	27	246	66	678	201	1,726
Allen	145	2,990	68	814	180	3,158
Ashland	144	2,903	149	2,098	150	1,875
Ashtabula	193	3,138	674	9,565	289	3,235
Athens			334	3,850	147	1,313
Auglaize	665	19,837	163	1,954	280	5,204
Belmont	225	3,598	321	3,853	345	3,467
Brown	27	762	121	1,007	1,329	11,875
Butler	17,908	566,105	140	2,117	208	2,210
Carroll	32	658	366	4,247	310	3,485
Champaign	58	1,340	192	2,140	50	610
Clarke	137	4,390	60	570	208	4,529
Clermont	85	1,412	176	2,029	730	7,748
Clinton	98	2,717	111	1,299	228	2,944
Columbiana	99	1,097	760	9,370	702	7,713
Coshocton	5	96	424	5,372	216	2,060
Crawford	295	7,317	99	1,622	192	4,216
Cuyahoga	386	8,127	78	1,158	908	14,611
Darke	1,404	47,260	195	3,003	490	10,154
Defiance	113	3,426	230	3,086	201	4,326
Delaware	16	251	306	3,264	324	3,993
Erie	1,759	44,057	371	5,230	115	1,923
Fairfield	861	28,198	56	740	180	1,865
Fayette			209	6,320	333	3,944
Franklin	91	2,040	234	2,422	251	3,743
Fulton	98	2,877	1,076	12,822	365	4,664
Gallia			201	3,010	248	2,174
Geauga	72	853	103	1,190	50	633
Greene	529	10,113	49	690	219	4,852
Guernsey	40	659	573	6,401	357	3,190
Hamilton	5,379	144,789	194	2,656	1,474	24,941
Hancock	131	3,614	100	1,189	152	2,245
Hardin	50	1,234	144	1,777	146	2,693
Harrison	24	271	140	1,848	145	1,599
Henry	55	1,354	256	3,202	923	18,031
Highland	7	115	52	493	798	7,217
Hocking	13	169	242	2,315	345	2,959
Holmes	99	2,240	424	4,804	364	3,814
Huron	639	12,183	246	2,891	84	1,440
Jackson			268	2,552	174	1,241
Jefferson	152	2,689	180	2,206	157	1,700
Knox	11	192	542	7,609	294	3,251
Lake	1,384	27,411	428	6,852	385	5,320
Lawrence	55	632	64	812	73	496
Licking	13	457	473	5,310	511	6,206

NORTH CAROLINA—Continued.

Counties.	INDIAN CORN.		OATS.		WHEAT.	
	Acres.	Bushels.	Acres.	Bushels.	Acres.	Bushels.
Surry	25,334	397,143	9,190	70,737	9,823	42,046
Swain	6,809	100,543	757	4,301	1,473	6,578
Transylvania	9,762	154,769	257	2,870	869	3,760
Tyrrell	8,300	108,839	781	7,622	261	2,067
Union	28,877	338,520	14,357	101,710	12,464	49,783
Wake	53,172	612,869	13,948	98,962	14,783	72,341
Warren	28,457	293,773	5,559	46,090	5,098	37,888
Washington	15,824	217,631	1,065	13,427	647	5,564
Watauga	8,227	148,204	1,828	23,205	2,957	22,247
Wayne	44,469	466,432	1,779	18,600	7,041	37,195
Wilkes	34,865	480,089	8,240	55,360	9,515	37,696
Wilson	27,288	299,957	1,590	13,682	2,804	21,113
Yadkin	21,735	343,070	11,289	79,443	10,190	48,762
Yancey	11,200	205,659	3,657	43,631	3,940	21,452

OHIO.

	Acres.	Bushels.	Acres.	Bushels.	Acres.	Bushels.
The State	3,281,923	111,877,124	910,388	28,664,505	2,556,134	46,014,869
Adams	41,252	987,430	9,988	170,133	20,032	213,892
Allen	39,924	1,401,217	9,172	301,021	32,802	677,827
Ashland	30,029	848,593	17,363	653,670	35,551	698,162
Ashtabula	16,661	563,699	22,438	762,470	14,121	194,735
Athens	23,761	698,400	2,544	40,127	19,508	220,875
Auglaize	40,280	1,264,623	10,047	348,750	34,982	706,944
Belmont	31,564	1,242,867	11,856	249,437	26,965	406,522
Brown	53,794	1,564,786	10,893	218,174	32,115	330,675
Butler	75,058	3,190,457	10,225	290,096	40,729	754,371
Carroll	15,567	450,511	14,629	439,698	17,540	233,658
Champaign	56,223	2,152,860	6,084	201,212	41,948	963,988
Clarke	49,536	1,730,532	4,821	164,402	37,536	839,147
Clermont	46,646	1,476,244	10,645	222,564	23,830	267,891
Clinton	69,169	2,382,670	4,669	132,917	32,937	602,788
Columbiana	22,613	776,600	19,559	584,374	23,228	312,064
Coshocton	37,235	1,125,266	10,393	274,342	35,883	604,393
Crawford	34,148	1,216,462	17,617	668,783	34,197	768,661
Cuyahoga	13,815	592,679	16,230	640,428	9,683	176,404
Darke	76,078	2,860,319	16,987	579,894	55,741	1,221,643
Defiance	23,792	834,141	11,152	386,639	28,842	542,215
Delaware	45,538	1,604,455	7,300	225,855	23,901	408,619
Erie	19,118	681,434	9,083	333,737	26,939	513,901
Fairfield	62,567	2,146,476	4,004	118,642	50,956	851,025
Fayette	82,222	2,766,255	1,319	33,698	31,809	509,444
Franklin	93,433	3,293,450	6,590	184,142	44,202	807,822
Fulton	27,171	1,064,787	13,671	501,932	29,549	609,063
Gallia	30,136	702,961	4,071	64,739	31,864	313,005
Geauga	7,434	245,255	10,499	382,071	5,673	78,477
Greene	61,344	2,302,443	4,452	155,481	46,064	1,066,941
Guernsey	24,796	777,828	8,864	154,837	20,323	253,347
Hamilton	41,073	1,639,115	8,600	203,055	15,595	259,801
Hancock	50,714	1,776,516	9,446	350,981	50,375	1,008,938
Hardin	39,539	1,212,919	5,617	200,709	32,308	614,661
Harrison	17,107	686,422	6,891	193,878	16,331	257,175
Henry	28,184	920,189	7,504	265,090	25,639	556,530
Highland	62,588	1,685,911	7,703	169,290	39,492	457,737
Hocking	17,862	471,492	2,952	48,898	13,165	148,568
Holmes	25,497	745,583	16,718	545,290	31,082	598,966
Huron	32,278	1,205,176	21,163	799,907	35,555	643,366
Jackson	18,547	401,883	6,006	91,128	12,119	96,522
Jefferson	17,248	643,830	10,287	297,964	10,151	284,360
Knox	40,744	1,252,181	10,496	303,098	33,386	518,008
Lake	8,167	309,919	6,860	231,584	7,338	125,464
Lawrence	24,261	454,080	5,184	78,440	17,199	152,081
Licking	58,314	1,977,935	9,322	279,364	40,227	621,670

OHIO—Continued.

Counties.	BARLEY.		BUCKWHEAT.		RYE.	
	Acres.	Bushels.	Acres.	Bushels.	Acres.	Bushels.
Logan	29	770	199	3,502	109	1,660
Lorain	1,500	38,979	109	3,409	107	1,486
Lucas	472	13,517	684	8,744	387	7,448
Madison			58	699	209	4,780
Mahoning	92	1,812	377	4,292	421	4,682
Marion	15	295	84	1,158	136	1,769
Medina	107	1,851	72	896	240	2,658
Meigs	115	2,102	453	5,746	324	3,110
Mercer	190	5,217	166	1,883	295	4,710
Miami	1,758	59,717	140	2,225	187	3,375
Monroe	18	125	720	7,622	1,099	9,991
Montgomery	3,685	129,178	115	1,905	347	5,212
Morgan	14	143	236	2,620	185	2,058
Morrow	46	714	307	3,189	314	3,552
Muskingum	73	1,360	221	6,741	460	4,622
Noble			228	2,658	225	2,554
Ottawa	407	10,409	104	1,527	305	6,557
Paulding	17	322	196	2,268	242	3,174
Perry	148	5,322	182	1,544	278	2,844
Pickaway	168	6,460	48	656	193	2,566
Pike	652	15,615	96	847	119	868
Portage	67	1,117	159	2,162	225	2,636
Preble	1,223	40,057	74	964	207	2,857
Putnam	69	1,473	187	1,956	774	11,312
Richland	211	5,078	364	4,540	311	3,617
Ross	86	3,230	89	877	289	3,202
Sandusky	358	9,621	117	1,766	232	4,320
Scioto	379	9,319	174	2,188	133	1,480
Seneca	120	2,800	75	955	135	1,743
Shelby	980	28,520	281	3,240	275	4,522
Stark	1,097	27,223	151	2,019	214	3,160
Summit	47	980	67	905	159	2,338
Trumbull	19	336	472	5,810	292	3,499
Tuscarawas	192	4,088	432	4,904	397	4,249
Union	17	480	134	1,827	128	1,414
Van Wert	75	1,334	264	2,698	460	7,601
Vinton			304	2,606	178	1,262
Warren	8,047	267,072	216	2,931	284	3,213
Washington	6	113	984	11,494	868	8,061
Wayne	354	8,043	146	1,492	384	3,547
Williams	90	1,807	242	3,165	152	2,268
Wood	933	25,883	559	7,772	1,110	21,973
Wyandot	73	1,182	117	1,193	51	858

OREGON.

	Acres.	Bushels.	Acres.	Bushels.	Acres.	Bushels.
The State	29,311	920,977	372	6,215	841	13,305
Baker	1,768	77,058	5	40	14	155
Benton	159	5,168	18	304	9	165
Clackamas	141	4,340	89	1,688	35	489
Clatsop	6	59			9	195
Columbia	10	415				
Coos	238	7,960	14	167		
Curry	109	3,440				
Douglas	1,495	39,254	6	88	19	280
Grant	861	22,724			13	140
Jackson	1,832	60,875			11	216
Josephine	299	5,421			48	591
Lake	744	18,330			122	1,105
Lane	1,893	44,478			36	556
Linn	2,221	51,322	41	648		
Marion	391	10,177	131	2,023	12	275

OHIO—Continued.

Counties.	INDIAN CORN.		OATS.		WHEAT.	
	Acres.	Bushels.	Acres.	Bushels.	Acres.	Bushels.
Logan	44,967	1,555,628	4,403	131,588	38,595	764,557
Lorain	19,503	809,325	14,807	627,916	21,486	375,301
Lucas	18,112	740,589	7,168	262,510	15,724	346,931
Madison	79,066	2,640,558	1,453	44,052	16,653	286,808
Mahoning	15,415	551,863	14,749	450,606	12,938	186,309
Marion	49,117	1,755,771	11,680	364,956	24,561	478,127
Medina	18,337	598,641	16,556	601,560	18,652	335,575
Meigs	19,875	562,335	3,578	57,551	22,726	236,060
Mercer	38,664	1,204,257	14,668	507,912	29,607	625,177
Miami	59,429	2,310,528	10,470	369,411	42,924	1,030,956
Monroe	22,622	646,486	10,081	170,209	20,443	251,624
Montgomery	55,603	1,925,859	15,204	512,850	42,864	966,024
Morgan	19,203	628,316	2,895	49,242	20,409	290,946
Morrow	28,552	873,944	12,641	395,070	16,592	285,422
Muskingum	38,607	1,219,012	6,807	120,045	34,627	504,894
Noble	23,968	830,252	4,987	90,851	19,703	247,804
Ottawa	15,540	617,862	4,106	150,229	17,253	363,173
Paulding	11,255	341,181	3,734	101,549	11,768	208,907
Perry	20,086	536,618	2,955	54,008	18,432	235,446
Pickaway	100,070	3,846,339	950	23,140	50,621	925,547
Pike	31,816	852,836	7,077	112,039	13,047	146,825
Portage	14,220	493,779	15,243	514,833	17,685	202,564
Preble	54,978	1,926,199	13,659	421,178	33,799	677,904
Putnam	40,307	1,380,644	5,670	169,784	29,263	576,771
Richland	32,933	868,950	24,600	821,672	39,220	771,513
Ross	74,414	2,626,536	3,354	59,260	41,102	667,891
Sandusky	34,996	1,443,647	11,422	451,514	49,181	1,061,379
Scioto	40,652	1,233,420	9,852	166,070	19,649	245,504
Seneca	40,046	1,415,590	16,608	631,274	68,490	1,446,333
Shelby	44,295	1,515,669	14,362	477,168	35,018	714,071
Stark	29,219	1,066,810	26,779	1,074,254	56,942	1,187,801
Summit	16,988	642,667	16,404	611,236	28,675	573,678
Trumbull	15,688	557,446	16,394	550,792	10,916	162,756
Tuscarawas	27,266	841,655	19,267	600,866	39,455	699,534
Union	54,460	2,012,783	5,586	145,628	22,744	383,665
Van Wert	31,967	1,100,213	8,179	265,660	21,656	444,225
Vinton	16,852	404,068	3,220	48,363	10,651	103,882
Warren	59,327	2,314,311	10,371	307,436	29,886	563,971
Washington	29,358	827,193	8,574	133,581	36,133	507,268
Wayne	34,690	1,238,075	26,607	1,019,083	55,557	1,210,281
Williams	29,028	1,090,658	15,500	558,163	33,749	645,208
Wood	57,039	1,976,372	16,850	594,501	33,796	750,327
Wyandot	39,766	1,454,370	8,365	294,264	34,430	740,935

OREGON.

	INDIAN CORN.		OATS.		WHEAT.	
	Acres.	Bushels.	Acres.	Bushels.	Acres.	Bushels.
The State	5,646	126,862	131,624	4,385,650	445,077	7,480,010
Baker	36	975	2,840	103,316	1,313	33,956
Benton	30	790	9,063	256,832	31,015	497,068
Clackamas	173	3,909	8,251	218,824	13,777	231,616
Clatsop			216	6,813	20	418
Columbia	15	667	174	5,322	161	3,041
Coos	272	8,892	536	17,584	1,792	42,044
Curry	70	2,520	337	11,100	63	1,565
Douglas	949	25,633	14,349	347,830	29,872	430,198
Grant	5	200	1,016	35,206	1,977	45,802
Jackson	2,132	41,564	4,519	141,676	10,601	219,478
Josephine	528	8,335	844	17,621	1,497	20,431
Lake			371	7,491	647	10,475
Lane	257	7,573	11,745	288,055	40,071	511,052
Linn	193	4,374	25,551	664,613	75,310	911,411
Marion	154	3,396	23,673	704,103	64,519	1,050,188

OREGON—Continued.

Counties.	BARLEY.		BUCKWHEAT.		RYE.	
	Acres.	Bushels.	Acres.	Bushels.	Acres.	Bushels.
Multnomah	47	1,189	7	86		
Polk	958	25,358			6	156
Tillamook	18	447				
Umatilla	10,641	363,097			46	1,171
Union	3,044	116,393			201	3,225
Wasco	1,742	47,013			220	3,029
Washington	121	3,276	31	678	13	291
Yam Hill	573	13,183	30	493	27	566

PENNSYLVANIA.

	BARLEY.		BUCKWHEAT.		RYE.	
	Acres.	Bushels.	Acres.	Bushels.	Acres.	Bushels.
The State	23,592	438,100	246,199	3,593,326	398,465	3,683,621
Adams	6	105	226	2,967	3,884	39,867
Allegheny	893	18,598	730	8,204	5,029	86,323
Armstrong			7,713	87,035	9,535	79,165
Beaver	171	3,164	1,311	15,270	1,843	18,209
Bedford	196	3,064	5,987	67,627	13,352	95,277
Berks	102	1,824	778	11,476	38,926	431,721
Blair	1,562	20,986	1,227	14,959	4,244	39,167
Bradford	1,455	29,104	23,525	424,168	3,597	36,891
Bucks	23	547	753	10,016	14,556	159,899
Butler	50	612	12,633	150,508	12,939	117,627
Cambria	350	4,661	3,356	50,022	3,744	33,370
Cameron			390	5,766	118	1,281
Carbon			1,666	20,740	6,138	41,200
Centre	1,947	28,315	1,858	32,688	4,146	41,884
Chester	33	871	335	5,067	1,466	19,694
Clarion	13	265	6,205	77,538	6,255	53,839
Clearfield	75	812	6,120	88,038	5,685	50,653
Clinton	555	6,943	2,486	33,942	1,597	15,151
Columbia	11	253	8,118	118,536	9,929	78,349
Crawford	155	3,027	8.421	128,807	571	6,227
Cumberland	116	2,553	107	1,242	3,139	33,053
Dauphin	7	182	542	6,584	5,559	56,414
Delaware	7	160	6	103	428	7,818
Elk	25	415	514	7,352	531	6,992
Erie	9,998	195,645	3,046	52,955	355	4,876
Fayette	12	164	2,763	31,380	981	8,549
Forest			903	13,509	378	4,039
Franklin	64	1,157	578	5,889	5,402	59,046
Fulton			3,068	28,022	4,888	26,695
Greene	49	535	1,052	11,316	731	6,417
Huntingdon	271	4,196	3,282	31,133	6,955	53,317
Indiana	23	352	9,035	109,159	9,262	77,166
Jefferson			6,544	78,401	6,662	59,157
Juiata	24	296	1,310	13,118	1,883	12,884
Lackawanna	31	612	4,217	68,650	2,626	29,325
Lancaster	59	967	309	5,281	6,751	77,818
Lawrence	103	1,853	2,585	34,939	636	6,655
Lebanon	6	79	69	1,305	6,548	68,466
Lehigh	24	528	730	12,303	27,441	242,568
Luzerne	6	190	10,254	162,257	12,948	118,219
Lycoming	38	501	7,615	109,821	7,510	60,826
McKean	31	511	451	6,929	87	1,077
Mercer	22	318	6,392	87,149	1,191	10,951
Mifflin	193	3,276	471	4,753	835	7,113
Monroe	6	123	6,532	86,393	12,896	89,770
Montgomery			153	2,234	13,854	194,636
Montour			1,201	15,193	2,131	17,863
Northampton	73	1,802	2,130	32,084	30,462	205,828
Northumberland	5	107	2,502	32,404	7,201	64,368
Perry			1,682	18,011	4,190	29,715

OREGON—Continued.

Counties.	INDIAN CORN.		OATS.		WHEAT.	
	Acres.	Bushels.	Acres.	Bushels.	Acres.	Bushels.
Multnomah	30	1,025	882	23,839	622	12,098
Polk	60	1,000	11,611	338,226	52,020	825,896
Tillamook			386	10,586	20	369
Umatilla	336	5,971	3,364	140,196	31,046	915,571
Union	56	1,110	6,724	251,344	11,422	284,463
Wasco	186	4,897	3,550	106,661	4,739	85,894
Washington	75	2,034	9,328	309,230	20,581	370,770
Yam Hill	89	1,097	12,294	379,182	51,992	957,816

PENNSYLVANIA.

The State	1,373,270	45,821,531	1,237,593	33,841,439	1,445,384	19,462,405
Adams	33,800	775,761	21,910	453,115	43,908	612,779
Allegheny	28,069	804,577	33,165	922,045	28,206	355,470
Armstrong	24,684	753,509	31,370	792,437	27,907	228,743
Beaver	17,331	531,857	17,929	470,294	17,732	201,823
Bedford	24,949	876,451	15,098	288,768	33,266	304,108
Berks	53,973	1,586,896	47,634	1,207,657	49,651	747,125
Blair	13,644	474,297	6,813	143,068	21,761	272,296
Bradford	22,908	721,662	42,974	1,365,814	17,318	217,344
Bucks	51,068	1,860,186	36,825	1,208,369	34,755	520,870
Butler	24,466	773,333	40,582	1,095,612	23,130	192,843
Cambria	10,405	336,113	14,558	346,563	11,047	117,099
Cameron	737	26,559	706	18,672	527	7,536
Carbon	4,072	78,406	3,397	70,560	971	12,778
Centre	25,151	898,185	10,376	250,351	37,310	389,804
Chester	47,097	1,964,532	33,283	1,137,089	43,235	775,312
Clarion	15,019	459,435	24,966	645,134	15,177	121,833
Clearfield	14,377	645,199	14,905	352,288	13,196	141,737
Clinton	9,016	341,735	5,774	157,565	11,786	142,879
Columbia	19,745	595,540	15,584	337,628	14,296	193,865
Crawford	24,618	829,369	32,072	1,128,674	18,088	232,140
Cumberland	39,256	1,219,107	33,584	937,166	53,089	834,517
Dauphin	28,222	877,155	24,968	607,302	30,601	444,082
Delaware	10,628	516,633	4,165	154,659	7,786	143,140
Elk	1,102	34,697	3,121	75,077	855	11,556
Erie	21,758	713,749	19,349	657,179	19,086	256,224
Fayette	28,569	920,889	17,167	405,442	30,105	381,810
Forest	979	27,871	1,931	48,672	689	7,261
Franklin	42,992	1,306,923	22,596	540,336	71,205	1,033,824
Fulton	10,906	243,644	4,877	87,976	11,502	87,560
Greene	30,441	1,083,255	14,588	326,934	28,920	317,890
Huntingdon	21,517	759,237	11,157	230,769	33,610	353,934
Indiana	29,146	914,695	31,260	775,383	31,358	309,752
Jefferson	12,050	341,031	17,402	452,435	12,085	115,361
Juniata	14,703	446,004	10,734	239,371	17,387	232,687
Lackawanna	4,371	140,314	8,045	237,107	1,119	14,047
Lancaster	80,284	3,293,292	44,613	1,412,694	108,277	1,929,767
Lawrence	15,639	609,540	17,454	538,362	19,349	280,046
Lebanon	23,837	804,214	20,422	628,597	31,377	482,610
Lehigh	25,128	784,760	20,477	552,497	17,334	192,923
Luzerne	14,973	478,648	12,636	295,574	6,478	85,112
Lycoming	24,887	830,332	19,422	490,065	23,418	287,699
McKean	1,253	39,729	4,316	133,676	666	8,599
Mercer	23,494	795,469	29,288	985,601	23,821	328,754
Mifflin	13,479	531,132	8,577	248,255	22,654	293,630
Monroe	8,599	187,202	5,619	116,328	1,133	14,573
Montgomery	38,175	1,521,097	25,651	840,085	25,875	446,763
Montour	9,193	278,144	7,371	177,590	7,545	93,148
Northampton	26,051	854,791	20,731	637,609	20,816	227,466
Northumberland	23,715	755,418	17,913	416,791	24,020	321,087
Perry	18,881	644,506	16,524	351,329	23,961	301,595

PENNSYLVANIA—Continued.

Counties.	BARLEY.		BUCKWHEAT.		RYE.	
	Acres.	Bushels.	Acres.	Bushels.	Acres.	Bushels.
Philadelphia	.....	......	50	892	958	19,612
Pike	.....	......	2,584	41,954	3,261	25,492
Potter	217	3,594	2,832	51,709	521	5,471
Schuylkill	6	173	3,010	40,896	15,216	136,900
Snyder	.....	......	1,109	10,878	4,131	34,287
Somerset	376	7,844	5,901	79,831	8,454	67,082
Sullivan	.....	......	1,915	33,880	368	3,774
Susquehanna	29	636	9,504	164,147	3,072	37,191
Tioga	1,893	40,611	10,633	190,238	395	3,707
Union	10	127	243	2,721	1,519	16,261
Venango	30	478	8,424	113,227	1,580	14,475
Warren	174	3,373	2,307	38,856	421	5,006
Washington	1,727	34,682	116	1,724	571	7,544
Wayne	18	301	7,300	142,966	3,265	34,764
Westmoreland	294	5,643	3,230	34,803	3,085	23,826
Wyoming	.....	......	9,275	165,310	5,228	49,665
York	28	471	3,425	55,080	13,770	141,052

RHODE ISLAND.

	BARLEY.		BUCKWHEAT.		RYE.	
The State	715	17,783	105	1,254	1,270	12,997
Bristol	22	456	......	......	78	896
Kent	53	1,062	30	281	300	2,721
Newport	413	12,249	......	......	120	1,374
Providence	178	2,871	67	867	454	4,861
Washington	49	1,145	8	106	318	3,145

SOUTH CAROLINA.

	BARLEY.		BUCKWHEAT.		RYE.	
The State	1,162	16,257	......	......	7,152	27,049
Abbeville	267	3,483	......	......	43	255
Aiken	......	......	......	......	332	986
Anderson	114	1,412	......	......	214	959
Barnwell	......	......	......	......	995	4,556
Beaufort	......	......	......	......	......	......
Charleston	......	......	......	......	37	365
Chester	......	......	......	......	113	376
Chesterfield	......	......	......	......	201	655
Clarendon	......	......	......	......	29	64
Colleton	86	442	......	......	126	652
Darlington	......	......	......	......	565	1,742
Edgefield	73	1,279	......	......	58	250
Fairfield	5	80	......	......	76	462
Georgetown	19	125	......	......	......	......
Greenville	65	995	......	......	640	2,494
Hampton	......	......	......	......	108	557
Horry	......	......	......	......	20	77
Kershaw	33	165	......	......	159	585
Lancaster	21	95	......	......	30	116
Laurens	244	5,447	......	......	58	372
Lexington	......	......	......	......	70	194
Marion	......	......	......	......	890	2,871
Marlborough	......	......	......	......	288	925
Newberry	61	1,283	......	......	14	107
Oconee	16	134	......	......	789	2,842
Orangeburgh	......	......	......	......	430	1,543
Pickens	12	127	......	......	237	1,077
Richland	......	......	......	......	5	14
Spartanburgh	9	130	......	......	93	375
Sumter	5	75	......	......	111	522

PENNSYLVANIA—Continued.

Counties.	INDIAN CORN.		OATS.		WHEAT.	
	Acres.	Bushels.	Acres.	Bushels.	Acres.	Bushels.
Philadelphia	4,163	188,814	1,093	38,541	2,861	63,513
Pike	2,543	99,733	1,795	37,731	401	4,951
Potter	2,397	73,465	10,455	288,193	2,533	28,509
Schuylkill	15,053	376,516	13,692	275,405	8,542	117,300
Snyder	14,707	480,105	12,060	268,875	19,809	235,894
Somerset	9,832	323,367	23,512	579,419	17,982	192,870
Sullivan	2,326	80,995	3,671	122,082	1,559	20,358
Susquehanna	13,383	436,249	24,676	760,579	4,593	55,805
Tioga	10,504	348,600	24,243	744,394	8,807	102,143
Union	12,561	459,227	10,602	272,868	16,901	247,417
Venango	12,546	343,518	20,912	558,839	7,481	73,973
Warren	5,061	158,090	9,615	304,653	3,382	50,042
Washington	37,443	1,308,294	27,411	845,416	37,301	614,260
Wayne	5,008	171,664	9,350	278,985	549	7,114
Westmoreland	43,077	1,670,943	42,556	1,134,604	56,381	721,907
Wyoming	8,346	273,006	9,951	272,181	5,019	58,079
York	63,053	1,739,865	46,120	1,006,110	81,805	1,211,340

RHODE ISLAND.

The State	11,893	372,967	5,575	159,339	17	240
Bristol	546	19,484	158	3,831		
Kent	1,212	32,007	435	6,802		
Newport	2,941	107,048	2,156	78,098		
Providence	2,814	96,402	479	7,484	9	124
Washington	4,380	118,026	2,347	63,124	8	116

SOUTH CAROLINA.

The State	1,303,404	11,767,099	261,445	2,715,505	170,902	962,358
Abbeville	51,569	471,955	23,544	249,981	14,396	107,008
Aiken	51,481	377,022	3,545	54,339	6,527	22,584
Anderson	49,953	492,646	12,776	94,613	16,734	101,050
Barnwell	84,108	607,610	10,808	140,150	3,778	18,057
Beaufort	14,735	135,755	213	2,901		
Charleston	29,569	279,068	1,773	23,996	16	198
Chester	40,409	357,308	10,440	87,583	7,342	35,768
Chesterfield	27,228	247,430	4,640	41,646	2,549	10,320
Clarendon	32,810	222,274	2,845	28,777	125	624
Colleton	43,544	376,532	5,931	66,097	186	805
Darlington	53,557	440,892	8,317	88,216	2,593	13,453
Edgefield	67,825	559,086	36,432	415,243	11,323	67,841
Fairfield	40,274	367,930	7,561	86,566	4,012	24,511
Georgetown	4,389	44,161	205	3,741		
Greenville	52,599	582,156	9,282	62,673	11,605	62,132
Hampton	30,825	227,884	5,325	58,595	23	147
Horry	13,391	103,895	157	1,057		
Kershaw	21,891	219,957	2,849	34,402	1,509	6,355
Lancaster	26,622	294,939	6,697	48,385	3,777	16,852
Laurens	45,066	361,933	15,860	149,410	9,804	62,243
Lexington	35,760	304,509	10,237	121,290	12,155	48,167
Marion	55,183	470,745	6,784	69,011	1,081	9,131
Marlborough	33,773	338,527	4,727	63,180	2,436	20,077
Newberry	34,005	315,863	13,904	177,062	9,258	64,136
Oconee	23,224	268,899	4,527	39,392	4,265	26,017
Orangeburgh	66,419	529,259	9,727	140,473	3,529	15,635
Pickens	27,070	314,064	2,882	23,987	4,904	31,663
Richland	19,431	171,040	2,158	30,904	514	3,916
Spartanburgh	56,225	593,454	11,287	74,572	14,808	79,901
Sumter	51,876	442,360	5,886	64,581	400	2,644

SOUTH CAROLINA—Continued.

Counties.	BARLEY.		BUCKWHEAT.		RYE.	
	Acres.	Bushels.	Acres.	Bushels.	Acres.	Bushels.
Union	67	800	....	....	43	133
Williamsburgh	10	50	....	....	33	143
York	45	126	....	....	336	783

TENNESSEE.

	Acres.	Bushels.	Acres.	Bushels.	Acres.	Bushels.
The State	2, 600	30, 019	4, 907	33, 434	32, 403	156, 419
Anderson	5	61	29	153	264	1, 208
Bedford	24	108	....	....	806	6, 145
Benton	....	....	....	....	18	118
Bledsoe	....	....	9	84	648	2, 405
Blount	5	13	21	114	295	1, 027
Bradley	....	....	6	37	141	693
Campbell	....	....	10	47	714	3, 725
Cannon	....	....	13	122	1, 158	6, 985
Carroll	....	....	....	....	45	198
Carter	30	282	715	4, 704	374	2, 094
Cheatham	....	....	....	....	20	96
Claiborne	....	....	28	135	434	2, 242
Clay	....	....	....	....	273	9.22
Cocke	10	115	99	725	482	1, 901
Coffee	....	....	33	207	685	4. 040
Crockett	....	....	....	....	36	219
Cumberland	....	....	33	247	786	3, 418
Davidson	229	3, 830	12	326	379	3, 069
Decatur	....	....	....	....	32	68
DeKalb	11	149	....	....	768	4, 043
Dickson	6	30	30	117	116	555
Dyer	....	....	....	....	46	325
Fayette	....	....	....	....	59	316
Fentress	....	....	32	275	545	2, 118
Franklin	144	1, 010	11	84	204	1, 282
Gibson	....	....	....	....	29	325
Giles	....	....	....	....	957	5, 020
Grainger	5	102	....	....	167	617
Greene	158	1, 288	624	3, 088	274	1, 237
Grundy	....	....	13	28	97	654
Hamblen	130	1, 906	23	121	76	432
Hamilton	....	....	....	....	679	2, 675
Hancock	....	....	23	140	278	1, 180
Hardeman	....	....	....	....	64	333
Hardin	....	....	....	....	84	407
Hawkins	9	73	146	839	214	1, 210
Haywood	....	....	....	....	85	319
Henderson	....	....	....	....	238	1, 424
Henry	....	....	....	....	151	961
Hickman	26	192	21	163	225	1, 221
Houston	....	....	....	....	....	....
Humphreys	....	....	....	....	34	177
Jackson	....	....	....	....	812	4, 153
James	....	....	....	....	34	139
Jefferson	17	111	42	235	112	445
Johnson	....	....	672	5, 132	822	4, 906
Knox	76	974	41	284	527	3, 102
Lake	....	....	....	....	....	....
Lauderdale	....	....	....	....	5	55
Lawrence	20	173	6	55	357	1, 684
Lewis	33	183	....	....	58	281
Lincoln	76	1, 070	19	213	268	1, 641
London	....	....	....	....	310	1, 212
McMinn	....	....	....	....	309	1, 383
McNairy	....	....	....	....	41	170

SOUTH CAROLINA—Continued.

Counties.	INDIAN CORN.		OATS.		WHEAT.	
	Acres.	Bushels.	Acres.	Bushels.	Acres.	Bushels.
Union	36, 710	379, 330	5, 562	42, 040	6, 710	33, 951
Williamsburgh	30, 291	220, 311	1, 070	9, 860	78	409
York	51, 532	626, 505	13, 824	119, 882	14, 175	75, 173

TENNESSEE.

	Acres.	Bushels.	Acres.	Bushels.	Acres.	Bushels.
The State	2, 904, 873	62, 764, 429	468, 566	4, 722, 190	1, 196, 563	7, 331, 353
Anderson	21, 047	369, 958	10, 230	86, 198	7, 343	44, 609
Bedford	68, 492	1, 682, 358	6, 270	87, 408	39, 589	257, 425
Benton	24, 788	562, 354	2, 368	26, 832	4, 600	19, 785
Bledsoe	17, 474	342, 240	2, 748	21, 282	3, 546	18, 106
Blount	31, 080	450, 011	12, 888	95, 367	20, 588	110, 196
Bradley	23, 794	337, 446	4, 652	25, 672	16, 608	88, 961
Campbell	22, 138	341, 945	8, 100	68, 834	4, 518	25, 549
Cannon	27, 812	821, 012	1, 952	22, 802	12, 991	94, 150
Carroll	46, 076	1, 018, 415	3, 413	37, 694	17, 354	88, 396
Carter	12, 403	243, 906	5, 046	51, 141	8, 226	55, 150
Cheatham	19, 719	457, 189	3, 309	42, 297	3, 368	18, 030
Claiborne	28, 475	496, 262	9, 136	74, 921	9, 128	44, 192
Clay	20, 010	412, 287	1, 955	15, 205	4, 790	24, 424
Cocke	28, 308	553, 567	5, 767	50, 165	16, 660	94, 763
Coffee	27, 962	658, 293	3, 127	34, 160	9, 574	58, 155
Crockett	25, 650	626, 762	1, 501	16, 171	9, 883	54, 431
Cumberland	8, 452	127, 636	1, 366	16, 826	517	2, 797
Davidson	52, 764	1, 436, 582	8, 141	133, 807	18, 051	157, 530
Decatur	19, 985	473, 924	2, 701	26, 399	3, 829	14, 911
DeKalb	31, 004	863, 207	2, 275	21, 202	13, 416	78, 803
Dickson	26, 351	616, 422	4, 200	50, 735	8, 518	45, 318
Dyer	27, 820	900, 726	1, 961	37, 371	11, 820	101, 523
Fayette	63, 419	1, 030, 505	3, 661	38, 129	3, 787	18, 004
Fentress	14, 591	210, 416	2, 482	15, 524	2, 705	11, 092
Franklin	41, 560	745, 293	5, 959	71, 980	20, 178	135, 816
Gibson	57, 838	1, 449, 633	3, 378	44, 282	26, 016	162, 477
Giles	67, 758	1, 545, 605	2, 592	33, 289	30, 795	190, 205
Grainger	25, 832	356, 128	10, 568	83, 078	12, 895	61, 563
Greene	39, 464	719, 465	16, 597	139, 134	39, 259	237, 302
Grundy	6, 364	114, 758	889	8, 507	1, 753	7, 855
Hamblen	16, 143	231, 184	6, 731	51, 270	11, 085	66, 057
Hamilton	23, 337	461, 070	4, 771	45, 378	7, 618	45, 925
Hancock	17, 132	292, 195	5, 678	41, 625	6, 162	32, 189
Hardeman	45, 207	767, 324	2, 554	26, 807	4, 758	23, 991
Hardin	30, 809	799, 739	3, 387	35, 620	5, 445	29, 248
Hawkins	35, 791	706, 899	12, 688	117, 578	20, 143	115, 636
Haywood	39, 878	730, 949	2, 976	29, 299	5, 326	29, 278
Henderson	37, 734	862, 249	4, 543	42, 176	9, 791	46, 941
Henry	51, 852	1, 128, 660	3, 171	35, 407	20, 853	124, 537
Hickman	30, 716	828, 117	2, 896	42, 488	7, 874	37, 491
Houston	8, 974	231, 311	841	13, 846	1, 864	9, 062
Humphreys	26, 387	826, 941	1, 968	24, 521	5, 426	25, 371
Jackson	27, 448	683, 019	2, 598	28, 714	6, 825	40, 294
James	14, 413	223, 701	2, 816	15, 148	6, 658	34, 657
Jefferson	29, 317	506, 592	9, 448	83, 035	21, 261	125, 849
Johnson	7, 555	147, 388	3, 364	39, 496	4, 488	31, 022
Knox	44, 129	752, 559	23, 068	228, 786	34, 417	227, 705
Lake	14, 730	536, 265	108	4, 266	1, 608	24, 293
Lauderdale	22, 580	580, 797	1, 375	17, 398	3, 889	24, 953
Lawrence	21, 673	434, 215	2, 812	30, 097	8, 053	43, 351
Lewis	5, 272	114, 010	339	4, 808	1, 139	4, 824
Lincoln	57, 460	1, 252, 915	2, 993	37, 309	37, 279	275, 453
London	22, 512	319, 283	10, 037	91, 298	14, 490	90, 555
McMinn	35, 313	480, 898	9, 865	78, 372	20, 196	119, 873
McNary	33, 501	678, 659	5, 093	47, 559	6, 726	30, 678

TENNESSEE—Continued.

Counties.	BARLEY.		BUCKWHEAT.		RYE.	
	Acres.	Bushels.	Acres.	Bushels.	Acres.	Bushels.
Macon					350	1,338
Madison					107	516
Marion					155	788
Marshall	19	165			392	2,051
Maury	390	6,270			236	1,513
Meigs			5	35	148	518
Monroe					403	1,835
Montgomery	18	400			200	1,154
Moore	15	300			182	992
Morgan			68	523	1,285	4,880
Obion					36	162
Overton			16	82	995	2,931
Perry	9	125			62	565
Polk			6	60	547	1,847
Putnam			12	58	787	3,289
Rhea			8	78	209	851
Roane	19	326	10	73	906	3,244
Robertson	179	2,472			104	311
Rutherford	40	590	10	87	483	3,739
Scott			44	369	742	3,003
Sequatchie					391	1,519
Sevier	12	15	7	32	343	1,353
Shelby	24	80			378	1,717
Smith	92	688			574	3,228
Stewart			5	70	17	90
Sullivan	167	1,533	1,085	7,523	337	2,063
Sumner	116	759	6	47	779	3,708
Tipton	9	51			43	205
Trousdale	10	84			154	878
Unicoi	7	40	168	1,283	459	2,266
Union			21	221	236	916
Van Buren					130	492
Warren			9	54	724	2,173
Washington	260	2,658	706	4,514	109	794
Wayne	23	08			505	2,514
Weakley					78	467
White			10	48	917	2,837
Williamson	37	499			413	2,265
Wilson	120	1,226			852	4,869

TEXAS.

	Acres.	Bushels.	Acres.	Bushels.	Acres.	Bushels.
The State	5,527	72,786	48	535	3,326	25,390
Anderson	7	85			31	479
Andrews						
Angelina						
Aransas						
Archer						
Armstrong						
Atascosa						
Austin					63	810
Bailey						
Bandera					15	43
Bastrop			7	16	8	68
Baylor						
Bee						
Bell	69	1,019			6	140
Bexar					52	177
Blanco	20	125			128	851
Borden						
Bosque	17	282			103	752
Bowie						
Brazoria						

Counties.	INDIAN CORN.		OATS.		WHEAT.	
	Acres.	Bushels.	Acres.	Bushels.	Acres.	Bushels.
Macon	21, 286	436, 804	3, 876	34, 581	6, 161	31, 495
Madison	46, 885	906, 255	3, 157	31, 542	9, 623	50, 918
Marion	21, 985	474, 115	4, 240	54, 582	2, 824	18, 275
Marshall	47, 927	1, 176, 536	4, 675	59, 567	30, 484	172, 5*4
Maury	85, 496	2, 177, 071	6, 068	91, 452	43, 510	271, 592
Meigs	21, 812	444, 103	5, 267	45, 124	8, 141	47, 797
Monroe	33, 928	566, 356	10, 116	80, 793	19, 773	114, 881
Montgomery	49, 832	1, 236, 561	7, 263	86, 026	17, 122	148, 534
Moore	14, 389	327, 956	1, 050	14, 739	8, 659	66, 866
Morgan	7, 889	115, 327	2, 660	19, 490	666	2, 832
Obion	45, 005	1, 501, 881	2, 105	35, 098	25, 368	230, 243
Overton	30, 336	550, 091	4, 193	32, 953	9, 609	10, 015
Perry	15, 007	423, 461	1, 461	23, 874	3, 113	16, 051
Polk	16, 009	239, 224	1, 827	10, 505	7, 133	37, 126
Putnam	25, 510	511, 610	2, 919	24, 160	8, 726	42, 033
Rhea	16, 453	362, 801	3, 848	38, 650	4, 764	31, 290
Roane	33, 261	607, 787	13, 305	130, 821	10, 416	54, 276
Robertson	45, 408	793, 702	9, 873	115, 678	21, 912	134, 426
Rutherford	75, 753	1, 590, 855	6, 482	74, 794	29, 250	172, 997
Scott	12, 586	185, 646	3, 606	23, 060	447	2, 207
Sequatchie	8, 267	145, 532	709	6, 337	1, 068	6, 735
Sevier	27, 761	493, 885	5, 923	53, 274	17, 450	89, 499
Shelby	55, 260	996, 210	5, 216	72, 674	3, 564	23, 437
Smith	37, 106	1, 071, 050	3, 724	47, 240	17, 645	104, 945
Stewart	28, 957	778, 404	2, 070	26, 629	5, 620	34, 855
Sullivan	25, 477	550, 374	13, 473	111, 662	21, 830	131, 319
Sumner	49, 245	917, 940	9, 188	96, 081	20, 445	140, 895
Tipton	32, 379	762, 731	2, 431	34, 096	7, 363	56, 137
Trousdale	15, 373	396, 384	2, 297	26, 197	6, 629	37, 2*4
Unicoi	5, 049	81, 852	2, 309	22, 501	1, 840	9, 365
Union	19, 844	319, 702	7, 524	62, 233	8, 015	39, 208
Van Buren	7, 771	139, 070	764	6, 008	2, 954	13, 007
Warren	36, 456	670, 848	5, 612	51, 613	15, 888	66, 163
Washington	20, 154	407, 633	11, 394	109, 579	23, 740	153, 204
Wayne	25, 674	583, 305	2, 109	27, 442	8, 791	40, 038
Weakley	50, 001	1, 307, 873	1, 795	22, 583	25, 479	171, 835
White	34, 639	637, 143	2, 775	24, 811	11, 354	44, 653
Williamson	61, 122	1, 439, 445	5, 912	85, 522	39, 685	315, 966
Wilson	68, 468	1, 806, 262	9, 978	132, 506	32, 083	188, 540

TEXAS.

	Acres.	Bushels.	Acres.	Bushels.	Acres.	Bushels.
The State	2, 468, 587	20, 065, 172	238, 010	4, 893, 359	373, 570	2, 567, 737
Anderson	29, 852	306, 722	2, 780	33, 810	17	119
Andrews						
Angelina	8, 957	77, 656	156	1, 507		
Aransas	104	890	9	100		
Archer	404	4, 095	33	510	59	371
Armstrong						
Atascosa	4, 475	20, 992	93	840		
Austin	26, 810	448, 481	519	13, 534	23	161
Bailey						
Bandera	3, 611	13, 505	259	3, 764	1, 200	3, 252
Bastrop	31, 786	401, 999	1, 345	33, 704	852	4, 869
Baylor	1, 308	13, 407	45	377	112	507
Bee	2, 966	18, 192				
Bell	40, 475	402, 322	5, 169	161, 324	10, 923	84, 267
Bexar	14, 601	93, 841	2, 159	26, 186	1, 597	7, 670
Blanco	5, 362	35, 380	597	8, 363	2, 106	8, 931
Borden						
Bosque	22, 491	202, 848	2, 273	53, 939	9, 503	74, 704
Bowie	13, 199	194, 782	600	6, 336	7	20
Brazoria	13, 044	234, 950	348	5, 335		

Counties.	BARLEY.		BUCKWHEAT.		RYE.	
	Acres.	Bushels.	Acres.	Bushels.	Acres.	Bushels.
Brazos					5	150
Briscoe						
Brown	20	155			8	36
Burleson						
Burnet	68	494			27	149
Caldwell						
Calhoun						
Callahan	16	25			19	61
Cameron						
Camp	12	90			5	10
Carson						
Cass	19	140			13	101
Castro						
Chambers						
Cherokee					96	832
Childress						
Clay	32	290			11	40
Cochran						
Coleman					7	70
Collin	179	3,425			77	788
Collingsworth						
Colorado						
Comal					74	340
Comanche	13	92			29	170
Concho						
Cooke	45	410			51	700
Corvell					10	125
Cottle						
Crockett						
Crosby						
Dallam						
Dallas	325	7,020			45	1,083
Dawson						
Deaf Smith						
Delta					10	170
Denton	95	1,270	6	90	30	512
De Witt					10	64
Dickens						
Dimmit						
Donley						
Duval						
Eastland	14	102				
Edwards						
Ellis	94	2,685			41	412
El Paso	776	7,860			12	320
Encinal						
Erath					24	185
Falls	64	568				
Fannin	108	1,386			48	299
Fayette					187	1,218
Fisher						
Floyd						
Fort Bend						
Franklin						
Freestone						
Frio						
Gaines						
Galveston						
Garza						
Gillespie					50	352
Goliad						
Gonzales					6	49
Gray						
Grayson	143	2,442	9	70	43	801
Gregg						

TEXAS—Continued.

Counties.	INDIAN CORN.		OATS.		WHEAT.	
	Acres.	Bushels.	Acres.	Bushels.	Acres.	Bushels
Brazos	16,542	165,100	626	14,435	8	25
Briscoe						
Brown	12,408	65,194	516	8,457	7,814	38,743
Burleson	14,692	171,552	320	7,549	118	567
Burnet	14,187	123,505	1,097	39,128	5,173	29,071
Caldwell	18,393	190,648	1,364	23,838	2,506	11,098
Calhoun	266	2,072				
Callahan	2,245	14,059	56	569	1,091	5,078
Cameron	9,526	187,695	25	125		
Camp	11,369	153,407	1,544	22,077	824	3,861
Carson						
Cass	34,410	427,683	3,188	35,150	363	1,651
Castro						
Chambers	1,839	30,214				
Cherokee	37,244	450,573	4,312	54,483	210	1,358
Childress						
Clay	8,778	92,766	1,343	11,959	2,282	15,351
Cochran						
Coleman	4,333	19,855	90	1,430	1,568	11,938
Collin	52,253	1,016,140	10,834	338,419	24,212	188,702
Collingsworth						
Colorado	29,711	532,486	227	5,446		
Comal	8,990	39,036	861	10,717	2,898	13,414
Comanche	14,267	85,454	460	6,839	5,074	29,141
Concho	40	300				
Cooke	32,353	514,429	4,388	73,596	7,960	62,306
Coryell	22,903	196,713	2,733	60,498	8,506	55,919
Cottle						
Crockett						
Crosby						
Dallam						
Dallas	44,004	575,667	8,306	209,281	26,854	186,460
Dawson						
Deaf Smith						
Delta	9,199	130,061	1,902	39,349	1,400	7,673
Denton	35,326	531,637	6,233	112,681	12,103	72,412
De Witt	19,146	135,016	639	6,185	500	1,842
Dickens						
Dimmit	80	215				
Donley	128	565				
Duval	456	1,117	25	250		
Eastland	5,867	25,479	89	1,123	1,941	7,069
Edwards	102	605			14	34
Ellis	42,899	377,121	5,533	153,527	18,500	176,215
El Paso	838	4,419	5	120	2,534	28,911
Encinal	28	300				
Erath	19,702	108,883	1,822	22,660	5,832	28,397
Falls	29,943	376,555	1,200	30,667	953	6,626
Fannin	48,124	922,738	9,698	205,880	7,753	54,504
Fayette	47,770	694,883	1,023	28,645	265	1,432
Fisher						
Floyd						
Fort Bend	16,710	326,648	284	4,240		
Franklin	9,804	144,287	1,519	26,986	489	2,466
Freestone	29,242	252,742	1,462	32,623	151	1,247
Frio	1,574	7,443			8	40
Gaines						
Galveston	655	16,367	44	1,115		
Garza						
Gillespie	5,297	13,985	527	5,387	3,533	13,395
Goliad	9,059	87,305	279	2,896	372	1,284
Gonzales	30,984	227,501	767	12,811	646	4,489
Gray	46	500				
Grayson	56,344	976,731	10,009	188,188	15,736	96,740
Gregg	13,411	120,819	827	7,161	22	103

TEXAS—Continued.

Counties.	BARLEY.		BUCKWHEAT.		RYE.	
	Acres.	Bushels.	Acres.	Bushels.	Acres.	Bushels.
Grimes					6	52
Guadalupe	20	450			111	1,154
Hale						
Hall						
Hamilton	6	73			8	22
Hansford						
Hardeman						
Hardin						
Harris			10	200		
Harrison					40	300
Hartley						
Haskell						
Hays	48	628			7	10
Hemphill						
Henderson					30	191
Hidalgo						
Hill	48	962	5	50	19	125
Hockley						
Hood	58	970			15	95
Hopkins					43	500
Houston					5	23
Howard						
Hunt	25	310	11	109	8	90
Hutchinson						
Jack	27	431			25	94
Jackson						
Jasper						
Jefferson						
Johnson	71	901			20	79
Jones						
Karnes					16	73
Kaufman	416	5,501			38	270
Kendall					147	226
Kent						
Kerr	19	205			54	182
Kimble						
King						
Kinney						
Knox						
Lamar	23	463			12	123
Lamb						
Lampasas	14	107			15	85
La Salle						
Lavaca					73	731
Lee					10	87
Leon					7	35
Liberty						
Limestone	12	65				
Lipscomb						
Live Oak						
Llano					14	123
Lubbock						
Lynn						
McCulloch						
McLennan	91	2,030			75	1,315
McMullen						
Madison						
Marion	5	55			5	53
Martin						
Mason					56	321
Matagorda						
Maverick						
Medina						
Menard					5	125
Milam	14	446			7	45

TEXAS—Continued.

Counties.	INDIAN CORN.		OATS.		WHEAT.	
	Acres.	Bushels.	Acres.	Bushels.	Acres.	Bushels.
Grimes	29,072	286,969	555	10,011	70	615
Guadalupe	23,501	191,399	2,260	33,216	4,489	21,124
Hale						
Hall						
Hamilton	12,941	73,052	723	12,569	3,772	24,154
Hansford						
Hardeman						
Hardin	2,491	21,689	194	1,525		
Harris	9,895	139,333	172	7,165		
Harrison	38,808	278,981	765	7,542	18	147
Hartley						
Haskell						
Hays	10,749	99,096	2,223	39,251	2,789	16,699
Hemphill						
Henderson	18,607	254,828	2,490	38,997	179	959
Hidalgo	2,117	42,465				
Hill	33,013	327,484	4,475	143,144	6,533	51,743
Hockley						
Hood	10,427	72,927	605	12,607	4,355	21,519
Hopkins	25,573	318,214	7,974	157,182	3,804	20,044
Houston	26,966	283,402	617	9,847	29	281
Howard						
Hunt	29,157	365,004	6,314	154,517	7,385	43,583
Hutchinson						
Jack	10,990	115,761	230	5,117	1,866	10,889
Jackson	3,787	37,175	45	880		
Jasper	9,763	97,366	1,097	10,134		
Jefferson	1,758	24,169				
Johnson	38,151	413,940	5,528	134,566	14,339	95,299
Jones	409	4,110	54	1,193	91	860
Karnes	5,184	13,115	48	507	52	153
Kaufman	24,386	354,781	4,522	115,215	8,921	70,701
Kendall	3,657	5,552	655	3,592	1,167	1,850
Kent						
Kerr	1,346	6,456	185	1,166	1,134	2,728
Kimble	152	1,155	10	110	5	30
King						
Kinney	1,575	28,340	255	5,700		
Knox	60	1,200				
Lamar	40,617	817,854	5,651	131,967	3,047	18,903
Lamb						
Lampasas	9,153	49,402	760	10,747	3,033	17,890
La Salle	28	280				
Lavaca	28,474	377,914	789	14,316	94	704
Lee	14,396	146,271	745	16,432	136	735
Leon	25,490	223,535	725	9,896		
Liberty	6,102	91,998	40	215		
Limestone	32,988	336,620	2,497	60,033	1,269	12,887
Lipscomb						
Live Oak	456	2,120				
Llano	7,700	60,200	209	2,805	1,145	4,209
Lubbock						
Lynn						
McCulloch	1,005	6,825	108	705	463	2,131
McLennan	48,357	515,648	9,091	287,545	18,682	197,520
McMullen			80	1,200		
Madison	9,694	74,350	322	4,803		
Marion	13,554	137,006	565	6,582	13	30
Martin						
Mason	3,033	8,933	69	1,014	958	4,492
Matagorda	4,747	74,563	14	580		
Maverick	685	7,454				
Medina	11,600	35,164	1,069	8,005	1,008	3,116
Menard	72	690				
Milam	32,725	386,792	1,946	50,168	593	3,241

Counties.	BARLEY.		BUCKWHEAT.		RYE.	
	Acres.	Bushels.	Acres.	Bushels.	Acres.	Bushels.
Mitchell						
Montague	26	299			17	142
Montgomery						
Moore						
Morris						17	69
Motley						
Nacogdoches						35	113
Navarro	61	1,075			94	596
Newton						
Nolan						
Nueces						
Ochiltree						
Oldham						
Orange						
Palo Pinto	13	190			10	100
Panola						6	30
Parker	127	1,683			53	301
Parmer						
Pecos	589	5,232				
Polk						
Potter						
Presidio	508	2,100				
Rains						
Randall						
Red River						11	110
Refugio						
Roberts						
Robertson						
Rockwall	16	78				
Runnels						
Rusk	9	58			35	331
Sabine						
San Augustine						
San Jacinto						
San Patricio						
San Saba	17	90			37	186
Shackelford	114	1,110				
Shelby						
Sherman						
Scurry						
Smith						61	266
Somervell						5	60
Starr						
Stephens	10	130				
Stonewall						
Swisher						
Tarrant	483	9,037			54	951
Taylor						
Terry						
Throckmorton	93	1,180				
Titus						
Tom Green	169	3,950				
Travis	32	227			14	120
Trinity						
Tyler						
Upshur						10	78
Uvalde						
Van Zandt	55	302				
Victoria						
Walker						8	15
Waller						
Washington						22	104
Webb						
Wharton						
Wheeler						

Counties.	INDIAN CORN.		OATS.		WHEAT.	
	Acres.	Bushels.	Acres.	Bushels.	Acres.	Bushels.
Mitchell						
Montague	15,571	195,584	1,018	13,206	2,101	14,958
Montgomery	13,702	115,017	88	800		
Moore						
Morris	11,062	144,914	1,256	15,706	275	1,398
Motley		6.				
Nacogdoches	25,102	218,205	886	9,600		
Navarro	40,133	521,402	4,268	121,548	2,872	25,160
Newton	7,508	69,842	513	4,946		
Nolan	64	330				
Nueces	3,165	60,615	13	160		
Ochiltree						
Oldham						
Orange	1,237	19,919				
Palo Pinto	9,301	60,628	305	5,416	2,425	11,844
Panola	27,452	192,090	1,825	18,749	44	205
Parker	24,987	243,245	2,253	30,561	12,306	81,688
Parmer						
Pecos	2,533	16,872	7	125	20	120
Polk	10,907	121,355	298	3,326		
Potter						
Presidio	3,313	35,450	203	1,850	1,025	11,423
Rains	5,477	75,655	1,055	25,881	553	4,226
Randall						
Red River	32,898	634,490	2,970	52,453	1,044	7,678
Refugio	2,238	27,375				
Roberts						
Robertson	34,255	422,889	1,407	36,873	67	560
Rockwall	6,715	88,713	961	26,305	2,515	20,966
Runnels						
Rusk	39,744	367,706	2,965	30,953	123	506
Sabine	8,322	66,363	295	2,613		
San Augustine	11,442	80,422	561	7,327		
San Jacinto	9,494	102,853	163	2,127		
San Patricio	1,219	4,358	14	70		
San Saba	8,281	41,079	675	9,053	3,148	13,751
Shackelford	699	3,916	18	290	228	1,457
Shelby	20,985	185,484	1,200	12,356	201	849
Sherman						
Scurry						
Smith	43,631	515,515	4,633	64,005	580	2,920
Somervell	5,629	58,236	238	3,793	1,603	13,356
Starr	834	16,805				
Stephens	3,824	26,974	254	3,081	2,187	11,191
Stonewall						
Swisher						
Tarrant	38,496	429,118	7,055	153,671	26,481	193,673
Taylor	73	1,000			157	1,610
Terry						
Throckmorton	887	8,197			605	3,944
Titus	11,379	179,550	1,997	30,045	372	1,926
Tom Green	468	7,085	108	1,900		
Travis	30,882	264,675	4,779	102,106	4,048	24,633
Trinity	9,184	96,584	159	1,671		
Tyler	11,055	123,887	1,343	11,748	5	25
Upshur	20,728	246,117	2,517	26,067	1,425	5,838
Uvalde	1,345	10,224	91	983	407	987
Van Zandt	21,635	302,427	4,034	76,744	1,506	8,231
Victoria	6,253	90,210	174	3,418	28	260
Walker	17,512	153,726	387	6,645	15	125
Waller	10,350	132,691	126	2,185		
Washington	43,610	571,663	776	22,727	49	234
Webb	626	3,524				
Wharton	9,477	245,717	5	50	5	25
Wheeler						

TEXAS—Continued.

Counties.	BARLEY.		BUCKWHEAT.		RYE.	
	Acres.	Bushels.	Acres.	Bushels.	Acres.	Bushels.
Wichita						
Wilbarger						
Williamson	10	133			534	2,129
Wilson						
Wise	122	2,154			12	115
Wood...........................	11	72			34	229
Young..........................	11	15			13	20
Yoakum.........................						
Zapata						
Zavala.........................						

UTAH.

	Acres.	Bushels.	Acres.	Bushels.	Acres.	Bushels.
The Territory	11,208	217,140			1,133	9,005
Beaver	387	6,482				
Box Elder	939	17,097			578	3,218
Cache	176	4,442			190	2,265
Davis........................	2,691	38,660			65	668
Emery........................	26	126				
Iron.........................	291	7,436				
Juab.........................	319	5,141				
Kane	74	1,066				
Millard	1,097	17,375			22	40
Morgan.......................	80	1,490				
Pi Ute.......................	267	3,863				
Rich	43	419				
Salt Lake....................	683	16,395			112	1,056
San Juan.....................	30	725				
San Pete.....................	287	6,126			42	357
Sevier	160	3,426				
Summit.......................	106	2,285				
Tooele.......................	60	1,259			32	602
Uintah						
Utah	1,774	47,561			45	520
Wasatch						
Washington	198	3,407				
Weber........................	1,580	31,677			67	859

VERMONT.

	Acres.	Bushels.	Acres.	Bushels.	Acres.	Bushels.
The State.............	10,552	267,625	17,649	356,618	6,319	71,733
Addison	809	17,633	1,212	20,324	882	10,520
Bennington..................	275	7,190	1,897	30,708	725	9,048
Caledonia....................	1,220	32,501	1,525	30,714	98	1,345
Chittenden	1,315	32,488	1,374	22,007	1,315	15,874
Essex........................	78	1,941	720	18,696	28	336
Franklin	1,647	38,389	1,052	20,230	651	6,672
Grand Isle...................	337	7,425	1,633	34,199	301	3,607
Lamoille	482	12,847	413	9,219	66	756
Orange	600	15,330	2,507	56,574	133	1,643
Orleans	1,924	52,600	1,002	23,835	64	931
Rutland	212	5,710	1,440	23,067	779	9,051
Washington	731	21,489	832	19,866	106	1,519
Windham.....................	519	11,865	484	9,282	458	4,500
Windsor......................	403	10,217	1,498	28,897	513	5,931

Counties.	INDIAN CORN.		OATS.		WHEAT.	
	Acres.	Bushels.	Acres.	Bushels.	Acres.	Bushels.
Wichita	1,361	18,325	10	70	50	532
Wilbarger	225	2,600				
Williamson	25,225	202,711	8,634	193,490	7,901	56,695
Wilson	7,999	57,467	43	320	96	355
Wise	27,400	357,494	2,267	43,963	4,121	26,749
Wood	18,635	253,079	2,801	40,729	2,282	10,644
Young	9,181	86,591	114	1,219	1,947	13,197
Yoakum						
Zapata	2,135	63,040	15	600		
Zavala	143	1,835	81	650		

UTAH.

	Acres.	Bushels.	Acres.	Bushels.	Acres.	Bushels.
The Territory	12,007	163,342	19,525	418,082	72,542	1,669,199
Beaver	84	517	223	4,331	1,610	18,270
Box Elder	780	9,024	737	15,088	5,306	75,200
Cache	624	9,228	1,358	29,343	10,258	208,553
Davis	891	11,443	550	18,454	7,453	92,347
Emery	17	195	69	762	237	2,496
Iron	494	9,193	353	6,761	1,366	19,386
Juab	89	708	155	3,234	927	11,324
Kane	639	7,621	39	1,136	632	11,933
Miller	110	875	569	8,340	1,470	14,550
Morgan	18	346	197	3,356	1,416	13,989
Pi Ute			528	6,565	913	7,706
Rich			665	14,750	599	9,018
Salt Lake	1,213	23,398	836	22,073	5,385	106,632
San Juan	8	74	16	262	59	1,041
San Pete	328	4,472	4,763	90,892	9,582	164,627
Sevier	126	1,447	2,806	52,245	4,598	70,528
Summit			903	22,171	1,976	36,320
Tooele	606	5,205	587	18,090	1,300	16,130
Uintah	41	880			67	1,780
Utah	2,933	41,310	2,215	50,264	7,326	125,685
Wasatch	5	70	485	16,144	1,620	29,174
Washington	157	1,636	29	537	473	6,672
Weber	2,844	35,700	1,442	33,284	7,969	124,929

VERMONT.

	Acres.	Bushels.	Acres.	Bushels.	Acres.	Bushels.
The State	55,249	2,014,271	99,548	3,742,282	20,748	337,257
Addison	5,295	162,964	13,539	452,882	3,054	46,549
Bennington	4,134	134,720	5,891	199,934	204	2,604
Caledonia	1,941	70,125	7,123	284,369	1,935	38,880
Chittenden	5,887	198,977	8,589	318,192	1,464	21,313
Essex	275	8,547	2,475	92,697	651	10,845
Franklin	4,356	145,214	9,261	360,615	2,153	29,129
Grande Isle	1,424	44,038	4,228	120,758	1,189	11,851
Lamoille	1,834	66,615	4,096	175,826	715	13,355
Orange	4,539	168,980	7,430	282,824	2,171	35,417
Orleans	1,441	49,032	8,275	325,425	2,432	47,556
Rutland	7,001	270,692	8,885	326,051	886	12,858
Washington	3,247	137,133	7,680	336,065	1,743	36,079
Windham	5,277	199,576	4,234	149,668	243	3,556
Windsor	8,508	357,658	7,842	316,976	1,908	27,263

VIRGINIA.

Counties.	BARLEY.		BUCKWHEAT.		RYE.	
	Acres.	Bushels.	Acres.	Bushels.	Acres.	Bushels.
The State	859	14,223	16,463	136,004	48,746	324,431
Accomac					60	411
Albemarle			55	649	285	1,671
Alexandria			20	275	159	1,539
Alleghany			121	895	58	232
Amelia			9	25		
Amherst			94	999	170	1,276
Appomattox					6	18
Augusta	182	3,733	196	1,791	1,955	16,000
Bath			220	1,963	320	2,196
Bedford			88	660	202	1,810
Bland			309	2,201	479	3,433
Botetourt	27	226	123	1,037	110	762
Brunswick					12	90
Buchanan			49	447	553	3,263
Buckingham			16	93	68	477
Campbell			13	134	79	412
Caroline			9	62	618	2,965
Carroll			2,008	14,544	6,155	33,138
Charles City					13	107
Charlotte			7	65	54	617
Chesterfield	5	23	78	720	83	499
Clarke			28	202	133	1,034
Craig			326	2,527	656	4,598
Culpeper			25	189	170	826
Cumberland			8	103	38	256
Dinwiddie					39	187
Elizabeth City						
Essex					462	2,336
Fairfax			357	4,630	699	6,172
Fauquier			150	1,312	779	4,293
Floyd			2,481	17,898	3,247	20,378
Fluvanna			5	25	21	92
Franklin			165	1,373	375	2,272
Frederick			977	9,561	1,746	11,634
Giles			280	2,542	657	4,237
Gloucester	20	40			71	582
Goochland	6	34	17	71	54	461
Grayson			942	7,035	4,648	31,825
Greene			40	390	547	3,801
Greenville						
Halifax					69	500
Hanover			22	170	95	776
Henrico	20	400			154	1,596
Henry					203	1,208
Highland			826	8,720	422	3,641
Isle of Wight					7	35
James City					12	61
King and Queen					211	1,150
King George					78	360
King William					94	368
Lancaster						
Lee			79	714	882	6,402
Loudoun			232	2,338	600	5,408
Louisa			8	79	40	277
Lunenburg	5	25			12	55
Madison			7	92	553	4,000
Matthews					18	154
Mecklenburg	13	109			73	489
Middlesex					47	152
Montgomery			970	7,027	990	5,419
Nansemond			36	410	24	193
Nelson			182	2,466	749	5,549
New Kent					40	200
Norfolk					5	50
Northampton						

VIRGINIA.

Counties.	INDIAN CORN.		OATS.		WHEAT.	
	Acres.	Bushels.	Acres.	Bushels.	Acres.	Bushels.
The State	1,768,127	29,119,761	563,443	5,333,181	901,177	7,826,174
Accomac	42,331	508,339	6,947	38,334	1,834	17,219
Albemarle	35,234	714,715	17,483	139,451	25,806	186,093
Alexandria	1,584	35,017	186	2,707	366	5,084
Alleghany	4,548	95,011	2,726	34,981	3,750	28,832
Amelia	16,112	176,685	8,467	74,598	5,996	51,919
Amherst	22,322	404,630	12,785	112,661	12,308	94,940
Appomattox	10,542	149,487	8,226	50,438	5,685	37,974
Augusta	31,324	727,235	8,570	122,337	44,966	522,341
Bath	4,427	90,845	1,437	20,927	3,462	26,557
Bedford	29,595	591,627	22,430	223,827	23,927	153,308
Bland	5,344	104,243	1,954	28,753	4,239	27,572
Botetourt	13,379	282,313	7,858	92,107	18,763	195,537
Brunswick	24,117	272,208	10,633	65,619	5,575	50,874
Buchanan	14,871	162,058	2,132	29,109	1,246	7,816
Buckingham	20,592	269,081	11,297	73,863	8,935	57,108
Campbell	19,794	316,606	18,188	120,034	9,830	58,987
Caroline	41,385	486,453	2,966	17,582	11,654	77,306
Carroll	16,229	241,912	7,140	74,509	5,505	4,599
Charles City	9,614	119,791	2,667	30,400	4,384	51,043
Charlotte	19,438	311,579	10,829	77,799	6,997	65,301
Chesterfield	20,817	245,645	10,708	79,607	6,092	57,577
Clarke	12,348	363,436	922	16,738	18,182	265,549
Craig	4,499	85,376	2,135	27,102	4,042	21,837
Culpeper	21,169	415,434	4,786	41,744	15,882	106,551
Cumberland	10,985	148,019	6,029	37,673	5,926	41,317
Dinwiddie	22,720	214,160	7,907	45,285	5,310	45,255
Elizabeth City	5,972	71,160	402	5,553	1,994	18,261
Essex	23,429	312,401	1,579	13,602	9,559	70,230
Fairfax	16,060	381,702	3,414	50,771	9,238	106,533
Fauquier	38,277	875,370	5,388	60,382	24,555	263,953
Floyd	13,449	226,574	9,521	130,370	8,044	46,263
Fluvanna	11,351	206,094	5,734	36,185	7,023	47,220
Franklin	24,097	450,021	16,524	180,756	16,756	104,468
Frederick	17,711	444,295	3,019	45,572	22,058	260,412
Giles	9,842	236,201	2,222	31,495	7,773	46,817
Gloucester	14,133	177,610	2,600	20,202	4,314	30,907
Goochland	13,876	207,856	6,649	58,443	8,260	73,728
Grayson	14,273	253,802	4,711	68,920	7,998	53,310
Greene	6,660	158,954	2,236	22,109	5,423	40,269
Greensville	12,745	145,674	1,857	18,525	451	3,493
Halifax	43,725	651,766	22,087	194,438	16,450	138,252
Hanover	30,630	356,283	11,847	86,381	13,146	101,705
Henrico	17,229	301,661	8,024	87,303	7,559	99,365
Henry	14,748	247,582	8,877	83,488	7,951	45,170
Highland	2,772	55,100	747	11,065	2,547	23,688
Isle of Wight	18,038	228,998	1,568	16,447	141	1,547
James City	6,231	66,774	1,061	7,311	1,081	9,315
King and Queen	21,232	252,546	1,334	10,526	5,260	34,071
King George	21,378	296,075	855	4,586	6,160	40,437
King William	16,944	218,184	2,434	13,206	8,542	78,476
Lancaster	6,723	78,248	395	2,815	2,816	25,413
Lee	30,267	628,753	8,420	82,805	13,222	91,812
Londonn	36,464	1,113,204	2,754	38,510	35,280	501,607
Louisa	23,807	303,863	10,329	50,254	11,928	72,854
Lunenburg	14,595	179,087	8,273	61,701	4,151	38,124
Madison	14,614	399,100	2,880	25,326	12,534	104,691
Matthews	10,023	146,184	795	7,281	1,598	12,472
Mecklenburg	34,268	462,512	15,811	185,345	10,548	86,303
Middlesex	9,625	93,433	568	3,211	3,030	17,987
Montgomery	15,697	332,709	5,576	79,121	12,271	69,701
Nansemond	25,750	280,854	2,147	29,647	407	5,486
Nelson	18,240	346,085	7,308	65,189	10,090	86,006
New Kent	9,391	121,910	3,384	29,090	2,970	21,545
Norfolk	31,171	403,849	1,459	18,443	63	442
Northampton	22,992	208,453	7,140	48,415	95	997

VIRGINIA—Continued.

Counties.	BARLEY.		BUCKWHEAT.		RYE.	
	Acres.	Bushels.	Acres.	Bushels.	Acres.	Bushels.
Northumberland	40	380	8	123	19	124
Nottoway			7	63	56	273
Orange					104	558
Page			220	1,900	2,275	15,160
Patrick			314	2,349	1,268	9,386
Pittsylvania					149	663
Powhatan					30	308
Prince Edward			18	185	11	65
Prince George			8	70		
Princess Anne					15	300
Prince William			202	1,925	265	1,720
Pulaski	24	252	530	3,812	531	3,124
Rappahannock			250	2,091	1,030	4,030
Richmond			54	471	353	1,626
Roanoke			130	1,183	530	3,522
Rockbridge	244	3,644	225	2,254	451	3,229
Rockingham	236	4,888	332	2,778	2,420	19,230
Russell			286	2,017	732	4,873
Scott			266	1,862	433	2,291
Shenandoah	17	317	220	1,940	1,901	16,602
Smyth			255	2,027	351	3,028
Southampton					341	2,600
Spottsylvania			44	522	67	374
Stafford			49	524	32	159
Surry						
Sussex			10	85	54	371
Tazewell			316	2,275	929	6,642
Warren			64	446	903	6,437
Warwick			26	560		
Washington	11	62	425	3,372	209	1,260
Westmoreland			5	65	42	231
Wise			337	2,674	1,289	6,513
Wythe	9	90	264	1,997	777	4,867
York						

WASHINGTON.

	Acres.	Bushels.	Acres.	Bushels.	Acres.	Bushels.
The Territory	14,680	506,537	106	2,498	518	7,124
Chehalis	24	1,070				
Clallam	171	7,065			18	218
Clarke	104	2,948	8	130	5	88
Columbia	3,881	180,015	6	50		
Cowlitz	32	977	15	265	9	174
Island	349	13,259				
Jefferson	5	135				
King	104	3,910	13	234		
Kitsap						
Klikitat	506	14,480			261	3,049
Lewis	15	390				
Mason						
Pacific						
Pierce	92	2,513	5	90	23	216
San Juan	162	6,078				
Skamania						
Snohomish	183	9,534				
Spokane	470	14,627				
Stevens	54	1,550				
Thurston	34	995			58	625
Wahkiakum					31	350
Walla Walla	6,183	214,719			26	538
Whatcom	427	23,728	9	229	19	271
Whitman	1,411	51,732	50	1,500	19	271
Yakima	473	15,912			68	1,595

VIRGINIA—Continued.

Counties.	INDIAN CORN.		OATS.		WHEAT.	
	Acres.	Bushels.	Acres.	Bushels.	Acres.	Bushels.
Northumberland	13,965	164,976	638	5,589	6,304	37,099
Nottoway	13,187	182,707	8,447	54,939	5,652	47,503
Orange	16,344	346,035	4,422	38,728	10,536	76,102
Page	9,335	205,432	941	11,250	12,396	122,648
Patrick	15,786	262,183	7,647	88,285	4,334	23,797
Pittsylvania	40,477	613,186	30,014	243,446	16,790	112,214
Powhatan	10,856	152,060	6,850	48,246	5,868	51,314
Prince Edward	14,446	192,462	7,664	59,870	5,195	45,838
Prince George	16,186	183,683	5,953	54,295	3,047	33,441
Princess Anne	28,573	306,602	1,138	13,451	109	790
Prince William	14,829	281,474	3,519	37,788	8,100	65,964
Pulaski	10,256	155,989	2,561	36,825	7,105	41,594
Rappahannock	15,734	320,978	2,626	31,946	8,917	64,716
Richmond	13,712	157,107	322	2,164	5,788	42,926
Roanoke	9,464	197,274	4,802	59,538	17,073	172,468
Rockbridge	18,988	432,645	5,852	60,593	24,144	203,097
Rockingham	28,938	657,834	4,127	54,833	43,838	507,080
Russell	19,030	419,106	5,619	46,117	8,623	79,280
Scott	30,456	529,968	11,457	79,698	13,683	72,912
Shenandoah	17,993	440,847	1,041	27,450	28,327	351,635
Smyth	12,692	325,055	5,536	99,607	8,272	68,412
Southampton	36,012	390,908	1,417	15,061	101	858
Spottsylvania	18,201	241,142	3,912	23,240	7,279	49,874
Stafford	15,434	216,333	2,255	15,101	7,127	40,697
Surry	9,013	84,616	1,930	10,675	60	241
Sussex	18,746	163,686	2,871	25,337	333	2,471
Tazewell	14,688	337,488	5,031	83,522	7,911	72,978
Warren	9,663	244,459	1,362	16,149	11,209	106,918
Warwick	5,622	70,519	322	3,775	228	3,658
Washington	24,543	536,301	12,582	159,180	16,163	107,973
Westmoreland	17,743	216,468	1,255	8,668	7,019	45,156
Wise	12,058	217,266	2,326	17,200	2,270	12,307
Wythe	13,305	205,484	5,951	112,616	10,397	70,713
York	8,693	104,326	725	6,836	1,471	15,079

WASHINGTON.

	INDIAN CORN.		OATS.		WHEAT.	
	Acres.	Bushels.	Acres.	Bushels.	Acres.	Bushels.
The Territory	2,117	39,183	37,962	1,571,706	81,554	1,921,322
Chehalis			484	17,952	731	19,966
Clallam	12	440	282	10,960	945	25,257
Clarke	86	1,640	2,507	72,734	2,958	51,584
Columbia	616	13,380	3,218	150,232	17,294	425,879
Cowlitz	10	158	609	27,894	1,038	24,042
Island			765	38,451	843	22,223
Jefferson			71	2,558	35	1,340
King	10	320	530	22,020	260	7,141
Kitsap						
Klikitat	237	4,210	1,012	33,488	5,143	74,352
Lewis			3,981	127,262	4,549	96,233
Mason			59	1,425		
Pacific			275	9,752	96	2,579
Pierce	5	114	1,201	31,935	448	6,593
San Juan			912	42,102	349	9,479
Skamania			78	1,960	26	500
Snohomish			682	32,469	172	5,251
Spokane	17	439	1,841	62,318	2,750	51,535
Stevens			856	27,778	567	12,672
Thurston			1,354	34,894	1,151	18,465
Wahkiakum			6	204		
Walla Walla	900	14,038	3,475	139,827	28,770	779,907
Whatcom	7	236	6,147	402,426	354	9,787
Whitman	46	910	6,328	231,922	10,225	204,762
Yakima	171	3,298	1,289	49,134	2,850	71,775

WEST VIRGINIA.

Counties.	BARLEY.		BUCKWHEAT.		RYE.	
	Acres.	Bushels.	Acres.	Bushels.	Acres.	Bushels.
The State............	424	9,740	30,334	285,298	17,279	113,181
Barbour...............			1,312	10,568	339	2,130
Berkeley	110	2,372	444	3,785	886	5,506
Boone			10	50	42	158
Braxton			93	049	26	253
Brooke	143	3,520	16	202	91	971
Cabell			54	539	54	432
Calhoun			153	1,222	57	332
Clay			33	271	23	177
Doddridge			374	3,382	123	1,068
Fayette			307	2,182	102	769
Gilmer...............			246	1,734	37	246
Grant................			435	4,351	471	2,711
Greenbrier			696	3,475	301	2,515
Hampshire			2,790	25,482	2,681	14,349
Hancock	7	129	184	1,993	179	1,622
Hardy................			1,176	9,170	1,418	8,863
Harrison.............			355	2,991	54	394
Jackson..............			631	6,151	184	1,735
Jefferson............			36	339	312	2,190
Kanawha..............			87	864	95	1,017
Lewis			233	1,880	26	236
Lincoln..............			18	153	66	389
Logan			8	51	114	657
McDowell			57	419	161	1,367
Marion...............			475	4,378	54	479
Marshall.............	11	195	548	6,294	310	3,360
Mason................			462	5,081	229	1,451
Mercer...............			481	3,436	322	2,127
Mineral			610	6,065	1,145	5,831
Monongalia...........			939	8,164	276	1,858
Monroe...............			841	6,600	249	1,679
Morgan			740	5,661	1,345	8,108
Nicholas.............			472	3,551	173	1,089
Ohio.................	147	3,443	6	74	71	996
Pendleton			1,367	11,510	901	5,871
Pleasants............			143	1,442	34	347
Pocahontas			566	5,608	295	1,907
Preston..............	6	81	6,423	73,974	1,151	8,690
Putnam			110	1,328	50	430
Raleigh..............			764	5,324	221	1,134
Randolph.............			833	6,052	390	2,962
Ritchie..............			605	5,532	184	1,300
Roane			188	1,706	78	470
Summers			274	2,375	154	964
Taylor			401	3,976	44	317
Tucker...............			661	5,784	196	1,247
Tyler................			488	5,424	97	721
Upshur...............			647	6,005	226	1,605
Wayne			41	254	278	1,730
Webster..............			91	1,174	49	480
Wetzel...............			470	4,858	192	1,550
Wirt.................			315	3,130	74	522
Wood.................			424	4,924	286	2,522
Wyoming			102	1,285	264	1,129

WEST VIRGINIA.

Counties.	INDIAN CORN.		OATS.		WHEAT.	
	Acres.	Bushels.	Acres.	Bushels.	Acres.	Bushels.
The State............	565,785	14,090,609	126,931	1,908,505	393,068	4,001,711
Barbour.....................	10,992	253,262	2,083	24,606	6,068	51,454
Berkeley....................	19,562	539,875	2,822	43,072	25,557	318,996
Boone........	8,563	160,615	1,798	14,123	1,360	7,425
Braxton...................	10,628	296,964	1,209	14,835	5,558	46,418
Brooke	4,244	162,809	2,021	61,290	3,890	62,623
Cabell.....................	14,078	271,431	1,760	19,581	8,068	78,805
Calhoun....................	6,586	157,191	622	7,239	3,089	21,550
Clay	4,390	90,052	1,184	11,853	1,035	6,583
Doddridge..................	7,089	241,832	626	9,428	6,125	57,138
Fayette	8,965	154,108	3,860	42,277	4,289	28,035
Gilmer	8,066	213,814	550	6,527	2,384	34,552
Grant	6,504	136,043	621	7,172	4,394	33,399
Greenbrier	11,658	251,695	6,382	100,913	7,786	72,941
Hampshire	12,898	287,228	4,446	58,783	11,821	102,931
Hancock....................	3,270	100,806	2,463	57,760	5,588	39,466
Hardy	8,710	236,082	1,232	17,952	4,958	50,416
Harrison....................	15,720	455,094	1,090	25,870	10,843	113,218
Jackson	17,575	404,287	1,846	28,373	14,500	131,988
Jefferson	20,804	673,425	841	17,731	31,072	496,705
Kanawha..................	26,136	549,410	5,138	55,835	10,680	86,755
Lewis	10,580	322,727	828	10,742	7,476	64,892
Lincoln....................	13,384	253,682	2,127	19,129	4,771	33,637
Logan	12,908	292,658	1,398	10,463	1,629	9,218
McDowell.................	4,534	67,776	1,372	14,829	526	4,353
Marion	13,667	390,487	3,105	46,481	11,701	112,506
Marshall.................	18,762	659,615	7,905	183,463	17,249	236,670
Mason....................	20,692	496,717	1,510	22,305	21,084	209,345
Mercer	7,437	114,123	3,400	42,759	5,605	38,538
Mineral....	6,465	131,032	1,867	23,120	5,590	47,402
Monongalia...............	15,216	441,587	4,607	72,988	12,881	96,916
Monroe....................	9,092	215,068	3,786	55,255	6,744	41,784
Morgan....................	5,878	114,503	1,360	17,577	5,249	123,393
Nicholas......	7,583	139,506	2,715	28,520	2,808	17,433
Ohio	7,195	305,847	2,033	90,061	4,769	88,329
Pendleton	6,975	143,622	1,275	12,212	5,340	44,936
Pleasants..................	5,829	152,527	496	6,341	5,081	53,059
Pocahontas................	3,519	80,943	1,889	32,990	2,891	27,790
Preston....................	10,823	245,266	9,988	197,395	7,112	65,913
Putnam	14,109	301,552	2,035	23,189	9,863	82,522
Raleigh...................	7,020	144,441	3,322	40,478	2,853	16,009
Randolph..................	5,539	128,610	1,013	25,873	2,772	25,713
Ritchie....................	10,769	276,743	1,234	16,141	8,038	65,074
Roane	14,490	347,905	1,322	18,418	9,767	68,899
Summers	7,776	149,180	2,375	31,075	4,440	33,783
Taylor....................	3,979	112,782 .	1,214	13,445	3,724	29,963
Tucker	2,193	63,632	1,012	15,221	935	6,973
Tyler.....................	10,132	279,506	1,444	17,937	8,543	79,310
Upshur	8,102	216,099	1,282	17,722	4,161	35,499
Wayne	24,308	501,506	4,324	38,560	7,183	56,613
Webster..................	2,896	84,861	578	7,266	626	5,074
Wetzel	15,426	483,463	3,019	49,205	10,927	112,110
Wirt	7,142	178,327	1,234	16,612	4,949	39,629
Wood	17,189	432,674	2,431	41,276	17,534	181,883
Wyoming..................	6,238	98,321	2,208	20,828	782	4,345

Counties.	BARLEY.		BUCKWHEAT.		RYE.	
	Acres.	Bushels.	Acres.	Bushels.	Acres.	Bushels.
The State	204,335	5,043,118	34,117	299,107	169,602	2,298,513
Adams	78	1,165	3,149	17,819	10,481	110,757
Ashland						
Barron	1,388	31,255	106	1,358	205	3,188
Bayfield						
Brown	2,022	47,011	184	1,780	2,862	44,337
Buffalo	2,085	51,481	179	1,977	774	11,714
Burnett	79	1,847	8	115	106	2,201
Calumet	6,294	157,021	89	1,108	239	4,020
Chippewa	1,513	39,849	114	1,597	255	3,863
Clark	392	8,019	189	2,796	431	6,456
Columbia	6,547	149,617	967	6,744	5,656	67,576
Crawford	1,715	28,150	340	4,168	1,478	19,610
Dane	21,361	480,624	914	8,784	5,555	84,890
Dodge	15,049	432,495	224	2,724	1,573	30,152
Door	692	15,013	61	932	789	13,023
Douglas						
Dunn	1,669	46,497	381	4,224	1,316	16,144
Eau Claire	831	21,635	156	2,064	764	9,902
Fond du Lac	12,075	313,497	439	5,688	989	17,223
Grant	2,998	52,961	724	8,072	4,827	63,200
Green	635	12,544	542	5,479	3,334	51,100
Green Lake	1,583	35,164	650	4,988	4,244	47,572
Iowa	1,841	41,377	471	4,613	1,816	22,970
Jackson	2,536	51,616	429	3,808	1,003	13,319
Jefferson	9,868	260,897	277	2,883	4,116	65,870
Juneau	455	10,065	3,701	35,036	4,010	44,797
Kenosha	1,275	32,615	195	2,121	770	13,313
Kewaunee	1,338	24,381	14	177	3,306	46,633
La Crosse	1,831	46,769	164	1,600	3,559	45,555
La Fayette	1,064	22,637	334	4,340	1,485	24,802
Langlade						
Lincoln	14	277	8	330	10	106
Manitowoc	5,290	119,536	29	505	5,306	87,869
Marathon	581	9,907	104	1,485	662	9,328
Marinette	60	1,373	15	225	302	5,235
Marquette	36	571	2,366	17,032	12,875	129,961
Milwaukee	7,036	212,779	104	2,202	3,468	80,683
Monroe	2,197	50,686	832	6,782	2,311	28,261
Oconto	258	5,725	73	1,021	440	6,952
Outagamie	2,964	77,881	244	3,466	1,269	18,735
Ozaukee	5,262	138,407	71	1,112	2,415	47,356
Pepin	357	9,170	224	2,717	1,434	16,521
Pierce	2,034	53,547	188	2,177	379	5,502
Polk	619	15,490	47	545	245	4,810
Portage	965	16,544	723	3,819	10,144	111,059
Price						
Racine	2,046	51,918	271	2,830	1,005	33,797
Richland	404	7,783	340	3,311	1,052	12,904
Rock	23,420	531,892	1,368	14,812	8,390	124,709
Saint Croix	1,073	27,981	110	1,810	209	3,132
Sauk	1,864	47,136	2,081	16,389	5,264	64,847
Shawano	417	7,907	80	822	1,740	22,301
Sheboygan	9,445	238,419	720	9,891	4,992	81,361
Taylor	5	96			16	343
Trempealeau	2,889	70,098	396	4,956	1,125	15,828
Vernon	4,270	93,445	181	2,213	1,622	22,082
Walworth	9,079	233,779	1,170	14,497	2,596	34,561
Washington	7,448	204,203	164	1,370	1,989	86,720
Waukesha	10,209	368,977	457	3,976	5,344	95,156
Waupaca	1,724	32,128	1,475	10,971	5,904	69,933
Waushara	446	7,612	4,611	21,024	15,029	164,486
Winnebago	1,824	47,150	603	9,231	1,004	14,307
Wood	79	1,507	61	588	1,728	17,511

WISCONSIN.

Counties.	INDIAN CORN.		OATS.		WHEAT.	
	Acres.	Bushels.	Acres.	Bushels.	Acres.	Bushels.
The State............	1, 015, 393	34, 230, 579	955, 597	32, 905, 320	1, 948, 160	24, 884, 669
Adams	11, 247	218, 785	5, 381	131, 223	7, 341	75, 813
Ashland	....	....	....	....	....	....
Barron	712	18, 956	5, 059	105, 747	8, 822	107, 688
Bayfield	....	....	....	....	5	65
Brown	2, 395	74, 994	12, 690	353, 048	23, 579	319, 915
Buffalo	9, 010	296, 862	14, 879	530, 295	64, 290	775, 887
Burnett................	177	6, 613	652	21, 335	2, 514	33, 888
Calumet	4, 463	161, 781	8, 928	315, 069	39, 076	483, 318
Chippewa	5, 600	141, 529	13, 634	488, 902	29, 375	337, 839
Clark.................	1, 894	70, 751	4, 355	146, 503	4, 542	56, 987
Columbia	39, 308	1, 242, 248	24, 334	869, 695	71, 525	751, 111
Crawford	18, 029	569, 150	13, 027	374, 364	26, 409	335, 279
Dane	86, 897	2, 983, 259	67, 099	2, 295, 708	89, 911	883, 870
Dodge	29, 642	1, 116, 628	28, 202	1, 162, 617	142, 809	1, 895, 433
Door.................	326	10, 527	4, 742	126, 634	12, 095	194, 299
Douglas	11	197	33	1, 026	38	641
Dunn	10, 721	317, 584	16, 823	581, 642	41, 619	451, 887
Eau Claire	7, 887	257, 114	13, 902	497, 429	44, 871	556, 955
Fond du Lac	21, 416	732, 372	26, 871	1, 100, 048	112, 201	1, 366, 263
Grant	94, 898	3, 408, 034	60, 443	1, 850, 707	41, 663	480, 707
Green	59, 745	2, 187, 550	37, 166	1, 348, 942	11, 774	192, 983
Green Lake...........	15, 998	506, 814	8, 800	319, 656	40, 676	455, 990
Iowa	47, 287	1, 673, 760	37, 670	1, 329, 712	29, 896	462, 545
Jackson	11, 137	260, 428	14, 277	410, 919	30, 222	308, 969
Jefferson	27, 089	992, 446	17, 051	625, 079	34, 596	554, 825
Juneau	11, 023	329, 789	13, 376	399, 888	10, 795	162, 450
Kenosha	15, 344	626, 128	14, 654	615, 954	5, 660	79, 145
Kewaunee............	85	2, 285	10, 005	240, 605	27, 445	370, 214
La Crosse............	11, 642	379, 578	12, 048	431, 376	43, 589	493, 240
La Fayette...........	63, 926	2, 505, 277	49, 997	1, 721, 316	9, 167	132, 616
Langlade	26	1, 030	185	5, 575	20	245
Lincoln	18	570	525	12, 980	341	3, 978
Manitowoc	668	21, 433	23, 732	700, 664	60, 894	803, 258
Marathon............	517	18, 647	7, 554	187, 179	7, 623	79, 464
Marinette............	196	5, 580	908	26, 989	1, 038	17, 435
Marquette............	14, 475	336, 845	4, 907	131, 094	11, 077	112, 240
Milwaukee	6, 556	232, 094	11, 573	497, 408	11, 732	190, 292
Monroe	13, 728	413, 908	17, 443	569, 489	40, 311	526, 806
Oconto..............	744	24, 758	2, 220	62, 547	4, 272	58, 843
Outagamie...........	17, 559	342, 766	15, 209	503, 593	40, 906	550, 455
Ozaukee.............	2, 940	112, 263	12, 464	409, 042	30, 683	406, 860
Pepin...............	5, 553	158, 013	4, 125	135, 341	15, 345	184, 396
Pierce	8, 968	313, 104	10, 323	404, 455	61, 169	793, 103
Polk	1, 360	45, 869	5, 040	168, 570	19, 953	288, 331
Portage..............	12, 131	278, 743	9, 749	225, 614	21, 853	204, 778
Price	....	....	19	352	50	502
Racine	15, 042	554, 377	18, 016	718, 942	13, 481	210, 434
Richland	25, 480	873, 042	11, 564	362, 987	21, 162	322, 572
Rock	74, 845	2, 555, 704	52, 528	1, 768, 454	23, 212	340, 976
Saint Croix	5, 617	186, 021	18, 982	728, 556	110, 304	1, 372, 511
Sauk	32, 124	963, 060	26, 863	943, 246	40, 714	620, 522
Shawano.............	2, 205	60, 342	5, 460	144, 924	12, 396	162, 561
Sheboygan...........	8, 813	336, 612	18, 142	678, 440	45, 407	610, 628
Taylor	33	1, 095	145	5, 004	89	1, 077
Trempealeau	13, 728	442, 092	19, 539	671, 173	72, 738	814, 256
Vernon	21, 655	707, 536	24, 810	829, 947	51. 316	657, 708
Walworth	40, 332	1, 571, 987	26, 305	1, 018, 578	26, 080	335, 228
Washington	12, 263	438, 785	15, 361	574. 344	59. 012	929. 114
Waukesha	23, 333	814, 988	19, 755	810, 989	42, 038	711. 839
Waupaca	11, 055	309, 122	9, 897	272, 947	21, 731	252. 925
Waushara	18, 126	493, 478	9, 538	248, 950	16, 746	174, 009
Winnebago	15, 075	589, 834	14, 957	556, 825	56, 627	814, 523
Wood	1. 529	43, 442	2, 101	54, 284	1, 323	11, 906

WYOMING.

Counties.	BARLEY.		BUCKWHEAT.		RYE.	
	Acres.	Bushels.	Acres.	Bushels.	Acres.	Bushels.
The Territory					6	78
Albany						
Carbon						
Crook						
Johnson						
Laramie						
Sweetwater					6	78
Uintah						

www.ingramcontent.com/pod-product-compliance
Lightning Source LLC
Chambersburg PA
CBHW020026030726
47499CB00007B/2290